PETER IBBETSON

❂ ❂ ❂

by George du Maurier

PASSE
AVENIR
Peter Ibbetson del. et

PETER IBBETSON

BY

GEORGE DU MAURIER

With a Preface by

DAPHNE DU MAURIER

Illustrated by the Author

THE HERITAGE PRESS

New York

P R E F A C E

GEORGE DU MAURIER, "Kicky" to his family and his friends, was born in Paris on the 6th of March, 1834. His father, Louis-Mathurin Busson du Maurier, was the son of Robert Mathurin Busson, an engraver in glass, who had left Paris in the very early days of the French Revolution, not because he had any respect for the *ancien régime*, but his creditors were after him and he hoped to start life afresh in London, where he was unknown. He believed the suffix "du Maurier" would give him standing amongst the English — it was the name of the farm-house in the Touraine where he had been born, close to the family glass-works. But the London fellow-craftsmen remained unimpressed, and in 1798 the *émigré* found himself serving a term of eight months in King's Bench prison, on a charge of breaking into a warehouse in Long Acre. He returned to France after the Peace of Amiens, in 1802, leaving his young wife and family behind him in London; but very soon war between France and England broke out anew, and Robert Busson never saw his wife and children again, or corresponded with them. He died in 1811, no longer an engraver in glass but a schoolmaster in Tours, having founded a *maison d'instruction* with his brother Pierre.

His son, Louis-Mathurin, grew up in London, educated by the famous Abbé Carron with the sons of other *émigrés*, and upon the Restoration of the French monarchy followed his compatriots to their country of origin. Like his father,

Louis-Mathurin was one of those charming irresponsible men who possess a spark of genius that unfortunately never becomes more than a spark. He sang like an angel, but his voice was not strong enough for stage or opera; he invented ingenious and strange machines which because of some flaw or other failed to work; he had a wizard's flair for speculation which just missed amassing him a fortune by the proverbial hair's breadth. Too proud and too delightfully inefficient to earn his own living, he was content to borrow money from those who were fond enough of him to lend it, and when friends proved difficult there was always his wife's annuity, hush-money from a royal prince.

Ellen Clarke, whom he had married in Paris in 1833, was the daughter of the notorious Mary-Anne Clarke, one-time mistress of the Duke of York, who had testified against her royal lover before the bar of the House of Commons and brought him to disgrace. The investigation was long over and done with when Louis-Mathurin married Ellen. She had been a child at the time of all the publicity, but the experience had left her caustic and a little sour. It could not have been very agreeable, hearing her mother lampooned in the streets of London, nor seeing her, some years later, taken away to King's Bench prison. Thus it was that George du Maurier, who was to write *Peter Ibbetson* in his middle years, had for grandparents two persons, a Frenchman and an Englishwoman, who had at different times suffered long months in the identical prison — a fact which almost certainly he never knew, but which nevertheless must have worked some strange unconscious influence upon him. It was not pure coincidence that made him choose for his hero a man condemned to life imprisonment.

Kicky was a happy little boy — or so he believed, when fifty years later he wrote about his childhood in *Peter Ibbetson* — and the scents and sounds of pre-imperial Paris, the rumble of wheels on cobbled stones, the crack of a whip, the white dust at the corner of the Rue de la Pompe, the chestnut trees in flower — even the smell of burnt bread, black coffee, and tobacco on the warm spring air — rise from the pages of his novel, proving that nothing is forgotten that we and

our forebears have known, experienced, and seen, but all images, like photographs, are printed on our subconscious minds forever.

Both Kicky, the eldest child, and his brother Eugene (Gyggy) were educated in Paris. During this time their impecunious father, Louis-Mathurin, was endeavouring to patent a lamp he had invented, which at one moment nearly blew them all to pieces. The venture failing, he persuaded his wife's brother, George Clarke, to enter into partnership with him in London, with the idea of clearing all the world's ports of seaweed. This enterprise, not surprisingly, came to nothing, but Louis-Mathurin set himself up in a laboratory near Pentonville in the happy expectation of one day making a fortune for himself and his family. He sent for his eldest son, who had just failed his baccalaureate. The reluctant Kicky dragged himself away from his beloved Paris and began to study chemistry under his father. It was a subject for which Kicky had not the slightest aptitude. The carefree child had grown into a thin, rather wistful young man, forever drawing the heads of beautiful women on the backs of envelopes, and he might have developed into just such another unsuccessful dreamer as his father, when the latter died, very suddenly, in the summer of 1856. Kicky at twenty-two was now the only hope of his widowed mother and his younger brother and sister, and their sole means of support was the annuity still regularly paid by the trustees of the long-dead Duke of York.

Kicky persuaded his mother to allow him to go to Paris to study art, and during the next eighteen months, although he worked hard and long at his drawing, he led the happy-go-lucky life of a student in the Quartier Latin, days of delight which he was afterwards to describe in his second novel, *Trilby*. This joyous existence might have continued long enough for him to develop into a great painter, but in 1858 the tragedy of his life occurred. He lost the sight of his left eye, and for a time it was feared he would lose the sight of both. The agony and misery of the months that followed he described later in his third novel, *The Martian*.

He moved from Antwerp, where he had been sharing a studio with a friend, to the little town of Malines; for a while he felt he would never recover from his blow, and even had dark thoughts of suicide. His mother, who came out to be with him, could give him no comfort. Money was scarce. His brother Gyggy, now a corporal in the French army, was a constant source of worry — always in debt as his father had been, and his grandfather the *émigré* before him; and his sister Isobel, a pretty girl of nineteen, must also be supported until she could find herself a husband. It seemed to Kicky at that time that he, who had hoped to be the family prop, had become its greatest liability. Then, like a miracle, his luck turned. He was told of an oculist at Grafrath, near Düsseldorf, who had cured hundreds of people near to blindness, and with rising hope Kicky and his mother set forth for Germany.

The oculist could not restore the sight of his left eye, but he did promise that, with care, the right one would remain sound to the end of his days. Kicky's natural optimism returned, and — what was more — there was a school for drawing in Düsseldorf itself. He and his mother at once plunged into the light-hearted society of Düsseldorf, and Isobel came out to join them.

In the spring of 1860 they were visited by a friend from the Quartier Latin, Tom Armstrong, who was now working in London. Tom Armstrong was very frank with Kicky. He told him he was allowing himself to drift, and would end up a second-rate artist in a German provincial town. He urged Kicky to go to London, where he would get introductions to the editor of *Punch* and other weekly papers. If a fellow wanted to earn his living by his pencil, London was the place to start.

Kicky agreed. It was time he supported his mother instead of his mother's supporting him. In May 1860 he borrowed ten pounds from her annuity and set off for London in the company of Tom Armstrong and a Mrs. and Miss Wightwick — the latter an ex-school-friend of Isobel's with whom he was already half in love. He found himself lodgings in Newman Street which (though he was unaware of it) were practically next door to the house in Cleveland Row where his glass-engraver grandfather, Robert Busson du Maurier, had lived as an *émigré* some sixty years before.

It was not long before the young artist succeeded in getting an introduction to Mark Lemon, editor of the widely-read *Punch*, and soon after his sketches began regularly to appear, with his signature "D.M." and later "du M" in the lower left-hand corner. Kicky had arrived. The time of waiting was over. Doubts of success, financial worries, ill-health, and loneliness belonged to the past; and although he was still to know some moments of stress and frustration during the next few years, he was sufficiently sure of himself and the future to make Emma Wightwick his wife on the 3rd of January, 1863. They were ideally happy, and remained so for the whole of their married life. A mutual friend had this to say about the pair in after years:

"Du Maurier was never a robust man, but had immense virility, and was one of those charming natures which give out hope, life, and amusement to all who come in contact with them. I should sum him up in one word—joyous. In the days I knew him he was not at all well off, and he had an increasing family, but he had married one of those wives of that period, the women who lived for their homes and their husbands. She was one of the loveliest creatures of her time; from her statuesque beauty her husband drew his inspiration, and has immortalised her over and over again in the pictures of *Punch*. She had quantities of lovely dark hair, and in those days often twisted a yellow riband among her locks with ravishing effect. It was always a delight to me to watch du Maurier draw, while Mrs. du Maurier sat and sewed, and the children played about the floor unchecked."

Kicky's graceful drawings soon became the best-known page in *Punch*, and he contributed to other popular periodicals too—such as *Once A Week* and *The Cornhill*—besides being in great demand as an illustrator of popular novels of the day, Mrs. Gaskell's amongst others. The du Mauriers went everywhere, and met

all the leading figures of artistic and social London: Frederick Leighton, Millais, William Morris, Burne-Jones, and Whistler. (Kicky had originally known Whistler as an art student in Paris, and had shared a studio with him in earlier days in London.)

In 1874 Kicky took a long lease of New Grove House, at Hampstead, which became his home for the next twenty years, much loved by himself and his five growing children. He used to tell his friends that Hampstead Heath reminded him of Passy and his childhood, that the trees grew close together like the trees in the Bois du Boulogne, and that the Leg o' Mutton pond was the same shape as the Mare d'Auteuil where he had fished for tadpoles as a small boy. He would take long walks across the heath, accompanied by the children and his enormous St. Bernard dog Chang, and then return to his studio and have them pose to him as models, which the children were always very willing to do. Summer holidays would be spent at Whitby or across the Channel at Dieppe, and the result of these excursions would soon be seen in the pages of *Punch*. It was a full and very happy life, with his wife his constant companion, and the only anxiety was the fear that he might lose the sight of his right eye. If this should happen, how would he provide for his family? What could a blind man do?

Kicky had from time to time tried his hand at writing, but never seriously. He would scribble occasionally, to amuse himself, mostly scraps about old days in Paris, and now it occurred to him — at fifty-six, with his eldest son in the Army and two of his daughters married — that he might weave a story from his memories, and illustrate it, and — who knows? — some indulgent publisher might care to print it. He found an exercise book and began to jot down his thoughts. Ideas for stories had constantly passed through his mind, and now that he was actually putting them down on paper he found it simple, almost too simple. He wrote, in fact, as somebody afterwards expressed it, with dangerous facility. Words poured from his pen.

He sat before his desk in the studio at New Grove House, Chang at his feet,

his wife Emma (Pem) sewing in the chair opposite, and his youngest daughter May playing the piano, and suddenly it was as though he were back again in the house in the Rue de la Pompe, his father and mother living, his mother's sad and very beautiful sister Mary coming to visit them, leading her little boy by the hand, and they were all of them setting forth for a walk in the Bois, he, Kicky, running ahead with his small cousin. It was strange—he had only to shut his eyes, and the figures were real, as living as Pem and May. He could smell the old scents of Passy, hear the long-dead voices, conjure the old ideals, the laughter, and the tears. He remembered the pageantry of his forgotten childhood, and it came alive for him once more with a new bloom upon it. His rather sharp-tongued mother shone with a gentle radiance she had not possessed, each and every figure of his boyhood became idealised and deeply loved; even his shadow self, the boy Kicky, re-named Gogo, grew up into a golden-bearded, broad-shouldered young giant, a dream-hero of greater substance than the small, slight artist, "pale almost to sallowness, with no hair on his face except a small moustache," whom his friend Tom Armstrong described from the old student Quartier Latin days.

And so *Peter Ibbetson* was born, the novel that was to be so greatly loved by the *fin de siècle* Victorians in England and the romantic Yankees across the Atlantic. As the poet John Masefield said, "Its effect upon that generation was profound. . . . I can think of no book which so startled and delighted the questing mind."

The conception was unusual and the story, of course, fictitious. The young and gentle hero-narrator, serving a life sentence because he had killed his uncle after provocation, was a figment of Kicky's imagination. But the dream encounters between the prisoner and the Duchess of Towers, their wandering into the past and into the future—here were the unconscious yearnings of the middle-aged artist himself, who, though happy and contented in his outer life, had within him all the passionate nostalgia of an expatriate whose ties with France had first been severed in childhood, then re-knit as a young man, and finally loosed forever. He was unaware that as he wrote he spilt upon the paper before him not only his own hidden longings but the frustration of his dead father, doomed to no settled home in either country, a wanderer between Paris and London, and the anguish of his *émigré* grandfather, serving a prison sentence in an alien capital. Even the romanticised Duchess of Towers, a more beautiful and more intellectual Emma, had to be transformed into the playmate of Peter Ibbetson's childhood and a blood-relative, so that the writer Kicky's deeply-felt longing for his own French kith-and-kin, about whom he thought so much and knew so little, could at long last be satisfied.

"I'm glad you approve of my literary style," Kicky told Tom Armstrong. "I took pains, of course — most delightful pains — and now I see that I should have taken more. It all came too easily, and I found it far more difficult to illustrate than to write! Whether it will go down with the British public is another matter. I count a great deal on people's curiosity to see how a poor devil of a *Punch* draughtsman will acquit himself in a new line!"

The British and American public not only approved but asked for more, and a few months later Kicky was hard at work on his second novel, *Trilby*, whose popularity was such that its author found himself famous overnight. *Trilby* was the first of the modern "best-sellers," and was a sensational literary event, but Kicky felt, in his heart of hearts, that *Peter Ibbetson*, his first-born, was the better book.

Today, the casual reader coming upon *Peter Ibbetson* for the first time, may find the unusual love story between the prisoner and Mary, Duchess of Towers, sentimental, even absurd. How could a man and a woman be content to meet only in their dreams? Is not Peter himself a "romantic" almost to absurdity, and the Duchess quite impossibly unselfish and "good"? Perhaps, but the author was an idealist, and wrote of life not as he had known it but as it might have been. Nor need the modern reader scoff at "dreaming true." Kicky, if he did not know it, was ahead of his time. In 1892 hypnosis was still a vague term, and telepathy an unknown word. A trained psychologist of today would not dismiss *Peter Ibbetson* as pure fantasy.

Kicky's third and last novel, *The Martian,* went one degree further into the quest of the unknown, with its hero — the author thinly disguised as Barty Josselin — protected and guided from infancy by a spirit from the planet Mars. But Kicky himself never lived to see the book published.

He had been in failing health for some months, with a wearisome cough and a pain below his heart, and he died on the 8th of October, 1896, aged sixty-two. Although for epitaph he had written on his Hampstead grave the lines from *Trilby* —

> *A little trust that when we die,*
> *We reap our sowing — and so good-bye*

— as his grand-daughter I should like to add a sentence from the closing words in *Peter Ibbetson,* which echo the same thought:

"All I know is this: *that all will be well for us all, and of such a kind that all who do not sigh for the moon will be well content.*"

DAPHNE DU MAURIER

Menabilly, Par, Cornwall

LIST *of* ILLUSTRATIONS

PETER IBBETSON

with an introduction by his cousin

*Lady * * * * * ("Madge Plunket")*

"O toi qui m'apparus dans ce désert du monde
Habitante du ciel, passagère en ces lieux!"
LAMARTINE

INTRODUCTION

INTRODUCTION

❂ ❂ ❂

The writer of this singular autobiography was my cousin, who died at the —— Criminal Lunatic Asylum, of which he had been an inmate three years.

He had been removed thither after a sudden and violent attack of homicidal mania (which fortunately led to no serious consequences), from —— Jail, where he had spent twenty-five years, having been condemned to penal servitude for life, for the murder of —— ——, his relative.

He had been originally sentenced to death.

It was at —— Lunatic Asylum that he wrote these memoirs, and I received the MS. soon after his decease, with the most touching letter, appealing to our early friendship, and appointing me his literary executrix.

It was his wish that the story of his life should be published just as he had written it.

I have found it unadvisable to do this. It would revive, to no useful purpose, an old scandal, long buried and forgotten, and thereby give pain or annoyance to people who are still alive.

Nor does his memory require rehabilitation among those who knew him,

or knew anything of him — the only people really concerned. His dreadful deed has long been condoned by all (and they are many) who knew the provocation he had received and the character of the man who had provoked him.

On mature consideration, and with advice, I resolved (in order that his dying wishes should not be frustrated altogether) to publish the memoir with certain alterations and emendations.

I have nearly everywhere changed the names of people and places; suppressed certain details, and omitted some passages of his life (most of the story of his school-days, for instance, and that of his brief career as a private in the Horse Guards) lest they should too easily lead to the identification and annoyance of people still alive, for he is strongly personal at times, and perhaps not always just; and some other events I have carefully paraphrased (notably his trial at the Old Bailey), and given for them as careful an equivalent as I could manage without too great a loss of verisimilitude.

I may as well state at once that, allowing for these alterations, every incident of his *natural* life as described by himself is absolutely true, to the minutest detail, as I have been able to ascertain.

For the early part of it — the life at Passy he describes with such affection — I can vouch personally; I am the Cousin "Madge" to whom he once or twice refers.

I well remember the genial abode where he lived with his parents (my dear uncle and aunt); and the lovely "Madame Seraskier," and her husband and daughter, and their house, "Parva sed Apta," and "Major Duquesnois," and the rest.

And although I have never seen him since he was twelve years old, when his parents died and he went to London (as most of my life has been spent abroad), I received occasional letters from him.

I have also been able to obtain much information about him from others, especially from a relative of the late "Mr. and Mrs. Lintot," who knew him well, and from several officers in his regiment who remember him; also from the "Vicar's daughter," whom he met at "Lady Cray's," and who perfectly recollects the conversation she had with him at dinner, his sudden indisposition, and his long interview with the "Duchess of Towers," under the ash-tree next morning; she was one of the croquet-players.

He was the most beautiful boy I ever saw, and so charming, lively, and amiable that everybody was fond of him. He had a horror of cruelty, especially to animals (quite singular in a boy of his age), and was very truthful and brave.

According to all accounts (and from a photograph in my possession), he grew up to be as handsome as a man can well be, a personal gift which he seems to have held of no account whatever, though he thought so much of it in others. But he also became singularly shy and reserved in manner, over-diffident and self-distrustful; of a melancholy disposition, loving solitude, living much alone, and taking nobody into his confidence; and yet inspiring both affection and respect. For he seems to have always been thoroughly gentlemanlike in speech, bearing, manner, and aspect.

It is possible, although he does not say so, that having first enlisted, and then entered upon a professional career under somewhat inauspicious conditions, he felt himself to have fallen away from the social rank (such as it was) that belonged to him by birth; and he may have found his associates uncongenial.

His old letters to me are charmingly open and effusive.

Of the lady whom (keeping her title and altering her name) I have called the "Duchess of Towers," I find it difficult to speak. That they only met twice, and in the way he describes, is a fact about which there can be no doubt.

It is also indubitable that he received in Newgate, on the morning after his sentence to death, an envelope containing violets, and the strange message he mentions. Both letter and violets are in my possession, and the words are in her handwriting; about that there can be no mistake.

It is certain, moreover, that she separated from her husband almost immediately after my cousin's trial and condemnation, and lived in comparative retirement from the world, as it is certain that he went suddenly mad, twenty-five years later, in —— Jail, a few hours after her tragic death, and before he could possibly have heard of it by the ordinary channels; and that he was sent to —— Asylum, where, after his frenzy had subsided, he remained for many days in a state of suicidal melancholia, until, to the surprise of all, he rose one morning in high spirits, and apparently cured of all serious symptoms of insanity; so he remained until his death. It was during the last year of his life that he wrote his autobiography, in French and English.

There is nothing to be surprised at, taking all the circumstances into consideration, that even so great a lady, the friend of queens and empresses, the bearer of a high title and an illustrious name, justly celebrated for her beauty and charm (and her endless charities), of blameless repute, and one of the most popular women in English society, should yet have conceived a very warm regard for my poor cousin; indeed, it was an open secret in the family of "Lord Cray" that she had done so. But for them she would have taken the whole world into her confidence.

After her death she left him what money had come to her from her father, which he disposed of for charitable ends, and an immense quantity of MS. in cipher—a cipher which is evidently identical with that he used himself in the annotations he put under innumerable sketches he was allowed to make during his long period of confinement, which (through her interest, and no doubt through his own good conduct) was rendered as bearable to him as possible. These sketches (which are very extraordinary) and her Grace's MS. are now in my possession.

They constitute a mystery into which I have not dared to pry.

From papers belonging to both I have been able to establish beyond doubt the fact (so strangely discovered) of their descent from a common French ancestress, whose name I have but slightly modified and the tradition of whom still lingers in the "Département de la Sarthe," where she was a famous person a century ago; and her violin, a valuable Amati, now belongs to me.

Of the non-natural part of his story I will not say much.

It is, of course, a fact that he had been absolutely and, to all appearance, incurably insane before he wrote his life.

There seems to have been a difference of opinion, or rather a doubt, among the authorities of the asylum as to whether he was mad after the acute but very violent period of his brief attack had ended.

Whichever may have been the case, I am at least convinced of this: that he was no romancer, and thoroughly believed in the extraordinary mental experience he has revealed.

At the risk of being thought to share his madness—if he *was* mad—I will conclude by saying that I, for one, believe him to have been sane, and to have told the truth all through.

MADGE PLUNKET

PART ONE

I am but a poor scribe, ill-versed in the craft of wielding words and phrases, as the cultivated reader (if I should ever happen to have one) will no doubt very soon find out for himself.

I have been for many years an object of pity and contempt to all who ever gave me a thought—to all but *one*! Yet of all that ever lived on this earth I have been, perhaps, the happiest and most privileged, as that reader will discover if he perseveres to the end.

My outer and my inner life have been as the very poles—asunder; and if, at the eleventh hour, I have made up my mind to give my story to the world, it is not in order to rehabilitate myself in the eyes of my fellow-men, deeply as I value their good opinion; for I have always loved them and wished them well, and would fain express my good-will and win theirs, if that were possible.

It is because the regions where I have found my felicity are accessible to all, and that many, better trained and better gifted, will explore them to far better purpose than I, and to the greater glory and benefit of mankind, when once I have given them the clew. Before I can do this, and in order to show how I came by this clew myself, I must tell, as well as I may, the tale of my checkered career—in telling which, moreover, I am obeying the last behest of one whose lightest wish was my law.

If I am more prolix than I need be, it must be set down to my want of experience in the art of literary composition—to a natural wish I have to show myself neither better nor worse than I believe myself to be; to the charm, the unspeakable charm, that personal reminiscences have for the person principally concerned, and which he cannot hope to impart, however keenly he may feel it, without gifts and advantages that have been denied to me.

And this leads me to apologize for the egotism of this Memoir, which is but an introduction to another and longer one that I hope to publish later. To write a story of paramount importance to mankind, it is true, but all about one's outer and one's inner self, to do this without seeming somewhat egotistical, requires something akin to genius—and I am but a poor scribe.

* * * * *

"Combien j'ai douce souvenance
Du joli lieu de ma naissance!"

These quaint lines have been running in my head at intervals through nearly all my outer life, like an oft-recurring burden in an endless ballad—

sadly monotonous, alas! the ballad, which is mine; sweetly monotonous the burden, which is by Chateaubriand.

I sometimes think that to feel the full significance of this refrain one must have passed one's childhood in sunny France, where it was written, and the remainder of one's existence in mere London—or worse than mere London—as has been the case with me. If I had spent all my life from infancy upward in Bloomsbury, or Clerkenwell, or Whitechapel, my early days would be shorn of much of their retrospective glamour as I look back on them in these my after-years.

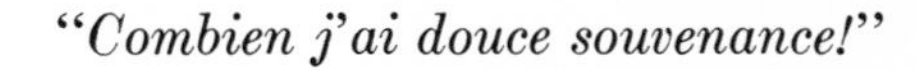
"Combien j'ai douce souvenance!"

It was on a beautiful June morning in a charming French garden, where the warm, sweet atmosphere was laden with the scent of lilac and syringa, and gay with butterflies and dragon-flies and humble-bees, that I began my conscious existence with the happiest day of all my outer life.

It is true that I had vague memories (with many a blank between) of a dingy house in the heart of London, in a long street of desolating straightness, that led to a dreary square and back again, and nowhere else for me; and then of a troubled and exciting journey that seemed of jumbled days and nights. I could recall the blue stage-coach with the four tall, thin, brown horses, so quiet and modest and well-behaved; the red-coated guard and his horn; the red-faced driver and his husky voice and many capes. Then the steamer with its glistening deck, so beautiful and white it seemed quite a desecration to walk upon it—this spotlessness did not last very long; and then two wooden piers with a light-house on each, and a quay, and blue-bloused workmen and red-legged little soldiers with mustaches, and bare-legged fisherwomen, all speaking a language that I knew as well as the other commoner language I had left behind; but which I had always looked upon as an exclusive possession of my father's and mother's and mine for the exchange of sweet confidence and the bewilderment of outsiders; and here were little boys and girls in the street, quite common children, who spoke it as well and better than I did myself.

After this came the dream of a strange, huge, top-heavy vehicle, that seemed like three yellow carriages stuck together, and a mountain of luggage at the top under an immense black tarpaulin, which ended in a hood; and beneath the hood sat a blue-bloused man with a singular cap, like a concertina, and mustaches, who cracked a loud whip over five squealing, fussy, pugnacious white and gray horses, with bells on their necks and bushy fox-tails on their foreheads, and their own tails carefully tucked up behind.

From the *coupé* where I sat with my father and mother I could watch them well as they led us through dusty roads with endless apple-trees or poplars on either side. Little barefooted urchins (whose papas and mammas wore wooden shoes and funny white nightcaps) ran after us for French half-pennies, which were larger than English ones, and pleasanter to have and to hold! Up hill and down we went; over sounding wooden bridges, through roughly paved streets in pretty towns to large court-yards, where five other quarrelsome steeds, gray and white, were waiting to take the place of the old ones—worn out, but quarreling still!

And through the night I could hear the gay music of the bells and hoofs, the rumbling of the wheels, the cracking of the eternal whip, as I fidgeted from one familiar lap to the other in search of sleep; and waking out of a doze I could see the glare of the red lamps on the five straining white and gray backs that dragged us so gallantly through the dark summer night.

Then it all became rather tiresome and intermittent and confused, till we reached at dusk next day a quay by a broad river; and as we drove along it, under thick trees, we met other red and blue and green lamped five-horsed diligences starting on their long journey just as ours was coming to an end.

Then I knew (because I was a well-educated little boy, and heard my father exclaim, "Here's Paris at last!") that we had entered the capital of France—a fact that impressed me very much—so much, it seems, that I went to sleep for thirty-six hours at a stretch, and woke up to find myself in the garden I have mentioned, and to retain possession of that self without break or solution of continuity (except when I went to sleep again) until now.

* * * * *

The happiest day in all my outer life!

For in an old shed full of tools and lumber at the end of the garden, and half-way between an empty fowl-house and a disused stable (each an Eden in itself) I found a small toy-wheelbarrow—quite the most extraordinary, the most unheard of and undreamed of, humorously, daintily, exquisitely fascinating object I had ever come across in all my brief existence.

I spent hours — enchanted hours — in wheeling brick-bats from the stable to the fowl-house, and more enchanted hours in wheeling them all back again, while genial French workmen, who were busy in and out of the house where we were to live, stopped every now and then to ask good-natured

questions of the "p'tit Anglais," and commend his knowledge of their tongue, and his remarkable skill in the management of a wheelbarrow. Well I remember wondering, with newly-aroused self-consciousness, at the intensity, the poignancy, the extremity of my bliss, and looking forward with happy confidence to an endless succession of such hours in the future.

But next morning, though the weather was as fine, and the wheelbarrow and the brick-bats and the genial workmen were there, and all the scents and sights and sounds were the same, the first fine careless rapture was not to be caught again, and the glory and the freshness had departed.

Thus did I, on the very dawning of life, reach at a single tide the high-water-mark of my earthly bliss—never to be reached again by me on this side of the ivory gate—and discover that to make the perfection of human happiness endure there must be something more than a sweet French garden, a small French wheelbarrow, and a nice little English boy who spoke French and had the love of approbation—a fourth dimension is required.

I found it in due time.

But if there were no more enchanted hours like the first, there were to be seven happy years that have the quality of enchantment as I look back on them.

* * * * *

Oh, the beautiful garden! Roses, nasturtiums and convolvulus, wall-flowers, sweet-pease and carnations, marigolds and sunflowers, dahlias and pansies and hollyhocks and poppies, and Heaven knows what besides! In my fond recollection they all bloom at once, irrespective of time and season.

To see and smell and pick all these for the first time at the susceptible age of five! To inherit such a kingdom after five years of Gower Street and Bedford Square! For all things are relative, and everything depends upon the point of view. To the owner of Chatsworth (and to his gardeners) my beautiful French Garden would have seemed a small affair.

And what a world of insects—Chatsworth could not beat *these* (indeed, is no doubt sadly lacking in them)—beautiful, interesting, comic, grotesque, and terrible; from the proud humble-bee to the earwig and his cousin, the devil's coach-horse; and all those rampant, many-footed things that pullulate in damp and darkness under big flat stones. To think that I have been friends with all these—roses and centipedes and all—and then to think that most of my outer life has been spent between bare white-washed walls, with never even a flea or a spider to be friends with again!

Our house (where, by the way, I had been born five years before), an old yellow house with green shutters and Mansard-roofs of slate, stood between this garden and the street—a long winding street, roughly flagged, with oil-lamps suspended across at long intervals; these lamps were let down with pulleys at dusk, replenished and lit, and then hauled up again to make darkness visible for a few hours on nights when the moon was away.

Opposite to us was a boys' school—"Maison d'Éducation, Dirigée par M. Jules Saindou, Bachelier et Maître ès Lettres et ès Sciences," and author of a treatise on geology, with such hauntingly terrific pictures of antediluvian reptiles battling in the primeval slime that I have never been able to forget them. My father, who was fond of science, made me a present of it on my sixth birthday. It cost me many a nightmare.

From our windows we could see and hear the boys at play—at a proper distance French boys sound just like English ones, though they do not look so, on account of their blue blouses and dusky, cropped heads—and we could see the gymnastic fixtures in the play-ground, M. Saindou's pride. "Le portique! la poutre! ! le cheval! ! ! et les barres parallèles! ! ! !" Thus they were described in M. Saindou's prospectus.

On either side of the street (which was called "the Street of the Pump"), as far as eye could reach looking west, were dwelling-houses just like our own, only agreeably different; and garden walls overtopped with the foliage

of horse-chestnut, sycamore, acacia, and lime; and here and there huge portals and iron gates defended by posts of stone gave ingress to mysterious abodes of brick and plaster and granite, many-shuttered, and embosomed in sun-shot greenery.

Looking east one could see in the near distance unsophisticated shops with old-fashioned windows of many panes—Liard, the grocer; Corbin, the poulterer; the butcher, the baker, the candlestick-maker.

And this delightful street, as it went on its winding way, led not to Bedford Square or the new University College Hospital, but to Paris through the Arc de Triomphe at one end, and to the river Seine at the other; or else, turning to the right, to St. Cloud through the Bois de Boulogne of Louis Philippe Premier, Roi des Français—as different from the Paris and the Bois de Boulogne of to-day as a diligence from an express train.

On one side of the beautiful garden was another beautiful garden, separated from ours by a high wall covered with peach and pear and plum and apricot trees; on the other, accessible to us through a small door in another lower wall clothed with jasmine, clematis, convolvulus, and nasturtium, was a long, straight avenue of almond-trees, acacia, laburnum, lilac, and may, so closely planted that the ivy-grown walls on either side could scarcely be seen. What lovely patches they made on the ground when the sun shone! One end of this abutted on "the Street of the Pump," from which it was fenced by tall, elaborately-carved iron gates between stone portals, and at the side was a "porte bâtarde," guarded by le Père et la Mère François, the old concierge and his old wife. Peace to their ashes, and Heaven rest their kindly, genial souls!

The other end of the avenue, where there was also an iron gate, admitted to a large private park that seemed to belong to nobody, and of which we were free—a very wilderness of delight, a heaven, a terror of tangled thickets and not too dangerous chalk cliffs, disused old quarries and dark caverns, prairies of lush grass, sedgy pools, turnip fields, forests of pine, groves and avenues of horse-chestnut, dank valleys of walnut-trees and hawthorn, which summer made dark at noon; bare, wind-swept mountainous regions whence one could reconnoitre afar; all sorts of wild and fearsome places for savages and wild beasts to hide and small boys to roam quite safely in quest of perilous adventure.

All this vast enclosure (full of strange singing, humming, whistling, buzzing, twittering, cooing, booming, croaking, flying, creeping, crawling, jumping, climbing, burrowing, splashing, diving things) had been neglected for ages — an Eden where one might gather and eat of the fruit of the tree of knowledge without fear, and learn lovingly the ways of life without losing one's innocence; a forest that had remade for itself a new virginity, and become primeval once more; where beautiful Nature had reasserted her own sweet will, and massed and tangled everything together as though a Beauty had been sleeping there undisturbed for close on a hundred years, and was only waiting for the charming Prince — or, as it turned out a few years later, alas! the speculative builder and the railway engineer — those princes of our day.

My fond remembrance would tell me that this region was almost boundless, well as I remember its boundaries. My knowledge of physical geography, as applied to this particular suburb of Paris, bids me assign more modest limits to this earthly paradise, which again was separated by an easily surmounted fence from Louis Philippe's Bois de Boulogne; and to this I cannot find it in my heart to assign any limits whatever, except the pretty old town from which it takes its name, and whose principal street leads to that magical combination of river, bridge, palace, gardens, mountain, and forest, St. Cloud.

What more could be wanted for a small boy fresh (if such be freshness) from the very heart of Bloomsbury?

That not a single drop should be lacking to the full cup of that small boy's felicity, there was a pond on the way from Passy to St. Cloud – a memorable pond, called "La Mare d'Auteuil," the sole aquatic treasure that Louis Philippe's Bois de Boulogne could boast. For in those ingenuous days there existed no artificial lake fed by an artificial stream, no Pré Catelan, no Jardin d'Acclimatation. The wood was just a wood, and nothing more – a dense, wild wood, that covered many hundreds of acres, and sheltered many thousands of wild live things. Though mysteriously deep in the middle, this famous pond (which may have been centuries old, and still exists) was not large; you might almost fling a stone across it anywhere.

Bounded on three sides by the forest (now shorn away), it was just hidden from the dusty road by a fringe of trees; and one could have it all to one's self, except on Sunday and Thursday afternoons, when a few love-sick Parisians remembered its existence, and in its loveliness forgot their own.

To be there at all was to be happy; for not only was it quite the most secluded, picturesque, and beautiful pond in all the habitable globe—that pond of ponds, the *only* pond—but it teemed with a far greater number and variety of wonderful insects and reptiles than any other pond in the world. Such, at least, I believed must be the case, for they were endless.

To watch these creatures, to learn their ways, to catch them (which we sometimes did), to take them home and be kind to them, and try to tame them, and teach them *our* ways (with never varying non-success, it is true, but in, oh, such jolly company!) became a hobby that lasted me, on and off, for seven years.

La Mare d'Auteuil! The very name has a magic, from all the associations that gathered round it during that time, to cling forever.

How I loved it! At night, snoozing in my warm bed, I would awesomely think of it, and how solemn it looked when I had reluctantly left it at dusk, an hour or two before; then I would picture it to myself, later, lying deep and cold and still under the stars, in the dark thicket, with all that weird, uncanny life seething beneath its stagnant surface.

Then gradually the water would sink, and the reeds, left naked, begin to move and rustle ominously, and from among their roots in the uncovered slush everything alive would make for the middle—hopping, gliding, writhing frantically. . . .

Down shrank the water; and soon in the slimy bottom, yards below, huge fat salamanders, long-lost and forgotten tadpoles as large as rats, gigantic toads, enormous flat beetles, all kinds of hairy, scaly, spiny, blear-eyed, bulbous, shapeless monsters without name, mud-colored offspring of the mire that had been sleeping there for hundreds of years, woke up, and crawled in and out, and wallowed and interwriggled, and devoured each other, like the great saurians and batrachians in my *Manuel de Géologie Élémentaire.* Édition illustrée à l'usage des enfants. Par Jules Saindou, Bachelier et Maître ès Lettres et ès Sciences.

Then would I wake up with a start, in a cold perspiration, an icy chill shooting through me that roughed my skin and stirred the roots of my hair, and ardently wish for to-morrow morning.

In after-years, and far away among the cold fogs of Clerkenwell, when the frequent longing would come over me to revisit "the pretty place of my birth," it was for the Mare d'Auteuil I longed the most; *that* was the loadstar, the very pole of my home-sick desires; always thither the wings of my hopeless fancy bore me first of all; it was, oh! to tread that sunlit grassy brink once more, and to watch the merry tadpoles swarm, and the green frog take its header like a little man, and the water-rat swim to his hole among the roots of the willow, and the horse-leech thread his undulating way between the water-lily stems; and to dream fondly of the delightful, irrevocable past, on the very spot of all where I and mine were always happiest!

"... *Qu'ils étaient beaux, les jours*
De France!"

In the avenue I have mentioned (*the* avenue, as it is still to me, and as I will always call it) there was on the right hand, half the way up, a *maison de santé*, or boarding-house, kept by one Madame Pelé; and there among others came to board and lodge, a short while after our advent, four or five gentlemen who had tried to invade France, with a certain grim Pretender at their head, and a tame eagle as a symbol of empire to rally round.

The expedition had failed; the Pretender had been consigned to a fortress; the eagle had found a home in the public slaughter-house of Boulogne-sur-Mer, which it adorned for many years, and where it fed as it had never probably fed before; and these, the faithful followers, le Colonel Voisil, le Major Duquesnois, le Capitaine Audenis, le Docteur Lombal (and one or two others whose names I have forgotten), were prisoners on

parole at Madame Pelé's, and did not seem to find their durance very vile.

I grew to know and love them all, especially the Major Duquesnois, an almost literal translation into French of Colonel Newcome. He took to me at once, in spite of my Englishness, and drilled me, and taught me the exercise as it was performed in the Vieille Garde; and told me a new fairy-tale, I verily believe, every afternoon for seven years. Scheherazade could do no more for a Sultan, and to save her own neck from the bowstring!

Cher et bien aimé "Vieux de la Vieille!" with his big iron-gray mustache, his black satin stock, his spotless linen, his long green frock-coat so baggy about the skirts, and the smart red ribbon in his button-hole! He little foresaw with what warm and affectionate regard his memory would be kept

forever sweet and green in the heart of his hereditary foe and small English tyrant and companion!

* * * * *

Opposite Madame Pelé's, and the only other dwelling besides hers and ours in the avenue, was a charming little white villa with a Grecian portico, on which were inscribed in letters of gold the words "Parva sed Apta"; but it was not tenanted till two or three years after our arrival.

In the genial French fashion of those times we soon got on terms of intimacy with these and other neighbors, and saw much of each other at all times of the day.

My tall and beautiful young mother (la belle Madame Pasquier, as she was gallantly called) was an Englishwoman who had been born and partly brought up in Paris.

My gay and jovial father (le beau Pasquier, for he was also tall and comely to the eye) was a Frenchman, although an English subject, who had been born and partly brought up in London; for he was the child of *émigrés* from France during the Reign of Terror.

He was gifted with a magnificent, a phenomenal voice—a barytone and tenor rolled into one; a marvel of richness, sweetness, flexibility, and power—and had intended to sing at the opera; indeed, he had studied for three years at the Paris Conservatoire to that end; and there he had carried all before him, and given rise to the highest hopes. But his family, who were Catholics of the blackest and Legitimists of the whitest dye—and as poor as church rats—had objected to such a godless and derogatory career; so the world lost a great singer, and the great singer a mine of wealth and fame.

However, he had just enough to live upon, and had married a wife (a heretic!) who had just about as much, or as little; and he spent his time, and both his money and hers, in scientific inventions—to little purpose, for well as he had learned how to sing, he had not been to any conservatoire where they teach one how to invent.

So that, as he waited "for his ship to come home," he sang only to amuse his wife, as they say the nightingale does; and to ease himself of superfluous energy, and to charm the servants, and le Père et la Mère François and the five followers of Napoleon, and all and everybody who cared to listen, and last and least (and most!), myself.

For this great neglected gift of his, on which he set so little store, was already to me the most beautiful and mysterious thing in the world; and next to this, my mother's sweet playing on the harp and piano, for she was an admirable musician.

It was her custom to play at night, leaving the door of my bedroom ajar, and also the drawing-room door, so that I could hear her till I fell asleep.

"When in death I shall calm recline,
Oh take my heart to my mistress dear!
Tell her it lived upon smiles and wine
Of the brightest hue while it lingered here!"

Sometimes, when my father was at home, the spirit would move him to hum or sing the airs she played, as he paced up and down the room on the track of a new invention.

And though he sang and hummed "pian-piano," the sweet, searching, manly tones seemed to fill all space.

The hushed house became a sounding-board, the harp a mere subservient tinkle, and my small, excitable frame would thrill and vibrate under the waves of my unconscious father's voice; and oh, the charming airs he sang!

His stock was inexhaustible, and so was hers; and thus an endless succession of lovely melodies went ringing through that happy period.

And just as when a man is drowning, or falling from a height, his whole past life is said to be mapped out before his mental vision as in a single flash, so seven years of sweet, priceless home love – seven times four changing seasons of simple, genial, præ-imperial Frenchness; an ideal house, with all its pretty furniture, and shape, and color; a garden full of trees and flowers; a large park, and all the wild live things therein; a town and its inhabitants; a mile or two of historic river; a wood big

enough to reach from the Arc de Triomphe to St. Cloud (and in it the pond of ponds); and every wind and weather that the changing seasons can bring—all lie embedded and embalmed for me in every single bar of at least a hundred different tunes, to be evoked at will for the small trouble and cost of just whistling or humming the same, or even playing it with one finger on the piano—when I had a piano within reach.

Enough to last me for a lifetime—with proper economy, of course—it will not do to exhaust, by too frequent experiment, the strange capacity of a melodic bar for preserving the essence of by-gone things, and days that are no more.

Oh, Nightingale! whether thou singest thyself, or, better still, if thy voice be not in thy throat, but in thy fiery heart and subtle brain, and thou makest songs for the singing of many others, blessed be thy name! The very sound of it is sweet in every clime and tongue: Nightingale, Rossignol, Usignuolo, Bulbul! Even Nachtigall does not sound amiss in the mouth of a fair English girl who has had a Hanoverian for a governess! and, indeed, it is in the Nachtigall's country that the best music is made!

And oh, Nightingale! never, never grudge thy song to those who love it—nor waste it upon those who do not. . . .

Thus serenaded, I would close my eyes, and lapped in darkness and warmth and heavenly sound, be lulled asleep—perchance to dream!

For my early childhood was often haunted by a dream, which at first I took for a reality—a transcendent dream of some interest and importance to mankind, as the patient reader will admit in time. But many years of my life passed away before I was able to explain and account for it.

I had but to turn my face to the wall, and soon I found myself in company with a lady who had white hair and a young face—a very beautiful young face.

Sometimes I walked with her, hand in hand—I being quite a small child

—and together we fed innumerable pigeons who lived in a tower by a winding stream that ended in a water-mill. It was too lovely, and I would wake.

Sometimes we went into a dark place, where there was a fiery furnace with many holes, and many people working and moving about—among them a man with white hair and a young face, like the lady, and beautiful red heels to his shoes. And under his guidance I would contrive to make in the furnace a charming little cocked hat of colored glass—a treasure! And the sheer joy thereof would wake me.

Sometimes the white-haired lady and I would sit together at a square box from which she made lovely music, and she would sing my favorite song—a song that I adored. But I always woke before this song came to an end, on account of the too insupportably intense bliss I felt on hearing it; and all I could remember when awake were the words "triste—comment—sale."

The air, which I knew so well in my dream, I could not recall.

It seemed as though some innermost core of my being, some childish holy of holies, secreted a source of supersubtle reminiscence, which, under some stimulus that now and again became active during sleep, exhaled itself in this singular dream—shadowy and slight, but invariably accompanied by a sense of felicity so measureless and so penetrating that I would always wake in a mystic flutter of ecstasy, the bare remembrance of which was enough to bless and make happy many a succeeding hour.

*   *   *   *   *

Besides this happy family of three, close by (in the Street of the Tower) lived my grandmother Mrs. Biddulph, and my Aunt Plunket, a widow, with her two sons, Alfred and Charlie, and her daughter Madge. They also were fair to look at—extremely so—of the gold-haired, white-skinned, well-grown Anglo-Saxon type, with frank, open, jolly manners, and no beastly British pride.

So that physically, at least, we reflected much credit on the English name, which was not in good odor just then at Passy-lès-Paris, where Waterloo was unforgotten. In time, however, our nationality was condoned on account of our good looks—"non Angli sed angeli!" as M. Saindou was gallantly pleased to exclaim when he called (with a prospectus of his school) and found us all gathered together under the big apple-tree on our lawn.

But English beauty in Passy was soon to receive a memorable addition to its ranks in the person of a certain Madame Seraskier, who came with an invalid little daughter to live in the house so modestly described in gold as "Parva sed Apta."

She was the English, or rather the Irish, wife of a Hungarian patriot and man of science, Dr. Seraskier (son of the famous violinist); an extremely tall, thin man, almost gigantic, with a grave, benevolent face, and a head like a prophet's; who was, like my father, very much away from his family—conspiring perhaps—or perhaps only inventing (like my father), and looking out "for his ship to come home!"

This fair lady's advent was a sensation—to me a sensation that never palled or wore itself away; it was no longer now "la belle Madame Pasquier," but "la divine Madame Seraskier"—beauty-blind as the French are apt to be.

She topped my tall mother by more than half a head; as was remarked by Madame Pelé, whose similes were all of the kitchen and dining-room, "elle lui mangerait des petits pâtés sur la tête!" And height, that lends dignity to ugliness, magnifies beauty on a scale of geometrical progression—2, 4, 8, 16, 32—for every consecutive inch, between five feet five, let us say, and five feet ten or eleven (or thereabouts), which I take to have been Madame Seraskier's measurement.

She had black hair and blue eyes—of the kind that turns violet in a novel—and a beautiful white skin, lovely hands and feet, a perfect figure, and features chiselled and finished and polished and turned out with such singular felicitousness that one gazed and gazed till the heart was full of a strange jealous resentment at any one else having the right to gaze on something so rare, so divinely, so sacredly fair—any one in the world but one's self!

But a woman can be all this without being Madame Seraskier—she was much more.

For the warmth and genial kindness of her nature shone through her eyes and rang in her voice. All was of a piece with her—her simplicity, her grace, her naturalness and absence of vanity; her courtesy, her sympathy, her mirthfulness.

I do not know which was the most irresistible: she had a slight Irish accent when she spoke English, a less slight English accent when she spoke French!

I made it my business to acquire both.

Indeed, she was in heart and mind and body what we should *all* be but for the lack of a little public spirit and self-denial (under proper guidance) during the last few hundred years on the part of a few thousand millions of our improvident fellow-creatures.

There should be no available ugly frames for beautiful souls to be hurried into by carelessness or mistake, and no ugly souls should be suffered to creep, like hermit-crabs, into beautiful shells never intended for them. The outward and visible form should mark the inward and spiritual grace; that it seldom does so is a fact there is no gainsaying. Alas! such beauty is such an exception that its possessor, like a prince of the blood royal, is pampered and spoiled from the very cradle, and every good and generous and unselfish impulse is corroded by adulation—that spontaneous tribute so lightly won, so quickly paid, and accepted so royally as a due.

So that only when by Heaven's grace the very beautiful are also very good, is it time for us to go down on our knees, and say our prayers in thankfulness and adoration; for the divine has been permitted to make itself manifest for a while in the perishable likeness of our poor humanity.

A beautiful face! a beautiful tune! Earth holds nothing to beat these, and of such, for want of better materials, we have built for ourselves the kingdom of Heaven.

"Plus oblige, et peut davantage
Un beau visage
Qu'un homme armé—
Et rien n'est meilleur que d'entendre
Air doux et tendre
Jadis aimé!"

* * * * *

My mother soon became the passionately devoted friend of the divine Madame Seraskier; and I, what would I not have done—what danger would I not have faced—what death would I not have died for her!

I did not die; I lived her protestant to be, for nearly fifty years. For nearly fifty years to recollect the rapture and the pain it was to look at her; that inexplicable longing ache, that dumb, delicious, complex, innocent distress, for which none but the greatest poets have ever found expression; and which, perhaps, they have not felt half so acutely, these glib and gifted ones, as *I* did, at the susceptible age of seven, eight, nine, ten, eleven, and twelve.

She had other slaves of my sex. The five Napoleonic heroes did homage each after his fashion: the good Major with a kind of sweet fatherly tender-

ness touching to behold; the others with perhaps less unselfish adoration; notably the brave Capitaine Audenis, of the fair waxed mustache and beautiful brown tail coat, so tightly buttoned with gilt buttons across his enormous chest, and imperceptible little feet so tightly imprisoned in shiny tipped female cloth boots, with buttons of mother-of-pearl; whose hobby was, I believe, to try and compensate himself for the misfortunes of war by more successful attempts in another direction. Anyhow he betrayed a warmth that made my small bosom a Gehenna, until she laughed and snubbed him into due propriety and shamefaced self-effacement.

It soon became evident that she favored two, at least, out of all this little masculine world—the Major and myself; and a strange trio we made.

Her poor little daughter, the object of her passionate solicitude, a very clever and precocious child, was the reverse of beautiful, although she would have had fine eyes but for her red lashless lids. She wore her thick hair cropped short, like a boy, and was pasty and sallow in complexion, hollow-cheeked, thick-featured, and overgrown, with long thin hands and feet, and arms and legs of quite pathetic length and tenuity; a silent and melancholy little girl, who sucked her thumb perpetually, and kept her own counsel. She would have to lie in bed for days together, and when she got well enough to sit up, I (to please her mother) would read to her *Le Robinson Suisse, Sandford and Merton, Evenings at Home, Les Contes de Madame Perrault,* the shipwreck from "Don Juan," of which we never tired, and the "Giaour," the "Corsair," and "Mazeppa"; and last, but not least, *Peter Parleys Natural History,* which we got to know by heart.

And out of this latter volume I would often declaim for her benefit what has always been to me the most beautiful poem in the world, possibly because it was the first I read for myself, or else because it is so intimately associated with those happy days. Under an engraving of a wild duck (after Bewick, I believe) were quoted W. C. Bryant's lines "To a Water-fowl."

They charmed me then and charm me now as nothing else has quite charmed me; I become a child again as I think of them, with a child's virgin subtlety of perception and magical susceptibility to vague suggestions of the Infinite.

Poor little Mimsey Seraskier would listen with distended eyes and quick comprehension. She had a strange fancy that a pair of invisible beings, "La fée Tarapatapoum," and "Le Prince Charmant" (two favorite characters of M. le Major's) were always in attendance upon us—upon her and me—and were equally fond of us both; that is, "La fée Tarapatapoum" of me, and "Le Prince Charmant" of her—and watched over us and would protect us through life.

"O! ils sont joliment bien ensemble, tous les deux—ils sont inséparables!" she would often exclaim, *apropos* of these visionary beings; and *apropos* of the water-fowl she would say—

"Il aime beaucoup cet oiseau-là, le Prince Charmant! dis encore, quand il vole si haut, et qu'il fait froid, et qu'il est fatigué, et que la nuit vient, mais qu'il ne veut pas descendre!"

And I would re-spout—

" '*All day thy wings have fanned,*
At that far height, the cold, thin atmosphere,
Yet stoop not, weary, to the welcome land,
Though the dark night be near!' "

And poor, morbid, precocious, overwrought Mimsey's eyes would fill, and she would meditatively suck her thumb and think unutterable things.

And then I would copy Bewick's wood-cuts for her, as she sat on the arm of my chair and patiently watched; and she would say: "La fée Tarapatapoum trouve que tu dessines dans la perfection!" and treasure up these little masterpieces—"pour l'album de la fée Tarapatapoum!"

There was one drawing she prized above all others — a steel engraving in a volume of Byron, which represented two beautiful beings of either sex, walking hand in hand through a dark cavern. The man was in sailor's garb; the lady, who went barefoot and lightly clad, held a torch; and underneath was written —

"And Neuha led her Torquil by the hand,
And waved along the vaults her flaming brand."

I spent hours in copying it for her, and she preferred the copy to the original, and would have it that the two figures were excellent portraits of her Prince and Fairy.

Sometimes during these readings and sketchings under the apple-tree on the lawn, the sleeping Médor (a huge nondescript sort of dog, built up of every breed in France, with the virtues of all and the vices of none) would wag his three inches of tail, and utter soft whimperings of welcome in his dream; and she would say —

"C'est le Prince Charmant qui lui dit: 'Médor, donne la patte!' "

Or our old tomcat would rise from his slumbers with his tail up, and rub an imaginary skirt; and it was —

"Regarde Mistigris! La fée Tarapatapoum est en train de lui frotter les oreilles!"

We mostly spoke French, in spite of strict injunctions to the contrary from our fathers and mothers, who were much concerned lest we should forget our English altogether.

In time we made a kind of ingenious compromise; for Mimsey, who was full of resource, invented a new language, or rather two, which we called Frankingle and Inglefrank, respectively. They consisted in anglicizing French nouns and verbs and then conjugating and pronouncing them Englishly, or *vice versa.*

For instance, it was very cold, and the school-room window was open, so she would say in Frankingle—

"Dispeach yourself to ferm the feneeter, Gogo. It geals to pier-fend! we shall be inrhumed!" or else, if I failed to immediately understand—"Gogo, il frise a splitter les stonnes—maque aste et chute le vindeau; mais chute-le donc vite! Je snize déjà!" which was Inglefrank.

With this contrivance we managed to puzzle and mystify the uninitiated, English and French alike. The intelligent reader, who sees it all in print, will not be so easily taken in.

When Mimsey was well enough, she would come with my cousins and me into the park, where we always had a good time—lying in ambush for red Indians, rescuing Madge Plunket from a caitiff knight, or else hunting snakes and field-mice and lizards, and digging for lizard's eggs, which we would hatch at home—that happy refuge for all manner of beasts, as well as little boys and girls. For there were squirrels, hedgehogs, and guinea-pigs; an owl, a raven, a monkey, and white mice; little birds that had strayed from the maternal nest before they could fly (they always died!), the dog Médor, and any other dog who chose; not to mention a gigantic rocking-horse made out of a real stuffed pony—the smallest pony that had ever been!

Often our united high spirits were too boisterous for Mimsey. Dreadful headaches would come on, and she would sit in a corner, nursing a hedgehog with one arm and holding her thumb in her mouth with the other. Only when we were alone together was she happy; and then, *moult tristement!*

On summer evenings whole parties of us, grown-up and small, would walk through the park and the Bois de Boulogne to the "Mare d'Auteuil"; as we got near enough for Médor to scent the water, he would bark and grin and gyrate, and go mad with excitement, for he had the gift of diving after stones, and liked to show it off.

There we would catch huge olive-colored water-beetles, yellow underneath; red-bellied newts; green frogs, with beautiful spots and a splendid parabolic leap; gold and silver fish, pied with purply brown. I mention them in the order of their attractiveness. The fish were too tame and easily caught, and their beauty of too civilized an order; the rare, flat, vicious dytiscus "took the cake."

Sometimes, even, we would walk through Boulogne to St. Cloud, to see the new railway and the trains—an inexhaustible subject of wonder and delight—and eat ices at the "Tête Noire" (a hotel which had been the scene of a terrible murder, that led to a cause célèbre); and we would come back through the scented night, while the glowworms were shining in the grass, and the distant frogs were croaking in the Mare d'Auteuil. Now and then a startled roebuck would gallop in short bounds across the path, from thicket to thicket, and Médor would go mad again, and wake the echoes of the new Paris fortifications, which were still in course of construction.

He had not the gift of catching roebucks!

If my father were of the party, he would yodel Tyrolese melodies, and sing lovely songs of Boieldieu, Hérold, and Grétry; or "Drink to me only with thine eyes," or else the "Bay of Dublin" for Madame Seraskier, who had the nostalgia of her beloved country whenever her beloved husband was away.

Or else we would break out into a jolly chorus and march to the tune—

"Marie, trempe ton pain,
Marie, trempe ton pain,
Marie, trempe ton pain dans la soupe;
Marie, trempe ton pain,
Marie, trempe ton pain,
Marie, trempe ton pain dans le vin!"

Or else—

> *"La— soupe aux choux— se fait dans la marmite;*
> *Dans— la marmite— se fait la soupe aux choux."*

which would give us all the nostalgia of supper!

Or else, again, if it were too hot to sing, or we were too tired, M. le Major, forsaking the realms of fairyland, and uncovering his high bald head as he walked, would gravely and reverently tell us of his great master, of Brienne, of Marengo, and Austerlitz; of the farewells at Fontainebleau, and the Hundred Days—never of St. Helena; he would not trust himself to speak to us of that! And gradually working his way to Waterloo, he would put his hat on, and demonstrate to us, by A + B, how, virtually, the English had lost the day, and why and wherefore. And on all the little party a solemn, awe-struck stillness would fall as we listened, and on some of us the sweet nostalgia of bed!

Oh, the good old time!

The night was consecrated for me by the gleam and scent and rustle of Madame Seraskier's gown, as I walked by her side in the deepening dusk—a gleam of yellow, or pale blue, or white—a scent of sandalwood—a rustle that told of a light, vigorous tread on firm, narrow, high-arched feet, that were not easily tired; of an anxious, motherly wish to get back to Mimsey, who was not strong enough for these longer expeditions.

On the shorter ones I used sometimes to carry Mimsey on my back most of the way home (to please her mother)—a frail burden, with her poor, long, thin arms round my neck, and her pale, cold cheek against my ear—she weighed nothing! And when I was tired M. le Major would relieve me, but not for long. She always wanted to be carried by Gogo (for so I was called, for no reason whatever, unless it was that my name was Peter).

She would start at the pale birches that shone out against the gloom, and

"LA BATAILLE DE VATERLO"

shiver if a bough scraped her, and tell me all about the Erl-king—"mais comme ils sont là tous les deux" (meaning the Prince and the Fairy) "il n'y a absolument rien à craindre."

And Mimsey was *si bonne camarade,* in spite of her solemnity and poor health and many pains, so grateful for small kindnesses, so appreciative of small talents, so indulgent to small vanities (of which she seemed to have no more share than her mother), and so deeply humorous in spite of her eternal gravity—for she was a real tomboy at heart—that I soon carried her, not only to please her mother, but to please herself, and would have done anything for her.

As for M. le Major, he gradually discovered that Mimsey was half a martyr and half a saint, and possessed all the virtues under the sun.

"Ah, vous ne la comprenez pas, cette enfant; vous verrez un jour quand ça ira mieux! vous verrez! elle est comme sa mère . . . elle a toutes les intelligences de la tête et du cœur!" and he would wish it had pleased Heaven that he should be her grandfather—on the maternal side.

L'art d'être grand-père! This weather-beaten, war-battered old soldier had learned it, without ever having had either a son or a daughter of his own. He was a *born* grandfather!

Moreover, Mimsey and I had many tastes and passions in common—music, for instance, as well as Bewick's wood-cuts and Byron's poetry, and roast chestnuts and domestic pets; and above all, the Mare d'Auteuil, which she preferred in the autumn, when the brown and yellow leaves were eddying and scampering and chasing each other round its margin, or drifting on its troubled surface, and the cold wet wind piped through the dishevelled boughs of the forest, under the leaden sky.

She said it was good to be there then, and think of home and the fireside; and better still, when home was reached at last, to think of the desolate pond we had left; and good, indeed, it was to trudge home by wood and park and avenue at dusk, when the bats were about, with Alfred and Charlie and Mimsey and Madge and Médor; swishing our way through the lush, dead leaves, scattering the beautiful, ripe horse-chestnut out of its split creamy case, or picking up acorns and beechnuts here and there as we went.

And, once home, it was good, very good, to think how dark and lonesome and shivery it must be out there by the *mare,* as we squatted and chatted and roasted chestnuts by the wood fire in the school-room before the candles were lit—*entre chien et loup,* as was called the French gloaming—while Thérèse was laying the tea-things, and telling us the news, and cutting bread and butter; and my mother played the harp in the drawing-room above; till the last red streak died out of the wet west behind the swaying tree-tops, and the curtains were drawn, and there was light, and the appetites were let loose.

I love to sit here, in my solitude and captivity, and recall every incident of that sweet epoch—to ache with the pangs of happy remembrance; than which, for the likes of me, great poets tell us there is no greater grief. This sorrow's crown of sorrow is my joy and my consolation, and ever has been; and I would not exchange it for youth, health, wealth, honor, and freedom; only for thrice happy childhood itself once more, over and over again, would I give up its thrice happy recollections.

* * * * *

That it should not be all beer and skittles with us, and therefore apt to pall, my cousins and I had to work pretty hard. In the first place, my dear mother did all she could to make me an infant prodigy of learning. She tried to teach me Italian, which she spoke as fluently as English or French (for she had lived much in Italy), and I had to translate the "Gerusalemme

Liberata" into both those latter languages — a task which has remained unfinished — and to render the "Allegro" and the "Penseroso" into Miltonian French prose, and "Le Cid" into Corneillian English. Then there were Pinnock's histories of Greece and Rome to master, and, of course, the Bible; and, every Sunday, the Collect, the Gospel, and the Epistle to get by heart. No, it was not all beer and skittles.

It was her pleasure to teach, but, alas! not mine to learn; and we cost each other many a sigh, but loved each other all the more, perhaps.

Then we went in the mornings, my cousins and I, to M. Saindou's, opposite, that we might learn French grammar and French-Latin and French-Greek. But on three afternoons out of the weekly six Mr. Slade, a Cambridge sizar stranded in Paris, came to anglicize (and neutralize) the Latin and Greek we had learned in the morning, and to show us what sorry stuff the French had made of them and of their quantities.

Perhaps the Greek and Latin quantities are a luxury of English growth — a mere social test — a little pitfall of our own invention, like the letter *h*, for the tripping up of unwary pretenders; or else, French education being so deplorably cheap in those days, the school-masters there could not afford to take such fanciful superfluities into consideration; it was not to be done at the price.

In France, be it remembered, the King and his greengrocer sent their sons to the same school (which did not happen to be M. Saindou's, by the way, where it was nearly all greengrocer and no King); and the fee for bed, board, and tuition, in all public schools alike, was something like thirty pounds a year.

The Latin, in consequence, was without the distinction that comes of exclusiveness, and quite lacked that aristocratic flavor, so grateful and comforting to scholar and ignoramus alike, which the costly British public-school system (and the British accent) alone can impart to a dead language.

When French is dead we shall lend it a grace it never had before; some of us even manage to do so already.

That is (no doubt) why the best French writers so seldom point their morals and adorn their tales, as ours do, with the usual pretty, familiar, and appropriate lines out of Horace or Virgil; and why Latin is so little quoted in French talk, except here and there by a weary shop-walker, who sighs—

"Varium et mutabile semper femina!" as he rolls up the unsold silk; or exclaims, "O rus! quando te aspiciam!" as he takes his railway ticket for Asnières on the first fine Sunday morning in spring.

But this is a digression, and we have wandered far away from Mr. Slade.

Good old Slade!

We used to sit on the stone posts outside the avenue gate and watch for his appearance at a certain distant corner of the winding street.

With his green tail coat, his stiff shirt collar, his thick flat thumbs stuck in the armholes of his nankeen waistcoat, his long flat feet turned inward, his reddish mutton-chop whiskers, his hat on the back of his head, and his clean, fresh, blooming, virtuous, English face—the sight of him was not sympathetic when he appeared at last.

Occasionally, in the course of his tuition, illness or domestic affairs would, to his great regret, detain him from our midst, and the beatitude we would experience when the conviction gradually dawned upon us that we were watching for him in vain was too deep for either words or deeds or outward demonstration of any sort. It was enough to sit on our stone posts and let it steal over us by degrees.

These beatitudes were few and far between. It would be infelicitous, perhaps, to compare the occasional absences of a highly respectable English tutor to an angel's visits, but so we felt them.

And then he would make up for it next afternoon, that conscientious Englishman; which was fair enough to our parents, but not to us. And then what extra severity, as interest for the beggarly loan of half an afternoon! What rappings on ink-stained knuckles with a beastly, hard, round, polished, heavy-wooded, business-like English ruler!

It was our way in those days to think that everything English was beastly — an expression our parents thought we were much too fond of using.

But perhaps we were not without some excuse for this unpardonable sentiment. For there was *another* English family in Passy — the Prendergasts, an older family than ours — that is, the parents (and uncles and aunts) were middle-aged, the grandmother dead, and the children grown up. We had not the honor of their acquaintance. But whether that was their misfortune and our fault (or *vice versa*) I cannot tell. Let us hope the former.

They were of an opposite type to ours, and, though I say it, their type was a singularly unattractive one; perhaps it may have been the original of those caricatures of our compatriots by which French comic artists have sought to avenge Waterloo. It was stiff, haughty, contemptuous. It had prominent front teeth, a high nose, a long upper lip, a receding jaw; it had dull, cold, stupid, selfish green eyes, like a pike's, that swerved neither to right nor left, but looked steadily over people's heads as it stalked along in its pride of impeccable British self-righteousness.

At the sudden sight of it (especially on Sundays) all the cardinal virtues became hateful on the spot, and respectability a thing to run away from. Even that smooth, close-shaven cleanliness was so Puritanically aggressive as to make one abhor the very idea of soap.

Its accent, when it spoke French (in shops), instead of being musical and sweet and sympathetic, like Madame Seraskier's, was barbarous and grotesque, with dreadful "ongs," and "angs," and "ows," and "ays"; and its manner overbearing, suspicious, and disdainful; and then we could hear its loud, insolent English asides; and though it was tall and straight and not outwardly deformed, it looked such a kill-joy skeleton at a feast, such a portentous carnival mask of solemn emptiness, such a dreary, doleful, unfunny figure of fun, that one felt Waterloo might some day be forgiven, even in Passy; but the Prendergasts, *never*!

I have lived so long away from the world that, for all I know, this ancient British type, this "grim, ungainly, ghastly, gaunt, and ominous bird of yore," may have become extinct, like another, but less unprepossessing bird—the dodo; whereby our state is the more gracious.

But in those days, and generalizing somewhat hastily as young people are apt to do, we grew to think that England must be full of Prendergasts, and did not want to go there.

To this universal English beastliness of things we made a few exceptions, it is true, but the list was not long: tea, mustard, pickles, gingerbread-nuts, and, of all things in the world, the English loaf of household bread that came to us once a week as a great treat and recompense for our virtues, and harmonized so well with Passy butter. It was too delicious! But there was always a difficulty, a dilemma—whether to eat it with butter alone, or with "cassonade" (French brown sugar) added.

Mimsey knew her own mind, and loved it with French brown sugar, and if she were not there I would save for her half of my slices, and carefully cassonade them for her myself.

On the other hand, we thought everything French the reverse of beastly—except all the French boys we knew, and at M. Saindou's there were about two hundred; then there were all the boys in Passy (whose name was legion, and who *did not* go to M. Saindou's), and we knew all the boys in Passy. So that we were not utterly bereft of material for good, stodgy, crusty, patriotic English prejudice.

Nor did the French boys fail to think us beastly in return, and sometimes to express the thought; especially the little vulgar boys, whose playground was the street—the *voyous de Passy*. They hated our white silk chimney-pot hats and large collars and Eton jackets, and called us "sacred godems," as their ancestors used to call ours in the days of Joan of Arc. Sometimes they would throw stones, and then there were collisions, and bleedings of impertinent little French noses, and runnings away of cowardly little French legs, and dreadful wails of "O là, là! O, là, là—maman!" when they were overtaken by English ones.

Not but what *our* noses were made to bleed now and then, unvictoriously, by a certain blacksmith—always the same young blacksmith—Boitard!

It is always a young blacksmith who does these things—or a young butcher.

Of course, for the honor of Great Britain, one of us finally licked him to such a tune that he has never been able to hold up his head since. It was about a cat. It came off at dusk, one Christmas Eve, on the "Isle of Swans," between Passy and Grenelle (too late to save the cat).

I was the hero of this battle. "It's now or never," I thought, and saw scarlet, and went for my foe like a maniac. The ring was kept by Alfred and Charlie, helped, oddly enough, by a couple of male Prendergasts, who so far forgot themselves as to take an interest in the proceedings. Madge and Mimsey looked on, terrified and charmed.

It did not last long, and was worthy of being described by Homer, or even in *Bell's Life*. That is one of the reasons why I will not describe it. The two Prendergasts seemed to enjoy it very much while it lasted, and when it was over they remembered themselves again, and said nothing, and stalked away.

* * * * *

As we grew older and wiser we had permission to extend our explorations to Meudon, Versailles, St. Germain, and other delightful places; to ride thither on hired horses, after having duly learned to ride at the famous "School of Equitation," in the Rue Duphot.

Also, we swam in those delightful summer baths in the Seine, that are so majestically called "Schools of Natation," and became past masters in "la coupe" (a stroke no other Englishman but ourselves has ever been quite able to manage), and in all the different delicate "nuances" of header-taking—"la coulante," "la hussarde," "la tête-bêche," "la tout ce que vous voudrez."

Also, we made ourselves at home in Paris, especially old Paris.

For instance, there was the island of St. Louis, with its stately old mansions *entre cour et jardin*, behind grim stone portals and high walls, where great magistrates and lawyers dwelt in dignified seclusion—the nobles of the robe; but where once had dwelt, in days gone by, the greater nobles

of the sword — crusaders, perhaps, and knights templars, like Brian de Bois Guilbert.

And that other more famous island, la Cité, where Paris itself was born, where Notre Dame reared its twin towers above the melancholy, gray, leprous walls and dirty brown roofs of the Hôtel-Dieu.

Pathetic little tumble-down old houses, all out of drawing and perspective, nestled like old spiders' webs between the buttresses of the great cathedral; and on two sides of the little square in front (the Place du Parvis Notre Dame) stood ancient stone dwellings, with high slate roofs and elaborately-wrought iron balconies. They seemed to have such romantic histories that I never tired of gazing at them, and wondering what the histories could be; and now I think of it, one of these very dwellings must have been the Hôtel de Gondelaurier, where, according to the most veracious historian that ever was, poor Esmeralda once danced and played the tambourine to divert the fair damosel Fleur-de-Lys de Gondelaurier and her noble friends, all of whom she so transcended in beauty, purity, goodness, and breeding (although she was but an untaught, wandering gypsy girl, out of the gutter); and there, before them all and the gay archer, she was betrayed to her final undoing by her goat, whom she had so imprudently taught how to spell the beloved name of "Phébus."

Close by was the Morgue, that gruesome building which the great etcher Méryon has managed to invest with some weird fascination akin to that it had for me in those days—and has now, as I see it with the charmed eyes of Memory.

La Morgue! what a fatal twang there is about the very name!

After gazing one's fill at the horrors within (as became a healthy-minded English boy) it was but a step to the equestrian statue of Henri Quatre, on the Pont-Neuf (the oldest bridge in Paris, by the way); there, astride his long-tailed charger, he smiled, *le roy vert et galant,* just midway between either bank of the historic river, just where it was most historic; and turned his back on the Paris of the Bourgeois King with the pear-shaped face and the mutton-chop whiskers.

And there one stood, spellbound in indecision, like the ass of Buridan between two sacks of oats; for on either side, north or south of the Pont-

Neuf, were to be found enchanting slums, all more attractive the ones than the others, winding up and down hill and roundabout and in and out, like haunting illustrations by Gustave Doré to *Drolatick Tales* by Balzac (not seen or read by me till many years later, I beg to say).

Dark, narrow, silent, deserted streets that would turn up afterwards in many a nightmare—with the gutter in the middle and towerlets and stone posts all along the sides; and high fantastic walls (where it was *défendu d'afficher*), with bits of old battlement at the top, and overhanging boughs of sycamore and lime, and behind them gray old gardens that dated from the days of Louis le Hutin and beyond! And suggestive names printed in old rusty iron letters at the street corners—"Rue Videgousset," "Rue Coupegorge," "Rue de la Vieille Truanderie," "Impasse de la Tour de Nesle," etc., that appealed to the imagination like a chapter from Hugo or Dumas.

And the way to these was by long, tortuous, busy thoroughfares, most irregularly flagged, and all alive with strange, delightful people in blue blouses, brown woollen tricots, wooden shoes, red and white cotton night-caps, rags and patches; most graceful girls, with pretty, self-respecting feet, and flashing eyes, and no head-dress but their own hair; gay, fat hags, all smile; thin hags, with faces of appalling wickedness or misery; precociously witty little gutter-imps of either sex; and such cripples! jovial hunchbacks, lusty blind beggars, merry creeping paralytics, scrofulous wretches who joked and punned about their sores; light-hearted, genial, mendicant monsters without arms or legs, who went ramping through the mud on their bellies from one underground wine-shop to another; and blue-chinned priests and barefooted brown monks and demure Sisters of Charity, and here and there a jolly chiffonnier with his hook, and his knapbasket behind; or a cuirassier, or a gigantic carbineer, or gay little "Hunter of Africa," or a couple of bold gendarmes riding abreast, with their towering black *bon-*

nets à poil; or a pair of pathetic little red-legged soldiers, conscripts just fresh from the country, with innocent light eyes and straw-coloured hair and freckled brown faces, walking hand in hand, and staring at all the pork-butchers' shops—and sometimes at the pork-butcher's wife!

Then a proletarian wedding procession—headed by the bride and bridegroom, an ungainly pair in their Sunday best—all singing noisily together. Then a pauper funeral, or a covered stretcher, followed by sympathetic eyes on its way to the Hôtel-Dieu; or the last sacrament, with bell and candle, bound for the bedside of some humble agonizer *in extremis*—and we all uncovered as it went by.

And then, for a running accompaniment of sound, the clanging chimes, the itinerant street cries, the tinkle of the *marchand de coco,* the drum, the *cor de chasse,* the organ of Barbary, the ubiquitous pet parrot, the knife-grinder, the bawling fried-potato monger, and, most amusing of all, the poodle-clipper and his son, strophe and antistrophe, for every minute the little boy would yell out in his shrill treble that "his father clipped poodles for thirty sous, and was competent also to undertake the management of refractory tomcats," upon which the father would growl in his solemn bass, "My son speaks the truth"—*L'enfant dit vrai!*

And rising above the general cacophony the din of the eternally cracking whip, of the heavy cartwheel jolting over the uneven stones, the stamp and neigh of the spirited little French cart-horse and the music of his many bells, and the cursing and swearing and *hue! dià!* of his driver! It was all entrancing.

*   *   *   *   *

Thence home—to quiet, innocent, suburban Passy—by the quays, walking on the top of the stone parapet all the way, so as to miss nothing (till a gendarme was in sight), or else by the Boulevards, the Rue de Rivoli, the

Champs Élysées, the Avenue de St. Cloud, and the Chaussée de la Muette. What a beautiful walk! Is there another like it anywhere as it was then, in the sweet early forties of this worn-out old century, and before this poor scribe had reached his teens?

Ah! it is something to have known that Paris, which lay at one's feet as one gazed from the heights of Passy, with all its pinnacles and spires and gorgeously-gilded domes, its Arch of Triumph, its Elysian Fields, its Field of Mars, its Towers of our Lady, its far-off Column of July, its Invalids, and Vale of Grace, and Magdalen, and Place of the Concord, where the obelisk reared its exotic peak by the beautiful unforgettable fountains.

There flowed the many-bridged winding river, always the same way, unlike our tidal Thames, and always full; just beyond it was spread that stately, exclusive suburb, the despair of the newly rich and recently ennobled, where almost every other house bore a name which read like a page of French history; and farther still the merry, wicked Latin quarter and the grave Sorbonne, the Pantheon, the Garden of Plants; on the hither side, in the middle distance, the Louvre, where the kings of France had dwelt for centuries; the Tuileries, where "the King of the French" dwelt then, and just for a little while yet.

Well I knew and loved it all; and most of all I loved it when the sun was setting at my back, and innumerable distant windows reflected the blood-red western flame. It seemed as though half Paris were on fire, with the cold blue east for a background.

Dear Paris!

Yes, it is something to have roamed over it as a small boy — a small English boy (that is, a small boy unattended by his mother or his nurse), curious, inquisitive, and indefatigable; full of imagination; all his senses keen with the keenness that belongs to the morning of life: the sight of a hawk, the hearing of a bat, almost the scent of a hound.

Indeed, it required a nose both subtle and unprejudiced to understand and appreciate and thoroughly enjoy that Paris—not the Paris of M. le Baron Haussmann, lighted by gas and electricity, and flushed and drained by modern science; but the "good old Paris" of Balzac and Eugène Sue and *Les Mystères*—the Paris of dim oil-lanterns suspended from iron gibbets (where once aristocrats had been hung); of water-carriers who sold water from their hand-carts, and delivered it at your door (*au cinquième*) for a penny a pail—to drink of, and wash in, and cook with, and all.

There were whole streets—and these by no means the least fascinating and romantic—where the unwritten domestic records of every house were afloat in the air outside it—records not all savory or sweet, but always full of interest and charm!

One knew at a sniff as one passed the *porte cochère* what kind of people lived behind and above; what they ate and what they drank, and what their trade was; whether they did their washing at home, and burned tallow or wax, and mixed chicory with their coffee, and were over-fond of Gruyère cheese—the biggest, cheapest, plainest, and most formidable cheese in the world; whether they fried with oil or butter, and liked their omelets overdone and garlic in their salad, and sipped black-currant brandy or anisette as a liqueur; and were overrun with mice, and used cats or mouse-traps to get rid of them, or neither; and bought violets, or pinks, or gillyflowers in season, and kept them too long; and fasted on Friday with red or white beans, or lentils, or had a dispensation from the Pope—or, haply, even dispensed with the Pope's dispensation.

For of such a telltale kind were the overtones in that complex, odorous clang.

I will not define its fundamental note—ever there, ever the same; big with a warning of quick-coming woe to many households; whose unheeded waves, slow but sure, and ominous as those that rolled on great occasions

from le Bourdon de Notre Dame (the Big Ben of Paris), drove all over the gay city and beyond, night and day—penetrating every corner, overflowing the most secret recesses, drowning the very incense by the altar-steps.

> "*Le pauvre en sa cabane où le chaume le couvre*
> *Est sujet à ses lois;*
> *Et la garde qui veille aux barrières du Louvre*
> *N'en défend point nos rois.*"

And here, as I write, the faint, scarcely perceptible, ghost-like suspicion of a scent—a mere nostalgic fancy, compound, generic, synthetic and all-embracing—an abstract olfactory symbol of the "Tout Paris" of fifty years ago, comes back to me out of the past; and fain would I inhale it in all its pristine fulness and vigour. For scents, like musical sounds, are rare sublimators of the essence of memory (this is a prodigious fine phrase—I hope it means something), and scents need not be seductive in themselves to recall the seductions of scenes and days gone by.

Alas! scents cannot be revived at will, like an

> "*Air doux et tendre*
> *Jadis aimé!*"

Oh, that I could hum or whistle an old French smell! I could evoke all Paris, sweet, præ-imperial Paris, in a single whiff!

* * * * *

In such fashion did we three small boys, like the three musketeers (the fame of whose exploits was then filling all France), gather and pile up sweet memories, to chew the cud thereof in after-years, when far away and apart.

Of all that *bande joyeuse*—old and young and middle-aged, from M. le Major to Mimsey Seraskier—all are now dead but me—all except dear

Madge, who was so pretty and light-hearted; and I have never seen her since.

* * * * *

Thus have I tried, with as much haste as I could command (being one of the plodding sort) to sketch that happy time, which came to an end suddenly and most tragically when I was twelve years old.

My dear and jovial happy-go-lucky father was killed in a minute by the explosion of a safety lamp of his own invention, which was to have superseded Sir Humphry Davy's, and made our fortune! What a brutal irony of fate.

So sanguine was he of success, so confident that his ship had come home at last, that he had been in treaty for a nice little old manor in Anjou (with a nice little old castle to match), called la Marière, which had belonged to his ancestors, and from which we took our name (for we were Pasquier de la Marière, of quite a good old family); and there we were to live on our own land, as *gentilshommes campagnards*, and be French for evermore, under a paternal, pear-faced bourgeois king as a temporary *pis-aller* until Henri Cinq, Comte de Chambord, should come to his own again, and make us counts and barons and peers of France—Heaven knows what for!

My mother, who was beside herself with grief, went over to London, where this miserable accident had occurred, and had barely arrived there when she was delivered of a still-born child, and died almost immediately; and I became an orphan in less than a week, and a penniless one. For it turned out that my father had by this time spent every penny of his own and my mother's capital, and had, moreover, died deeply in debt. I was too young and too grief-stricken to feel anything but the terrible bereavement, but it soon became patent to me that an immense alteration was to be made in my mode of life.

"FAREWELL TO PASSY"

A relative of my mother's, Colonel Ibbetson (who was well off), came to Passy to do his best for me, and pay what debts had been incurred in the neighborhood, and settle my miserable affairs.

After a while it was decided by him and the rest of the family that I should go back with him to London, there to be disposed of for the best, according to his lights.

And on a beautiful June morning, redolent of lilac and syringa, and gay with dragon-flies and butterflies and humble-bees, my happy childhood ended as it had begun. My farewells were heart-rending (to me), but showed that I could inspire affection as well as feel it, and that was some compensation for my woe.

"Adieu, cher Monsieur Gogo. Bonne chance, et le Bon Dieu vous bénisse," said le Père et la Mère François. Tears trickled down the Major's hooked nose on to his mustache, now nearly white.

Madame Seraskier strained me to her kind heart, and blessed and kissed me again and again, and rained her warm tears on my face; and hers was the last figure I saw as our fly turned into the Rue de la Tour on our way to London, Colonel Ibbetson exclaiming—

"Gad! who's the lovely young giantess that seems so fond of you, you little rascal, hey? By George! you young Don Giovanni, I'd have given something to be in your place! And who's that nice old man with the long green coat and the red ribbon? A *vieille moustache*, I suppose; looks almost like a gentleman. Precious few Frenchmen can do that!"

Such was Colonel Ibbetson.

And then and there, even as he spoke, a little drop of sullen, chill dislike to my guardian and benefactor, distilled from his voice, his aspect, the expression of his face, and his way of saying things, suddenly trickled into my consciousness—never to be wiped away!

As for poor Mimsey, her grief was so overwhelming that she could not come out and wish me good-bye like the others; and it led, as I afterwards heard, to a long illness, the worst she ever had; and when she recovered it was to find that her beautiful mother was no more.

Madame Seraskier died of the cholera, and so did le Père et la Mère François, and Madame Pelé, and one of the Napoleonic prisoners (not M. le Major), and several other people we had known, including a servant of our own, Thérèse, the devoted Thérèse, to whom we were all devoted in return. That malodorous tocsin, which I have compared to the big bell of Notre Dame, had warned, and warned, and warned in vain.

The *maison de santé* was broken up. M. le Major and his friends went and roosted on parole elsewhere, until a good time arrived for them, when their lost leader came back and remained—first as President of the French Republic, then as Emperor of the French themselves. No more parole was needed after that.

My grandmother and Aunt Plunket and her children fled in terror to Tours, and Mimsey went to Russia with her father.

Thus miserably ended that too happy septennate, and so no more at present of

"Le joli lieu de ma naissance!"

PART TWO

PART TWO

The next decade of my outer life is so uninteresting, even to myself, that I will hurry through it as fast as I can. It will prove dull reading, I fear.

My Uncle Ibbetson (as I now called him) took to me and arranged to educate and start me in life, and make "a gentleman" of me—an "English gentleman." But I had to change my name and adopt his; for some reason I did not know, he seemed to hate my father's very name. Perhaps it was because he had injured my father through life in many ways, and my father had always forgiven him; a very good reason! Perhaps it was because he had proposed to my mother three times when she was a girl, and had been thrice refused! (After the third time, he went to India for seven years, and just before his departure my father and mother were married, and a year after that I was born.)

So Pierre Pasquier de la Marière, *alias* Monsieur Gogo, became Master Peter Ibbetson, and went to Bluefriars, the gray-coat school, where he spent six years—an important slice out of a man's life, especially at that age.

I hated the garb, I hated the surroundings—the big hospital at the back, and that reek of cruelty, drunkenness, and filth, the cattle-market—where every other building was either a slaughter-house, a gin-palace, or a pawnbroker's shop; more than all I hated the gloomy jail opposite, where they sometimes hanged a man in public on a Monday morning. This dismal prison haunted my dreams when I wanted to dream of Passy, of my dear dead father and mother and Madame Seraskier.

For the first term or two they were ever in my thoughts, and I was always trying to draw their profiles on desks and slates and copybooks, till at last all resemblance seemed to fade out of them; and then I drew M. le Major till his side face became quite demoralized and impossible, and ceased to be like anything in life. Then I fell back on others: le Père François, with his eternal *bonnet de coton* and sabots stuffed with straw; the dog Médor, the rocking-horse, and all the rest of the menagerie; the diligence that brought me away from Paris; the heavily jack-booted couriers in shiny hats and pigtails, and white breeches, and short-tailed blue coats covered with silver buttons, who used to ride through Passy, on their way to and fro between the Tuileries and St. Cloud, on little, neighing, gray stallions with bells round their necks and tucked-up tails, and beautiful heads like the horses' heads in the Elgin Marbles.

In my sketches they always looked and walked and trotted the same way: to the left, or westward as it would be on the map. M. le Major, Madame Seraskier, Médor, the diligences and couriers, were all bound westward by common consent—all going to London, I suppose, to look after me, who was so dotingly fond of them.

Some of the boys used to admire these sketches and preserve them—some of the bigger boys would value my idealized (!) profiles of Madame Seraskier, with eyelashes quite an inch in length, and an eye three times the size of her mouth; and thus I made myself an artistic reputation for a while. But it did not last long, for my vein was limited; and soon another boy came to the school, who surpassed me in variety and interest of subject, and could draw profiles looking either way with equal ease; he is now a famous Academician, and seems to have preserved much of his old facility.*

* * * * *

Thus, on the whole, my school career was neither happy nor unhappy, nor did I distinguish myself in any way, nor (though I think I was rather liked than otherwise) make any great or lasting friendships; on the other hand, I did not in any way disgrace myself, nor make a single enemy that I knew of. Except that I grew out of the common tall and very strong, a more commonplace boy than I must have seemed (after my artistic vein had run itself dry) never went to a public school. So much for my outer life at Bluefriars.

But I had an inner world of my own, whose capital was Passy, whose

*NOTE.—*I have here omitted several pages, containing a description in detail of my cousin's life "at Bluefriars"; and also the portraits (not always flattering) which he has written of masters and boys, many of whom are still alive, and some of whom have risen to distinction; but these sketches would be without special interest unless the names were given as well, and that would be unadvisable for many reasons. Moreover, there is not much in what I have left out that has any bearing on his subsequent life, or the development of his character.*

Madge Plunket

fauna and flora were not to be surpassed by anything in Regent's Park or the Zoological Gardens.

It was good to think of it by day, to dream of it by night, *although I had not yet learned how to dream!*

There were soon other and less exclusive regions, however, which I

shared with other boys of that by-gone day. Regions of freedom and delight, where I heard the ominous crack of Deerslayer's rifle, and was friends with Chingachgook and his noble son—the last, alas! of the Mohicans: where Robin Hood and Friar Tuck made merry, and exchanged buffets with Lion-hearted Richard under the green-wood tree: where Quentin Durward, happy squire of dames, rode midnightly by their side through the gibbet-and-gypsy-haunted forests of Touraine. . . . Ah! I had my dream of chivalry!

Happy times and climes! One must be a gray-coated school-boy, in the heart of foggy London, to know that nostalgia.

Not, indeed, but what London has its merits. Sam Weller lived there, and Charley Bates, and the irresistible Artful Dodger—and Dick Swiveller, and his adorable Marchioness, who divided my allegiance with Rebecca of York and sweet Diana Vernon.

It was good to be an English boy in those days, and care for such friends as these! But it was good to be a French boy also; to have known Paris, to possess the true French feel of things—and the language.

Indeed, bilingual boys—boys double-tongued from their very birth (especially in French and English)—enjoy certain rare privileges. It is not a bad thing for a school-boy (since a school-boy he must be) to hail from two mother-countries if he can, and revel now and then in the sweets of home-sickness for that of his two mother-countries in which he does not happen to be; and read *Les Trois Mousquetaires* in the cloisters of Bluefriars, or *Ivanhoe* in the dull, dusty prison-yard that serves for a playground in so many a French *lycée*!

Without listening, he hears all round him the stodgy language of every day, and the blatant shouts of his school-fellows, in the voices he knows so painfully well—those shrill trebles, those cracked barytones and frog-like early basses! There they go, bleating and croaking and yelling; Dick, Tom, and Harry, or Jules, Hector, and Alphonse! How vaguely tiresome and trivial and commonplace they are—those too familiar sounds; yet what an additional charm they lend to that so utterly different but equally familiar word-stream that comes silently flowing into his consciousness through his rapt eyes! The luxurious sense of mental exclusiveness and self-sequestration is made doubly complete by the contrast!

And for this strange enchantment to be well and thoroughly felt, both his languages must be native; not acquired, however perfectly. Every single word must have its roots deep down in a personal past so remote for him as to be almost unremembered; the very sound and printed aspect of each must be rich in childish memories of home; in all the countless, nameless, priceless associations that make it sweet and fresh and strong, and racy of the soil.

Oh! Porthos, Athos, and D'Artagnan—how I loved you, and your immortal squires, Planchet, Grimaud, Mousqueton! How well and wittily you spoke the language I adored—better even than good Monsieur Lallemand,

the French master at Bluefriars, who could wield the most irregular subjunctives as if they had been mere feathers—trifles light as air.

Then came the Count of Monte-Cristo, who taught me (only too well) his terrible lesson of hatred and revenge; and *Les Mystères de Paris*, *Le Juif Errant*, and others.

But no words that I can think of in either mother-tongue can express what I felt when first, through these tear-dimmed eyes of mine, and deep into my harrowed soul, came silently flowing the never-to-be-forgotten history of poor Esmeralda,* my first love! whose cruel fate filled with pity, sorrow, and indignation the last term of my life at school. It was the most important, the most solemn, the most epoch-making event of my school life. I read it, reread it, and read it again. I have not been able to read it since; it is rather long! but how well I remember it, and how short it seemed then! and oh! how short those well-spent hours!

That mystic word 'Ανάγκη! I wrote it on the flyleaf of all my books. I carved it on my desk. I intoned it in the echoing cloisters! I vowed I would make a pilgrimage to Notre Dame some day, that I might hunt for it in every hole and corner there, and read it with my own eyes, and feel it with my own forefinger.

And then that terrible prophetic song the old hag sings in the dark slum—how it haunted me, too! I could not shake it out of my troubled consciousness for months:

"*Grouille, grève, grève, grouille,*
File, file, ma quenouille:
File sa corde au bourreau
Qui siffle dans le préau.

* * *

" 'Ανάγκη! 'Ανάγκη! 'Ανάγκη!"

* * *

**Notre-Dame de Paris*, par Victor Hugo.

Yes; it was worth while having been a little French boy just for a few years.

I especially found it so during the holidays, which I regularly spent at Bluefriars; for there was a French circulating library in Holborn, close by — a paradise. It was kept by a delightful old French lady who had seen better days, and was very kind to me, and did not lend me all the books I asked for!

Thus irresistibly beguiled by these light wizards of our degenerate age, I dreamed away most of my school life, utterly deaf to the voices of the older enchanters — Homer, Horace, Virgil — whom I was sent to school on purpose to make friends with; a deafness I lived to deplore, like other dunces, when it was too late.

* * * * *

And I was not only given to dream by day — I dreamed by night; my sleep was full of dreams — terrible nightmares, exquisite visions, strange scenes full of inexplicable reminiscence; all vague and incoherent, like all men's dreams that have hitherto been; *for I had not yet learned how to dream.*

A vast world, a dread and beautiful chaos, an ever-changing kaleidoscope of life, too shadowy and dim to leave any lasting impression on the busy, waking mind; with here and there more vivid images of terror or delight, that one remembered for a few hours with a strange wonder and questioning, as Coleridge remembered his Abyssinian maid who played upon the dulcimer (a charming and most original combination).

The whole cosmos is in a man's brains — as much of it, at least, as a man's brains will hold; perhaps it is nowhere else. And when sleep relaxes the will, and there are no earthly surroundings to distract attention — no duty, pain, or pleasure to compel it—riderless Fancy takes the bit in its teeth, and the whole cosmos goes mad and has its wild will of us.

Ineffable false joys, unspeakable false terror and distress, strange phantoms only seen as in a glass darkly, chase each other without rhyme or reason, and play hide-and-seek across the twilit field and through the dark recesses of our clouded and imperfect consciousness.

And the false terrors and distress, however unspeakable, are no worse than such real terrors and distress as are only too often the waking lot of man, or even so bad; but the ineffable false joys transcend all possible human felicity while they last, and a little while it is! We wake, and wonder, and recall the slight foundation on which such ultra-human bliss has seemed to rest. What matters the foundation if but the bliss be there, and the brain has nerves to feel it?

Poor human nature, so richly endowed with nerves of anguish, so splendidly organized for pain and sorrow, is but slenderly equipped for joy.

What hells have we not invented for the afterlife! Indeed, what hells we have often made of this, both for ourselves and others, and at really such a very small cost of ingenuity, after all!

Perhaps the biggest and most benighted fools have been the best hell-makers.

Whereas the best of our heavens is but a poor perfunctory conception, for all that the highest and cleverest among us have done their very utmost to decorate and embellish it, and make life there seem worth living. So impossible it is to imagine or invent beyond the sphere of our experience.

Now, these dreams of mine (common to many) of the false but ineffable joys, are they not a proof that there exist in the human brain hidden capacities, dormant potentialities of bliss, unsuspected hitherto, to be developed some day, perhaps, and placed within the reach of all, wakers and sleepers alike?

A sense of ineffable joy, attainable at will, and equal in intensity and duration to (let us say) an attack of sciatica, would go far to equalize the sorrowful, one-sided conditions under which we live.

* * * * *

But there is one thing which, as a school-boy, I never dreamed – namely, that I, and one other holding a torch, should one day, by common consent, find our happiness in exploring these mysterious caverns of the brain; and should lay the foundations of order where only misrule had been before: and out of all those unreal, waste, and transitory realms of illusion, evolve a real, stable, and habitable world, which all who run may reach.

* * * * *

At last I left school for good, and paid a visit to my Uncle Ibbetson in Hopshire, where he was building himself a lordly new pleasure-house on his own land, as the old one he had inherited a year or two ago was no longer good enough for him.

It was an uninteresting coast on the German Ocean, without a rock, or a cliff, or a pier, or a tree; even without cold gray stones for the sea to break on – nothing but sand! – a bourgeois kind of sea, charmless in its best moods, and not very terrible in its wrath, except to a few stray fishermen whom it employed, and did not seem to reward very munificently.

Inland it was much the same. One always thought of the country as gray, until one looked and found that it was green; and then, if one were old and wise, one thought no more about it, and turned one's gaze inward. Moreover, it seemed to rain incessantly.

But it was the country and the sea, after Bluefriars and the cloisters—after Newgate, St. Bartholomew, and Smithfield.

And one could fish and bathe in the sea after all, and ride in the country, and even follow the hounds, a little later; which would have been a joy beyond compare if one had not been blessed with an uncle who thought one rode like a French tailor, and told one so, and mimicked one, in the presence of charming young ladies who rode in perfection.

In fact, it was heaven itself by comparison, and would have remained so longer but for Colonel Ibbetson's efforts to make a gentleman of me—an English gentleman.

What is a gentleman? It is a grand old name; but what does it mean?

At one time, to say of a man that he is a gentleman, is to confer on him the highest title of distinction we can think of; even if we are speaking of a prince.

At another, to say of a man that he is *not* a gentleman is almost to stigmatize him as a social outcast, unfit for the company of his kind—even if it is only one haberdasher speaking of another.

Who is a gentleman, and yet who *is not*?

The Prince of Darkness was one, and so was Mr. John Halifax, if we are to believe those who knew them best; and so was one "Pelham," according to the late Sir Edward Bulwer, Earl of Lytton, etc.; and it certainly seemed as if *he* ought to know.

And I was to be another, according to Roger Ibbetson, Esquire, of Ibbetson Hall, late Colonel of the ——, and it certainly seemed as if he ought to know too! The word was as constantly on his lips (when talking to *me*) as though, instead of having borne her Majesty's commission, he were a hairdresser's assistant who had just come into an independent fortune.

This course of tuition began pleasantly enough, before I left London, by his sending me to his tailors, who made me several beautiful suits; es-

pecially an evening suit, which has lasted me for life, alas; and these, after the uniform of the gray-coat school, were like an initiation to the splendors of freedom and manhood.

Colonel Ibbetson—or Uncle Ibbetson, as I used to call him—was my mother's first cousin; my grandmother, Mrs. Biddulph, was the sister of his father, the late Archdeacon Ibbetson, a very pious, learned, and exemplary divine, of good family.

But his mother (the Archdeacon's second wife) had been the only child and heiress of an immensely rich pawnbroker, by name Mendoza; a Portuguese Jew, with a dash of colored blood in his veins besides, it was said; and, indeed, this remote African strain still showed itself in Uncle Ibbetson's thick lips, wide-open nostrils, and big black eyes with yellow whites—and especially in his long, splay, lark-heeled feet, which gave both himself and the best bootmaker in London a great deal of trouble.

Otherwise, and in spite of his ugly face, he was not without a certain soldier-like air of distinction, being very tall and powerfully built. He wore stays, and an excellent wig, for he was prematurely bald; and he carried his hat on one side, which (in my untutored eyes) made him look very much like a "*swell,*" but not quite like a *gentleman.*

To wear your hat jauntily cocked over one eye, and yet "look like a gentleman!"

It can be done, I am told; and has been, and is even still! It is not, perhaps, a very lofty achievement—but such as it is, it requires a somewhat rare combination of social and physical gifts in the wearer; and the possession of either Semitic or African blood does not seem to be one of these.

Colonel Ibbetson could do a little of everything—sketch (especially a steam-boat on a smooth sea, with beautiful thick smoke reflected in the water), play the guitar, sing chansonnettes and canzonets, write society verses, quote De Musset—

"Avez-vous vu dans Barcelone
Une Andalouse au sein bruni?"

He would speak French whenever he could, even to an English ostler, and then recollect himself suddenly, and apologize for his thoughtlessness; and even when he spoke English, he would embroider it with little twopenny French tags and idioms: "Pour tout potage"; "Nous avons changé tout cela"; "Que diable allait-il faire dans cette galère?" etc.; or Italian, "Chi lo sa?" "Pazienza!" "Ahimè!" or even Latin, "Eheu fugaces," and "Vidi tantum!" for he had been an Eton boy. It must have been very cheap Latin, for I could always understand it myself! He drew the line at German and Greek; fortunately, for so do I. He was a bachelor, and his domestic arrangements had been irregular, and I will not dwell upon them; but his house, as far as it went, seemed to promise better things.

His architect, Mr. Lintot, an extraordinary little man, full of genius and quite self-made, became my friend and taught me to smoke, and drink gin and water.

He did his work well; but of an evening he used to drink more than was good for him, and rave about Shelley, his only poet. He would recite "The

Skylark" (his only poem) with uncertain *h's*, and a rather cockney accent –

> *" 'Ail to thee, blythe sperrit!*
> *Bird thou never wert,*
> *That from 'eaven, or near it*
> *Po'rest thy full 'eart*
> *In profuse strains of hunpremeditated hart."*

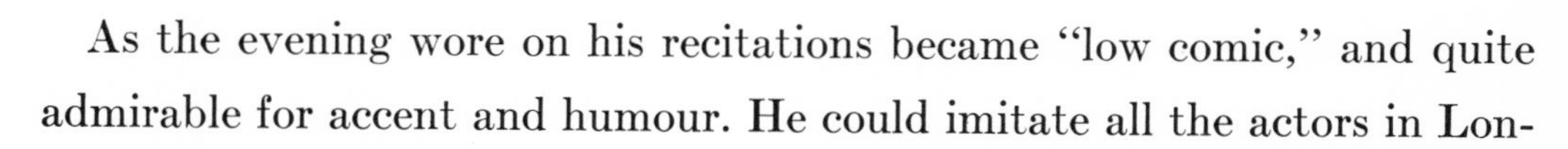

As the evening wore on his recitations became "low comic," and quite admirable for accent and humour. He could imitate all the actors in Lon-

don (none of which I had seen) so well as to transport me with delight and wonder; and all this with nobody but me for an audience, as we sat smoking and drinking together in his room at the "Ibbetson Arms."

I felt grateful to adoration.

Later still, he would become sentimental again; and dilate to me on the joys of his wedded life, on the extraordinary intellect and beauty of Mrs. Lintot. First he would describe to me the beauties of her mind, and compare her to "L. E. L." and Felicia Hemans. Then he would fall back on her physical perfections; there was nobody worthy to be compared to her in these—but I draw the veil.

He was very egotistical. Whatever he did, whatever he liked, whatever belonged to him, was better than anything else in the world; and he was cleverer than any one else, except Mrs. Lintot, to whom he yielded the palm; and then he would cheer up and become funny again.

In fact his self-satisfaction was quite extraordinary; and what is more extraordinary still, it was not a bit offensive—at least, to me; perhaps because he was such a tiny little man; or because much of this vanity of his seemed to have no very solid foundation, for it was not of the gifts I most admired in him that he was vainest; or because it came out most when he was most tipsy, and genial tipsiness redeems so much; or else because he was most vain about things I should never have been vain about myself; and the most unpardonable vanity in others is that which is secretly our own, whether we are conscious of it or not.

And then he was the first funny man I had ever met. What a gift it is! He was always funny when he tried to be, whether one laughed with him or at him, and I loved him for it. Nothing on earth is more pathetically pitiable than the funny man when he still tries and succeeds no longer.

The moment Lintot's vein was exhausted, he had the sense to leave off and begin to cry, which was still funny; and then I would help him upstairs to his room, and he would jump out of his clothes and into his bed and be asleep in a second, with the tears still trickling down his little nose—and even that was funny!

But next morning he was stern and alert and indefatigable, as though

gin and poetry and conjugal love had never been, and fun were a capital crime.

Uncle Ibbetson thought highly of him as an architect, but not otherwise; he simply made use of him.

"He's a terrible little snob, of course, and hasn't got an *h* in his head" (as if *that* were a capital crime); "but he's very clever—look at that campanile—and then he's cheap, my boy, cheap."

There were several fine houses in fine parks not very far from Ibbetson Hall; but although Uncle Ibbetson appeared in name and wealth and social position to be on a par with their owners, he was not on terms of intimacy with any of them, or even of acquaintance, as far as I know, and spoke of them with contempt, as barbarians—people with whom he had nothing in common. Perhaps they, too, had found out this incompatibility, especially the ladies; for, school-boy as I was, I was not long in discovering that his manner towards those of the other sex was not always such as to please either them or their husbands or fathers or brothers. The way he looked at them was enough. Indeed, most of his lady friends and acquaintances through life had belonged to the *corps de ballet*, the *demi-monde*, etc.—not, I should imagine, the best school of manners in the world.

On the other hand, he was very friendly with some families in the town; the doctor's, the rector's, his own agent's (a broken-down brother officer and bosom friend, who had ceased to love him since he received his pay); and he used to take Mr. Lintot and me to parties there; and he was the life of those parties.

He sang little French songs, with no voice, but quite a good French accent, and told little anecdotes with no particular point, but in French and Italian (so that the point was never missed); and we all laughed and admired without quite knowing why, except that he was the lord of the manor.

"ONE OF UNCLE IBBETSON'S WALTZES"

On these festive occasions poor Lintot's confidence and power of amusing seemed to desert him altogether; he sat glum in a corner.

Though a radical and a sceptic, and a peace-at-any-price man, he was much impressed by the social status of the army and the church.

Of the doctor, a very clever and accomplished person, and the best educated man for miles around, he thought little; but the rector, the colonel, the poor captain, even, now a mere land-steward, seemed to fill him with respectful awe. And for his pains he was cruelly snubbed by Mrs. Captain and Mrs. Rector and their plain daughters, who little guessed what talents he concealed, and thought him quite a common little man, hardly fit to turn over the leaves of their music.

It soon became pretty evident that Ibbetson was very much smitten with a Mrs. Deane, the widow of a brewer, a very handsome woman indeed, in her own estimation and mine, and everybody else's, except Mr. Lintot's, who said, "Pooh, you should see my wife!"

Her mother, Mrs. Glyn, excelled us all in her admiration of Colonel Ibbetson.

For instance, Mrs. Deane would play some common little waltz of the cheap kind that is never either remembered or forgotten, and Mrs. Glyn would exclaim, "*Is* not that *lovely*?"

And Ibbetson would say: "Charming! charming! Whose is it? Rossini's? Mozart's?"

"Why, no, my dear colonel. Don't you remember? *It's your own!*"

"Ah, so it is! I had quite forgotten." And general laughter and applause would burst forth at such a natural mistake on the part of our great man.

Well, I could neither play nor sing, and found it far easier by this time to speak English than French, especially to English people who were ignorant of any language but their own. Yet sometimes Colonel Ibbetson would seem quite proud of me.

"Deux mètres, bien sonnés!" he would say, alluding to my stature, "et le profil d'Antinoüs!" which he would pronounce without the two little dots on the *u*.

And afterwards, if he had felt his evening a pleasant one, if he had sung all he knew, if Mrs. Deane had been more than usually loving and self-surrendering, and I had distinguished myself by skilfully turning over the leaves when her mother had played the piano, he would tell me, as we walked home together, that I "did credit to his name, and that I would make an excellent figure in the world as soon as I had *décrassé* myself; that I must get another dress-suit from his tailor, just an eighth of an inch longer in the tails; that I should have a commission in his old regiment (the Eleventeenth Royal Bounders), a deuced crack cavalry regiment; and see the world and break a few hearts (it is not for nothing that our friends have pretty wives and sisters); and finally marry some beautiful young heiress of title, and make a home for him when he was a poor solitary old fellow. Very little would do for him: a crust of bread, a glass of wine and water, and a clean napkin, a couple of rooms, and an old piano and a few good books. For, of course, Ibbetson Hall would be mine and every penny he possessed in the world."

All this in confidential French—lest the very clouds should hear us—and with the familiar thee and thou of blood-relationship, which I did not care to return.

It did not seem to bode very serious intentions towards Mrs. Deane, and would scarcely have pleased her mother.

Or else, if something had crossed him, and Mrs. Deane had flirted outrageously with somebody else, and he had not been asked to sing (or somebody else had), he would assure me in good round English that I was the most infernal lout that ever disgraced a drawing-room, or ate a man out of house and home, and that he was sick and ashamed of me. "Why can't you sing, you d——d French milksop? That d——d roulade-monger of a father of yours could sing fast enough, if he could do nothing else, confound him! Why can't you talk French, you infernal British booby? Why can't you hand round the tea and muffins, confound you! Why, twice Mrs. Glyn dropped her pocket-handkerchief and had to pick it up herself! What, 'at the other end of the room,' were you? Well, you should have skipped *across* the room, and picked it up, and handed it to her with a pretty speech, like a gentleman! When I was your age I was *always* on the lookout for ladies' pocket-handkerchiefs to drop—or their fans! I never missed *one*!"

Then he would take me out to shoot with him (for it was quite essential that an English gentleman should be a sportsman)—a terrible ordeal to both of us.

A snipe that I did not want to kill in the least would sometimes rise and fly right and left like a flash of lightning, and I would miss it—always; and he would d——n me for a son of a confounded French Micawber, and miss the next himself, and get into a rage and thrash his dog, a pointer that I was very fond of. Once he thrashed her so cruelly that I saw scarlet, and nearly yielded to the impulse of emptying both my barrels in his broad back. If I had done so it would have passed for a mere mishap, after all, and saved many future complications.

One day he pointed out to me a small bird pecking in a field—an extremely pretty bird—I think it was a skylark—and whispered to me in his most sarcastic manner—

"Look here, you Peter without any salt, do you think, if you were to kneel down and rest your gun comfortably on this gate without making a noise, and take a careful aim, you could manage to shoot that bird *sitting*? I've heard of some Frenchmen who would be equal to *that*!"

"'AIL TO THEE, BLYTHE SPERRIT!"

I said I would try, and, resting my gun as he told me, I carefully aimed a couple of yards above the bird's head, and mentally ejaculating,

" 'Ail to thee, blythe sperrit!"

I fired both barrels (for fear of any after-mishap to Ibbetson), and the bird naturally flew away.

After this he never took me out shooting with him again; and, indeed, I had discovered to my discomfiture that I, the friend and admirer and would-be emulator of Natty Bumppo the Deerslayer, I, the familiar of the last of the Mohicans and his scalp-lifting father, could not bear the sight of blood—least of all, of blood shed by myself, and for my own amusement.

The only beast that ever fell to my gun during those shootings with Uncle Ibbetson was a young rabbit, and that more by accident than design, although I did not tell Uncle Ibbetson so.

As I picked it off the ground, and felt its poor little warm narrow chest, and the last beats of its heart under its weak ribs, and saw the blood on its fur, I was smitten with pity, shame, and remorse; and settled with myself that I would find some other road to English gentlemanhood than the slaying of innocent wild things whose happy life seems so well worth living.

I must eat them, I suppose, but I would never shoot them any more; my hands, at least, should be clean of blood henceforward.

Alas, the irony of fate!

*   *   *   *   *

The upshot of all this was that he confided to Mrs. Deane the task of licking his cub of a nephew into shape. She took me in hand with right good-will, and began by teaching me how to dance, that I might dance with her at the coming hunt ball; and I did so nearly all night, to my infinite joy and triumph, and to the disgust of Colonel Ibbetson, who could dance much better than I—to the disgust, indeed, of many smart men in red coats and black, for she was considered the belle of the evening.

Of course I fell, or fancied I fell, in love with her. To her mother's extreme distress, she gave me every encouragement, partly for fun, partly to annoy Colonel Ibbetson, whom she had apparently grown to hate. And, indeed, from the way he often spoke of her to me (this trainer of English gentlemen), he well deserved that she should hate him. He never had the slightest intention of marrying her—that is certain; and yet he had made her the talk of the place.

And here I may state that Ibbetson was one of those singular men who go through life afflicted with the mania that they are fatally irresistible to women.

He was never weary of pursuing them—not through any special love of gallantry for its own sake, I believe, but from the mere wish to appear as a Don Giovanni in the eyes of others. Nothing made him happier than to be seen whispering mysteriously in corners with the prettiest woman in the room. He did not seem to perceive that for one woman silly or vain or vulgar enough to be flattered by his idiotic persecution, a dozen would loathe the very sight of him, and show it plainly enough.

This vanity had increased with years and assumed a very dangerous form. He became indiscreet, and, more disastrous still, he told lies! The very dead—the honored and irreproachable dead—were not even safe in their graves. It was his revenge for unforgotten slights.

He who kisses and tells, he who tells even though he has not kissed—what can be said for him, what should be done to him?

Ibbetson one day expiated this miserable craze with his life, and the man who took it—more by accident than design, it is true—has not yet found it in his heart to feel either compunction or regret.

* * * * *

So there was a great row between Ibbetson and myself. He d——d and confounded and abused me in every way, and my father before me, and finally struck me; and I had sufficient self-command not to strike him back, but left him then and there with as much dignity as I could muster.

Thus unsuccessfully ended my brief experience of English country life—a little hunting and shooting and fishing, a little dancing and flirting; just enough of each to show me I was unfit for all.

A bitter-sweet remembrance, full of humiliation, but not altogether without charm. There was the beauty of sea and open sky and changing country weather; and the beauty of Mrs. Deane, who made a fool of me to revenge herself on Colonel Ibbetson for trying to make a fool of her, whereby he became the laughing-stock of the neighborhood for at least nine days.

And I revenged myself on both—heroically, as I thought; though where the heroism comes in, and where the revenge, does not appear quite patent.

For I ran away to London, and enlisted in her Majesty's Household Cavalry, where I remained a twelvemonth, and was happy enough, and learned a great deal more good than harm.

Then I was bought out and articled to Mr. Lintot, architect and surveyor: a conclave of my relatives agreeing to allow me ninety pounds a year for three years; then all hands were to be washed of me altogether.*

* * * * *

So I took a small lodging in Pentonville, to be near Mr. Lintot, and worked hard at my new profession for three years, during which nothing of importance occurred in my outer life. After this Lintot employed me as a salaried clerk, and I do not think he had any reason to complain of me, nor did he make any complaint. I was worth my hire, I think, and something over; which I never got and never asked for.

Nor did I complain of him; for with all his little foibles of vanity, irascibility, and egotism, and a certain close-fistedness, he was a good fellow and a very clever one.

His paragon of a wife was by no means the beautiful person he had made her out to be, nor did anybody but he seem to think her so.

She was a little older than himself; very large and massive, with stern but not irregular features, and a very high forehead; she had a slight tendency to baldness, and colorless hair that she wore in an austere curl on each side of her face, and a menacing little topknot on her occiput. She had been a Unitarian and a governess, was fond of good long words, like Dr. Johnson, and very censorious.

*NOTE.—*I have thought it better to leave out, in its entirety, my cousin's account of his short career as a private soldier. It consists principally of personal descriptions that are not altogether unprejudiced; he seems never to have quite liked those who were placed in authority above him, either at school or in the army.*

But one of my husband's intimate friends, General ——, who was cornet in the Life Guards in my poor cousin's time, writes me that "he remembers him well, as far and away the tallest and handsomest lad in the whole regiment, of immense physical strength, unimpeachable good conduct, and a thorough gentleman from top to toe."

Madge Plunket

Her husband's occasional derelictions in the matter of grammar and accent must have been very trying to her!

She knew her own mind about everything under the sun, and expected that other people should know it, too, and be of the same mind as herself. And yet she was not proud; indeed, she was a very dragon of humility, and had raised injured meekness to the rank of a militant virtue. And well she knew how to be master and mistress in her own house!

But with all this she was an excellent wife to Mr. Lintot and a devoted mother to his children, who were very plain and subdued (and adored their father); so that Lintot, who thought her Venus and Diana and Minerva in one, was the happiest man in all Pentonville.

And, on the whole, she was kind and considerate to me, and I always did my best to please her.

Moreover (a gift for which I could never be too grateful), she presented me with an old square piano, which had belonged to her mother, and had done duty in her school-room, till Lintot gave her a new one (for she was a highly cultivated musician of the severest classical type). It became the principal ornament of my small sitting-room, which it nearly filled, and on it I tried to learn my notes, and would pick out with one finger the old beloved melodies my father used to sing, and my mother play on the harp.

To sing myself was, it seems, out of the question; my voice (which I trust was not too disagreeable when I was content merely to speak) became as that of a bull-frog under a blanket whenever I strove to express myself in song; my larynx refused to produce the notes I held so accurately in my mind, and the result was disaster.

On the other hand, in my mind I could sing most beautifully. Once on a rainy day, inside an Islington omnibus, I mentally sang "Adelaida" with the voice of Mr. Sims Reeves—an unpardonable liberty to take; and although it is not for me to say so, I sang it even better than he, for I made myself shed tears—so much so that a kind old gentleman sitting opposite seemed to feel for me very much.

I also had the faculty of remembering any tune I once heard, and would whistle it correctly ever after—even one of Uncle Ibbetson's waltzes!

As an instance of this, worth recalling, one night I found myself in Guildford Street, walking in the same direction as another belated individual (only on the other side of the road), who, just as the moon came out of a cloud, was moved to whistle.

He whistled exquisitely, and, what was more, he whistled quite the most

beautiful tune I had ever heard. I felt all its changes and modulations, its majors and minors, just as if a whole band had been there to play the accompaniment, so cunning and expressive a whistler was he.

And so entranced was I that I made up my mind to cross over and ask him what it was—"Your melody or your life!" But he suddenly stopped at No. 48, and let himself in with his key before I could prefer my humble request.

Well, I went whistling that tune all next day, and for many days after, without ever finding out what it was; till one evening, happening to be at the Lintots, I asked Mrs. Lintot (who happened to be at the piano) if she knew it, and began to whistle it once more. To my delight and surprise she straightway accompanied it all through (a wonderful condescension in so severe a purist), and I did not make a single wrong note.

"Yes," said Mrs. Lintot, "it's a pretty, catchy little tune—of a kind to achieve immediate popularity."

Now, I apologize humbly to the reader for this digression; but if he be musical he will forgive me, for that tune was the "Serenade" of Schubert, and I had never even heard Schubert's name!

And having thus duly apologized, I will venture to transgress and digress anew, and mention here a kind of melodic malady, a singular obsession to which I am subject, and which I will call unconscious musical cerebration.

I am never without some tune running in my head—never for a moment; not that I am always aware of it; existence would be insupportable if I were. What part of my brain sings it, or rather in what part of my brain it sings itself, I cannot imagine—probably in some useless corner full of cobwebs and lumber that is fit for nothing else.

But it never leaves off; now it is one tune, now another; now a song *without* words, now *with;* sometimes it is near the surface, so to speak, and I am vaguely conscious of it as I read or work, or talk or think; sometimes to make sure it is there I have to dive for it deep into myself, and I never fail to find it after a while, and bring it up to the top. It is the "Carnival of Venice," let us say; then I let it sink again, and it changes without my knowing; so that when I take another dive the "Carnival of Venice" has become "Il Mio Tesoro," or the "Marseillaise," or "Pretty Little Polly Perkins of Paddington Green." And Heaven knows what tunes, unheard

and unperceived, this internal barrel-organ has been grinding meanwhile.

Sometimes it intrudes itself so persistently as to become a nuisance, and the only way to get rid of it is to whistle or sing myself. For instance, I may be mentally reciting for my solace and delectation some beloved lyric like "The Water-fowl," or "Tears, Idle Tears," or "Break, Break, Break"; and all the while, between the lines, this fiend of a subcerebral vocalist, like a wandering minstrel in a distant square, insists on singing, "Cheer, Boys, Cheer," or, "Tommy, make room for your uncle" (tunes I cannot abide), with words, accompaniment, and all, complete, and not quite so refined an accent as I could wish; so that I have to leave off my recitation and whistle "J'ai du Bon Tabac" in quite a different key to exorcise it.

But this, at least, I will say for this never still small voice of mine: its intonation is always perfect; it keeps ideal time, and its quality, though rather thin and somewhat nasal and quite peculiar, is not unsympathetic. Sometimes, indeed (as in that Islington omnibus), I can compel it to imitate, *à s'y méprendre*, the tones of some singer I have recently heard, and thus make for myself a ghostly music which is not to be despised.

Occasionally, too, and quite unbidden, it would warble little impromptu inward melodies of my own composition, which often seemed to me extremely pretty, old-fashioned, and quaint; but one is not a fair judge of one's own productions, especially during the heat of inspiration; and I had not the means of recording them, as I had never learned the musical notes. What the world has lost!

Now whose this small voice was I did not find out till many years later, *for it was not mine!*

* * * * *

In spite of such rare accomplishments and resources within myself, I was

not a happy or contented young man; nor had my discontent in it anything of the divine.

I disliked my profession, for which I felt no particular aptitude, and would fain have followed another—poetry, science, literature, music, painting, sculpture; for all of which I most unblushingly thought myself better fitted by the gift of nature.

I disliked Pentonville, which, although clean, virtuous, and respectable, left much to be desired on the score of shape, color, romantic tradition, and local charm; and I would sooner have lived anywhere else: in the Champs Élysées, let us say—yes, indeed, even on the fifth branch of the third tree on the left-hand side as you leave the Arc de Triomphe, like one of those classical heroes in Henri Murger's *Vie de Bohème*.

I disliked my brother apprentices, and did not get on well with them, especially a certain very clever but vicious and deformed youth called Judkins, who seemed to have conceived an aversion for me from the first; he is now an associate of the Royal Academy. They thought I gave myself airs because I did not share in their dissipations; such dissipations as I could have afforded would have been cheap and nasty indeed.

Yet such pothouse dissipation seemed to satisfy them, since they took not only a pleasure in it, but a pride.

They even took a pride in a sick headache, and liked it, if it were the result of a debauch on the previous night; and were as pompously mock-modest about a black eye, got in a squabble at the Argyll Rooms, as if it had been the Victoria Cross. To pass the night in a police cell was such glory that it was worth while pretending they had done so when it was untrue.

They looked upon me as a muff, a milksop, and a prig, and felt the greatest contempt for me; and if they did not openly show it, it was only because they were not quite so fond of black eyes as they made out.

So I left them to their inexpensive joys, and betook myself to pursuits of my own, among others to the cultivation of my body, after methods I had learned in the Life Guards. I belonged to a gymnastic and fencing and boxing club, of which I was a most assiduous frequenter; a more persevering dumb-beller and Indian-clubber never was, and I became in time an all-round athlete, as wiry and lean as a greyhound, just under fifteen stone, and four inches over six feet in height, which was considered very tall thirty years ago; especially in Pentonville, where the distinction often brought me more contumely than respect.

Altogether a most formidable person; but that I was of a timid nature, afraid to hurt, and the peacefulest creature in the world.

My old love for slums revived, and I found out and haunted the worst in London. They were very good slums, but they were not the slums of Paris—they manage these things better in France.

Even Cow Cross (where the Metropolitan Railway now runs between King's Cross and Farringdon Street)—Cow Cross, that whilom labyrinth of slaughter-houses, gin-shops, and thieves' dens, with the famous Fleet Ditch running underneath it all the while, lacked the fascination and mystery of mediæval romance. There were no memories of such charming people as Le roi des Truands and Gringoire and Esmeralda; with a sigh one had to fall back on visions of Fagin and Bill Sykes and Nancy.

Quelle dégringolade!

And as to the actual denizens! One gazed with a dull, wondering pity at the poor, pale, rickety children; the slatternly, coarse women who never smiled (except when drunk); the dull, morose, miserable men. How they lacked the grace of French deformity, the ease and lightness of French depravity, the sympathetic distinction of French grotesqueness. How unterrible they were, who preferred the fist to the noiseless and insidious knife! who fought with their hands instead of their feet, quite loyally; and

reserved the kicks of their hobnailed boots for their recalcitrant wives!

And then there was no Morgue; one missed one's Morgue badly.

And Smithfield! It would split me truly to the heart (as M. le Major used to say) to watch the poor beasts that came on certain days to make a short station in that hideous cattle-market, on their way to the slaughter-house.

What bludgeons have I seen descend on beautiful, bewildered, dazed, meek eyes, so thickly fringed against the country sun; on soft, moist, tender nostrils that clouded the poisonous reek with a fragrance of the far-off fields! What torture of silly sheep and genially cynical pigs!

The very dogs seemed demoralized, and brutal as their masters. And there one day I had an adventure, a dirty bout at fisticuffs, most humiliating in the end for me, and which showed that chivalry is often its own reward, like virtue, even when the chivalrous are young and big and strong, and have learned to box.

A brutal young drover wantonly kicked a sheep, and, as I thought, broke her hind-leg, and in my indignation I took him by the ear and flung him round onto a heap of mud and filth. He rose and squared at me in a most plucky fashion; he hardly came up to my chin, and I refused to fight him. A crowd collected round us, and as I tried to explain to the by-standers the cause of our quarrel, he managed to hit me in the face with a very muddy fist.

"Bravo, little 'un!" shouted the crowd, and he squared up again. I felt wretchedly ashamed and warded off all his blows, telling him that I could not hit him or I should kill him.

"Yah!" shouted the crowd again; "go it, little 'un! Let 'im 'ave it! The long 'un's showing the white feather," etc., and finally I gave him a slight backhander that made his nose bleed and seemed to demoralize him completely. "Yah!" shouted the crowd; "'it one yer own size!"

I looked round in despair and rage, and picking out the biggest man I could see, said, "Are *you* big enough?" The crowd roared with laughter.

"Well, guv'ner, I dessay I might do at a pinch," he replied; and I tried to slap his face, but missed it, and received such a tremendous box on the ear that I was giddy for a second or two, and when I recovered I found him still grinning at me. I tried to hit him again and again, but always missed; and at last, without doing me any particular damage, he laid me flat three times running onto the very heap where I had flung the drover, the crowd applauding madly. Dazed, hatless, and panting, and covered with filth, I stared at him in hopeless impotence. He put out his hand, and said, "You're all right, ain't yer, guv'ner? I 'ope I 'aven't 'urt yer! My name's Tom Sayers. If you'd a 'it me, I should 'a' gone down like a ninepin, and I ain't so sure as I should ever 'ave got up again."

He was to become the most famous fighting-man in England!

I wrung his hand and thanked him, and offered him a sovereign, which he refused; and then he led me into a room in a public-house close by, where he washed and brushed me down, and insisted on treating me to a glass of brandy-and-water.

I have had a fondness for fighting-men ever since, and a respect for the noble science I had never felt before. He was many inches shorter than I, and did not look at all the Hercules he was.

He told me I was the strongest built man for a youngster that he had ever seen, barring that I was "rather leggy." I do not know if he was sincere or not, but no possible compliment could have pleased me more. Such is the vanity of youth.

And here, although it savors somewhat of vaingloriousness, I cannot resist the temptation of relating another adventure of the same kind, but in which I showed to greater advantage.

It was on a boxing-day (oddly enough), and I was returning with Lintot

and one of his boys from a walk in the Highgate Fields. As we plodded our dirty way homeward through the Caledonian Road we were stopped by a crowd outside a public-house. A gigantic drayman (they always seem bigger than they really are) was squaring up to a poor drunken lout of a navvy not half his size, who had been put up to fight him, and who was quite incapable of even an attempt at self-defence; he could scarcely lift his arms. I thought at first it was only horse-play; and as little Joe Lintot wanted to see, I put him up on my shoulder, just as the drayman, who had been drinking, but was not drunk, and had a most fiendishly brutal face, struck the poor tipsy wretch with all his might between the eyes, and felled him (it was like pole-axing a bullock), to the delight of the crowd.

Little Joe, a very gentle and sensitive boy, began to cry; and his father, who had the pluck of a bull-terrier, wanted to interfere, in spite of his diminutive stature. I was also beside myself with indignation, and pulling off my coat and hat, which I gave to Lintot, made my way to the drayman, who was offering to fight any three men in the crowd, an offer that met with no response.

"Now, then, you cowardly skunk!" I said, tucking up my shirt-sleeves; "stand up, and I will knock every tooth down your ugly throat."

His face went the colors of a mottled Stilton cheese, and he asked what I meddled with him for. A ring formed itself, and I felt the sympathy of the crowd *with* me this time—a very agreeable sensation!

"Now, then, up with your arms! I'm going to kill you!"

"*I* ain't going to fight you, mister; I ain't going to fight *nobody*. Just you let me alone!"

"Oh yes, you are, or else you're going down on your marrow-bones to beg pardon for being a brutal, cowardly skunk"; and I gave him a slap on the face that rang like a pistol-shot—a most finished, satisfactory, and successful slap this time. My finger-tips tingle at the bare remembrance.

THE BIG DRAYMAN

He tried to escape, but was held opposite to me. He began to snivel and whimper, and said he had never meddled with me, and asked what should I meddle with him for?

"Then down on your knees—quick—this instant!" and I made as if I were going to begin serious business at once, and no mistake.

So down he plumped on his knees, and there he actually fainted from sheer excess of emotion.

As I was helped on with my coat, I tasted, for once in my life, the sweets of popularity, and knew what it was to be the idol of a mob.

Little Joey Lintot and his brothers and sisters, who had never held me in any particular regard before that I knew of, worshipped me from that day forward.

And I should be insincere if I did not confess that on that one occasion I was rather pleased with myself, although the very moment I stood opposite the huge, hulking, beer-sodden brute (who had looked so formidable from afar) I felt, with a not unpleasant sense of relief, that he did not stand a chance. He was only big, and even at that I beat him.

The real honors of the day belonged to Lintot, who, I am convinced, was ready to act the David to that Goliath. He had the real stomach for fighting, which I lacked, as very tall men are often said to do.

And that, perhaps, is why I have made so much of my not very wonderful prowess on that occasion; not, indeed, that I am physically a coward—at least, I do not think so. If I thought I were I should avow it with no more shame than I should avow that I had a bad digestion, or a weak heart, which makes cowards of us all.

It is that I hate a row, and violence, and bloodshed, even from a nose—any nose, either my own or my neighbor's.

* * * * *

There are slums at the east end of London that many fashionable people know something of by this time; I got to know them by heart. In addition to the charm of the mere slum, there was the eternal fascination of the seafaring element; of Jack ashore—a lovable creature who touches nothing but what he adorns it in his own peculiar fashion.

I constantly haunted the docks, where the smell of tar and the sight of ropes and masts filled me with unutterable longings for the sea—for distant lands—for anywhere but where it was my fate to be.

I talked to ship captains and mates and sailors, and heard many marvellous tales, as the reader may well believe, and framed for myself visions

of cloudless skies, and sapphire seas, and coral reefs, and groves of spice, and dusky youths in painted plumage roving, and friendly isles where a lovely half-clad, barefooted Neuha would wave her torch, and lead me, her Torquil, by the hand through caverns of bliss!

Especially did I haunt a wharf by London Bridge, from whence two steamers—the *Seine* and the *Dolphin,* I believe—started on alternate days for Boulogne-sur-Mer.

I used to watch the happy passengers bound for France, some of them, in their holiday spirits, already fraternizing together on the sunny deck, and fussing with camp-stools and magazines and novels and bottles of bitter beer, or retiring before the funnel to smoke the pipe of peace.

The sound of the boiler getting up steam—what delicious music it was! Would it ever get up steam for me? The very smell of the cabin, the very feel of the brass gangway and the brass-bound, oil-clothed steps were delightful; and down-stairs, on the snowy cloth, were the cold beef and ham, the beautiful fresh mustard, the bottles of pale ale and stout. Oh, happy travellers, who could afford all this, and France into the bargain!

Soon would a large white awning make the afterdeck a paradise, from which, by-and-by, to watch the quickly gliding panorama of the Thames. The bell would sound for non-passengers like me to go ashore—"Que diable allait-il faire dans cette galère!" as Uncle Ibbetson would have said. The steamer, disengaging itself from the wharf with a pleasant yohoing of manly throats and a slow, intermittent plashing of the paddle-wheels, would carefully pick its sunny, eastward way among the small craft of the river, while a few handkerchiefs were waved in a friendly, make-believe farewell—*auf Wiedersehen!*

Oh, to stand by that unseasonably sou'-westered man at the wheel, and watch St. Paul's and London Bridge and the Tower of London fade out of sight—never, never to see them again. No *auf Wiedersehen* for me!

Sometimes I would turn my footsteps westward and fill my hungry, jealous eyes with a sight of the gay summer procession in Hyde Park, or listen to the band in Kensington Gardens, and see beautiful, well-dressed women, and hear their sweet, refined voices and happy laughter; and a longing would come into my heart more passionate than my longing for the sea and France and distant lands, and quite as unutterable. I would even forget Neuha and her torch.

After this it was a dreary downfall to go and dine for tenpence all by myself, and finish up with a book at my solitary lodgings in Pentonville. The book would not let itself be read; it sulked and had to be laid down, for "beautiful woman! beautiful girl!" spelled themselves between me and the printed page. Translate me those words into French, O ye who can even render Shakespeare into French Alexandrines—"Belle femme? Belle fille?" Ha! ha!

If you want to get as near it as you can, you will have to write, "Belle Anglaise," or "Belle Américaine"; only then will you be understood, even in France!

Ah! elle était bien belle, Madame Seraskier!

At other times, more happily inspired, I would slake my thirst for nature by long walks into the country. Hampstead was my Passy—the Leg-of-Mutton Pond my Mare d'Auteuil; Richmond was my St. Cloud, with Kew Gardens for a Bois de Boulogne; and Hampton Court made a very fair Versailles—how incomparably fairer, even a pupil of Lintot's should know.

And after such healthy fatigue and fragrant impressions the tenpenny dinner had a better taste, the little front parlor in Pentonville was more like a home, the book more like a friend.

For I read all I could get in English or French. Novels, travels, history, poetry, science—everything came as grist to that most melancholy mill, my mind.

I tried to write; I tried to draw; I tried to make myself an inner life apart from the sordid, commonplace ugliness of my outer one—a private oasis of my own; and to raise myself a little, if only mentally, above the circumstances in which it had pleased the Fates to place me.*

*NOTE.—*It is with great reluctance that I now come to my cousin's account of the deplorable opinions he held, at that period of his life, on the most important subject that can ever engross the mind of man.*

I have left out much, *but I feel that in suppressing it altogether, I should rob his sad story of all its moral significance; for it cannot be doubted that most of his unhappiness is attributable to the defective religious training of his childhood, and that his parents (otherwise the best and kindest people I have ever known) incurred a terrible responsibility when they determined to leave him "unbiassed," as he calls it, at that tender and susceptible age when the mind is*

"Wax to receive, and marble to retain."

Madge Plunket

It goes without saying that, like many thoughtful youths of a melancholy temperament, impecunious and discontented with their lot, and much given to the smoking of strong tobacco (on an empty stomach), I continuously brooded on the problems of existence—free-will and determinism, the whence and why and whither of man, the origin of evil, the immortality of the soul, the futility of life, etc., and made myself very miserable over such questions.

Often the inquisitive passer-by, had he peeped through the blinds of No.— Wharton Street, Pentonville, late at night, would have been rewarded by the touching spectacle of a huge, rawboned ex-private in her Majesty's Life Guards, with his head bowed over the black and yellow key-board of a venerable square piano-forte (on which he could not play), dropping the bitter tear of loneliness and *Weltschmerz* combined.

It never once occurred to me to seek relief in the bosom of any Church.

Some types are born and not made. I was a born "infidel"; if ever there was a congenital agnostic, one agnostically constituted from his very birth, it was I. Not that I had ever heard such an expression as agnosticism; it is an invention of late years. . . .

"J'avais fait de la prose toute ma vie sans le savoir!"

But almost the first conscious dislike I can remember was for the black figure of the priest, and there were several of these figures in Passy.

Monsieur le Major called them *maîtres corbeaux*, and seemed to hold them in light esteem. Dr. Seraskier hated them; his gentle Catholic wife had grown to distrust them. My loving, heretic mother loved them not; my father, a Catholic born and bred, had an equal aversion. They had persecuted his gods—the thinkers, philosophers, and scientific discoverers —Galileo, Bruno, Copernicus; and brought to his mind the cruelties of the

Holy Inquisition, the Massacre of St. Bartholomew; and I always pictured them as burning little heretics alive if they had their will—Eton jackets, white chimney-pot hats, and all!

I have no doubt they were in reality the best and kindest of men.

The parson (and parsons were not lacking in Pentonville) was not so insidiously repellent as the blue-cheeked, blue-chinned Passy priest; but he was by no means to me a picturesque or sympathetic apparition, with his weddedness, his whiskers, his black trousers, his frock-coat, his tall hat, his little white tie, his consciousness of being a "gentleman" by profession. Most unattractive, also, were the cheap, brand-new churches wherein he spoke the word to his dreary-looking, Sunday-clad flock, with scarcely one of whom his wife would have sat down to dinner—especially if she had been chosen from among them.

To watch that flock pouring in of a Sunday morning, or afternoon, or evening, at the summons of those bells, and pouring out again after the long service, and banal, perfunctory sermon, was depressing. Weekdays, in Pentonville, were depressing enough; but Sundays were depressing beyond words, though nobody seemed to think so but myself. Early training had acclimatized them.

I have outlived those physical antipathies of my salad days; even the sight of an Anglican bishop is no longer displeasing to me, on the contrary; and I could absolutely rejoice in the beauty of a cardinal.

Indeed, I am now friends with both a parson and a priest, and do not know which of the two I love and respect the most. They ought to hate me, but they do not; they pity me too much, I suppose. I am too negative to rouse in either the deep theological hate; and all the little hate that the practice of love and charity has left in their kind hearts is reserved for each other—an unquenchable hate in which they seem to glory, and which rages all the more that it has to be concealed. It saddens me to think that I am a bone of contention between them.

And yet, for all my unbelief, the Bible was my favorite book, and the Psalms my adoration; and most truly can I affirm that my mental attitude has ever been one of reverence and humility.

But every argument that has ever been advanced against Christianity (and I think I know them all by this time) had risen spontaneously and unprompted within me, and they have all seemed to me unanswerable, and indeed, as yet, unanswered. Nor had any creed of which I ever heard appeared to me either credible or attractive or even sensible, but for the central figure of the Deity—a Deity that in no case could ever be mine.

The awe-inspiring and unalterable conception that had wrought itself into my consciousness, whether I would or no, was that of a Being infinitely more abstract, remote, and inaccessible than any the genius of mankind has ever evolved after its own image and out of the needs of its own heart—inscrutable, unthinkable, unspeakable; above all human passions, beyond the reach of any human appeal; One upon whose attributes it was futile to speculate—One whose name was *It*, not *He*.

The thought of total annihilation was uncongenial, but had no terror.

Even as a child I had shrewdly suspected that hell was no more than a vulgar threat for naughty little boys and girls, and heaven than a vulgar bribe, from the casual way in which either was meted out to me as my probable portion, by servants and such people, according to the way I behaved. Such things were never mentioned to me by either my father or mother, or M. le Major, or the Seraskiers—the only people in whom I trusted.

But for the bias against the priest, I was left unbiassed at that tender and susceptible age. I had learned my catechism and read my Bible, and

used to say the Lord's Prayer as I went to bed, and "God bless papa and mamma," and the rest, in the usual perfunctory manner.

Never a word against religion was said in my hearing by those few on whom I had pinned my childish faith; on the other hand, no such importance was attached to it, apparently, as was attached to the virtues of truthfulness, courage, generosity, self-denial, politeness, and especially consideration for others, high or low, human and animal alike.

I imagine that my parents must have compromised the matter between them, and settled that I should work out all the graver problems of existence for myself, when I came to a thinking age, out of my own conscience, and such knowledge of life as I should acquire, and such help as they would no doubt have given me, according to their lights, had they survived.

I did so, and made myself a code of morals to live by, in which religion had but a small part.

For me there was but one sin, and that was cruelty, because I hated it; though Nature, for inscrutable purposes of her own, almost teaches it as a virtue. All sins that did not include cruelty were merely sins against health, or taste, or common-sense, or public expediency.

Free-will was impossible. We could only *seem* to will freely, and that only within the limits of a small triangle, whose sides were heredity, education, and circumstance—a little geometrical arrangement of my own, of which I felt not a little proud, although it does not quite go on all-fours—perhaps because it is only a triangle.

That is, we could will fast enough—*too* fast; but could not will *how* to will—fortunately, for we were not fit as yet, and for a long time to come, to be trusted, constituted as we are!

Even the characters of a novel must act according to the nature, training, and motives their creator the novelist has supplied them with, or we put the novel down and read something else; for human nature must be con-

sistent with itself in fiction as well as in fact. Even in its madness there must be a method, so how could the will be free?

To pray for any personal boon or remission of evil—to bend the knee, or lift one's voice in praise or thanksgiving for any earthly good that had befallen one, either through inheritance, or chance, or one's own successful endeavor—was in my eyes simply futile; but, putting its futility aside, it was an act of servile presumption, of wheedling impertinence, not without suspicion of a lively sense of favors to come.

It seemed to me as though the Jews—a superstitious and business-like people, who know what they want and do not care how they get it—must have taught us to pray like that.

It was not the sweet, simple child innocently beseeching that to-morrow might be fine for its holiday, or that Santa Claus would be generous; it was the cunning trader, fawning, flattering, propitiating, bribing with fulsome, sycophantic praise (an insult in itself), as well as burnt-offerings, working for his own success here and hereafter, and his enemy's confounding.

It was the grovelling of the dog, without the dog's single-hearted love, stronger than even its fear or its sense of self-interest.

What an attitude for one whom God had made after His own image—even towards his Maker!

* * * * *

The only permissible prayer was a prayer for courage or resignation; for that was a prayer turned inward, an appeal to what is best in ourselves—our honor, our stoicism, our self-respect.

And for a small detail, grace before and after meals seemed to me especially self-complacent and iniquitous, when there were so many with scarcely ever a meal to say grace for. The only decent and proper grace was to give half of one's meal away—not, indeed, that I was in the habit of

doing so! But at least I had the grace to reproach myself for my want of charity, and that was my only grace.

* * * * *

Fortunately, since we had no free-will of our own, the tendency that impelled us was upward, like the sparks, and bore us with it willy-nilly—the good and the bad, and the worst and the best.

By seeing this clearly, and laying it well to heart, the motive was supplied to us for doing all we could in furtherance of that upward tendency—*pour aider le bon Dieu*—that we might rise the faster and reach Him the sooner, if He were! And when once the human will has been set going, like a rocket or a clock or a steam-engine, and in the right direction, what can it not achieve?

We should in time control circumstance instead of being controlled thereby; education would day by day become more adapted to one consistent end; and, finally, conscience-stricken, we should guide heredity with our own hands instead of leaving it to blind chance; unless, indeed, a well-instructed paternal government wisely took the reins, and only sanctioned the union of people who were thoroughly in love with each other, after due and careful elimination of the unfit.

Thus, cruelty should at least be put into harness, and none of its valuable energy wasted on wanton experiments, as it is by Nature.

And thus, as the boy is father to the man, should the human race one day be father to—what?

That is just where my speculations would arrest themselves; that was the × of a sum in rule of three, not to be worked out by Peter Ibbetson, Architect and Surveyor, Wharton Street, Pentonville.

As the orang-outang is to Shakespeare, so is Shakespeare to . . . ×?

As the female chimpanzee is to the Venus of Milo, so is the Venus of Milo to . . . ×?

Finally, multiply these two ×'s by each other, and try to conceive the result!

* * * * *

Such was, crudely, the simple creed I held at this time; and, such as it was, I had worked it all out for myself, with no help from outside—a poor thing, but mine own; or, as I expressed it in the words of De Musset, "Mon verre n'est pas grand—mais je bois dans mon verre."

For though such ideas were in the air, like wholesome clouds, they had not yet condensed themselves into printed words for the million. People did not dare to write about these things, as they do at present, in popular novels and cheap magazines, that all who run may read, and learn to think a little for themselves, and honestly say what they think, without having to dread a howl of execration, clerical and lay.

And it was not only that I thought like this and could not think otherwise; it was that I felt like this and could not feel otherwise; and I should have appeared to myself as wicked, weak, and base had I ever even *desired* to think or feel otherwise, however personally despairing of this life—a traitor to what I jealously guarded as my best instincts.

And yet to me the faith of others, if but unaggressive, humble, and sincere, had often seemed touching and pathetic, and sometimes even beautiful, as childish things seem sometimes beautiful, even in those who are no longer children, and should have put them away. It had caused many heroic lives, and rendered many obscure lives blameless and happy; and then its fervor and passion seemed to burn with a lasting flame.

At brief moments now and then, and especially in the young, unfaith can be as fervent and as passionate as faith, and just as narrow and unreasonable, as *I* found; but alas! its flame was intermittent, and its light was not a kindly light.

It had no food for babes; it could not comfort the sick or sorry, nor

resolve into submissive harmony the inner discords of the soul; nor compensate us for our own failures and shortcomings, nor make up to us in any way for the success and prosperity of others who did not choose to think as we did.

It was without balm for wounded pride, or stay for weak despondency, or consolation for bereavement; its steep and rugged thoroughfares led to no promised land of beatitude, and there were no soft resting-places by the way.

Its only weapon was steadfastness; its only shield, endurance; its earthly hope, the common weal; its earthly prize, the opening of all roads to knowledge, and the release from a craven inheritance of fear; its final guerdon—sleep? Who knows?

Sleep was not bad.

So that simple, sincere, humble, devout, earnest, fervent, passionate, and over-conscientious young unbelievers like myself had to be very strong and brave and self-reliant (which I was not), and very much in love with what they conceived to be the naked Truth (a figure of doubtful personal attractions at first sight), to tread the ways of life with that unvarying cheerfulness, confidence, and serenity which the believer claims as his own special and particular appanage.

So much for my profession of unfaith, shared (had I but known it) by many much older and wiser and better educated than I, and only reached by them after great sacrifice of long-cherished illusions, and terrible pangs of soul-questioning—a struggle and a wrench that I was spared through my kind parents' thoughtfulness when I was a little boy.

* * * * *

It thus behooved me to make the most of this life; since, for all I knew, or believed, or even hoped to the contrary, to-morrow we must die.

Not, indeed, that I might eat and drink and be merry; heredity and education had not inclined me that way, I suppose, and circumstances did not allow it; but that I might try and live up to the best ideal I could frame out of my own conscience and the past teaching of mankind. And man, whose conception of the Infinite and divine has been so inadequate, has furnished us with such human examples (ancient and modern, Hebrew, Pagan, Buddhist, Christian, Agnostic, and what not) as the best of us can only hope to follow at a distance.

I would sometimes go to my morning's work, my heart elate with lofty hope and high resolve.

How easy and simple it seemed to lead a life without fear, or reproach, or self-seeking, or any sordid hope of personal reward, either here or hereafter!—a life of stoical endurance, invincible patience and meekness, indomitable cheerfulness and self-denial!

After all, it was only for another forty or fifty years at the most, and what was that? And after that—*que sçais-je?*

The thought was inspiring indeed!

By luncheon-time (and luncheon consisted of an Abernethy biscuit and a glass of water, and several pipes of shag tobacco, cheap and rank) some subtle change would come over the spirit of my dream.

Other people did not have high resolves. Some people had very bad tempers, and rubbed one very much the wrong way. . . .

What a hideous place was Pentonville to slave away one's life in! . . .

What a grind it was to be forever making designs for little new shops in Rosoman Street, and not making them well, it seemed! . . .

Why should a squinting, pock-marked, bowlegged, hunch-backed little Judkins (a sight to make a recruiting-sergeant shudder) forever taunt one with having enlisted as a private soldier? . . .

And then why should one be sneeringly told to "hit a fellow one's own

size," merely because, provoked beyond endurance, one just grabbed him by the slack of his trousers and gently shook him out of them onto the floor, terrified but quite unhurt? . . .

And so on, and so on; constant little pin-pricks, sordid humiliations, ugliness, meannesses, and dirt, that called forth in resistance all that was lowest and least commendable in one's self.

One has attuned one's nerves to the leading of a forlorn hope, and a gnat gets into one's eye, or a little cinder grit, and there it sticks; and there is no question of leading any forlorn hope, after all, and never will be; all *that* was in the imagination only: it is always gnats and cinder grits, gnats and cinder grits.

By the evening I had ignominiously broken down, and was plunged in the depths of an exasperated pessimism too deep even for tears, and would have believed myself the meanest and most miserable of mankind, but that everybody else, without exception, was even meaner and miserabler than myself.

They could still eat and drink and be merry. I could not, and did not even want to.

* * * * *

And so on, day after day, week after week, for months and years. . . .

Thus I grew weary in time of my palling individuality, ever the same through all these uncontrollable variations of mood.

Oh, that alternate ebb and flow of the spirits! It is a disease, and, what is most distressing, it is no real change; it is more sickeningly monotonous than absolute stagnation itself. And from that dreary seesaw I could never escape, except through the gates of dreamless sleep, the death in life; for even in our dreams we are still ourselves. There was no rest!

I loathed the very sight of myself in the shop-windows as I went by; and yet I always looked for it there, in the forlorn hope of at least finding some alteration, even for the worse. I passionately longed to be somebody else; and yet I never met anybody else I could have borne to be for a moment.

And then the loneliness of us!

Each separate unit of our helpless race is inexorably bounded by the inner surface of his own mental periphery, a jointless armor in which there is no weak place, never a fault, never a single gap of egress for ourselves, of ingress for the nearest and dearest of our fellow-units. At only five points can we just touch each other, and all that is—and that only by the function of our poor senses—from the outside. In vain we rack them that we may get a little closer to the best beloved and most implicitly trusted; ever in vain, from the cradle to the grave.

Why should so fantastic a thought have persecuted me so cruelly? I knew nobody with whom I should have felt such a transfusion of soul even tolerable for a second. I cannot tell! But it was like a gadfly which drove me to fatigue my body that I should have by day the stolid peace of mind that comes of healthy physical exhaustion; that I should sleep at night the dreamless sleep—the death in life!

"Of such materials wretched men are made!" Especially wretched young men; and the wretcheder one is, the more one smokes; and the more one smokes, the wretcheder one gets—a vicious circle!

Such was my case. I grew to long for the hour of my release (as I expressed it pathetically to myself), and caressed the idea of suicide. I even composed for myself a little rhymed epitaph in French which I thought very neat—

Je n'étais point. Je fus.

Je ne suis plus.

*   *   *   *   *

Oh, to perish in some noble cause—to die saving another's life, even another's worthless life, to which he clung!

I remember formulating this wish, in all sincerity, one moonlit night as I walked up Frith Street, Soho. I came upon a little group of excited people gathered together at the foot of a house built over a shop. From a broken window-pane on the second floor an ominous cloud of smoke rose like a column into the windless sky. An ordinary ladder was placed against the house, which, they said, was densely inhabited; but no fire-engine or fire-escape had arrived as yet, and it appeared useless to try and rouse the inmates by kicking and beating at the door any longer.

A brave man was wanted—a very brave man, who would climb the ladder, and make his way into the house through the broken window. Here was a forlorn hope to lead at last!

Such a man was found. To my lasting shame and contrition, it was not I.

He was short and thick and middle-aged, and had a very jolly red face and immense whiskers—quite a common sort of man, who seemed by no means tired of life.

His heroism was wasted, as it happened; for the house was an empty one, as we all heard, to our immense relief, before he had managed to force a passage into the burning room. His whiskers were not even singed!

Nevertheless, I slunk home, and gave up all thoughts of self-destruction—even in a noble cause; and there, in penance, I somewhat hastily committed to flame the plodding labor of many midnights—an elaborate copy in pen and ink, line for line, of Rethel's immortal wood-engraving "Der Tod als Freund," which Mrs. Lintot had been kind enough to lend me—and under which I had written, in beautiful black Gothic letters and red capitals (and without the slightest sense of either humor or irreverence), the following poem, which had cost me infinite pains:

I.

F, i, fi — n, i, ni!
Bon Dieu Père, j'ai fini . . .
Vous qui m'avez tant puni,
Dans ma triste vie,
Pour tant d'horribles forfaits
Que je ne commis jamais,
Laissez-moi jouir en paix
De mon agonie!

II.

Les faveurs que je Vous dois,
Je les compte sur mes doigts:
Tout infirme que je sois,
Ça se fait bien vite!
Prenez patience, et comptez
Tous mes maux — puis computez
Toutes Vos sévérités —
Vous me tiendrez quitte!

III.

Né pour souffrir, et souffrant —
Bas, honni, bête, ignorant,
Vieux, laid, chétif — et mourant
Dans mon trou sans plainte,
Je suis aussi sans désir
Autre que d'en bien finir —
Sans regret, sans repentir —
Sans espoir ni crainte!

IV.

Père inflexible et jaloux,
Votre Fils est mort pour nous!
Aussi, je reste envers Vous
Si bien sans rancune,
Que je voudrais, sans façon,
Faire, au seuil de ma prison,
Quelque petite oraison . . .
Je n'en sais pas une!

V.

J'entends sonner l'Angélus
Qui rassemble Vos Élus:
Pour moi, du bercail exclus,
C'est la mort qui sonne!
Prier ne profite rien . . .
Pardonner est le seul bien:
C'est le Vôtre, et c'est le mien:
Moi, je Vous pardonne!

VI.

Soyez d'un égard pareil!
S'il est quelque vrai sommeil
Sans ni rêve, ni réveil,
Ouvrez-m'en la porte—
Faites que l'immense Oubli
Couvre, sous un dernier pli,
Dans mon corps enseveli,
Ma conscience morte!

Oh me duffer! What a hopeless failure was I in all things, little and big.

PART THREE

PART THREE

I had no friends but the Lintots and their friends. "Les amis de nos amis sont nos amis!"

My cousin Alfred had gone into the army, like his father before him. My cousin Charlie had gone into the Church, and we had drifted completely apart. My grandmother was dead. My Aunt Plunket, a great invalid, lived in Florence. Her daughter, Madge, was in India, happily married to a young soldier who is now a most distinguished general.

The Lintots held their heads high as representatives of a liberal profession, and an old Pentonville family. People were generally exclusive in those days—an exclusiveness that was chiefly kept up by the ladies. There were charmed circles even in Pentonville.

Among the most exclusive were the Lintots. Let us hope, in common justice, that those they excluded were at least able to exclude others.

I have eaten their bread and salt, and it would ill become me to deny that their circle was charming as well as charmed. But I had no gift for making friends, although I was often attracted by people the very opposite of myself; especially by little, clever, quick, but not too familiar men; but even if they were disposed to make advances, a miserable shyness and stiffness of manner on my part, that I could not help, would raise a barrier of ice between us.

They were most hospitable people, these good Lintots, and had many friends, and gave many parties, which my miserable shyness prevented me from enjoying to the full. They were both too stiff and too free.

In the drawing-room, Mrs. Lintot and one or two other ladies, severely dressed, would play the severest music in a manner that did not mitigate its severity. They were merciless! It was nearly always Bach, or Hummel, or

Scarlatti, each of whom, they would say, could write both like an artist and a gentleman—a very rare but indispensable combination, it seemed.

Other ladies, young and middle-aged, and a few dumb-struck youths like myself, would be suffered to listen, but never to retaliate—never to play or sing back again.

If one ventured to ask for a song without words by Mendelssohn—or a song with words, even by Schubert, even with German words—one was rebuked and made to blush for the crime of musical frivolity.

Meanwhile, in Lintot's office (built by himself in the back garden), grave men and true, pending the supper hour, would smoke and sip spirits-and-water, and talk shop; formally at first, and with much politeness. But gradually, feeling their way, as it were, they would relax into social unbuttonment, and drop the "Mister" before each other's names (to be resumed next morning), and indulge in lively professional chaff, which would soon become personal and free and boisterous—a good-humored kind of warfare in which I did not shine, for lack of quickness and repartee. For instance, they would ask one whether one would rather be a bigger fool than one looked, or look a bigger fool than one was; and whichever way one answered the question, the retort would be that "that was impossible!" amid roars of laughter from all but one.

So that I would take a middle course, and spend most of the evening on the stairs and in the hall, and study (with an absorbing interest much too well feigned to look natural) the photographs of famous cathedrals and public buildings till supper came; when, by assiduously attending on the ladies, I would cause my miserable existence to be remembered, and forgiven; and soon forgotten again, I fear.

I hope I shall not be considered an overweening coxcomb for saying that, on the whole, I found more favor with the ladies than with the gentlemen; especially at supper-time.

After supper there would be a change—for the better, some thought. Lintot, emboldened by good-cheer and good-fellowship, would become unduly, immensely, uproariously funny, in spite of his wife. He had a genuine gift of buffoonery. His friends would whisper to each other that Lintot was "on," and encourage him. Bach and Hummel and Scarlatti were put on the shelf, and the young people would have a good time. There were comic songs and Negro melodies, with a chorus all round. Lintot would sing "Vilikins and his Dinah," in the manner of Mr. Robson, so well that even Mrs. Lintot's stern mask would relax into indulgent smiles. It was irresistible. And when the party broke up, we could all (thanks to our host) honestly thank our hostess "for a very pleasant evening," and cheerfully, yet almost regretfully, wish her good-night.

It is good to laugh sometimes—wisely if one can; if not, *quocumque modo!* There are seasons when even "the crackling of thorns under a pot" has its uses. It seems to warm the pot—all the pots—and all the emptiness thereof, if they be empty.

* * * * *

Once, indeed, I actually made a friend, but he did not last me very long.

It happened thus: Mrs. Lintot gave a grander party than usual. One of the invited was Mr. Moses Lyon, the great picture-dealer—a client of Lintot's; and he brought with him young Raphael Merridew, the already famous painter, the most attractive youth I had ever seen. Small and slight, but beautifully made, and dressed in the extreme of fashion, with a handsome face, bright and polite manners, and an irresistible voice, he became his laurels well; he would have been sufficiently dazzling without them. Never had those hospitable doors in Myddelton Square been opened to so brilliant a guest.

I was introduced to him, and he discovered that the bridge of my nose was just suited for the face of the sun-god in his picture of "The Sun-god and the Dawn-maiden," and begged I would favor him with a sitting or two.

Proud indeed was I to accede to such a request, and I gave him many sittings. I used to rise at dawn to sit, before my work at Lintot's began; and to sit again as soon as I could be spared.

It seems I not only had the nose and brow of a sun-god (who is not supposed to be a very intellectual person), but also his arms and his torso; and sat for these, too. I have been vain of myself ever since.

During these sittings, which he made delightful, I grew to love him as David loved Jonathan.

We settled that we would go to the Derby together in a hansom. I engaged the smartest hansom in London days beforehand. On the great Wednesday morning I was punctual with it at his door in Charlotte Street. There was another hansom there already—a smarter hansom still than mine, for it was a private one—and he came down and told me he had altered his mind, and was going with Lyon, who had asked him the evening before.

"One of the first picture-dealers in London, my dear fellow. Hang it all, you know, I couldn't refuse—awfully sorry!"

So I drove to the Derby in solitary splendor, but the bright weather, the humors of the road, all the gay scenes were thrown away upon me, such was the bitterness of my heart.

In the early afternoon I saw Merridew lunching on the top of a drag, among some men of smart and aristocratic appearance. He seemed to be the life of the party, and gave me a good-humored nod as I passed. I soon found Lyon sitting disconsolate in his hansom, scowling and solitary; he invited me to lunch with him, and disembosomed himself of a load of bitterness as intense as mine (which I kept to myself). The shrewd Hebrew

tradesman was sunk in the warm-hearted, injured friend. Merridew had left Lyon for the Earl of Chiselhurst, just as he had left me for Lyon.

That was a dull Derby for us both!

A few days later I met Merridew, radiant as ever. All he said was:

"Awful shame of me to drop old Lyon for Chiselhurst, eh? But an earl, my dear fellow! Hang it all, you know! Poor old Mo' had to get back in his hansom all by himself, but he's bought the 'Sun-god' all the same."

Merridew soon dropped me altogether, to my great sorrow, for I forgave him his Derby desertion as quickly as Lyon did, and would have forgiven him anything. He was one of those for whom allowances are always being made, and with a good grace.

He died before he was thirty, poor boy! but his fame will never die. The "Sun-god" (even with the bridge of that nose which had been so wofully put out of joint) is enough by itself to place him among the immortals. Lyon sold it to Lord Chiselhurst for three thousand pounds—it had cost him five hundred. It is now in the National Gallery.

Poetical justice was satisfied!

* * * * *

Nor was I more fortunate in love than in friendship.

All the exclusiveness in the world cannot exclude good and beautiful maidens, and these were not lacking, even in Pentonville.

There is always one maiden much more beautiful and good than all the others—like Esmeralda among the ladies of the Hôtel de Gondelaurier. There was such a maiden in Pentonville, or rather Clerkenwell, close by. But her station was so humble (like Esmeralda's) that even the least exclusive would have drawn the line at *her!* She was one of a large family, and they sold tripe and pig's feet, and food for cats and dogs, in a very small shop opposite the western wall of the Middlesex House of Detention. She

"A DULL DERBY FOR US BOTH"

was the eldest, and the busy, responsible one at this poor counter. She was one of Nature's ladies, one of Nature's goddesses — a queen! Of that I felt sure every time I passed her shop, and shyly met her kind, frank, uncoquettish gaze. A time was approaching when I should have to overcome my shyness, and tell her that she of all women was the woman for me, and that it was indispensable, absolutely indispensable, that we two should be made one — immediately! at once! forever!

But before I could bring myself to this she married somebody else, and we had never exchanged a single word!

If she is alive now she is an old woman — a good and beautiful old woman, I feel sure, wherever she is, and whatever her rank in life. If she should read this book, which is not very likely, may she accept this small tribute from an unknown admirer; for whom, so many years ago, she beautified and made poetical the hideous street that still bounds the Middlesex House of Detention on its western side; and may she try to think not the less of it because since then its writer has been on the wrong side of that long, blank wall, of that dreary portal where the agonized stone face looks down on the desolate slum:

"Per me si va tra la perduta gente . . . !"

* * * * *

After this disappointment I got myself a big dog (like Byron, Bismarck, and Wagner), but not in the spirit of emulation. Indeed, I had never heard of either Bismarck or Wagner in those days, or their dogs, and I had lost my passion for Byron and any wish to emulate him in any way; it was simply for the want of something to be fond of, and that would be sure to love me back again.

He was not a big dog when I bought him, but just a little ball of orange-tawny fluff that I could carry with one arm. He cost me all the money I had saved up for a holiday trip to Passy. I had seen his father, a champion St. Bernard, at a dog-show, and felt that life would be well worth living with such a companion; but *his* price was five hundred guineas. When I saw the irresistible son, just six weeks old, and heard that he was only one-fiftieth part of his sire's value, I felt that Passy must wait, and became his possessor.

I gave him of the best that money could buy—real milk at fivepence a quart, three quarts a day. I combed his fluff every morning, and washed him three times a week, and killed all his fleas one by one—a labor of love. I weighed him every Saturday, and found he increased at the rate of from six to nine pounds weekly; and his power of affection increased as the square of his weight. I christened him Porthos, because he was so big and fat and jolly; but in his noble puppy face and his beautiful pathetic eyes I already foresaw for his middle age that distinguished and melancholy grandeur which characterized the sublime Athos, Comte de la Fère.

He was a joy. It was good to go to sleep at night and know he would be there in the morning. Whenever we took our walks abroad, everybody turned round to look at him and admire, and to ask if he was good-tem-

pered, and what his particular breed was, and what I fed him on. He became a monster in size—a beautiful, playful, gracefully galumphing, and most affectionate monster, and I, his happy Frankenstein, congratulated myself on the possession of a treasure that would last twelve years at least, or even fourteen, with the care I meant to take of him. But he died of distemper when he was eleven months old.

I do not know if little dogs cause as large griefs when they die as big ones; but I settled there should be no more dogs—big or little—for me.

* * * * *

After this I took to writing verses and sending them to magazines, where they never appeared. They were generally about my being reminded, by a tune, of things that had happened a long time ago: my poetic, like my artistic vein, was limited.

Here are the last I made, thirty years back. My only excuse for giving them is that they are so *singularly prophetic.*

The reminding tune (an old French chime which my father used to sing) is very simple and touching; and the old French words run thus:

"Orléans, Beaugency!
Notre Dame de Cléry!
Vendôme! Vendôme!
Quel chagrin, quel ennui
De compter toute la nuit
Les heures — les heures!"

That is all. They are supposed to be sung by a mediæval prisoner who cannot sleep; and who, to beguile the tediousness of his insomnia, sets any words that come into his head to the tune of the chime which marks the hours from a neighboring belfry. I tried to fancy that his name was Pasquier de la Marière, and that he was my ancestor.

THE CHIME

There is an old French air,
A little song of loneliness and grief —
Simple as nature, sweet beyond compare —
And sad — past all belief!

Nameless is he that wrote
The melody — but this much I opine:

Whoever made the words was some remote
French ancestor of mine.

I know the dungeon deep
Where long he lay — and why he lay therein;
And all his anguish, that he could not sleep
For conscience of a sin.

I see his cold, hard bed;
I hear the chimes that jingled in his ears
As he pressed nightly, with that wakeful head,
A pillow wet with tears.

Oh, restless little chime!
It never changed — but rang its roundelay
For each dark hour of that unhappy time
That sighed itself away.

And ever, more and more,
Its burden grew of his lost self a part —
And mingled with his memories, and wore
Its way into his heart.

And there it wove the name
Of many a town he loved, for one dear sake,
Into its web of music; thus he came
His little song to make.

Of all that ever heard
And loved it for its sweetness, none but I
Divined the clew that, as a hidden word,
The notes doth underlie.

That wail from lips long dead
Has found its echo in this breast alone!
Only to me, by blood-remembrance led,
Is that wild story known!

And though 'tis mine, by right
Of treasure-trove, to rifle and lay bare—
A heritage of sorrow and delight
The world would gladly share—

Yet must I not unfold
For evermore, nor whisper late or soon,
The secret that a few slight bars thus hold
Imprisoned in a tune.

For when that little song
Goes ringing in my head, I know that he,
My luckless lone forefather, dust so long,
Relives his life in me!

I sent them to ——*'s Magazine*, with the six French lines on which they were founded at the top. ——*'s Magazine* published only the six French lines—the only lines in my handwriting that ever got into print. And they date from the fifteenth century!

Thus was my little song lost to the world, and for a time to me. But long, long afterwards I found it again, where Mr. Longfellow once found a song of *his:* "in the heart of a friend"—surely the sweetest bourne that can ever be for any song!

Little did I foresee that a day was not far off when real blood-remembrance would carry me—but that is to come.

*   *   *   *   *

Poetry, friendship, and love having failed, I sought for consolation in art, and frequented the National Gallery, Marlborough House (where the Vernon collection was), the British Museum, the Royal Academy, and other exhibitions.

I prostrated myself before Titian, Rembrandt, Velasquez, Veronese, Da Vinci, Botticelli, Signorelli—the older the better; and tried my best to honestly feel the greatness I knew and know to be there; but for want of proper training I was unable to reach those heights, and, like most outsiders, admired them for the wrong things, for the very beauties they lack—such transcendent, ineffable beauties of feature, form, and expression as an outsider always looks for in an old master, and often persuades himself he finds there—and oftener still, *pretends* he does!

I was far more sincerely moved (although I did not dare to say so) by some works of our own time—for instance, by the "Vale of Rest," the "Autumn Leaves," "The Huguenot" of young Mr. Millais—just as I found such poems as *Maud* and *In Memoriam*, by Mr. Alfred Tennyson, infinitely more precious and dear to me than Milton's *Paradise Lost* and Spenser's *Faerie Queene*.

Indeed, I was hopelessly modern in those days—quite an every-day young man; the names I held in the warmest and deepest regard were those of then living men and women. Darwin, Browning, and George Eliot did not, it is true, exist for me as yet; but Tennyson, Thackeray, Dickens, Millais, John Leech, George Sand, Balzac, the old Dumas, Victor Hugo, and Alfred de Musset!

I have never beheld them in the flesh; but, like all the world, I know their outer aspect well, and could stand a pretty stiff examination in most they have ever written, drawn, or painted.

Other stars of magnitude have risen since, but of the old galaxy four at least still shine out of the past with their ancient lustre undimmed in my

"MONSIEUR N'EST PAS DÉGOÛTÉ!"

eyes—Thackeray; dear John Leech, who still has power to make me laugh as I like to laugh; and for the two others it is plain that the Queen, the world, and I are of a like mind as to their deserts, for one of them is now an ornament to the British peerage, the other a baronet and a millionaire; only I would have made dukes of them straight off, with precedence over the Archbishop of Canterbury, if they would care to have it so.

It is with a full but humble heart that I thus venture to record my long indebtedness, and pay this poor tribute, still fresh from the days of my unquestioning hero-worship. It will serve, at least, to show my reader (should I ever have one sufficiently interested to care) in what mental latitudes and longitudes I dwelt, who was destined to such singular experience—a kind of reference, so to speak—that he may be able to place me at a glance, according to the estimation in which he holds these famous and perhaps deathless names.

It will be admitted, at least, that my tastes were normal, and shared by a large majority—the tastes of an every-day young man at that particular period of the nineteenth century—one much given to athletics and cold tubs, and light reading and cheap tobacco, and endowed with the usual discontent; the last person for whom or from whom or by whom to expect anything out of the common.

* * * * *

But the splendor of the Elgin Marbles! I understood that at once—perhaps because there is not so much to understand. Mere physically beautiful people appeal to us all, whether they be in flesh or marble.

By some strange intuition, or natural instinct, I *knew* that people ought to be built like that, before I had ever seen a single statue in that wondrous room. I had divined them—so completely did they realize an æsthetic ideal I had always felt.

I had often, as I walked the London streets, peopled an imaginary world of my own with a few hundreds of such beings, made flesh and blood, and pictured them as a kind of beneficent aristocracy seven feet high, with minds and manners to match their physique, and set above the rest of the world for its good; for I found it necessary (so that my dream should have a point) to provide them with a foil in the shape of millions of such people as we meet every day. I was egotistic and self-seeking enough, it is true, to enroll myself among the former, and had chosen for my particular use and wear just such a frame as that of the Theseus, with, of course, the nose and hands and feet (of which time has bereft him) restored, and all mutilations made good.

And for my mistress and companion I had duly selected no less a person than the Venus of Milo (no longer armless), of which Lintot possessed a plaster-cast, and whose beauties I had foreseen before I ever beheld them with the bodily eye.

"Monsieur n'est pas dégoûté!" as Ibbetson would have remarked.

*   *   *   *   *

But most of all did I pant for the music which is divine.

Alas, that concerts and operas and oratorios should not be as free to the impecunious as the National Gallery and the British Museum – a privilege which is not abused!

Impecunious as I was, I sometimes had pence enough to satisfy this craving, and discovered in time such realms of joy as I had never dreamed of; such monarchs as Mozart, Handel, and Beethoven, and others, of whom my father knew apparently so little; and yet they were more potent enchanters than Grétry, Hérold, and Boieldieu, whose music he sang so well.

I discovered, moreover, that they could do more than charm – they could drive my weary self out of my weary soul, and for a space fill that weary soul with courage, resignation, and hope. No Titian, no Shakespeare, no Phidias could ever accomplish that—not even Mr. William Makepeace Thackeray or Mr. Alfred Tennyson.

My sweetest recollections of this period of my life (indeed, the only sweet recollections) are of the music I heard, and the places where I heard it; it was an enchantment! With what vividness I can recall it all! The eager anticipation for days; the careful selection, beforehand, from such an *embarras de richesses* as was duly advertised; then the long waiting in the street, at the doors reserved for those whose portion is to be the gallery. The hard-won seat aloft is reached at last, after a selfish but good-humored struggle up the long stone staircase (one is sorry for the weak, but a famished ear has no conscience). The gay and splendid house is crammed; the huge chandelier is a golden blaze; the delight of expectation is in the air, and also the scent of gas, and peppermint, and orange-peel, and music-loving humanity, whom I have discovered to be of sweeter fragrance than the common herd.

The orchestra fills, one by one; instruments tune up—a familiar cacophony, sweet with seductive promise. The conductor takes his seat—applause—a hush—three taps—the baton waves once, twice, thrice—the eternal fountain of magic is let loose, and at the very first jet

"The cares that infest the day
Shall fold their tents, like the Arabs,
And as silently steal away."

Then lo! the curtain rises, and straightway we are in Seville—Seville, after Pentonville! Count Almaviva, lordly, gallant, and gay beneath his disguise, twangs his guitar, and what sounds issue from it! For every instrument that was ever invented is in that guitar—the whole orchestra!

"*Ecco ridente il cielo . . .* ," so sings he (with the most beautiful male

voice of his time) under Rosina's balcony; and soon Rosina's voice (the most beautiful female voice of hers) is heard behind her curtains — so girlish, so innocent, so young and light-hearted, that the eyes fill with involuntary tears.

Thus encouraged, he warbles that his name is Lindoro, that he would fain espouse her; that he is not rich in the goods of this world, but gifted with an inordinate, inexhaustible capacity for love (just like Peter Ibbetson); and vows that he will always warble to her, in this wise, from dawn till when daylight sinks behind the mountain. But what matter the words?

"Go on, my love, go on, *like this!*" warbles back Rosina — and no wonder — till the dull, despondent, commonplace heart of Peter Ibbetson has room for nothing else but sunny hope and love and joy! And yet it is all mere sound — impossible, unnatural, unreal nonsense!

Or else, in a square building, decent and well-lighted enough, but not otherwise remarkable — the very chapel of music — four business-like gentlemen, in modern attire and spectacles, take their places on an unpretentious platform amid refined applause; and soon the still air vibrates to the trembling of sixteen strings — only that and nothing more!

But in that is all Beethoven, or Schubert, or Schumann has got to say to us for the moment, and what a say it is! And with what consummate precision and perfection it is said — with what a mathematical certainty, and yet with what suavity, dignity, grace, and distinction!

They are the four greatest players in the world, perhaps; but they forget themselves, and we forget them (as it is their wish we should), in the master whose work they interpret so reverently, that we may yearn with his mighty desire and thrill with his rapture and triumph, or ache with his heavenly pain and submit with his divine resignation.

Not all the words in all the tongues that ever were — dovetail them, rhyme them, alliterate them, torture them as you will — can ever pierce to

the uttermost depths of the soul of man, and let in a glimpse of the Infinite, as do the inarticulate tremblings of those sixteen strings.

Ah, songs without words are the best!

Then a gypsy-like little individual, wiry and unkempt, who looks as if he had spent his life listening to the voices of the night in Heaven knows what Lithuanian forests, with wolves and wild-boars for his familiars, and the wind in the trees for his teacher, seats himself at the great brass-bound oaken Broadwood piano-forte. And under his phenomenal fingers, a haunting, tender, world-sorrow, full of questionings—a dark mystery of moonless, starlit nature—exhales itself in nocturnes, in impromptus, in preludes—in mere waltzes and mazourkas even! But waltzes and mazourkas such as the most frivolous would never dream of dancing to. A capricious, charming sorrow—not too deep for tears, if one be at all inclined to shed them—so delicate, so fresh, and yet so distinguished, so ethereally civilized and worldly and well-bred that it has crystallized itself into a drawing-room ecstasy, to last forever. It seems as though what was death (or rather euthanasia) to him who felt it, is play for us—surely an immortal sorrow whose recital will never, never pall—the sorrow of Chopin.

Though why Chopin should have been so sorry we cannot even guess; for mere sorrow's sake, perhaps; the very luxury of woe—the real sorrow which has no real cause (like mine in those days); and that is the best and cheapest kind of sorrow to make music of, after all!

And this great little gypsy pianist, who plays his Chopin so well; evidently he has not spent his life in Lithuanian forests, but hard at the keyboard, night and day; and he has had a better master than the wind in the trees—namely, Chopin himself (for it is printed in the programme). It was his father and mother before him, and theirs, who heard the voices of the night; but he remembers it all, and puts it all into his master's music, and makes us remember it, too.

Or else behold the chorus, rising tier upon tier, and culminating in the giant organ. But their thunder is just hushed.

Some Lilliputian figure, male or female, as the case may be, rises on its little legs amid the great Lilliputian throng, and through the sacred stillness there peals forth a perfect voice (by no means Lilliputian). It bids us "Rest in the Lord," or else it tells us that "He was despised and rejected of men"; but, again, what matter the words? They are almost a hindrance, beautiful though they be.

The hardened soul melts at the tones of the singer, at the unspeakable pathos of the sounds that cannot lie; one almost believes—one believes at least in the belief of others. At last one understands, and is purged of intolerance and cynical contempt, and would kneel with the rest, in sheer human sympathy!

Oh, wretched outsider that one is (if it all be true)—one whose heart, so hopelessly impervious to the written word, so helplessly callous to the spoken message, can be reached only by the organized vibrations of a trained larynx, a metal pipe, a reed, a fiddle-string—by invisible, impalpable, incomprehensible little air-waves in mathematical combination, that beat against a tiny drum at the back of one's ear. And these mathematical combinations and the laws that govern them have existed forever, before Moses, before Pan, long before either a larynx or a tympanum had been evolved. They are absolute!

Oh, mystery of mysteries!

Euterpe, Muse of Muses, what a personage hast thou become since first thou sattest for thy likeness (with that ridiculous lyre in thy untaught hands) to some Greek who could carve so much better than thou couldst play!

Four strings; but not the fingerable strings of Stradivarius. Nay, I beg thy pardon—five; for thy scale was pentatonic, I believe. Orpheus himself

had no better, it is true. It was with just such an instrument that he all but charmed his Eurydice out of Hades. But, alas, she went back; on second thoughts, she liked Hades best!

Couldst thou fire and madden and wring the heart, and then melt and console and charm it into the peace that passeth all understanding, with those poor five rudimentary notes, and naught between?

Couldst thou, out of those five sounds of fixed, unalterable pitch, make, not a sixth sound, but a star?

What were they, those five sounds? "Do, re, mi, fa, sol?" What must thy songs without words have been, if thou didst ever make any?

Thou wast in very deed a bread-and-butter miss in those days, Euterpe, for all that thy eight twin sisters were already grown up, and out; and now thou toppest them all by half a head, at least. "Tu leur mangerais des petits pâtés sur la tête—comme Madame Seraskier!"

And oh, how thou beatest them all for beauty! In *my* estimation, at least—like—like Madame Seraskier again!

And hast thou done growing at last?

Nay, indeed; thou art not even yet a bread-and-butter miss—thou art but a sweet baby, one year old, and seven feet high, tottering midway between some blessed heaven thou hast only just left and the dull home of us poor mortals.

The sweet one-year-old baby of our kin puts its hands upon our knees and looks up into our eyes with eyes full of unutterable meaning. It has so much to say! It can only say "ga-ga" and "ba-ba"; but with oh! how searching a voice, how touching a look—that is, if one is fond of babies! We are moved to the very core; we want to understand, for it concerns us all; we were once like that ourselves—the individual and the race—but for the life of us we cannot *remember*.

And what canst *thou* say to us yet, Euterpe, but thy "ga-ga" and thy "ba-ba," the inarticulate sweetness whereof we feel and cannot comprehend? But how beautiful it is—and what a look thou hast, and what a voice—that is, if one is fond of music!

"Je suis las des mots —je suis las d'entendre
Ce qui peut mentir;
J'aime mieux les sons, qu'au lieu de comprendre
Je n'ai qu'à sentir."

* * * * *

Next day I would buy or beg or borrow the music that had filled me with such emotion and delight, and take it home to my little square piano, and try to finger it all out for myself. But I had begun too late in life.

To sit, longing and helpless, before an instrument one cannot play, with a lovely score one cannot read! Even Tantalus was spared such an ordeal as that.

It seemed hard that my dear father and mother, so accomplished in music themselves, should not even have taught me the musical notes, at an age when it was so easy to learn them; and thus have made me free of that wonder-world of sound in which I took such an extraordinary delight, and might have achieved distinction—perhaps.

But no, my father had dedicated me to the Goddess of Science from before my very birth; that I might some day be better equipped than he for the pursuit, capture, and utilization of Nature's sterner secrets. There must be no dallying with light Muses. Alas! I have fallen between two stools!

And thus, Euterpe absent, her enchantment would pass away; her handwriting was before me, but I had not learned how to decipher it, and my weary self would creep back into its old prison—my soul.

Self-sickness—*Selbstschmerz, le mal de soi!* What a disease! It is not to be found in any dictionary, medical or otherwise.

I ought to have been whipped for it, I know; but nobody was big enough, or kind enough, to whip me!

* * * * *

At length there came a day when that weary, weak, and most ridiculous self of mine was driven out—and exorcised for good—by a still more potent enchanter than even Handel or Beethoven or Schubert!

There was a certain Lord Cray, for whom Lintot had built some laborers' cottages in Hertfordshire, and I sometimes went there to superintend the workmen. When the cottages were finished, Lord Cray and his wife (a very charming, middle-aged lady) came to see them, and were much pleased with all that had been done, and also seemed to be much interested in *me*, of all people in the world! and a few days later I received a card of invitation to their house in town for a concert.

At first I felt much too shy to go; but Mr. Lintot insisted that it was my duty to do so, as it might lead to business; so that when the night came, I screwed up my courage to the sticking-place, and went.

That evening was all enchantment, or would have been but for the somewhat painful feeling that I was such an outsider.

But I was always well content to be the least observed of all observers, and felt happy in the security that here I should at least be left alone; that no perfect stranger would attempt to put me at my ease by making me the butt of his friendly and familiar banter; that no gartered duke, or belted earl (I have no doubt they were as plentiful there as blackberries, though they did not wear their insignia) would pat me on the back and ask me if I would sooner look a bigger fool than I was, or be a bigger fool than I looked. (I have not found a repartee for that insidious question yet; that is why it rankles so.)

I had always heard that the English were a stiff people. There seemed to be no stiffness at Lady Cray's; nor was there any facetiousness; it put one

"PARIGI, O CARA . . ."

at one's ease merely to look at them. They were mostly big, and strong, and healthy, and quiet, and good-humored, with soft and pleasantly-modulated voices. The large, well-lighted rooms were neither hot nor cold; there were beautiful pictures on the walls, and an exquisite scent of flowers came from an immense conservatory. I had never been to such a gathering before; all was new and a surprise, and very much to my taste, I confess. It was my first glimpse of "Society"; and last—but one!

There were crowds of people—but no crowd; everybody seemed to know everybody else quite intimately, and to resume conversations begun an hour ago somewhere else.

Presently these conversations were hushed, and Grisi and Mario sang! It was as much as I could do to restrain my enthusiasm and delight. I could have shouted out loud—I could almost have sung myself!

In the midst of the applause that followed that heavenly duet, a lady and gentleman came into the room, and at the sight of that lady a new interest came into my life; and all the old half-forgotten sensations of mute pain and rapture that the beauty of Madame Seraskier used to make me feel as a child were revived once more; but with a depth and intensity, in comparison, that were as a strong man's barytone to a small boy's treble.

It was the quick, sharp, cruel blow, the *coup de poignard*, that beauty of the most obvious, yet subtle, consummate, and highly-organized order can deal to a thoroughly prepared victim.

And what a thoroughly prepared victim was I! A poor, shy, over-susceptible, virginal savage—Uncas, the son of Chingachgook, astray for the first time in a fashionable London drawing-room.

A chaste mediæval knight, born out of his due time, ascetic both from reverence and disgust, to whom woman in the abstract was the one religion; in the concrete, the cause of fifty disenchantments a day!

A lusty, love-famished, warm-blooded pagan, stranded in the middle of the nineteenth century; in whom some strange inherited instinct had planted a definite, complete, and elaborately-finished conception of what the ever-beloved shape of woman should be—from the way the hair should grow on her brow and her temples and the nape of her neck, down to the very rhythm that should regulate the length and curve and position of every single individual toe! and who had found, to his pride and delight, that his preconceived ideal was as near to that of Phidias as if he had lived in the time of Pericles and Aspasia.

For such was this poor scribe, and such he had been from a child, until this beautiful lady first swam into his ken.

She was so tall that her eyes seemed almost on a level with mine, but she moved with the alert lightness and grace of a small person. Her thick, heavy hair was of a dark coppery brown, her complexion clear and pale, her eyebrows and eyelashes black, her eyes a light bluish gray. Her nose was short and sharp, and rather tilted at the tip, and her red mouth large and very mobile; and here, deviating from my preconceived ideal, she showed me how tame a preconceived ideal can be. Her perfect head was small, and round her long, thick throat two slight creases went parallel, to make what French sculptors call *le collier de Vénus;* the skin of her neck was like a white camellia, and slender and square-shouldered as she was, she did not show a bone. She was that beautiful type the French define as *la fausse maigre*, which does not mean a "false, thin woman."

She seemed both thoughtful and mirthful at once, and genial as I had never seen any one genial before—a person to confide in, to tell all one's troubles to, without even an introduction! When she laughed she showed both top and bottom teeth, which were perfect, and her eyes nearly closed, so that they could no longer be seen for the thick lashes that fringed both upper and under eyelids; at which time the expression of her face was so keenly, cruelly sweet that it went through one like a knife. And then the

laugh would suddenly cease, her full lips would meet, and her eyes beam out again like two mild gray suns, benevolently humorous and kindly inquisitive, and full of interest in everything and everybody around her. But there—I cannot describe her any more than one can describe a beautiful tune.

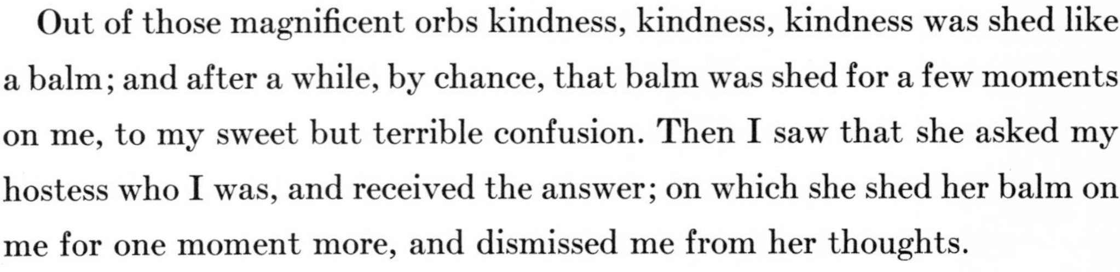

Out of those magnificent orbs kindness, kindness, kindness was shed like a balm; and after a while, by chance, that balm was shed for a few moments on me, to my sweet but terrible confusion. Then I saw that she asked my hostess who I was, and received the answer; on which she shed her balm on me for one moment more, and dismissed me from her thoughts.

Madame Grisi sang again—Desdemona's song from *Othello*—and the beautiful lady thanked the divine singer, whom she seemed to know quite intimately; and I thought her thanks—Italian thanks—even diviner than the song—not that I could quite understand them or even hear them well—I was too far; but she thanked with eyes and hands and shoulders—slight, happy movements—as well as words; surely the sweetest and sincerest words ever spoken.

She was much surrounded and made up to—evidently a person of great importance; and I ventured to ask another shy man standing in my corner who she was, and he answered—

"The Duchess of Towers."

She did not stay long, and when she departed all turned dull and commonplace that had seemed so bright before she came; and seeing that it was not necessary to bid my hostess good-night and thank her for a pleasant evening, as we did in Pentonville, I got myself out of the house and walked back to my lodgings an altered man.

I should probably never meet that lovely young duchess again, and certainly never know her; but her shaft had gone straight and true into my very heart, and I felt how well barbed it was, beyond all possibility of its ever being torn out of that blessed wound; might this never heal; might it bleed on forever!

She would be an ideal in my lonely life, to live up to in thought and word and deed. An instinct which I felt to be infallible told me she was as good as she was fair—

"Dowered with the hate of hate, the scorn of scorn,
The love of love."

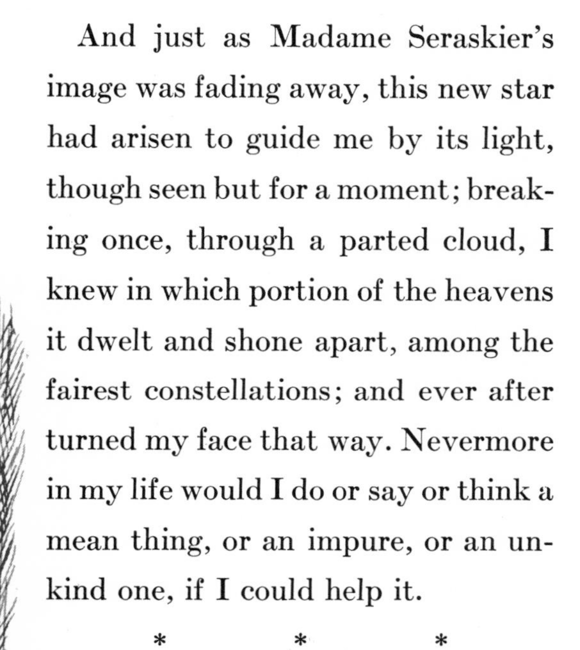

And just as Madame Seraskier's image was fading away, this new star had arisen to guide me by its light, though seen but for a moment; breaking once, through a parted cloud, I knew in which portion of the heavens it dwelt and shone apart, among the fairest constellations; and ever after turned my face that way. Nevermore in my life would I do or say or think a mean thing, or an impure, or an unkind one, if I could help it.

* * *

Next day, as we walked to the Foundling Hospital for divine service, Mrs. Lintot severely deigned—under protest, as it were—to cross-examine me on the adventures of the evening.

I did not mention the Duchess of Towers, nor was I able to describe the different ladies' dresses; but I described everything else in a manner I thought calculated to interest her deeply—the flowers, the splendid pictures and curtains and cabinets, the beautiful music, the many lords and ladies gay.

She disapproved of them all.

Existence on such an opulent scale was unconducive to any qualities of real sterling value, either moral or intellectual. Give *her*, for one, plain living and high thinking!

"By-the-way," she asked, "what kind of supper did they give you? Something extremely *recherché*, I have no doubt. Ortolans, nightingales' tongues, pearls dissolved in wine?"

Candor obliged me to confess there had been no supper, or that if there had I had managed to miss it. I suggested that perhaps everybody had dined late; and all the pearls, I told her, were on the ladies' necks and in their hair; and not feeling hungry, I could not wish them anywhere else; and the nightingales' tongues were in their throats to sing heavenly Italian duets with.

"And they call that hospitality!" exclaimed Lintot, who loved his supper; and then, as he was fond of summing up and laying down the law when once his wife had given him the lead, he did so to the effect that though the great were all very well in their superficial way, and might possess many external charms for each other, and for all who were so deplorably weak as to fall within the sphere of their attraction, there was a gulf between the likes of them and the likes of us, which it would be better not to try and bridge if one wished to preserve one's independence and one's self-respect; unless, of course, it led to business; and this, he feared, it would never do with me.

"They take you up one day and they drop you like a 'ot potato the next;

and, moreover, my dear Peter," he concluded, affectionately linking his arm in mine, as was often his way when we walked together (although he was twelve good inches shorter than myself), "inequality of social condition is a bar to any real intimacy. It is something like disparity of physical stature. One can walk arm in arm only with a man of about one's own size."

This summing up seemed so judicious, so incontrovertible, that feeling quite deplorably weak enough to fall within the sphere of Lady Cray's attraction if I saw much of her, and thereby losing my self-respect, I was deplorably weak enough not to leave a card on her after the happy evening I had spent at her house.

Snob that I was, I dropped her—"like a 'ot potato"—for fear of her dropping me.

Besides which I had on my conscience a guilty, snobby feeling that in merely external charms at least these fine people were more to my taste than the charmed circle of my kind old friends the Lintots, however inferior they might be to these (for all that I knew) in sterling qualities of the heart and head—just as I found the outer aspect of Park Lane and Piccadilly more attractive than that of Pentonville, though possibly the latter may have been the more wholesome for such as I to live in.

But people who can get Mario and Grisi to come and sing for them (and the Duchess of Towers to come and listen); people whose walls are covered with beautiful pictures; people for whom the smooth and harmonious ordering of all the little external things of social life has become a habit and a profession—such people are not to be dropped without a pang.

So with a pang I went back to my usual round as though nothing had happened; but night and day the face of the Duchess of Towers was ever present to me, like a fixed idea that dominates a life.

*   *   *   *   *

On reading and rereading these past pages, I find that I have been unpardonably egotistic, unconscionably prolix and diffuse; and with such small beer to chronicle!

And yet I feel that if I strike out this, I must also strike out that; which would lead to my striking out all, in sheer discouragement; and I have a tale to tell which is more than worth the telling!

Once having got into the way of it, I suppose, I must have found the temptation to talk about myself irresistible.

It is evidently a habit easy to acquire, even in old age—perhaps especially in old age, for it has never been my habit through life. I would sooner have talked to you about yourself, reader, or about you to somebody else—your friend, or even your enemy; or about them to you.

But, indeed, at present, and until I die, I am without a soul to talk to about anybody or anything worth speaking of, so that most of my talking is done in pen and ink—a one-sided conversation, O patient reader, with yourself. I am the most lonely old man in the world, although perhaps the happiest.

Still, it is not always amusing where I live, cheerfully awaiting my translation to another sphere.

There is the good chaplain, it is true, and the good priest; who talk to me about myself a little too much, methinks; and the doctor, who talks to me about the priest and the chaplain, which is better. He does not seem to like them. He is a very witty man.

But, my brother maniacs!

They are lamentably *comme tout le monde*, after all. They are only interesting when the mad fit seizes them. When free from their awful complaint they are for the most part very common mortals: conventional Philistines, dull dogs like myself, and dull dogs do not like each other.

Two of the most sensible (one a forger, the other a kleptomaniac on an important scale) are friends of mine. They are fairly well educated, respectable city men, clean, solemn, stodgy, punctilious, and resigned, but they are both unhappy; not because they are cursed with the double brand of madness and crime, and have forfeited their freedom in consequence; but because they find there are so few "ladies and gentlemen" in a criminal lunatic asylum, and they have always been used to "the society of ladies and gentlemen." Were it not for this, they would be well content to live here. And each is in the habit of confiding to me that he considers the other a very high-minded, trustworthy fellow, and all that, but not altogether "quite a gentleman." I do not know what they consider me; they probably confide that to each other.

Can anything be less odd, less eccentric or interesting?

Another, when quite sane, speaks English with a French accent and demonstrative French gestures, and laments the lost glories of the French régime, and affects to forget the simplest English words. He doesn't know a word of French, however. But when his madness comes on, and he is put into a strait-waistcoat, all his English comes back, and very strong, fluent, idiomatic English it is, of the cockneyest kind, with all its *h's* duly transposed.

Another (the most unpleasant and ugliest person here) has chosen me for the confidant of his past amours; he gives me the names and dates and all. The less I listen the more he confides. He makes me sick. What can I do to prevent his believing that I believe him? I am tired of killing people for lying about women. If I call him a liar and a cad, it may wake in him Heaven knows what dormant frenzy—for I am quite in the dark as to the nature of his mental infirmity.

Another, a weak but amiable and well-intentioned youth, tries to think that he is passionately fond of music; but he is so exclusive, if you please, that he can only endure Bach and Beethoven, and when he hears Mendelssohn or Chopin, is obliged to leave the room. If I want to please him I whistle "Le Bon Roi Dagobert," and tell him it is the *motif* of one of Bach's fugues; and to get rid of him I whistle it again and tell him it is one of Chopin's impromptus. What his madness is I can never be quite sure, for he is very close, but have heard that he is fond of roasting cats alive; and that the mere sight of a cat is enough to rouse his terrible propensity, and drive all wholesome, innocent, harmless, natural affectation out of his head.

There is a painter here who (like others one has met outside) believes himself the one living painter worthy of the name. Indeed, he has forgotten the names of all the others, and can only despise and abuse them in the lump. He triumphantly shows you his own work, which consists of just the kind of crude, half-clever, irresponsible, impressionist daubs you would expect from an amateur who talks in that way; and you wonder why on earth he should be in a lunatic asylum, of all places in the world. And (just as would happen outside, again) some of his fellow-sufferers take him at his own valuation and believe him a great genius; some of them want to kick him for an impudent impostor (but that he is so small); and the majority do not care.

His mania is arson, poor fellow; and when the terrible wish comes over him to set the place on fire he forgets his artistic conceit, and his mean, weak, silly face becomes almost grand.

And with the female inmates it is just the same. There is a lady who has spent twenty years of her life here. Her father was a small country doctor, called Snogget; her husband an obscure, hard-working curate; and she is absolutely normal, commonplace, and even vulgar. For her hobby is to discourse of well-born and titled people and county families, with whom (and with no others) it has always been her hope and desire to mix; and is still, though her hair is nearly white, and she is still here. She thinks and talks and cares about nothing else but "smart people," and has conceived a very warm regard for me, on account of Lieutenant-colonel Ibbetson, of Ibbetson Hall, Hopshire; not because I killed him and was sentenced to be hanged for it, or because he was a greater criminal than I (all of which is interesting enough); but because he was my relative, and that through him I must be distantly connected, she thinks, with the Ibbetsons of Lechmere — whoever they may be, and whom neither she nor I have ever met (indeed, I had never heard of them), but whose family history she knows almost by heart. What can be tamer, duller, more prosaic, more sordidly humdrum, more hopelessly sane, more characteristic of common, under-bred, provincial feminine cackle?

And yet this woman, in a fit of conjugal jealousy, murdered her own children; and her father went mad in consequence, and her husband cut his throat.

In fact, during their lucid intervals it would never enter one's mind that they were mad at all, they are so absolutely like the people one meets every day in the world — such narrow-minded idiots, such deadly bores! One might as well be back in Pentonville or Hopshire again, or live in Passionate Brompton (as I am told it is called); or even in Belgravia, for that matter!

For we have a young lord and a middle-aged baronet — a shocking pair, who should not be allowed to live; but for family influence they would be doing their twenty years' penal servitude in jail, instead of living comfortably sequestered here. Like Ouida's high-born heroes, they "stick to their order," and do not mingle with the rest of us. They ignore us so completely that we cannot help looking up to them in spite of their vices — just as we should do outside.

And we, of the middle class, we stick to our order, too, and do not mingle with the small shop-keepers — who do not mingle with the laborers, artisans, and mechanics — who (alas, for them!) have nobody to look down upon but each other — but they do not; and are the best-bred people in the place.

Such are we! It is only when our madness is upon us that we cease to be commonplace, and wax tragical and great, or else original and grotesque and humorous, with that true deep humor that compels both our laughter and our tears, and leaves us older, sadder, and wiser than it found us.

"Sunt lacrimae rerum, et mentem mortalia tangunt."

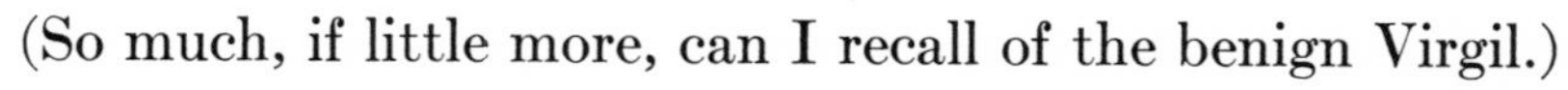

(So much, if little more, can I recall of the benign Virgil.)

And now to my small beer again, which will have more of a head to it henceforward.

* * * * *

Thus did I pursue my solitary way, like Bryant's Water-fowl, only with a less definite purpose before me—till at last there dawned for me an ever-memorable Saturday in June.

I had again saved up enough money to carry my long longed-for journey to Paris into execution. The *Seine*'s boiler got up its steam, the *Seine*'s white awning was put up for me as well as others; and on a beautiful cloudless English morning I stood by the man at the wheel, and saw St. Paul's and London Bridge and the Tower fade out of sight; with what hope and joy I cannot describe. I almost forgot that I was me!

And next morning (a beautiful French morning) how I exulted as I went up the Champs Élysées and passed under the familiar Arc de Triomphe on my way to the Rue de la Pompe, Passy, and heard all around the familiar tongue that I still knew so well, and rebreathed the long-lost and half-forgotten, but now keenly remembered, fragrance of the *genius loci;* that vague, light, indescribable, almost imperceptible scent of a place, that is so heavily laden with the past for those who have lived there long ago—the most subtly intoxicating ether that can be!

When I came to the meeting of the Rue de la Tour and the Rue de la

TO "THE ELYSIAN FIELDS" ONCE MORE!

Pompe, and, looking in at the grocer's shop at the corner, I recognized the handsome mustachioed groceress, Madame Liard (whose mustache twelve prosperous years had turned gray), I was almost faint with emotion. Had any youth been ever so moved by that face before?

There, behind the window (which was now of plate-glass), and among splendid Napoleonic wares of a later day, were the same old India-rubber balls in colored net-work; the same quivering lumps of fresh paste in brown paper, that looked so cool and tempting; the same three-sou boxes of water-colors (now marked seventy-five centimes), of which I had consumed so many in the service of Mimsey Seraskier! I went in and bought one, and resmelt with delight the smell of all my by-gone dealings there, and received her familiar sounding—

"Merci, monsieur! faudrait-il autre chose?" as if it had been a blessing; but I was too shy to throw myself into her arms and tell her that I was the "lone, wandering, but not lost" Gogo Pasquier. She might have said—

"Eh bien, et après?"

The day had begun well.

Like an epicure, I deliberated whether I should walk to the old gate in the Rue de la Pompe, and up the avenue and back to our old garden, or make my way round to the gap in the park hedge that we had worn of old by our frequent passage in and out, to and from the Bois de Boulogne.

I chose the latter as, on the whole, the more promising in exquisite gradations of delight.

The gap in the park hedge, indeed! The park hedge had disappeared, the very park itself was gone, cut up, demolished, all parcelled out into small gardens, with trim white villas, except where a railway ran through a deep cutting in the chalk. A train actually roared and panted by, and choked me with its filthy steam as I looked round in stupefaction on the ruins of my long-cherished hope.

If that train had run over me and I had survived it, it could not have given me a greater shock; it all seemed too cruel and brutal an outrage.

A winding carriage-road had been pierced through the very heart of the wilderness; and on this, neatly-paled little brand-new gardens abutted, and in these I would recognize, here and there, an old friend in the shape of some well-remembered tree that I had often climbed as a boy, and which had been left standing out of so many, but so changed by the loss of its old surroundings that it had a tame, caged, transplanted look—almost apologetic, and as if ashamed of being found out at last!

Nothing else remained. Little hills and cliffs and valleys and chalk-pits that had once seemed big had been levelled up, or away, and I lost my bearings altogether, and felt a strange, creeping chill of blankness and bereavement.

But how about the avenue and my old home? I hastened back to the Rue de la Pompe with the quick step of aroused anxiety. The avenue was gone—blocked within a dozen yards of the gate by a huge brick building covered with newly-painted trellis-work! My old house was no more, but in its place a much larger and smarter edifice of sculptured stone. The old gate at least had not disappeared, nor the porter's lodge; and I feasted my sorrowful eyes on these poor remains, that looked snubbed and shabby and out of place in the midst of all this new splendor.

Presently a smart concierge, with a beautiful pink-ribboned cap, came out and stared at me for a while, and inquired if monsieur desired anything.

I could not speak.

"Est-ce que monsieur est indisposé? Cette chaleur! Monsieur ne parle pas le français, peut-être?"

When I found my tongue I explained to her that I had once lived there in a modest house overlooking the street, but which had been replaced by this much more palatial abode.

"O, oui, monsieur — on a balayé tout ça!" she replied.

"Balayé!" What an expression for *me* to hear!

And she explained how the changes had taken place, and how valuable the property had become. She showed me a small plot of garden, a fragment of my old garden, that still remained, and where the old apple-tree might still have been, but that it had been sawed away. I saw the stump; that did duty for a rustic table.

Presently, looking over a new wall, I saw another small garden, and in it the ruins of the old shed where I had found the toy wheelbarrow—soon to disappear, as they were building there too.

I asked after all the people I could think of, beginning with those of least interest—the butcher, the baker, the candlestick-maker.

Some were dead; some had retired and had left their "commerce" to their children and children-in-law. Three different school-masters had kept the school since I had left. Thank Heaven, there was still the school—much altered, it is true. I had forgotten to look for it.

She had no remembrance of my name, or the Seraskiers'—I asked, with a beating heart. We had left no trace. Twelve short years had effaced all memory of us! But she told me that a gentleman, *décoré, mais tombé en enfance,* lived at a *maison de santé* in the Chaussée de la Muette, close by, and that his name was le Major Duquesnois; and thither I went, after rewarding and warmly thanking her.

I inquired for le Major Duquesnois, and I was told he was out for a walk, and I soon found him, much aged and bent, and leaning on the arm of a Sister of Charity. I was so touched that I had to pass him two or three times before I could speak. He was so small—so pathetically small!

It was a long time before I could give him an idea of who I was—Gogo Pasquier!

Then after a while he seemed to recall the past a little.

"Ha, ha! Gogo—gentil petit Gogo!—oui—oui—l'exercice? Portez . . . arrrmes! arrmes . . . bras? Et Mimsé? bonne petite Mimsé! toujours mal à la tête?"

He could just remember Madame Seraskier; and repeated her name several times and said, "Ah! elle était bien belle, Madame Seraskier!"

In the old days of fairy-tale telling, when he used to get tired and I still wanted him to go on, he had arranged that if, in the course of the story, he suddenly brought in the word "Cric," and I failed to immediately answer "Crac," the story would be put off till our next walk (to be continued in our next!) and he was so ingenious in the way he brought in the terrible word that I often fell into the trap, and had to forego my delight for that afternoon.

I suddenly thought of saying "Cric!" and he immediately said "Crac!" and laughed in a touching, senile way—"Cric!—Crac! c'est bien ça!" and then he became quite serious and said—

"Et la suite au prochain numéro!"

After this he began to cough, and the good Sister said—

"Je crains que monsieur ne le fatigue un peu!"

So I had to bid him good-bye; and after I had squeezed and kissed his

hand, he made me a most courtly bow, as though I had been a complete stranger.

I rushed away, tossing up my arms like a madman in my pity and sorrow for my dear old friend, and my general regret and disenchantment. I made for the Bois de Boulogne, there to find, instead of the old rabbit-and-roebuck-haunted thickets and ferneries and impenetrable undergrowth, a huge artificial lake, with row-boats and skiffs, and a rockery that would have held its own in Rosherville gardens. And on the way thither, near the iron gates in the fortifications, whom should I meet but one of my friends the couriers, on his way from St. Cloud to the Tuileries! There he rode with his arms jogging up and down, and his low glazed hat, and his immense jack-boots, just the same as ever, never rising in his stirrups, as his horse trotted to the jingle of the sweet little chime round its neck.

Alas! his coat was no longer the innocent, unsophisticated blue and silver livery of the bourgeois king, but the hateful green and gold of another régime.

Farther on the Mare d'Auteuil itself had suffered change and become respectable—imperially respectable. No more frogs or newts or water-beetles, I felt sure; but gold and silver fish in vulgar Napoleonic profusion.

No words that I can find would give any idea of the sadness and longing that filled me as I trod once more that sunlit grassy brink—the goal of my fond ambition for twelve long years.

It was Sunday, and many people were about—many children, in their best Sunday clothes and on their best behavior, discreetly throwing crumbs to the fish. A new generation, much quieter and better dressed than my cousins and I, who had once so filled the solitude with the splashing of our nets, and the excited din of our English voices.

As I sat down on a bench by the old willow (where the rat lived), and gazed and gazed, it almost surprised me that the very intensity of my desire did not of itself suffice to call up the old familiar faces and forms, and conjure away these modern intruders. The power to do this seemed almost within my reach; I willed and willed and willed with all my might, but in

vain; I could not cheat my sight or hearing for a moment. There they remained, unconscious and undisturbed, those happy, well-mannered, well-appointed little French people, and fed the gold and silver fish; and there, with an aching heart, I left them.

Oh, surely, surely, I cried to myself, we ought to find some means of possessing the past more fully and completely than we do. Life is not worth living for many of us if a want so desperate and yet so natural can never be satisfied. Memory is but a poor, rudimentary thing that we had better be without, if it can only lead us to the verge of consummation like this, and madden us with a desire it cannot slake. The touch of a vanished hand, the sound of a voice that is still, the tender grace of a day that is dead, should be ours forever, at our beck and call, by some exquisite and quite conceivable illusion of the senses.

Alas! alas! I have hardly the hope of ever meeting my beloved ones again in another life. Oh, to meet their too dimly remembered forms in *this*, just as they once were, by some trick of my own brain! To see them with the eye, and hear them with the ear, and tread with them the old obliterated ways as in a waking dream! It would be well worth going mad to become such a self-conjurer as that.

Thus musing sadly, I reached St. Cloud, and *that*, at least, and the Boulogne that led to it, had not been very perceptibly altered, and looked as though I had only left them a week ago. The sweet aspect from the bridge, on either side and beyond, filled me with the old enchantment. There, at least, the glory had not departed.

I hastened through the gilded gates and up the broad walk to the grand cascade. There, among the lovely wreathed urns and jars of geranium, still sat or reclined or gesticulated, the old, unalterable gods; there squatted the grimly genial monsters in granite and marble and bronze, still spouting their endless gallons for the delectation of hot Parisian eyes. Unchanged, and to all appearance unchangeable (save that they were not nearly so big as I had imagined), their cold, smooth, ironical patience shamed and braced me into better cheer. Beautiful, hideous, whatever you please, they seemed to revel in the very sense of their insensibility of their eternal stability—their stony scorn of time and wind and weather, and the peevish, weak-kneed, short-lived discontent of man. It was good to fondly pat them on the back once more—when one could reach them—and cling to them for a little while, after all the dust and drift and ruin I had been tramping through all day.

Indeed, they woke in me a healthy craving for all but forgotten earthly joys — even for wretched meat and drink — so I went and ordered a sumptuous repast at the Tête Noire — a brand-new Tête Noire, alas! quite white, all in stone and stucco, and without a history!

It was a beautiful sunset. Waiting for my dinner, I gazed out of the first-floor window, and found balm for my disappointed and regretful spirit in all that democratic joyousness of French Sunday life. I had seen it over and over again just like that in the old days; *this*, at least, was like coming back home to something I had known and loved.

The cafés on the little "Place" between the bridge and the park were full to overflowing. People chatting over their *consommations* sat right out, almost into the middle of the square, so thickly packed that there was scarcely room for the busy, lively, white-aproned waiters to move between them. The air was full of the scent of trodden grass and macaroons and French tobacco, blown from the park; of gay French laughter and the music of *mirlitons;* of a light dusty haze, shot with purple and gold by the setting sun. The river, alive with boats and canoes, repeated the glory of the sky, and the well-remembered, thickly-wooded hills rose before me, culminating in the Lanterne de Diogène.

I could have threaded all that maze of trees blindfolded.

Two Roman pifferari came on to the Place and began to play an extraordinary and most exciting melody that almost drew me out of the window; it seemed to have no particular form, no beginning or middle or end; it went soaring higher and higher, like the song of a lark, with never a pause for breath, to the time of a maddening jig—a tarantella, perhaps—always on the strain and stress, always getting nearer and nearer to some shrill climax of ecstasy quite high up and away, beyond the scope of earthly music; while the persistent drone kept buzzing of the earth and the impossibility to escape. All so gay, so sad, there is no name for it!

Two little deformed and discarded-looking dwarfs, beggars, brother and sister, with large toothless gaps for mouths and no upper lip, began to dance; and the crowd laughed and applauded. Higher and higher, nearer and nearer to the impossible, rose the quick, piercing notes of the piffero. Heaven seemed almost within reach—the nirvana of music after its quick madness—the region of the ultra-treble that lies beyond the ken of ordinary human ears!

A carriage and four, with postilions and "guides," came clattering royally down the road from the palace, and dispersed the crowd as it bowled on its way to the bridge. In it were two ladies and two gentlemen. One of the ladies was the young Empress of the French; the other looked up at my window—for a moment, as in a soft flash of summer lightning, her face seemed ablaze with friendly recognition—with a sweet glance of kindness and interest and surprise—a glance that pierced me like a sudden shaft of light from heaven.

It was the Duchess of Towers!

I felt as though the bagpipes had been leading up to this! In a moment more the carriage was out of sight, the sun had quite gone down, the pifferari had ceased to play and were walking round with the hat, and all was over.

I dined, and made my way back to Paris on foot through the Bois de Boulogne, and by the Mare d'Auteuil, and saw my old friend the water-rat swim across it, trailing the gleam of his wake after him like a silver comet's tail.

"Allons-nous-en, gens de la noce!
Allons-nous-en, chacun chez nous!"

So sang a festive wedding-party as it went merrily arm in arm through the long high street of Passy, with a gleeful trust that would have filled the heart with envy but for sad experience of the vanity of human wishes.

Chacun chez nous! How charming it sounds!

Was each so sure that when he reached his home he would find his heart's desire? Was the bridegroom himself so very sure?

The heart's desire – the heart's regret! I flattered myself that I had pretty well sounded the uttermost depths of both on that eventful Sunday!

PART FOUR

PART FOUR

I got back to my hotel in the Rue de la Michodière.

Prostrate with emotion and fatigue, the tarantella still jingling in my ears, and that haunting, beloved face, with its ineffable smile still printed on the retina of my closed eyes, I fell asleep.

And then I dreamed a dream, and the first phase of my real, inner life began!

All the events of the day, distorted and exaggerated and jumbled together after the usual manner of dreams, wove themselves into a kind of nightmare and oppression. I was on my way to my old abode; everything that I met or saw was grotesque and impossible, yet had now the strange, vague charm of association and reminiscence, now the distressing sense of change and loss and desolation.

As I got near to the avenue gate, instead of the school on my left there was a prison; and at the door a little thick-set jailer, three feet high and much deformed, and a little deformed jaileress no bigger than himself, were cunningly watching me out of the corners of their eyes, and toothlessly smiling. Presently they began to waltz together to an old, familiar tune, with their enormous keys dangling at their sides; and they looked so funny

that I laughed and applauded. But soon I perceived that their crooked faces were not really funny; indeed, they were fatal and terrible in the extreme, and I was soon conscious that these deadly dwarfs were trying to waltz between me and the avenue gate for which I was bound – to cut me off, that they might run me into the prison, where it was their custom to hang people of a Monday morning.

In an agony of terror I made a rush for the avenue gate, and there stood the Duchess of Towers, with mild surprise in her eyes and a kind smile – a heavenly vision of strength and reality.

“You are not dreaming true!” she said. “Don’t be afraid—those little people don’t exist! Give me your hand and come in here.”

And as I did so she waved the troglodytes away, and they vanished; and I felt that this was no longer a dream, but something else—some strange thing that had happened to me, some new life that I had woke up to.

For at the touch of her hand my consciousness, my sense of being I, myself, which hitherto in my dream (as in all previous dreams up to then) had been only partial, intermittent, and vague, suddenly blazed into full, consistent, practical activity—just as it is in life, when one is well awake and much interested in what is going on—only with perceptions far keener and more alert.

I knew perfectly who I was and what I was, and remembered all the events of the previous day. I was conscious that my real body, undressed and in bed, now lay fast asleep in a small room on the fourth floor of an *hôtel garni* in the Rue de la Michodière. I knew this perfectly; and yet here was my body, too, just as substantial, with all my clothes on; my boots rather dusty, my shirt-collar damp with the heat, for it was hot. With my disengaged hand I felt in my trousers-pocket; there were my London latch-keys, my purse, my penknife; my handkerchief in the breast-pocket of my coat, and in its tail-pockets my gloves and pipe-case, and the little water-color box I had bought that morning. I looked at my watch; it was going, and marked eleven. I pinched myself, I coughed, I did all one usually does under the pressure of some immense surprise, to assure myself that I was awake; and I *was*, and yet here I stood, actually hand in hand with a great lady to whom I had never been introduced (and who seemed much tickled at my confusion); and staring now at her, now at my old school.

The prison had tumbled down like a house of cards, and lo! in its place was M. Saindou’s *maison d’éducation*, just as it had been of old. I even recognized on the yellow wall the stamp of a hand in dry mud, made fifteen years ago by a day boy called Parisot, who had fallen down in the gutter close by, and thus left his mark on getting up again; and it had remained there for months, till it had been whitewashed away in the holidays. Here it was anew, after fifteen years.

The swallows were flying and twittering. A yellow omnibus was drawn up to the gates of the school; the horses stamped and neighed, and bit each other, as French horses always did in those days. The driver swore at them perfunctorily.

A crowd was looking on—le Père et la Mère François, Madame Liard, the grocer's wife, and other people, whom I remembered at once with delight. Just in front of us a small boy and girl were looking on, like the rest, and I recognized the back and the cropped head and thin legs of Mimsey Seraskier.

A barrel-organ was playing a pretty tune I knew quite well, and had forgotten.

The school gates opened, and M. Saindou, proud and full of self-importance (as he always was), and half a dozen boys whose faces and names were quite familiar to me, in smart white trousers and shining boots, and silken white bands round their left arms, got into the omnibus, and were driven away in a glorified manner—as it seemed—to heaven in a golden chariot. It was beautiful to see and hear.

I was still holding the duchess's hand, and felt the warmth of it through her glove; it stole up my arm like a magnetic current. I was in Elysium; a heavenly sense had come over me that at last my periphery had been victoriously invaded by a spirit other than mine—a most powerful and beneficent spirit. There was a blessed fault in my impenetrable armor of self, after all, and the genius of strength and charity and loving-kindness had found it out.

"Now you're dreaming true," she said. "Where are those boys going?"

"To church, to make their *première communion,*" I replied.

"That's right. You're dreaming true because I've got you by the hand. Do you know that tune?"

I listened, and the words belonging to it came out of the past and I said them to her, and she laughed again, with her eyes screwed up deliciously.

"Quite right—quite!" she exclaimed. "How odd that you should know them! How well you pronounce French for an Englishman! For you are Mr. Ibbetson, Lady Cray's architect?"

I assented, and she let go my hand.

The street was full of people—familiar forms and faces and voices, chatting together and looking down the road after the yellow omnibus; old attitudes, old tricks of gait and manner, old forgotten French ways of speech—all as it was long ago. Nobody noticed us, and we walked up the now deserted avenue.

The happiness, the enchantment of it all! Could it be that I was dead, that I had died suddenly in my sleep, at the hotel in the Rue de la Michodière! Could it be that the Duchess of Towers was dead too—had been killed by some accident on her way from St. Cloud to Paris? and that, both having died so near each other, we had begun our eternal afterlife in this heavenly fashion?

That was too good to be true, I reflected; some instinct told me that this was not death, but transcendent earthly life—and also, alas! that it would not endure forever!

I was deeply conscious of every feature in her face, every movement of her body, every detail of her dress—more so than I could have been in actual life—and said to myself, "Whatever this is, it is no dream." But I felt there was about me the unspeakable elation which can come to us only in our waking moments when we are at our very best; and then only feebly, in comparison with this, and to many of us never. It never had to me, since that morning when I had found the little wheelbarrow.

I was also conscious, however, that the avenue itself had a slight touch of the dream in it. It was no longer quite right, and was getting out of drawing and perspective, so to speak. I had lost my stay—the touch of her hand.

"Are you still dreaming true, Mr. Ibbetson?"

"I am afraid not quite," I replied.

"You must try by yourself a little—try hard. Look at this house; what is written on the portico?"

I saw written in gold letters the words, "Tête Noire," and said so.

She rippled with laughter, and said, "No; try again"; and just touched me with the tip of her finger for a moment.

I tried again, and said, "Parvis Notre Dame."

"That's rather better," she said, and touched me again; and I read, "Parva sed Apta," as I had so often read there before in old days.

"And now look at that old house over there," pointing to my old home; "how many windows are there in the top story?"

I said seven.

"No; there are five. Look again!" and there were five; and the whole house was exactly, down to its minutest detail, as it had been once upon a time. I could see Thérèse through one of the windows, making my bed.

"That's better," said the duchess; "you will soon do it — it's very easy — *ce n'est que le premier pas!* My father taught me; you must always sleep on your back with your arms above your head, your hands clasped under it and your feet crossed, the right one over the left, unless you are left-handed; and you must never for a moment cease thinking of where you want to be in your dream till you are asleep and get there; and you must never forget in your dream where and what you were when awake. You must join the dream on to reality. Don't forget. And now I will say good-bye; but before I go give me both hands and look round everywhere as far as your eyes can see."

It was hard to look away from her; her face drew my eyes, and through them all my heart; but I did as she told me, and took in the whole familiar scene, even to the distant woods of Ville d'Avray, a glimpse of which was visible through an opening in the trees; even to the smoke of a train making its way to Versailles, miles off; and the old telegraph, working its black arms on the top of Mont Valérien.

"Is it all right?" she asked. "That's well. Henceforward, whenever you come here, you will be safe as far as your sight can reach — from this spot — all through my introduction. See what it is to have a friend at court! No more little dancing jailers! And then you can gradually get farther by yourself.

"Out there, through that park, leads to the Bois de Boulogne — there's a gap in the hedge you can get through; but mind and make everything plain in front of you — *true*, before you go a step farther, or else you'll have to wake and begin it all over again. You have only to will it, and think of yourself as awake, and it will come — on condition, of course, that you have been there before. And mind, also, you must take care how you touch things or people — you may hear, and see, and smell; but you mustn't touch, nor pick flowers or leaves, nor move things about. It blurs the dream, like breathing on a window-pane. I don't know why, but it does. You must remember that everything here is dead and gone by. With you and me it is different; we're alive and real — that is, *I* am; and there would seem to be no mistake about your being real too, Mr. Ibbetson, by the grasp of your hands. But you're *not*; and why you are here, and what business you have in this, my particular dream, I cannot understand; no living person has ever come into it before. I can't make it out. I suppose it's because I saw your reality this afternoon, looking out of the window at the 'Tête Noire,' and you are just a stray figment of my overtired brain — a very agreeable figment, I admit; but you don't exist here just now — you can't possibly; you are somewhere else, Mr. Ibbetson; dancing at Mabille, perhaps, or fast asleep somewhere, and dreaming of French churches and palaces, and public fountains, like a good young British architect—otherwise I shouldn't talk to you like this, you may be sure!

"Never mind. I am very glad to dream that I have been of use to you, and you are very welcome here, if it amuses you to come—especially as you are only a false dream of mine, for what else *can* you be? And now I must leave you, so good-bye."

She disengaged her hands, and laughed her angelic laugh, and then turned towards the park. I watched her tall, straight figure and blowing skirts, and saw her follow some ladies and children into a thicket that I remembered well, and she was soon out of sight.

I felt as if all warmth had gone out of my life; as if a joy had taken flight; as if a precious something had withdrawn itself from my possession, and the gap in my periphery had closed again.

Long I stood in thought, with my eyes fixed on the spot where she had disappeared; and I felt inclined to follow, but then considered this would not have been discreet. For although she was only a false dream of mine, a mere recollection of the exciting and eventful day, a stray figment of my overtired and excited brain—a *more* than agreeable figment (what else *could* she be!)—she was also a great lady, and had treated me, a perfect stranger and a perfect nobody, with singular courtesy and kindness; which I repaid, it is true, with a love so deep and strong that my very life was hers, to do what she liked with, and always had been since I first saw her, and always would be as long as there was breath in my body! But this did not constitute an acquaintance without a proper introduction, even in France—even in a dream. Even in dreams one must be polite, even to stray figments of one's tired, sleeping brain.

And then what business had *she*, in *this*, *my* particular dream—as she herself had asked of me?

But *was* it a dream? I remembered my lodgings at Pentonville, that I had left yesterday morning. I remembered what I was—why I came to Paris; I remembered the very bedroom at the Paris hotel where I was now fast asleep, its loudly-ticking clock, and all the meagre furniture. And here was I, broad awake and conscious, in the middle of an old avenue that had long ceased to exist—that had been built over by a huge brick edifice covered with newly-painted trellis-work. I saw it, this edifice, myself, only twelve hours ago. And yet here was everything as it had been when I was a child; and all through the agency of this solid phantom of a lovely young English duchess, whose warm gloved hands I had only this minute been holding in mine! The scent of her gloves was still in my palm. I looked at my watch; it marked twenty-three minutes to twelve. All this had happened in less than three-quarters of an hour!

Pondering over all this in hopeless bewilderment, I turned my steps towards my old home, and, to my surprise, was just able to look over the garden wall, which I had once thought about ten feet high.

Under the old apple-tree in full bloom sat my mother, darning small socks; with her flaxen side-curls (as it was her fashion to wear them) half-concealing her face. My emotion and astonishment were immense. My heart beat fast. I felt its pulse in my temples, and my breath was short.

At a little green table that I remembered well sat a small boy, rather quaintly dressed in a by-gone fashion, with a frill round his wide shirt-collar, and his golden hair cut quite close at the top, and rather long at the sides and back. It was Gogo Pasquier. He seemed a very nice little boy. He had pen and ink and copy-book before him, and a gilt-edged volume bound in red morocco. I knew it at a glance; it was *Elegant Extracts.* The dog Médor lay asleep in the shade. The bees were droning among the nasturtiums and convolvulus.

A little girl ran up the avenue from the porter's lodge and pushed the garden gate, which rang the bell as it opened, and she went into the garden, and I followed her; but she took no notice of me, nor did the others. It was Mimsey Seraskier.

I went and sat at my mother's feet, and looked long in her face.

I must not speak to her, nor touch her—not even touch her busy hand with my lips, or I should "blur the dream."

I got up and looked over the boy Gogo's shoulder. He was translating Gray's *Elegy* into French; he had not got very far, and seemed to be stumped by the line—

"And leaves the world to darkness and to me."

Mimsey was silently looking over his other shoulder, her thumb in her mouth, one arm on the back of his chair. She seemed to be stumped also: it was an awkward line to translate.

I stooped and put my hand to Médor's nose, and felt his warm breath. He wagged his rudiment of a tail, and whimpered in his sleep. Mimsey said—

"Regarde Médor, comme il remue la queue! *C'est le Prince Charmant qui lui chatouille le bout du nez.*"

Said my mother, who had not spoken hitherto: "Do speak English, Mimsey, please."

Oh, my God! My mother's voice, so forgotten, yet so familiar, so unutterably dear! I rushed to her, and threw myself on my knees at her feet, and seized her hand and kissed it, crying, "Mother, mother!"

A strange blur came over everything; the sense of reality was lost. All became as a dream—a beautiful dream—but only a dream; and I woke.

*   *   *   *   *

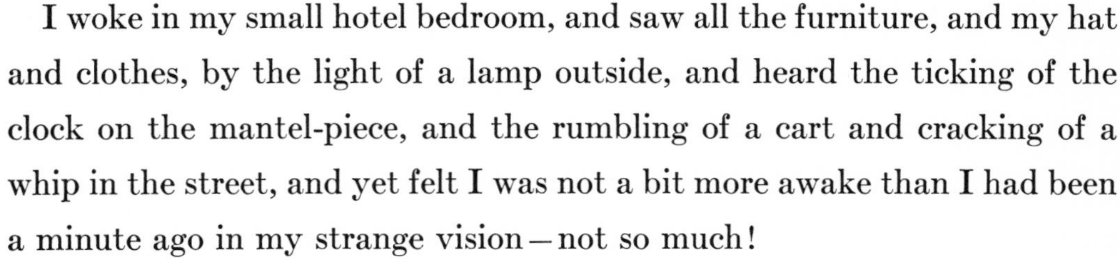

I woke in my small hotel bedroom, and saw all the furniture, and my hat and clothes, by the light of a lamp outside, and heard the ticking of the clock on the mantel-piece, and the rumbling of a cart and cracking of a whip in the street, and yet felt I was not a bit more awake than I had been a minute ago in my strange vision—not so much!

I heard my watch ticking its little tick on the mantel-piece by the side of the clock, like a pony trotting by a big horse. The clock struck twelve. I got up and looked at my watch by the light of the gas-lit streets; it marked the same. My dream had lasted an hour—I had gone to bed at half-past ten.

I tried to recall it all, and did so to the smallest particular—all except the tune the organ had played, and the words belonging to it; they were on the tip of my tongue, and refused to come further. I got up again and walked about the room, and felt that it had not been like a dream at all; it was more "recollectable" than all my real adventures of the previous day. It had ceased to be like a dream, and had become an actuality from the moment I first touched the duchess's hand to the moment I kissed my mother's, and the blur came. It was an entirely new and utterly bewildering experience that I had gone through.

In a dream there are always breaks, inconsistencies, lapses, incoherence, breaches of continuity, many links missing in the chain; only at points is the impression vivid enough to stamp itself afterwards on the waking mind, and even then it is never so really vivid as the impression of real life, although it ought to have seemed so in the dream. One remembers it well on

awaking, but soon it fades, and then it is only one's remembrance of it that one remembers.

There was nothing of this in my dream.

It was something like the "camera-obscura" on Ramsgate pier: one goes in and finds one's self in total darkness; the eye is prepared; one is thoroughly expectant and wide-awake.

Suddenly there flashes on the sight the moving picture of the port and all the life therein, and the houses and cliffs beyond; and farther still the green hills, the white clouds, and blue sky.

Little green waves chase each other in the harbor, breaking into crisp white foam. Sea-gulls wheel and dash and dip behind masts and ropes and pulleys; shiny brass fittings on gangway and compass flash in the sun without dazzling the eye; gay Lilliputians walk and talk, their white teeth, no bigger than a pin's point, gleam in laughter, with never a sound; a steamboat laden with excursionists comes in, its paddles churning the water, and you cannot hear them. Not a detail is missed—not a button on a sailor's jacket, not a hair on his face. All the light and color of sea and earth and sky, that serve for many a mile, are here concentrated within a few square feet. And what color it is! A painter's despair! It is light itself, more beautiful than that which streams through old church windows of stained glass. And all is framed in utter darkness, so that the fully dilated pupils can see their very utmost. It seems as though all had been painted life-size and then shrunk, like a Japanese picture on crape, to a millionth of its natural size, so as to intensify and mellow the effect.

It is all over: you come out into the open sunshine, and all seems garish and bare and bald and commonplace. All magic has faded out of the scene; everything is too far away from everything else; everybody one meets seems coarse and Brobdingnagian and too near. And one has been looking at the like of it all one's life!

Thus with my dream, compared to common, waking, every-day experience; only instead of being mere flat, silent little images moving on a dozen square feet of Bristol-board, and appealing to the eye alone, the things and people in my dream had the same roundness and relief as in life, and were life-size; one could move among them and behind them, and feel as if one could touch and clasp and embrace them if one dared. And the ear, as well as the eye, was made free of this dark chamber of the brain: one heard their speech and laughter as in life. And that was not all, for soft breezes fanned the cheek, the sparrows twittered, the sun gave out its warmth, and the scent of many flowers made the illusion complete.

And then the Duchess of Towers! She had been not only visible and audible like the rest, but tangible as well, to the fullest extent of the sensibility that lay in my nerves of touch; when my hands held hers I felt as though I were drawing all her life into mine.

With the exception of that one figure, all had evidently been as it *had* been in *reality* a few years ago, to the very droning of an insect, to the very fall of a blossom!

Had I gone mad by any chance? I had possessed the past, as I had longed to do a few hours before.

What are sight and hearing and touch and the rest?

Five senses in all.

The stars, worlds upon worlds, so many billions of miles away, what are they for us but mere shiny specks on a net-work of nerves behind the eye? How does one *feel* them there?

The sound of my friend's voice, what is it? The clasp of his hand, the pleasant sight of his face, the scent of his pipe and mine, the taste of the bread and cheese and beer we eat and drink together, what are they but figments (stray figments, perhaps) of the brain – little thrills through nerves made on purpose, and without which there would be no stars, no pipe, no bread and cheese and beer, no voice, no friend, no me?

And is there, perchance, some sixth sense embedded somewhere in the thickness of the flesh—some survival of the past, of the race, of our own childhood even, etiolated by disuse? or some rudiment, some effort to begin, some priceless hidden faculty to be developed into a future source of bliss and consolation for our descendants? some nerve that now can only be made to thrill and vibrate in a dream, too delicate as yet to ply its function in the light of common day?

And was I, of all people in the world—I, Peter Ibbetson, architect and surveyor, Wharton Street, Pentonville—most futile, desultory, and uneducated dreamer of dreams—destined to make some great psychical discovery?

Pondering deeply over these solemn things, I sent myself to sleep again, as was natural enough—but no more to dream. I slept soundly until late in the morning, and breakfasted at the Bains Deligny, a delightful swimming-bath near the Pont de la Concorde (on the other side), and spent most of the day there, alternately swimming, and dozing, and smoking cigarettes, and thinking of the wonders of the night before, and hoping for their repetition on the night to follow.

I remained a week in Paris, loafing about by day among old haunts of my childhood—a melancholy pleasure—and at night trying to "dream true," as my dream duchess had called it. Only once did I succeed.

I had gone to bed thinking most persistently of the "Mare d'Auteuil," and it seemed to me that as soon as I was fairly asleep I woke up there, and knew directly that I had come into a "true dream" again, by the reality and the bliss. It was transcendent *life* once more—a very ecstasy of remembrance made actual, and *such* an exquisite surprise!

There was M. le Major, in his green frock-coat, on his knees near a little hawthorn-tree by the brink, among the water-logged roots of which there dwelt a cunning old dytiscus as big as the bowl of a tablespoon—a prize we had often tried to catch in vain.

M. le Major had a net in his hand, and was watching the water intently; the perspiration was trickling down his nose; and around him, in silent expectation and suspense, were grouped Gogo and Mimsey and my three cousins, and a good-humored freckled Irish boy I had quite forgotten, and I suddenly remembered that his name was Johnstone, that he was very combative, and that he lived in the Rue Basse (now Rue Raynouard).

On the other side of the pond my mother was keeping Médor from the water, for fear of his spoiling the sport, and on the bench by the willow sat Madame Seraskier—lovely Madame Seraskier—deeply interested. I sat down by her side and gazed at her with a joy there is no telling.

An old woman came by, selling conical wafer-cakes, and singing—"*V'là l'plaisir, mesdames—V'là l'plaisir!*" Madame Seraskier bought ten sous' worth—a mountain!

M. le Major made a dash with his net—unsuccessfully, as usual. Médor was let loose, and plunged with a plunge that made big waves all round the *mare*, and dived after an imaginary stone, amid general shouts and shrieks of excitement. Oh, the familiar voices! I almost wept.

Médor came out of the water without his stone and shook himself, twisting and barking and grinning and gyrating, as was his way, quite close to me. In my delight and sympathy I was ill-advised enough to try and stroke him, and straight the dream was "blurred"—changed to an ordinary dream, where all things were jumbled up and incomprehensible; a dream pleasant enough, but different in kind and degree—an *ordinary* dream; and in my distress thereat I woke, and failed to dream again (as I wished to dream) that night.

Next morning (after an early swim) I went to the Louvre, and stood spellbound before Leonardo da Vinci's "Lisa Gioconda," trying hard to find where the wondrous beauty lay that I had heard so extravagantly extolled; and not trying very successfully, for I had seen Madame Seraskier once more, and felt that "Gioconda" was a fraud.

Presently I was conscious of a group just behind me, and heard a pleasant male English voice exclaim—

"And now, duchess, let me present you to my first and last and only

love, Mona Lisa." I turned round, and there stood a soldier-like old gentleman and two ladies (one of whom was the Duchess of Towers), staring at the picture.

As I made way for them I caught her eye, and in it again, as I felt sure, a kindly look of recognition—just for half a second. She evidently recollected having seen me at Lady Cray's, where I had stood all the evening alone in a rather conspicuous corner. I was so exceptionally tall (in those days of not such tall people as now) that it was easy to notice and remember me, especially as I wore my beard, which it was unusual to do then among Englishmen.

She little guessed how *I* remembered *her;* she little knew all she was and had been to me—in life and in a dream!

My emotion was so great that I felt it in my very knees; I could scarcely walk; I was as weak as water. My worship for the beautiful stranger was becoming almost a madness. She was even more lovely than Madame Seraskier. It was cruel to be like that.

It seems that I was fated to fall down and prostrate myself before very tall, slender women, with dark hair and lily skins and light angelic eyes. The fair damsel who sold tripe and pigs' feet in Clerkenwell was also of that type, I remembered; and so was Mrs. Deane. Fortunately for me it is not a common one!

All that day I spent on quays and bridges, leaning over parapets, and looking at the Seine, and nursing my sweet despair, and calling myself the biggest fool in Paris, and recalling over and over again that gray-blue kindly glance—my only light, the Light of the World for ME!

* * * * *

My brief holiday over, I went back to London—to Pentonville—and resumed my old occupations; but the whole tenor of my existence was changed.

The day, the working-day (and I worked harder than ever, to Lintot's great satisfaction), passed as in an unimportant dream of mild content and cheerful acquiescence in everything, work or play.

There was no more quarrelling with my destiny, nor wish to escape from myself for a moment. My whole being, as I went about on business or recreation bent, was suffused with the memory of the Duchess of Towers as with a warm inner glow that kept me at peace with all mankind and myself, and thrilled by the hope, the enchanting hope, of once more meeting her image at night in a dream, in or about my old home at Passy, and perhaps even feeling once more that ineffable bliss of touching her hand. Though why should she be there?

When the blessed hour came round for sleep, the real business of my life began. I practised "dreaming true" as one practises a fine art, and after many failures I became a professed expert – a master.

I lay straight on my back, with my feet crossed, and my hands clasped above my head in a symmetrical position; I would fix my will intently and persistently on a certain point in space and time that was within my memory – for instance, the avenue gate on a certain Christmas afternoon, when I remembered waiting for M. le Major to go for a walk – at the same time never losing touch of my own present identity as Peter Ibbetson, architect, Wharton Street, Pentonville; all of which is not so easy to manage as one might think, although the dream duchess had said, "Ce n'est que le premier pas qui coûte"; and finally one night, instead of dreaming the ordinary dreams I had dreamed all my life (but twice), I had the rapture of *waking up*, the minute I was fairly asleep, by the avenue gate, and of seeing Gogo Pasquier sitting on one of the stone posts and looking up the snowy street for the major. Presently he jumped up to meet his old friend, whose bottle-green-clad figure had just appeared in the distance. I saw and heard their warm and friendly greeting, and walked unperceived by their side through Auteuil to the *mare*, and back by the fortifications, and listened to the thrilling adventures of one Fier-à-bras, which, I confess, I had completely forgotten.

As we passed all three together through the "Porte de la Muette," M. le Major's powers of memory (or invention) began to flag a little—for he suddenly said, "*Cric!*" But Gogo pitilessly answered, "*Crac!*" and the story had to go on, till we reached at dusk the gate of the Pasquiers' house, where these two most affectionately parted, after making an appointment for the morrow; and I went in with Gogo, and sat in the school-room while Thérèse gave him his tea, and heard her tell him all that had happened in Passy that afternoon. Then he read and summed and translated with his mother till it was time to go up to bed, and I sat by his bedside as he was lulled asleep by his mother's harp . . . how I listened with all my ears and heart, till the sweet strain ceased for the night! Then out of the hushed house I stole, thinking unutterable things—through the snow-clad garden, where Médor was baying the moon—through the silent avenue and park—

through the deserted streets of Passy—and on by desolate quays and bridges to dark quarters of Paris; till I fell awake in my tracks and found that another dreary and commonplace day had dawned over London—but no longer dreary and commonplace for me, with such experiences to look back and forward to—such a strange inheritance of wonder and delight!

I had a few more occasional failures, such as, for instance, when the thread between my waking and sleeping life was snapped by a moment's carelessness, or possibly by some movement of my body in bed, in which case the vision would suddenly get blurred, the reality of it destroyed, and an ordinary dream rise in its place. My immediate consciousness of this was enough to wake me on the spot, and I would begin again, *da capo*, till all went as I wished.

Evidently our brain contains something akin both to a photographic plate and a phonographic cylinder, and many other things of the same kind not yet discovered; not a sight or a sound or a smell is lost; not a taste or a feeling or an emotion. Unconscious memory records them all, without our even heeding what goes on around us beyond the things that attract our immediate interest or attention.

Thus night after night I saw reacted before me scenes not only fairly remembered, but scenes utterly forgotten, and yet as unmistakably true as the remembered ones, and all bathed in that ineffable light, the light of other days—the light that never was on sea or land, and yet the light of absolute truth.

How it transcends in value as well as in beauty the garish light of common day, by which poor humanity has hitherto been content to live and die, disdaining through lack of knowledge the shadow for the substance, the spirit for the matter! I verified the truth of these sleeping experiences in every detail: old family letters I had preserved, and which I studied on awaking, confirmed what I had seen and heard in my dream; old stories

explained themselves. It was all by-gone truth, garnered in some remote corner of the brain, and brought out of the dim past as I willed, and made actual once more.

And strange to say, and most inexplicable, I saw it all as an independent spectator, an outsider, not as an actor going again through scenes in which he has played a part before!

Yet many things perplexed and puzzled me.

For instance, Gogo's back, and the back of his head, when I stood behind him, were as visible and apparently as true to life as his face, and I had never seen his back or the back of his head; it was much later in life that I learned the secret of two mirrors. And then, when Gogo went out of the room, sometimes apparently passing through me as he did so and coming out at the other side (with a momentary blurring of the dream), the rest would go on talking just as reasonably, as naturally, as before. Could the trees and walls and furniture have had ears and eyes, those long-vanished trees and walls and furniture that existed now only in my sleeping brain, and have retained the sound and shape and meaning of all that passed when Gogo, my only conceivable remembrancer, was away?

Françoise, the cook, would come into the drawing-room to discuss the dinner with my mother when Gogo was at school; and I would hear the orders given, and later I would assist at the eating of the meal (to which Gogo would invariably do ample justice), and it was just as my mother had ordered. Mystery of mysteries!

What a pleasant life it was they led together, these ghosts of a by-gone time! Such a genial, smooth, easy-going, happy-go-lucky state of things – half bourgeois, half Bohemian, and yet with a well-marked simplicity, refinement, and distinction of bearing and speech that were quite aristocratic.

The servants (only three – Thérèse the house-maid, Françoise the cook, and English Sarah, who had been my nurse and was now my mother's

LE BEAU PASQUIER DRINKS TO HIS KING

maid) were on the kindliest and most familiar terms with us, and talked to us like friends, and interested themselves in our concerns, and we in theirs; I noticed that they always wished us each good-morning and good-night—a pretty French fashion of the Passy bourgeoisie in Louis Philippe's time (he was a bourgeois king).

Our cuisine was bourgeoise also. Peter Ibbetson's mouth watered (after his tenpenny London dinner) to see and smell the steam of "soupe à la bonne femme," "soupe aux choux," "pot au feu," "blanquette de veau," "bœuf à la mode," "cotelettes de porc à la sauce piquante," "vinaigrette de bœuf bouilli"—that endless variety of good things on which French people grow fat so young—and most excellent claret (at one franc a bottle in those happy days): its bouquet seemed to fill the room as soon as the cork was drawn!

Sometimes, such a repast ended, "le beau Pasquier," in the fulness of his heart, would suddenly let off impossible fireworks of vocalization, ascending rockets of chromatic notes which would explode softly very high up and come down in full cadences, trills, roulades, like beautiful colored stars; and Thérèse would exclaim, "Ah q'c'est beau!" as if she had been present at a real pyrotechnic display; and Thérèse was quite right. I have never heard the like from any human throat, and should not have believed it possible. Only Joachim's violin can do such beautiful things so beautifully.

Or else he would tell us of wolves he had shot in Brittany, or wild-boars in Burgundy—for he was a great sportsman—or of his adventures as a *garde du corps* of Charles Dix, or of the wonderful inventions that were so soon to bring us fame and fortune; and he would loyally drink to Henri Cinq; and he was so droll and buoyant and witty that it was as good to hear him speak as to hear him sing.

But there was another and a sad side to all this strange comedy of vanished lives.

They built castles in the air, and made plans, and talked of all the wealth and happiness that would be theirs when my father's ship came home, and of all the good they would do, pathetically unconscious of the near future; which, of course, was all past history to their loving audience of one.

And then my tears would flow with the unbearable ache of love and pity combined; they would fall and dry on the waxed floors of my old home in Passy, and I would find them still wet on my pillow in Pentonville when I woke. . . .

* * * * *

Soon I discovered by practice that I was able for a second or two to be more than a mere spectator—to be an actor once more; to turn myself (Ibbetson) into my old self (Gogo), and thus be touched and caressed by those I had so loved. My mother kissed me and I felt it; just as long as I could hold my breath I could walk hand in hand with Madame Seraskier, or feel Mimsey's small weight on my back and her arms round my neck for four or five yards as I walked, before blurring the dream; and the blur would soon pass away, if it did not wake me, and I was Peter Ibbetson once more, walking and sitting among them, hearing them talk and laugh, watching them at their meals, in their walks; listening to my father's songs, my mother's sweet playing, and always unseen and unheeded by them. Moreover, I soon learned to touch things without sensibly blurring the dream. I would cull a rose, and stick it in my buttonhole, and there it remained—but lo! the very rose I had just culled was still on the rose-bush also! I would pick up a stone and throw it at the wall, where it disappeared without a sound—and the very same stone still lay at my feet, however often I might pick it up and throw it!

No waking joy in the world can give, can equal in intensity, these complex joys I had when asleep; waking joys seem so slight, so vague in com-

parison — so much escapes the senses through lack of concentration and undivided attention — the waking perceptions are so blunt.

It was a life within a life — an intenser life — in which the fresh perceptions of childhood combined with the magic of dream-land, and in which there was but one unsatisfied longing; but its name was Lion.

It was the passionate longing to meet the Duchess of Towers once more in that land of dreams.

* * * * *

Thus for a time I went on, more solitary than ever, but well compensated for all my loneliness by this strange new life that had opened itself to me, and never ceasing to marvel and rejoice — when one morning I received a note from Lady Cray, who wanted some stables built at Cray, their country-seat in Hertfordshire, and begged I would go there for the day and night.

I was bound to accept this invitation, as a mere matter of business, of course; as a friend, Lady Cray seemed to have dropped me long ago, "like a 'ot potato," blissfully unconscious that it was I who had dropped her.

But she received me as a friend — an old friend. All my shyness and snobbery fell from me at the mere touch of her hand.

I had arrived at Cray early in the afternoon, and had immediately set about my work, which took several hours, so that I got to the house only just in time to dress for dinner.

When I came into the drawing-room there were several people there, and Lady Cray presented me to a young lady, the vicar's daughter, whom I was to take in to dinner.

I was very much impressed on being told by her that the company assembled in the drawing-room included no less a person than Sir Edwin Landseer. Many years ago I had copied an engraving of one of his pictures

MARY IS LATE

for Mimsey Seraskier. It was called "The Challenge," or "Coming Events cast their Shadows before Them." I feasted my eyes on the wondrous little man, who seemed extremely chatty and genial, and quite unembarrassed by his fame.

A guest was late, and Lord Cray, who seemed somewhat peevishly impatient for his food, exclaimed—

"Mary wouldn't be Mary if she were punctual!"

Just then Mary came in—and Mary was no less a person than the Duchess of Towers!

My knees trembled under me; but there was no time to give way to any such tender weakness. Lord Cray walked away with her; the procession filed into the dining-room, and somewhere at the end of it my young vicaress and myself.

The duchess sat a long way from me, but I met her glance for a moment, and fancied I saw again in it that glimmer of kindly recognition.

My neighbor, who was charming, asked me if I did not think the Duchess of Towers the most beautiful woman I had ever seen.

I assented with right good-will, and was told that she was as good as she was beautiful, and as clever as she was good (as if I did not know it); that she would give away the very clothes off her back; that there was no trouble she would not take for others; that she did not get on well with her husband, who drank, and was altogether bad and vile; that she had a great sorrow—an only child, an idiot, to whom she was devoted, and who would some day be the Duke of Towers; that she was highly accomplished, a great linguist, a great musician, and about the most popular woman in all English society.

Ah! who loved the Duchess of Towers better than this poor scribe, in whose soul she lived and shone like a bright particular star—like the sun; and who, without his knowing, was being rapidly drawn into the sphere of her attraction, as Lintot called it; one day to be finally absorbed, I trust, forever!

"And who was this wonderful Duchess of Towers before she married?" I asked.

"She was a Miss Seraskier. Her father was a Hungarian, a physician, and a political reformer—a most charming person; that's where she gets her manners. Her mother, whom she lost when she was quite a child, was a very beautiful Irish girl of good family, a first cousin of Lord Cray's—a Miss Desmond, who ran away with the interesting patriot. They lived somewhere near Paris. It was there that Madame Seraskier died of cholera— . . . What is the matter—are you ill?"

I made out that I was faint from the heat, and concealed as well as I could the flood of emotion and bewilderment that overwhelmed me.

I dared not look again at the Duchess of Towers.

"Oh! little Mimsey dear, with your poor thin arms round my neck, and your cold, pale cheek against mine. I felt them there only last night! To have grown into such a splendid vision of female health and strength and beauty as this—with that enchanting, ever-ready laugh and smile! Why, of course, those eyes, so lashless then, so thickly fringed to-day!—how could I have mistaken them? Ah, Mimsey, you never smiled or laughed in those days, or I should have known your eyes again! Is it possible—is it possible?"

Thus I went on to myself till the ladies left, my fair young companion expressing her kind anxiety and polite hope that I would soon be myself again.

I sat silent till it was time to join the ladies (I could not even follow the witty and brilliant anecdotes of the great painter, who held the table); and then I went up to my room. I could not face *her* again so soon after what I had heard.

The good Lord Cray came to make kind inquiries, but I soon satisfied him that my indisposition was nothing. He stayed on, however, and talked; his dinner seemed to have done him a great deal of good, and he wanted to smoke (and somebody to smoke with), which he had not been able to do in the dining-room on account of some reverend old bishop who was present. So he rolled himself a little cigarette, like a Frenchman, and puffed away to his heart's content.

He little guessed how his humble architect wished him away, until he began to talk of the Duchess of Towers – "Mary Towers," as he called her – and to tell me how "Towers" deserved to be kicked, and whipped at the

cart's tail. "Why, she's the best and most beautiful woman in England, and as sharp as a needle! If it hadn't been for her, he'd have been in the bankruptcy court long ago," etc. "There's not a duchess in England that's fit to hold the candle to her, either for looks or brains, or breedin' either. Her mother (the loveliest woman that ever lived, except Mary) was a connection of mine; that's where she gets her manners!" etc.

Thus did this noble earl make music for me—sweet and bitter music.

Mary! It is a heavenly name, especially on English lips, and spelled in the English mode with the adorable *y*! Great men have had a passion for it—Byron, Shelley, Burns. But none, methinks, a greater passion than I, nor with such good cause.

And yet there must be a bad Mary now and then, here or there, and even an ugly one. Indeed, there was once a Bloody Mary who was both! It seems incredible!

Mary, indeed! Why not Hecuba? For what was I to the Duchess of Towers?

When I was alone again I went to bed, and tried to sleep on my back, with my arms up, in the hope of a true dream; but sleep would not come, and I passed a white night, as the French say. I rose early and walked about the park, and tried to interest myself in the stables till it was breakfast-time. Nobody was up, and I breakfasted alone with Lady Cray, who was as kind as she could be. I do not think she could have found me a very witty companion. And then I went back to the stables to think, and fell into a doze.

At about twelve I heard the sound of wooden balls, and found a lawn where some people were playing "croquet." It was quite a new game, and a few years later became the fashion.

I sat down under a large weeping-ash close to the lawn; it was like a tent, with chairs and tables underneath.

Presently Lady Cray came there with the Duchess of Towers. I wanted to fly, but was rooted to the spot.

Lady Cray presented me, and almost immediately a servant came with a message for her, and I was left with the One Woman in the World! My heart was in my mouth, my throat was dry, my pulse was beating in my temples.

She asked me, in the most natural manner, if I played "croquet."

"Yes—no—at least, sometimes—that is, I never heard of it—oh—I forget!" I groaned at my idiocy, and hid my face in my hands. She asked if I were still unwell, and I said no; and then she began to talk quite easily about anything, everything, till I felt more at my ease.

Her voice! I had never heard it well but in a dream, and it was the same—a very rich and modulated voice—low—contralto, with many varied and delightful inflexions; and she used more action in speaking than the generality of Englishwomen, thereby reminding me of Madame Seraskier. I noticed that her hands were long and very narrow, and also her feet, and remembered that Mimsey's were like that—they were considered poor Mimsey's only beauty. I also noticed an almost imperceptible scar on her left temple, and remembered with a thrill that I had noticed it in my dream as we walked up the avenue together. In waking life I had never been near enough to her to notice a small scar, and Mimsey had no scar of the kind in the old days—of that I felt sure, for I had seen much of Mimsey lately.

I grew more accustomed to the situation, and ventured to say that I had once met her at Lady Cray's in London.

"Oh yes; I remember. Giulia Grisi sang the 'Willow Song!' " And then she crinkled up her eyes, and laughed, and blushed, and went on: "I noticed you standing in a corner, under the famous Gainsborough. You reminded me of a dear little French boy I once knew who was very kind to me when I was a little girl in France, and whose father you happen to be like. But I found that you were Mr. Ibbetson, an English architect, and, Lady Cray tells me, a very rising one."

"I *was* a little French boy once. I had to change my name to please a relative, and become English—that is, I was always *really* English, you know."

"Good heavens, what an extraordinary thing! What *was* your name, then?"

"Pasquier—Gogo Pasquier!" I groaned, and the tears came into my eyes, and I looked away. The duchess made no answer, and when I turned and looked at her she was looking at me, very pale, her lips quite white, her hands tightly clasped in her lap, and trembling all over.

I said, "You used to be little Mimsey Seraskier, and I used to carry you pickaback!"

"Oh don't! oh don't!" she said, and began to cry.

I got up and walked about under the ash-tree till she had dried her eyes. The croquet-players were intent upon their game.

I again sat down beside her; she had dried her eyes, and at length she said—

"What a dreadful thing it was about your poor father and mother, and *my* dear mother! Do you remember her? She died a week after you left. I went to Russia with papa—Dr. Seraskier. What a terrible break-up it all was!"

And then we gradually fell to talking quite naturally about old times, and dear dead people. She never took her eyes off mine. After a while I said—

"I went to Passy, and found everything changed and built over. It nearly drove me mad to see. I went to St. Cloud, and saw you driving with the Empress of the French. That night I had such an extraordinary dream! I dreamed I was floundering about the Rue de la Pompe, and had just got to the avenue gate, and you were there."

"Good heavens!" she whispered, and turned white again, and trembled all over, "what do you mean?"

"Yes," I said, "you came to my rescue. I was pursued by gnomes and horrors." . . .

She. "Good heavens! by—by two little jailers, a man and his wife, who danced and were trying to hem you in?"

It was now my turn to ejaculate "Good heavens!" We both shook and trembled together.

I said: "You gave me your hand, and all came straight at once. My old school rose in place of the jail."

She. "With a yellow omnibus? And boys going off to their *première communion?*"

I. "Yes; and there was a crowd—le Père et la Mère François, and Madame Liard, the grocer's wife, and—and Mimsey Seraskier, with her cropped head. And an organ was playing a tune I knew quite well, but cannot now recall." . . .

She. "Wasn't it 'Maman, les p'tits bateaux?' "

I. "Oh, of *course!*

" '*Maman, les p'tits bateaux*
Qui vont sur l'eau,
Ont-ils des jambes?' "

She. "That's it!

" '*Eh oui, petit bêta!*
S'ils n'avaient pas
Ils n'march'raient pas!' "

She sank back in her chair, pale and prostrate. After a while—

She. "And then I gave you good advice about how to dream true, and we got to my old house, and I tried to make you read the letters on the portico, and you read them wrong, and I laughed."

I. "Yes; I read 'Tête Noire.' Wasn't it idiotic?"

She. "And then I touched you again and you read 'Parvis Notre Dame.' "

I. "Yes! and you touched me *again*, and I read 'Parva sed Apta'—small but fit."

She. "Is *that* what it means? Why, when you were a boy, you told me *sed apta* was all one word, and was the Latin for 'Pavilion.' I believed it ever since, and thought 'Parva sed Apta' meant *petit pavillon!*"

I. "I blush for my bad Latin! After this you gave me good advice again, about not touching anything or picking flowers. I never have. And then you went away into the park—the light went out of my life, sleeping or waking. I have never been able to dream of you since. I don't suppose I shall ever meet you again after to-day!"

After this we were silent for a long time, though I hummed and hawed now and then, and tried to speak. I was sick with the conflict of my feelings. At length she said—

"Dear Mr. Ibbetson, this is all so extraordinary that I must go away and think it all over. I cannot tell you what it has been to me to meet you once more. And that double dream, common to us both! Oh, I am dazed beyond expression, and feel as if I were dreaming now—except that this all seems so unreal and impossible—so untrue! We had better part now. I don't know if I shall ever meet you again. You will be often in my thoughts, but never in my dreams again—that, at least, I can command—nor I in yours; it must not be. My poor father taught me how to dream before he died, that I might find innocent consolation in dreams for my waking troubles, which are many and great, as his were. If I can see that any good may come of it, I will write—but no—you must not expect a letter. I will now say good-bye and leave you. You go to-day, do you not? That is best. I think this had better be a final adieu. I cannot tell you of what interest you are to me and always have been. I thought you had died long ago. We shall often think of each other—that is inevitable—*but never, never dream. That will not do.*

"Dear Mr. Ibbetson, I wish you all the good that one human being can wish another. And now good-bye, and may God in heaven bless you!"

She rose, trembling and white, and her eyes wet with tears, and wrung both my hands, and left me as she had left me in the dream.

The light went out of my life, and I was once more alone—more wretchedly and miserably alone than if I had never met her.

I went back to Pentonville, and outwardly took up the thread of my monotonous existence, and ate, drank, and worked, and went about as usual, but as one in an ordinary dream. For now dreams—true dreams—had become the only reality for me.

So great, so inconceivable and unexampled a wonder had been wrought in a dream that all the conditions of life had been altered and reversed.

I and another human being had met—actually and really met—in a double dream, a dream common to us both, and clasped each other's hands! And each had spoken words to the other which neither ever would or ever could forget.

And this other human being and I had been enshrined in each other's memory for years—since childhood—and were now linked together by a

tie so marvellous, an experience so unprecedented, that neither could ever well be out of the other's thoughts as long as life and sense and memory lasted.

Her very self, as we talked to each other under the ash-tree at Cray, was less vividly present to me than that other and still dearer self of hers with whom I had walked up the avenue in that balmy dream atmosphere, where we had lived and moved and had our being together for a few short moments, yet each believing the other at the time to be a mere figment of his own (and her) sleeping imagination; such stuff as dreams are made of!

And lo! it was all true—as true as the common experience of every-day life—more (ten times more), because through our keener and more exalted sense perceptions, and less divided attention, we were more conscious of each other's real inner being—linked closer together for a space—than two mortals had probably ever been since the world began.

That clasp of the hands in the dream—how infinitely more it had conveyed of one to the other than even that sad farewell clasp at Cray!

In my poor outer life I waited in vain for a letter; in vain I haunted the parks and streets—the street where she lived—in the hope of seeing her once more. The house was shut; she was away—in America, as I afterwards learned—with her husband and child.

At night, in the familiar scenes I had learned so well to conjure up, I explored every nook and corner with the same yearning desire to find a trace of her. I was hardly ever away from "Parva sed Apta." There were Madame Seraskier and Mimsey and the major, and my mother and Gogo, at all times, in and out, and of course as unconscious of my solid presence as though I had never existed. And as I looked at Mimsey and her mother I wondered at my obtuseness in not recognizing at the very first glance who the Duchess of Towers had been, and whose daughter. The height, the voice, the eyes, certain tricks of gait and gesture—how could I have failed to know her again after such recent dream opportunities?

And Seraskier, towering among them all, as his daughter now towered among women. I saw that he lived again in his daughter; *his* was the smile that closed up the eyes, as *hers* did; had Mimsey ever smiled in those days, I should have known her again by this very characteristic trait.

Of this daughter of his (the Mimsey of the past years, not the duchess of to-day) I never now could have enough, and made her go through again and again all the scenes with Gogo, so dear to my remembrance, and to hers. I was, in fact, the Prince Charmant, of whose unseen attendance she had been conscious in some inconceivable way. What a strange foresight! But where was the fée Tarapatapoum? Never there during this year of unutterable longing; she had said it; never, never again should I be in her dream, or she in mine, however constantly we might dwell in each other's thoughts.

So sped a twelvemonth after that last meeting in the flesh at Cray.

* * * * *

And now, with an unwilling heart and most reluctant pen, I must come to the great calamity of my life, which I will endeavor to tell in as few words as possible.

The reader, if he has been good enough to read without skipping, will remember the handsome Mrs. Deane, to whom I fancied I lost my heart, in Hopshire, a few years back.

I had not seen her since—had, indeed, almost forgotten her—but had heard vaguely that she had left Hopshire, and come to London, and married a wealthy man much older than herself.

Well, one day I was in Hyde Park, gazing at the people in the drive, when a spick-and-span and very brand-new open carriage went by, and in it sat Mrs. Deane (that was), all alone in her glory, and looking very sulky indeed. She recognized me and bowed, and I bowed back again, with just a moment's little flutter of the heart—an involuntary tribute to auld langsyne – and went on my way, wondering that I could ever have admired her so.

Presently, to my surprise, I was touched on the elbow. It was Mrs. Deane again – I will call her Mrs. Deane still. She had got out and followed me on foot. It was her wish that I should drive round the park with her and talk of old times. I obeyed, and for the first and last time found myself forming part of that proud and gay procession I had so often watched with curious eyes.

She seemed anxious to know whether I had ever made it up with Colonel Ibbetson, and pleased to hear that I had not, and that I probably never should, and that my feeling against him was strong and bitter and likely to last.

She appeared to hate him very much.

She inquired kindly after myself and my prospects in life, but did not seem deeply interested in my answers – until later, when I talked of my French life, and my dear father and mother, when she listened with eager sympathy, and I was much touched. She asked if I had portraits of them; I had – most excellent miniatures; and when we parted I had promised to call upon her next afternoon, and bring these miniatures with me.

She seemed a languid woman, much ennuyée, and evidently without a large circle of acquaintance. She told me I was the only person in the whole park whom she had bowed to that day. Her husband was in Hamburg, and she was going to meet him in Paris in a day or two.

I had not so many friends but what I felt rather glad than otherwise to have met her, and willingly called, as I had promised, with the portraits.

She lived in a large, new house, magnificently upholstered, near the Marble Arch. She was quite alone when I called, and asked me immediately if I had brought the miniatures; and looked at them quite eagerly, and then at me, and exclaimed –

"Good heavens, you are your father's very image!"

Indeed, I had always been considered so.

Both his eyebrows and mine, especially, met in a singular and characteristic fashion at the bridge of the nose, and she seemed much struck by this. He was represented in the uniform of Charles X's *gardes du corps,* in which he had served for two years, and had acquired the nickname of "le beau Pasquier." Mrs. Deane seemed never to tire of gazing at it, and remarked that my father "must have been the very ideal of a young girl's dream" (an indirect compliment which made me blush after what she had just said of the likeness between us. I almost began to wonder whether she was going to try and make a fool of me again, as she had so successfully done a few years ago).

Then she became interested again in my early life and recollections, and wanted to know whether my parents were fond of each other. They were a most devoted and lover-like pair, and had loved each other at first sight and until death, and I told her so; and so on until I became quite excited, and imagined she must know of some good fortune to which I was entitled, and had been kept out of by the machinations of a wicked uncle.

For I had long discovered in my dreams that he had been my father's bitterest enemy and the main cause of his financial ruin, by selfish, heartless, and dishonest deeds too complicated to explain here—a regular Shylock.

I had found this out by listening (in my dreams) to long conversations between my father and mother in the old drawing-room at Passy, while Gogo was absorbed in his book; and every word that had passed through Gogo's inattentive ears into his otherwise preoccupied little brain had been recorded there as in a phonograph, and was now repeated over and over again for Peter Ibbetson, as he sat unnoticed among them.

I asked her, jokingly, if she had discovered that I was the rightful heir to Ibbetson Hall by any chance.

She replied that nothing would give her greater pleasure, but there was no such good fortune in store for either her or me; that she had discovered long ago that Colonel Ibbetson was the greatest blackguard unhung, and nothing new she might discover could make him worse.

I then remembered how he would often speak of her, even to me, and hint and insinuate things which were no doubt untrue, and which I disbelieved. Not that the question of their truth or untruth made him any the less despicable and vile for telling.

She asked me if he had ever spoken of her to me, and after much persuasion and cunning cross-examination I told her as much of the truth as I dared, and she became a tigress. She assured me that he had managed so to injure and compromise her in Hopshire that she and her mother had to leave, and she swore to me most solemnly (and I thoroughly believe she spoke the truth) that there had never been any relation between them that she could not have owned to before the whole world.

She had wished to marry him, it is true, for his wealth and position; for both she and her mother were very poor, and often hard put to it to make both ends meet and keep up a decent appearance before the world; and he had singled her out and paid her marked attention from the first, and given her every reason to believe that his attentions were serious and honorable.

At this juncture her mother came in, Mrs. Glyn, and we renewed our old acquaintance. She had quite forgiven me my school-boy admiration for her daughter; all her power of hating, like her daughter's, had concentrated itself on Ibbetson; and as I listened to the long story of their wrongs and his infamy, I grew to hate him worse than ever, and was ready to be their champion on the spot, and to take up their quarrel there and then.

But this would not do, it appeared, for their name must nevermore be in any way mixed up with his.

Then suddenly Mrs. Glyn asked me if I knew when he went to India.

I could satisfy her, for I knew that it was just after my parents' marriage, nearly a year before my birth; upon which she gave the exact date of his departure with his regiment, and the name of the transport, and everything; and also, to my surprise, the date of my parents' marriage at Marylebone Church, and of my baptism there fifteen months later—just fourteen weeks after my birth in Passy. I was growing quite bewildered with all this knowledge of my affairs, and wondered more and more.

We sat silent for a while, the two women looking at each other and at me and at the miniatures. It was getting gruesome. What could it all mean?

Presently Mrs. Glyn, at a nod from her daughter, addressed me thus:

"Mr. Ibbetson, your uncle, as you call him, though he is not your uncle, is a very terrible villain, and has done you and your parents a very foul wrong. Before I tell you what it is (and I think you ought to know) you must give me your word of honor that you will do or say nothing that will get our name publicly mixed up in any way with Colonel Ibbetson's. The injury to my daughter, now she is happily married to an excellent man, would be irreparable."

With a beating heart I solemnly gave the required assurance.

"Then, Mr. Ibbetson, it is right that you should know that Colonel Ibbetson, when he was paying his infamous addresses to my daughter, gave her unmistakably to understand that you were his natural son, by his cousin, Miss Catherine Biddulph, afterwards Madame Pasquier de la Marière!"

"Oh, oh, oh!" I cried, "surely you must be mistaken—he knew it was impossible—he had been refused by my mother three times—he went to India nearly a year before I was born—he——"

Then Mrs. Deane said, producing an old letter from her pocket:

"Do you know his handwriting and his crest? Do you happen to recollect once bringing me a note from him at Ibbetson Hall? Here it is," and she

handed it to me. It was unmistakably his, and I remembered it at once, and this is what it said:

"For Heaven's sake, dear friend, don't breathe a word to any living soul of what you were clever enough to guess last night! There is a likeness, of course.

"Poor Antinoüs! He is quite ignorant of the true relationship, which has caused me many a pang of shame and remorse. . . .

" 'Que voulez-vous? Elle était ravissante!' . . . We were cousins, much thrown together; 'both were so young, and one so beautiful!' . . . I was but a penniless cornet in those days—hardly more than a boy. Happily an unsuspecting Frenchman of good family was there who had loved her long, and she married him. 'Il était temps!' . . .

"Can you forgive me this 'entraînement de jeunesse?' I have repented in sackcloth and ashes, and made what reparation I could by adopting and giving my name to one who is a perpetual reminder to me of a moment's infatuation. He little knows, poor boy, and never will, I hope. 'Il n'a plus que moi au monde!'

"Burn this as soon as you have read it, and never let the subject be mentioned between us again.

"R. ('Qui sait aimer')."

Here was a thunderbolt out of the blue!

I sat stunned and saw scarlet, and felt as if I should see scarlet forever.

After a long silence, during which I could feel my pulse beat to bursting-point in my temples, Mrs. Glyn said:

"Now, Mr. Ibbetson, I hope you will do nothing rash—nothing that can bring my daughter's name into any quarrel between yourself and your uncle. For the sake of your mother's good name, you will be prudent, I

know. If he could speak like this of his cousin, with whom he had been in love when he was young, what lies would he not tell of my poor daughter? He *has*—terrible lies! Oh, what we have suffered! When he wrote that letter I believe he really meant to marry her. He had the greatest trust in her, or he would never have committed himself so foolishly."

"Does he know of this letter's existing?" I asked.

"No. When he and my daughter quarrelled she sent him back his letters—all but this one, which she told him she had burned immediately after reading it, as he had told her to do."

"May I keep it?"

"Yes. I know you may be trusted, and my daughter's name has been removed from the outside, as you see. No one but ourselves has ever seen it, nor have we mentioned to a soul what it contains, as we never believed it for a moment. Two or three years ago we had the curiosity to find out when and where your parents had married, and when you were born, and when *he* went to India. It was no surprise to us at all. We then tried to find *you*, but soon gave it up, and thought it better to leave matters alone. Then we heard he was in mischief again – just the same sort of mischief; and then my daughter saw you in the park, and we concluded you ought to know."

Such was the gist of that memorable conversation, which I have condensed as much as I could.

When I left these two ladies I walked twice rapidly round the park. I saw scarlet often during that walk. Perhaps I looked scarlet. I remember people staring at me.

Then I went straight to Lintot's, with the impulse to tell him my trouble and ask his advice.

He was away from home, and I waited in his smoking-room for a while, reading the letter over and over again.

Then I decided not to tell him, and left the house, taking with me as I did so (but without any definite purpose) a heavy loaded stick, a most formidable weapon, even in the hands of a boy, and which I myself had given to Lintot on his last birthday. 'Ανάγκη!

Then I went to my usual eating-house near the circus and dined. To the surprise of the waiting-maid, I drank a quart of bitter ale and two glasses of sherry. It was my custom to drink water. She plied me with questions as to whether I was ill or in trouble. I answered her no, and at last begged she would leave me alone.

Ibbetson lived in St. James's Street. I went there. He was out. It was nine o'clock, and his servant seemed uncertain when he would return. I came back at ten. He was not yet home, and the servant, after thinking a while, and looking up and down the street, and finding my appearance decent and by no means dangerous, asked me to go up-stairs and wait, as I told him it was a matter of great importance.

So I went and sat in my uncle's drawing-room and waited.

The servant came with me and lit the candles, and remarked on the weather, and handed me the *Saturday Review* and *Punch.* I must have looked quite natural—as I tried to look—and he left me.

I saw a Malay creese on the mantel-piece and hid it behind a picture-frame. I locked a door leading to another drawing-room where there was a grand piano, and above it a trophy of swords, daggers, battle-axes, etc., and put the key in my pocket.

The key of the room where I waited was inside the door.

All this time I had a vague idea of possible violence on his part, but no idea of killing him. I felt far too strong for that. Indeed, I had a feeling of quiet, irresistible strength—the result of suppressed excitement.

I sat down and meditated all I would say. I had settled it over and over again, and read and reread the fatal letter.

The servant came up with glasses and soda-water. I trembled lest he should observe that the door to the other room was locked, but he did not. He opened the window and looked up and down the street. Presently he said, "Here's the colonel at last, sir," and went down to open the door.

I heard him come in and speak to his servant. Then he came straight up, humming "*la donna e mobile,*" and walked in with just the jaunty, airy manner I remembered. He was in evening dress, and very little changed. He seemed much surprised to see me, and turned very white.

"Well, my Apollo of the T square, *pourquoi cet honneur?* Have you come, like a dutiful nephew, to humble yourself and beg for forgiveness?"

I forgot all I meant to say (indeed, nothing happened as I had meant), but rose and said, "I have come to have a talk with you," as quietly as I could, though with a thick voice.

He seemed uneasy, and went towards the door.

I got there before him, and closed it, and locked it, and put the key in my pocket.

He darted to the other door and found it locked.

Then he went to the mantel-piece and looked for the creese, and not finding it, he turned round with his back to the fireplace and his arms akimbo, and tried to look very contemptuous and determined. His chin was quite white under his dyed mustache — like wax — and his eyes blinked nervously.

I walked up to him and said: "You told Mrs. Deane that I was your natural son."

"It's a lie! Who told you so?"

"She did — this afternoon."

"It's a lie — a spiteful invention of a cast-off mistress!"

"She never was your mistress!"

"You fool! I suppose she told you that too. Leave the room, you pitiful green jackass, or I'll have you turned out," and he rang the bell.

"Do you know your own handwriting?" I said, and handed him the letter.

He read a line or two and gasped out that it was a forgery, and rang the bell again, and looked again behind the clock for his creese. Then he lit the letter at a candle and threw it in the fireplace, where it blazed out.

I made no attempt to prevent him.

The servant tried to open the door, and Ibbetson went to the window and called out for the police. I rushed to the picture where I had hidden the creese, and threw it on the table. Then I swung him away from the window by his coat-tails, and told him to defend himself, pointing to the creese.

He seized it, and stood on the defensive; the servant had apparently run down-stairs for assistance.

"Now, then," I said, "down on your knees, you infamous cur, and confess; it's your only chance."

"Confess what, you fool?"

"That you're a coward and a liar; that you wrote that letter; that Mrs. Deane was no more your mistress than my mother was!"

There was a sound of people running up-stairs. He listened a moment and hissed out:

"They *both* were, you idiot! How can I tell for certain whether you are my son or not? It all comes to the same. Of course I wrote the letter. Come on, you cowardly assassin, you bastard parricide!" . . . and he ad-

vanced on me with his creese low down in his right hand, the point upward, and made a thrust, shrieking out, "Break open the door! quick!" They did; but too late!

I saw crimson!

He missed me, and I brought down my stick on his left arm, which he held over his head, and then on his head, and he fell, crying:

"Oh my God! O Christ!"

I struck him again on his head as he was falling, and once again when he was on the ground. It seemed to crash right in.

That is why and how I killed Uncle Ibbetson.

PART FIVE

PART FIVE

"Grouille, grève, grève, grouille,
File, file, ma quenouille!
File sa corde au bourreau
Qui siffle dans le préau. . . ."

So sang the old hag in *Notre-Dame de Paris!*

So sang to me night and day, for many nights and days, the thin small voice that always went piping inside me, now to one tune, now to another, but always the same words — that terrible refrain that used to haunt me so when I was a school-boy at Bluefriars!

* * *

Oh, to be a school-boy again in a long gray coat and ridiculous pink stockings — innocent and free — with Esmeralda for my only love, and Athos and Porthos and D'Artagnan for my bosom friends, and no worse tribulation than to be told on a Saturday afternoon that the third volume was in hand — *volume trois en lecture!*

* * *

Sometimes, I remember, I could hardly sleep on a Sunday night, for pity of the poor wretch who was to be hanged close by on the Monday morning, and it has come to that with *me!*

* * *

Oh, Mary, Mary, Duchess of Towers, sweet friend of my childhood, and love of my life, what must you think of me now?

* * *

How blessed are the faithful! How good it must be to trust in God and heaven, and the forgiveness of sin, and be as a little child in all but innocence! A whole career of crime wiped out in a moment by just one cheap little mental act of faith at the eleventh hour, in the extreme terror of well-merited dissolution; and all the evil one has worked through life (that goes on breeding evil for ages to come) taken off one's shoulders like a filthy garment, and just cast aside, anywhere, anyhow, for the infecting of others — who do not count.

* * *

What matter if it be a fool's paradise? Paradise is paradise, for whoever owns it!

* * *

They say a Sicilian drum-major, during the French occupation of Palermo, was sentenced to be shot. He was a well-known coward, and it was feared he would disgrace his country at the last moment in the presence of the French soldiers, who had a way of being shot with a good grace and a light heart: they had grown accustomed to it.

For the honor of Sicily his confessor told him, in the strictest confidence, that his sentence was a mock one, and that he would be fired at with blank cartridges.

It was a pious fraud. All but two of the twelve cartridges had bullets, and he fell, riddled through and through. No Frenchman ever died with a lighter heart, a better grace. He was superb, and the national honor was saved.

Thrice happy Sicilian drum-major, if the story be true! That trust in blank cartridges was his paradise.

* * *

Oh, it is uphill work to be a stoic when the moment comes and the tug! But when the tug lasts for more than a moment—days and nights, days and nights! Oh, happy Sicilian drum-major!

* * *

Pray? Yes, I will pray night and morning, and all day long, to whatever there is left of inherited strength and courage in that luckless, misbegotten waif, Peter Ibbetson; that it may bear him up a little while yet; that he may not disgrace himself in the dock or on the gallows.

* * *

Repent? Yes, of many things. But of the thing for which I am here? Never!

* * *

It is a ghastly thing to be judge and jury and executioner all in one, and for a private and personal wrong—to condemn and strike and kill.

Pity comes after—when it is too late, fortunately—the wretched weakness of pity! Pooh! no Calcraft will ever pity *me*, and I do not want him to.

* * *

He had his long, snaky knife against my stick; he, too, was a big strong man, well skilled in self-defence! Down he went, and I struck him again and again. "O my God! O Christ!" he shrieked. . . .

"It will ring in my heart and my ears till I die—till I die!"

* * *

There was no time to lose—no time to think for the best. It is all for the best as it is. What might he not have said if he had lived!

* * *

Thank Heaven, pity is not remorse or shame; and what crime could well be worse than his? To rob one's dearly beloved dead of their fair fame!

* * *

He might have been mad, perhaps, and have grown in time to believe the lies he told himself. Such things have been. But such a madman should no more be suffered to live than a mad dog. The only way to kill the lie was to kill the liar—that is, if one *can* ever kill a lie!

* * *

Poor worm! after all, he could not help it, I suppose! he was *built* like that! and *I* was built to kill him for it, and be hanged. 'Ανάγκη!

What an exit for "Gogo—gentil petit Gogo!"

* * *

Just opposite that wall, on the other side, was once a small tripe and trotter shop, kept by a most lovely daughter of the people, so fair and good in my eyes that I would have asked her to be my wife. What would she think of me now? That I should have dared to aspire! What a King Cophetua!

* * *

What does everybody think? I can never breathe the real cause to a soul. Only two women know the truth, and they will take good care not to tell. Thank Heaven for that!

* * *

What matters what anybody thinks? "It will be all the same a hundred years hence." That is the most sensible proverb ever invented.

* * *

But meanwhile!

* * *

The judge puts on the black cap, and it is all for you! Every eye is fixed on you, so big and young and strong and full of life! Ugh!

* * *

They pinion you, and you have to walk and be a man, and the chaplain exhorts and prays and tries to comfort. Then a sea of faces; people opposite, who have been eating and drinking and making merry, waiting for *you!* A cap is pulled over your eyes—oh, horror! horror! horror!

* * *

"Heureux tambour-major de Sicile!"

* * *

"Il faut laver son linge sale en famille, et c'est ce que j'ai fait. Mais ça va me coûter cher!"

* * *

Would I do it all over again? Oh, let me hope, yes!

* * *

Ah, he died too quick; I dealt him those four blows in less than as many seconds. It was five minutes, perhaps—or, at the most, ten—from the moment he came into the room to that when I finished him and was caught red-handed. And I—what a long agony!

* * *

Oh, that I might once more dream a "true dream," and see my dear people once more! But it seems that I have lost the power of dreaming true since that fatal night. I try and try, but it will not come. My dreams are dreadful; and, oh, the *waking!*

* * *

After all, my life hitherto, but for a few happy years of childhood, has not been worth living; it is most unlikely that it ever would have been, had I lived to a hundred! Oh, Mary! Mary!

* * *

And penal servitude! Better any death than that. It is good that my secret must die with me—that there will be no extenuating circumstances, no recommendation to mercy, no commutation of the swift penalty of death.

"File, file . . .
File sa corde au bourreau!"

*　　*　　*　　*　　*

By such monotonous thoughts, and others as dreary and hopeless, recurring again and again in the same dull round, I beguiled the terrible time that intervened between Ibbetson's death and my trial at the Old Bailey.

It all seems very trivial and unimportant now—not worth recording—even hard to remember.

But at the time my misery was so great, my terror of the gallows so poignant, that each day I thought I must die of sheer grief before another twenty-four hours could possibly pass over me.

The intolerable strain would grow more and more severe till a climax of tension was reached, and a hysterical burst of tears would relieve me for a while, and I would feel reconciled to my fate, and able to face death like a man. . . . Then the anguish would gradually steal over me again, and the uncontrollable weakness of the flesh. . . .

And each of these two opposite moods, while it lasted, made the other seem impossible, and as if it never could come back again; yet back it came with the regularity of a tide—the most harrowing seesaw that ever was.

I had always been unstable like that; but whereas I had hitherto oscillated between high elation and despondency, it was now from a dumb, resigned despair to the wildest agony and terror.

I sought in vain for the only comfort it was in me to seek; but when, overdone with suffering, I fell asleep at last, I could no longer dream true; I could dream only as other wretches dream.

I always dreamed those two little dancing deformed jailers, man and wife, had got me at last; and that I shrieked aloud for my beloved duchess to succor me, as they ran me in, each butting at me sideways, and showing their toothless gums in a black smile, and poisoning me with their hot sour breath! The gate was there, and the avenue, all distorted and quite unlike; and, opposite, a jail; but no powerful Duchess of Towers to wave the horror away.

* * * * *

It will be remembered by some, perhaps, how short was my trial.

The plea of "not guilty" was entered for me. The defence set up was insanity, based on the absence of any adequate motive. This defence was soon disposed of by the prosecution; witnesses to my sanity were not wanting, and motives enough were found in my past relations with Colonel Ibbetson to "make me—a violent, morose, and vindictive-natured man—imbrue my hands in the gore of my relative and benefactor—a man old enough to be my father—who, indeed, might have been my father, for the love he had bestowed upon me, with his honored name, when I was left a penniless, foreign orphan on his hands."

Here I laughed loud and long, and made a most painful impression, as is duly recorded in the reports of the trial.

The jury found me guilty quite early in the afternoon of the second day, without leaving the box; and I, "preserving to the last the callous and unmoved demeanor I had borne all through the trial," was duly sentenced to death without any hope of mercy, but with an expression of regret on the part of the judge—a famous hanging judge—that a man of my education and promise should be brought by his own evil nature and uncontrollable passions to so deplorable an end.

Now whether the worst of certainties is better than suspense—whether my nerves of pain had been so exercised during the period preceding my trial that I had really become callous, as they say a man's back does after a certain number of strokes from the "cat"—certain it was that I knew the worst, and acquiesced in it with a surprised sense of actual relief, and found it in me to feel it not unbearable.

Such, at least, was my mood that night. I made the most of it. It was almost happiness by comparison with what I had gone through. I remember eating with a heartiness that surprised me. I could have gone straight from my dinner to the gallows, and died with a light heart and a good grace—like a Sicilian drum-major.

I resolved to write the whole true story to the Duchess of Towers, with an avowal of my long and hopeless adoration for her, and the expression of a hope that she would try to think of me only as her old playfellow, and as she had known me before this terrible disaster. And thinking of the letter I would write till very late, I fell asleep in my cell, with two warders to watch over me; and then——Another phase of my inner life began.

* * * * *

Without effort, without let or hindrance of any kind, I was at the avenue gate.

The pink and white may, the lilacs and laburnums were in full bloom, the sun made golden paths everywhere. The warm air was full of fragrance, and alive with all the buzz and chirp of early summer.

I was half crying with joy to reach the land of my true dreams again, to feel at home once more—*chez moi! chez moi!*

La Mère François sat peeling potatoes at the door of her *loge;* she was singing a little song about *cinq sous, cinq sous, pour monter notre ménage.* I had forgotten it, but it all came back now.

The facetious postman, Yverdon, went in at the gate of my old garden; the bell rang as he pushed it, and I followed him.

Under the apple-tree, which was putting forth shoots of blossom in profusion, sat my mother and father and Monsieur le Major. My mother took the letter from the postman's hand as he said, "Pour vous? Oh yes, Madame Pasquier, God sev ze Kveen!" and paid the postage. It was from Colonel Ibbetson, then in Ireland, and not yet a colonel.

Médor lay snoring on the grass, and Gogo and Mimsey were looking at the pictures in the *musée des familles*.

In a garden chair lolled Dr. Seraskier, apparently asleep, with his long porcelain pipe across his knees.

Madame Seraskier, in a yellow nankeen gown with gigot sleeves, was cutting curl-papers out of the *Constitutionnel*.

I gazed on them all with unutterable tenderness. I was gazing on them perhaps for the last time.

I called out to them by name.

"Oh, speak to me, beloved shades! Oh, my father! oh, mother, I want

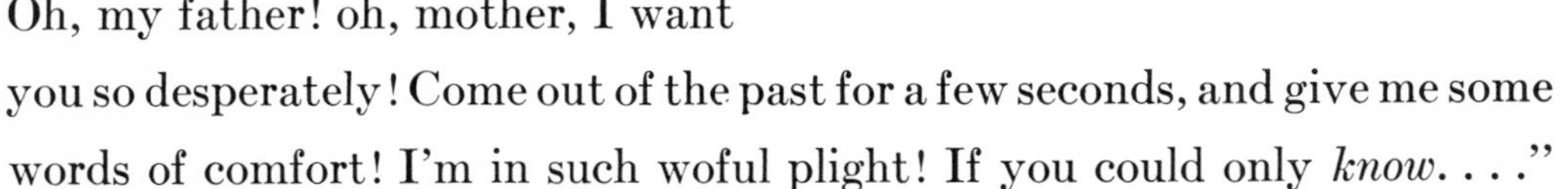

you so desperately! Come out of the past for a few seconds, and give me some words of comfort! I'm in such woful plight! If you could only *know*. . . ."

But they could neither hear nor see me.

Then suddenly another figure stepped forth from behind the apple-tree—no old-fashioned, unsubstantial shadow of by-gone days that one can only

see and hear, and that cannot hear and see one back again; but one in all the splendid fulness of life, a pillar of help and strength—Mary, Duchess of Towers!

I fell on my knees as she came to me with both hands extended.

"Oh, Mr. Ibbetson, I have been seeking and waiting for you here night after night! I have been frantic! If you hadn't come at last, I must have thrown everything to the winds, and gone to see you in Newgate, waking and before the world, to have a talk with you—an *abboccamento.* I suppose you couldn't sleep, or were unable to dream."

I could not answer at first. I could only cover her hands with kisses, as I felt her warm life-current mixing with mine—a rapture!

And then I said—

"I swear to you by all I hold most sacred—by *my* mother's memory and *yours*—by yourself—that I never meant to take Ibbetson's life, or even strike him; the miserable blow was dealt. . . ."

"As if you need tell me that! As if I didn't know you of old, my poor friend, kindest and gentlest of men! Why, I am holding your hands, and see into the very depths of your heart!"

(I put down all she said as she said it. Of course I am not, and never have been, what her old affectionate regard made me seem in her eyes, any more than I am the bloodthirsty monster I passed for. Woman-like, she was the slave of her predilections.)

"And now, Mr. Ibbetson," she went on, "let me first of all tell you, for a certainty, that the sentence will be commuted. I saw the Home Secretary three or four hours ago. The real cause of your deplorable quarrel with your uncle is an open secret. His character is well known. A Mrs. Gregory (whom you knew in Hopshire as Mrs. Deane) has been with the Home Secretary this afternoon. Your chivalrous reticence at the trial. . . ."

"Oh," I interrupted, "I don't care to live any longer! Now that I have

met you once more, and that you have forgiven me and think well of me in spite of everything, I am ready to die. There has never been anybody but you in the world for *me* — never a ghost of a woman, never even a friend since my mother died and yours. Between that time and the night I first saw you at Lady Cray's concert, I can scarcely be said to have lived at all. I fed on scraps of remembrance. You see I have no talent for making new friends, but oh, such a genius for fidelity to old ones! I was waiting for Mimsey to come back again, I suppose, the one survivor to me of that sweet time, and when she came at last I was too stupid to recognize her. She suddenly blazed and dazzled into my poor life like a meteor, and filled it with a maddening love and pain. I don't know which of the two has been the sweetest; both have been my life. You cannot realize what it has been. Trust me, I have lived my fill. I am ready and willing to die. It is the only perfect consummation I can think of. Nothing can ever equal this moment — nothing on earth or in heaven. And if I were free to-morrow, life would not be worth having without *you*. I would not take it as a gift."

She sat down by me on the grass with her hands clasped across her knees, close to the unconscious shadows of our kith and kin, within hearing of their happy talk and laughter.

Suddenly we both heard Mimsey say to Gogo —

"O, ils sont joliment bien ensemble, le Prince Charmant et la fée Tarapatapoum!"

We looked at each other and actually laughed aloud. The Duchess said —

"Was there ever, since the world began, such a *mise en scène*, and for such a meeting, Mr. Ibbetson? Think of it! Conceive it! *I* arranged it all. I chose a day when they were all together. As they would say in America, *I* am the boss of this particular dream."

And she laughed again, through her tears, that enchanting ripple of a laugh that closed her eyes and made her so irresistible.

BELOVED SHADES

"Was there ever," said I—"ever since the world began, such ecstasy as I feel now? After this what can there be for me but death—well earned and well paid for? Welcome and lovely death!"

"You have not yet thought, Mr. Ibbetson—you have not realized what life may have in store for you if—if all you have said about your affection for me is true. Oh, it is too terrible for me to think of, I know, that you, scarcely more than a boy, should have to spend the rest of your life in miserable confinement and unprofitable monotonous toil. But there is *another* side to that picture.

"Now listen to your old friend's story—poor little Mimsey's confession. I will make it as short as I can.

"Do you remember when you first saw me, a sickly, plain, sad little girl, at the avenue gate, twenty years ago?

"Le Père François was killing a fowl—cutting its throat with a clasp-knife—and the poor thing struggled frantically in his grasp as its blood flowed into the gutter. A group of boys were looking on in great glee, and all the while Père François was gossiping with M. le Curé, who didn't seem to mind in the least. I was fainting with pity and horror. Suddenly you came out of the school opposite with Alfred and Charlie Plunket, and saw it all, and in a fit of noble rage you called Père François a 'sacred pig of assassin'—which, as you know, is very rude in French—and struck him as near his face as you could reach.

"Have you forgotten that? Ah, *I* haven't! It was not an effectual deed, perhaps, and certainly came too late to save the fowl. Besides, Père François struck you back again, and left some of the fowl's blood on your cheek. It was a baptism! You became on the spot my hero—my angel of light. Look at Gogo over there. Is he beautiful enough? That was *you*, Mr. Ibbetson.

"M. le Curé said something about 'ces *Anglais*' who go mad if a man

whips his horse, and yet pay people to box each other to death. Don't you really remember? Oh, the recollection to *me!*

"And that little language we invented and used to talk so fluently! Don't you *rappel* it to yourself? 'Ne le *récollectes* tu pas?' as we would have said in those days, for it used to be *thee* and *thou* with us then.

"Well, at all events, you must remember how for five happy years we were so often together; how you drew for me, read to me, played with me; took my part in everything, right or wrong; carried me pickaback when I was tired. Your drawings—I have them all. And oh! you were so funny sometimes! How you used to make mamma laugh, and M. le Major! Just look at Gogo again. Have you forgotten what he is doing now? I haven't. . . . He has just changed the *musée des familles* for the *Penny Magazine*, and is explaining Hogarth's pictures of the 'Idle and Industrious Apprentices' to Mimsey, and they are both agreed that the idle one is much the less objectionable of the two!

"Mimsey looks passive enough, with her thumb in her mouth, doesn't she? Her little heart is so full of gratitude and love for Gogo that she can't speak. She can only suck her thumb. Poor, sick, ungainly child! She would like to be Gogo's slave—she would die for Gogo. And her mother adores Gogo too; she is almost jealous of dear Madame Pasquier for having so sweet a son. In just one minute from now, when she has cut that last curl-paper, poor long-dead mamma will call Gogo to her and give him a good 'Irish hug,' and make him happy for a week. Wait a minute and see. *There!* What did I tell you?

"Well, all that came to an end. Madame Pasquier went away and never came back, and so did Gogo. Monsieur and Madame Pasquier were dead, and dear mamma died in a week from the cholera. Poor heart-broken Mimsey was taken away to St. Petersburg, Warsaw, Leipsic, Venice, all over Europe, by her father, as heart-broken as herself.

"It was her wish and her father's that she should become a pianist by profession, and she studied hard for many years in almost every capital, and under almost every master in Europe, and she gave promise of success.

"And so, wandering from one place to another, she became a young woman—a greatly petted and spoiled and made-much-of young woman, Mr. Ibbetson, although she says it who shouldn't; and had many suitors of all kinds and countries.

"But the heroic and angelic Gogo, with his lovely straight nose, and his hair *aux enfants d'Édouard,* and his dear little white silk chimney-pot hat and Eton jacket, was always enshrined in her memory, in her inmost heart, as the incarnation of all that was beautiful and brave and good. But alas! what had become of this Gogo in the mean time? Ah, he was never even heard of—he was dead!

"Well, this long-legged, tender-hearted, grown-up young Mimsey of nineteen was attracted by a very witty and accomplished English attaché at Vienna—a Mr. Harcourt, who seemed deeply in love with her, and wished her to be his wife.

"He was not rich, but Dr. Seraskier liked and trusted him so much that he dispossessed himself of almost everything he had to enable this young couple to marry—and they did. And truth compels me to admit that for a year they were very happy and contented with fate and each other.

"Then a great misfortune befell them both. In a most unexpected manner, through four or five consecutive deaths in Mr. Harcourt's family, he became, first, Lord Harcourt, and then the Duke of Towers. And since then, Mr. Ibbetson, I have not had an hour's peace or happiness.

"In the first place a son was born to me—a cripple, poor dear! and deformed from his birth; and as he grew older it soon became evident that he was also born without a mind.

"Then my unfortunate husband changed completely; he drank and gam-

bled and worse, till we came to live together as strangers, and only spoke to each other in public and before the world. . . ."

"Ah," I said, "you were still a great lady — an English duchess!"

I could not endure the thought of that happy twelvemonth with that bestial duke! I, sober, chaste, and clean — of all but blood, alas! — and a condemned convict!

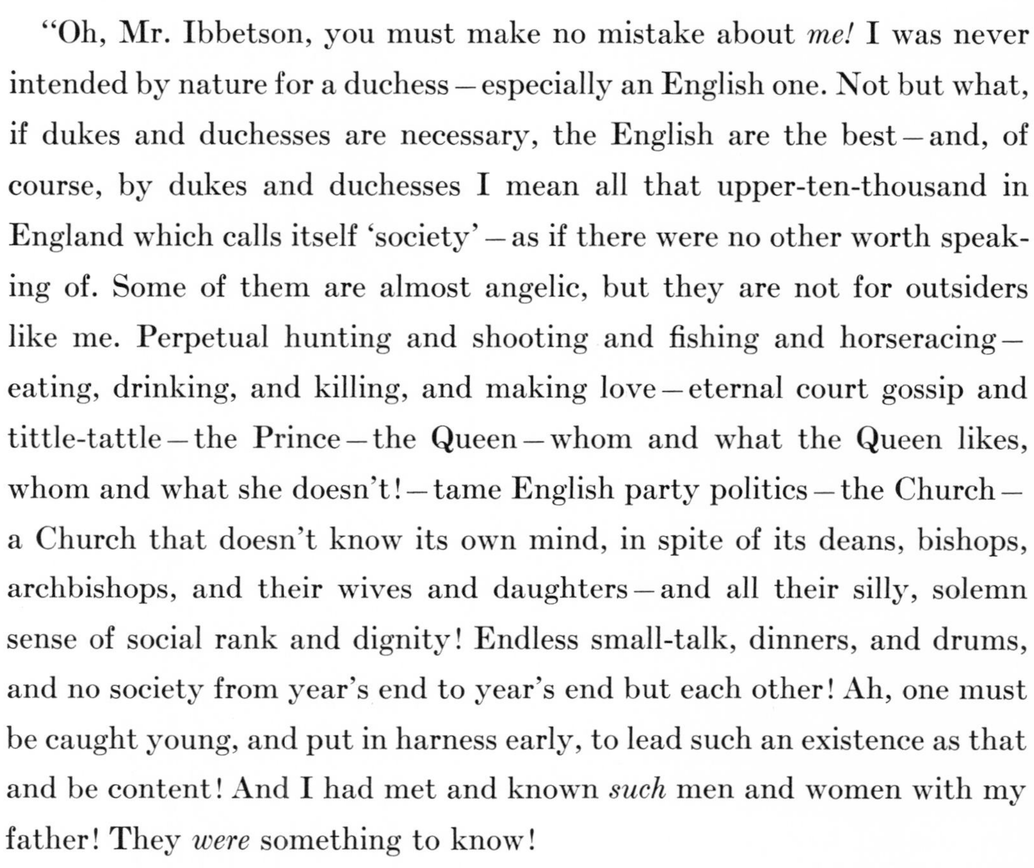

"Oh, Mr. Ibbetson, you must make no mistake about *me!* I was never intended by nature for a duchess — especially an English one. Not but what, if dukes and duchesses are necessary, the English are the best — and, of course, by dukes and duchesses I mean all that upper-ten-thousand in England which calls itself 'society' — as if there were no other worth speaking of. Some of them are almost angelic, but they are not for outsiders like me. Perpetual hunting and shooting and fishing and horseracing — eating, drinking, and killing, and making love — eternal court gossip and tittle-tattle — the Prince — the Queen — whom and what the Queen likes, whom and what she doesn't! — tame English party politics — the Church — a Church that doesn't know its own mind, in spite of its deans, bishops, archbishops, and their wives and daughters — and all their silly, solemn sense of social rank and dignity! Endless small-talk, dinners, and drums, and no society from year's end to year's end but each other! Ah, one must be caught young, and put in harness early, to lead such an existence as that and be content! And I had met and known *such* men and women with my father! They *were* something to know!

"There is another society in London and elsewhere — a freemasonry of intellect and culture and hard work — *la haute bohème du talent* — men and women whose names are or ought to be household words all over the world; many of them are good friends of mine, both here and abroad; and that society, which was good enough for my father and mother, is quite good enough for me.

"I am a republican, Mr. Ibbetson—a cosmopolite—a born Bohemian!

" '*Mon grand-père était rossignol;*
Ma grand'mère était hirondelle!'

"Look at my dear people there—look at your dear people! What waifs and strays, until their ship comes home, which we know it never will! Our

fathers forever racking their five wits in the pursuit of an idea! Our mothers forever racking theirs to save money and make both ends meet! . . . Why, Mr. Ibbetson, you are nearer to the *rossignol* than I am. Do you remember your father's voice? Shall I ever forget it! He sang to me only last night, and in the midst of my harrowing anxiety about you I was beguiled into listening outside the window. He sang Rossini's '*Cujus Animam.*' He *was* the nightingale; that was his vocation, if he could but have known it. And you are my brother Bohemian; that is *yours!* . . . Ah, *my* vocation! It was to be the wife of some busy brain-worker — man of science — conspirator — writer — artist — architect, if you like; to fence him round and shield him from all the little worries and troubles and petty vexations of life. I am a woman of business *par excellence* — a manager, and all that. He would have had a warm, well-ordered little nest to come home to after hunting his idea!

"Well, I thought myself the most unhappy woman alive, and wrapped myself up in my affection for my much-afflicted little son; and as I held him to my breast, and vainly tried to warm and mesmerize him into feeling and intelligence, Gogo came back into my heart, and I was forever thinking, 'Oh, if I had a son like Gogo what a happy woman I should be!' and pitied Madame Pasquier for dying and leaving him so soon, for I had just begun to dream true, and had seen Gogo and his sweet mother once again.

"And then one night — one never-to-be-forgotten night — I went to Lady Cray's concert, and saw you standing in a corner by yourself; and I thought, with a leap of my heart, 'Why, that must be Gogo, grown dark, and with a beard and mustache like a Frenchman!' But alas, I found that you were only a Mr. Ibbetson, Lady Cray's architect, whom she had asked to her house because he was 'quite the handsomest young man she had ever seen!'

"You needn't laugh. You looked very nice, I assure you!

"Well, Mr. Ibbetson, although you were not Gogo, you became suddenly so interesting to me that I never forgot you — you were never quite out of my mind. I wanted to counsel and advise you, and take you by the hand, and be an elder sister to you, for I felt myself already older than you in the world and its ways. I wanted to be twenty years older still, and to have you for my son. I don't know *what* I wanted! You seemed so lonely, and fresh, and unspotted from the world, among all those smart worldlings, and yet so big and strong and square and invincible—oh, so strong! And then you looked at me with such sincere and sweet and chivalrous admiration and sympathy—there, I cannot speak of it—and then you were *so* like what Gogo might have become! Oh, you made as warm and devoted a friend of me at first sight as any one might desire!

"And at the same time you made me feel so self-conscious and shy that I dared not ask to be introduced to you—I, who scarcely know what shyness is.

"Dear Giulia Grisi sang '*Sedut' al Pie d'un' Salice,*' and that tune has always been associated in my mind with your image ever since, and always will be. Your dear mother used to play it on the harp. Do you remember?

"Then came that extraordinary dream, which you remember as well as I do: *wasn't* it a wonder? You see, my dear father had learned a strange secret of the brain—how in sleep to recall past things and people and places as they had once been seen or known by him—even unremembered things. He called it 'dreaming true,' and by long practice, he told me, he had brought the art of doing this to perfection. It was the one consolation of his troubled life to go over and over again in sleep all his happy youth and childhood, and the few short years he had spent with his beloved young wife. And before he died, when he saw I had become so unhappy that life seemed to have no longer any possible hope of pleasure for me, he taught me his very simple secret.

"Thus have I revisited in sleep every place I have ever lived in, and especially this, the beloved spot where I first as a little girl knew *you!*

"That night when we met again in our common dream I was looking at the boys from Saindou's school going to their *première communion*, and thinking very much of you, as I had seen you, when awake, a few hours before, looking out of the window at the 'Tête Noire'; when you suddenly appeared in great seeming trouble and walking like a tipsy man; and my vision was disturbed by the shadow of a prison — alas! alas! — and two little jailers jingling their keys and trying to hem you in.

"My emotion at seeing you again so soon was so great that I nearly woke. But I rescued you from your imaginary terrors and held you by the hand. You remember all the rest.

"I could not understand why you should be in my dream, as I had almost always dreamed true — that is, about things that *had* been in my life — not about things that *might* be; nor could I account for the solidity of your hand, nor understand why you didn't fade away when I took it, and blur the dream. It was a most perplexing mystery that troubled many hours of both my waking and sleeping life. Then came that meeting with you at Cray, and part of the mystery was accounted for, for you were my old friend Gogo, after all. But it is still a mystery, an awful mystery, that two people should meet as we are meeting now in one and the same dream — should dovetail so accurately into each other's brains. What a link between us two, Mr. Ibbetson, already linked by such memories!

"After meeting you at Cray I felt that I must never meet you again, either waking or dreaming. The discovery that you were Gogo, after all, combined with the preoccupation which as a mere stranger you had already caused me for so long, created such a disturbance in my spirit that — that — there, you must try and imagine it for yourself.

"Even before that revelation at Cray I had often known you were here in my dream, and I had carefully avoided you . . . though little dreaming you were here in your own dream too! Often from that little dormer-window up there I have seen you wandering about the park and avenue in seeming search of *me*, and wondered why and how you came. You drove me into attics and servants' bedrooms to conceal myself from you. It was quite a game of hide-and-seek—*cache-cache*, as we used to call it.

"But after our meeting at Cray I felt there must be no more *cache-cache;* I avoided coming here at all; you drove me away altogether.

"Now try to imagine what I felt when the news of your terrible quarrel with Mr. Ibbetson burst upon the world. I was beside myself! I came here night after night; I looked for you everywhere—in the park, in the Bois de Boulogne, at the Mare d'Auteuil, at St. Cloud—in every place I could think of! And now here you are at last—at last!

"Hush! Don't speak yet! I have soon done!

"Six months ago I lost my poor little son, and, much as I loved him, I cannot wish him back again. In a fortnight I shall be legally separated from my wretched husband—I shall be quite alone in the world! And then, Mr. Ibbetson—oh, *then*, dearest friend that child or woman ever had—every hour that I can steal from my waking existence shall henceforward be devoted to you as long as both of us live, and sleep the same hours out of the twenty-four. My one object and endeavor shall be to make up for the wreck of your sweet and valuable young life. 'Stone walls shall not a prison make, nor iron bars a cage!' [And here she laughed and cried together, so that her eyes, closing up, squeezed out her tears, and I thought, "Oh, that I might drink them!"]

"And now I will leave you. I am a weak and loving woman, and must not stay by your side till I can do so without too much self-reproach.

"And indeed I feel I shall soon fall awake from sheer exhaustion of joy. Oh, selfish and jealous wretch that I am, to talk of joy!

"I cannot help rejoicing that no other woman can be to you what I hope to be. No other woman can ever come *near* you! I am your tyrant and your slave—your calamity has made you mine forever; but all my life—all—all

—shall be spent in trying to make you forget yours, and I think I shall succeed."

"Oh, don't make such dreadful haste!" I exclaimed. "Am *I* dreaming true? What is to prove all this to me when I wake? Either I am the most abject and wretched of men, or life will never have another unhappy moment. How am I to *know?*"

"Listen. Do you remember 'Parva sed Apta, le petit pavillon,' as you used to call it? That is still my home when I am here. It shall be yours, if you like, when the time comes. You will find much to interest you there. Well, to-morrow early, in your cell, you will receive from me an envelope with a slip of paper in it, containing some violets, and the words 'Parva sed Apta—à bientôt' written in violet ink. Will that convince you?"

"Oh yes, yes!"

"Well, then, give me your hands, dearest and best—both hands! I shall soon be here again, by this apple-tree; I shall count the hours. Good-bye!" and she was gone, and I woke.

I woke to the gaslit darkness of my cell. It was just before dawn. One of the warders asked me civilly if I wanted anything, and gave me a drink of water.

I thanked him quietly, and recalled what had just happened to me, with a wonder, an ecstasy, for which I can find no words.

No, it had *not* been a *dream*—of that I felt quite sure—not in any one single respect; there had been nothing of the dream about it except its transcendent, ineffable enchantment.

Every inflexion of that beloved voice, with its scarcely perceptible foreign accent that I had never noticed before; every animated gesture, with its subtle reminiscence of both her father and her mother; her black dress trimmed with gray; her black and gray hat; the scent of sandal-wood about her—all were more distinctly and vividly impressed upon me than if she

had just been actually, and in the flesh, at my bedside. Her tones still rang in my ears. My eyes were full of her: now her profile, so pure and chiselled; now her full face, with her gray eyes (sometimes tender and grave and wet with tears, sometimes half closed in laughter) fixed on mine; her lithe sweet body curved forward, as she sat and clasped her knees; her arched and slender smooth straight feet so delicately shod, that seemed now and then to beat time to her story. . . .

And then that strange sense of the transfusion of life at the touching of the hands! Oh, it was *no dream!* Though what it was I cannot tell. . . .

I turned on my side, happy beyond expression, and fell asleep again—a dreamless sleep that lasted till I was woke and told to dress.

Some breakfast was brought to me, and *with it an envelope, open, which contained some violets, and a slip of paper, scented with sandal-wood, on which were written, in violet ink, the words—*

"Parva sed Apta — à bientôt!

Tarapatapoum."

I will pass over the time that elapsed between my sentence and its commutation; the ministrations and exhortations of the good chaplain; the kind and touching farewells of Mr. and Mrs. Lintot, who had also believed that I was Ibbetson's son (I undeceived them); the visit of my old friend Mrs. Deane . . . and her strange passion of gratitude and admiration.

I have no doubt it would all be interesting enough, if properly remembered and ably told. But it was all too much like a dream — anybody's dream — not one of *mine* — all too slight and flimsy to have left an abiding remembrance, or to matter much.

In due time I was removed to the jail at ——, and bade farewell to the world, and adapted myself to the conditions of my new outer life with a good grace and with a very light heart.

The prison routine, leaving the brain so free and unoccupied; the healthy labor, the pure air, the plain, wholesome food were delightful to me — a much-needed daily mental rest after the tumultuous emotions of each night.

For I was soon back again in Passy, where I spent every hour of my sleep, you may be sure, never very far from the old apple-tree, which went through all its changes, from bare bough to tender shoots and blossoms, from blossom to ripe fruit, from fruit to yellow falling leaf, and then to bare boughs again, and all in a few peaceful nights, which were my days. I flatter myself by this time that I know the habits of a French apple-tree, and its caterpillars!

And all the dear people I loved, and of whom I could never tire, were about — all but one. *The* One!

At last she arrived. The garden door was pushed, the bell rang, and she came across the lawn, radiant and tall and swift, and opened wide her arms. And there, with our little world around us — all that we had ever loved and cared for, but quite unseen and unheard by them — for the first time in my life since my mother and Madame Seraskier had died I held a woman in my arms, and she pressed her lips to mine.

Round and round the lawn we walked and talked, as we had often done fifteen, sixteen, twenty years ago. There were many things to say. "The Charming Prince" and the "Fairy Tarapatapoum" were "prettily well together"—at last!

The time sped quickly—far too quickly. I said—

"You told me I should see your house—'Parva sed Apta'—that I should find much to interest me there." . . .

She blushed a little and smiled, and said—

"You mustn't expect *too* much," and we soon found ourselves walking thither up the avenue. Thus we had often walked as children, and once – a memorable once – besides.

There stood the little white house with its golden legend, as I had seen it a thousand times when a boy – a hundred since.

How sweet and small it looked in the mellow sunshine! We mounted the stone *perron*, and opened the door and entered. My heart beat violently.

Everything was as it had always been, as far as I could see. Dr. Seraskier sat in a chair by the window reading Schiller, and took no notice of us. His hair moved in the gentle breeze. Overhead we heard the rooms being swept and the beds made.

I followed her into a little lumber-room, where I did not remember to have been before; it was full of odds and ends.

"Why have you brought me here?" I asked.

She laughed and said –

"Open the door in the wall opposite."

There was no door, and I said so.

Then she took my hand, and lo! there *was* a door! And she pushed, and we entered another suite of apartments that never could have been there before; there had never been room for them – nor ever could have been – in all Passy!

"Come," she said, laughing and blushing at once; for she seemed nervous and excited and shy – "do you remember –

" '*And Neuha led her Torquil by the hand,*

And waved along the vault her flaming brand!'

– do you remember your little drawing out of *The Island*, in the green morocco Byron? Here it is, in the top drawer of this beautiful cabinet. Here are all the drawings you ever did for me – plain and colored – with dates, explanations, etc., all written by myself – *l'album de la fée Tarapatapoum.*

They are only duplicates. I have the real ones at my house in Hampshire.

"The cabinet also is a duplicate;—isn't it a beauty?—it's from the Czar's Winter Palace. Everything here is a duplicate, more or less. See, this is a

little dining-room;—did you ever see anything so perfect?—it is the famous *salle à manger* of Princesse de Chevagné. I never use it, except now and then to eat a slice of English household bread with French butter and 'cassonade.' Little Mimsey, out there, does so sometimes, when Gogo brings her one, and it makes big Mimsey's mouth water to see her, so she has to go and do likewise. Would you like a slice?

"You see the cloth is spread, *deux couverts*. There is a bottle of famous champagne from Mr. De Rothschild's; there's plenty more where that came from. The flowers are from Chatsworth, and this is a lobster salad for *you*. Papa was great at lobster salads and taught me. I mixed it myself a fortnight ago, and, as you see, it is as fresh and sweet as if I had only just made it, and the flowers haven't faded a bit.

"Here are cigarettes and pipes and cigars. I hope they are good. I don't smoke myself.

"Isn't all the furniture rare and beautiful? I have robbed every palace in Europe of its very best, and yet the owners are not a penny the worse. You should see up-stairs.

"Look at those pictures—the very pick of Raphael and Titian and Velasquez. Look at that piano—I have heard Liszt play upon it over and over again, in Leipsic!

"Here is my library. Every book I ever read is there, and every binding I ever admired. I don't often read them, but I dust them carefully. I've arranged that dust shall fall on them in the usual way to make it real, and remind one of the outer life one is so glad to leave. All has to be taken very seriously here, and one must put one's self to a little trouble. See, here is my father's microscope, and under it a small spider caught on the premises by myself. It is still alive. It seems cruel, doesn't it? but it only exists in our brains.

"Look at the dress I've got on—feel it; how every detail is worked out. And you have unconsciously done the same: that's the suit you wore that morning at Cray under the ash-tree—the nicest suit I ever saw. Here is a spot of ink on your sleeve as real as can be (bravo!). And this button is coming off—quite right; I will sew it on with a dream needle, and dream thread, and a dream thimble!

"This little door leads to every picture-gallery in Europe. It took me a long time to build and arrange them all by myself—quite a week of nights. It is very pleasant to walk there with a good catalogue, and make it rain cats and dogs outside.

"Through this curtain is an opera box—the most comfortable one I've ever been in; it does for theatres as well, and oratorios and concerts and scientific lectures. You shall see from it every performance I've ever been at, in half a dozen languages; you shall hold my hand and understand them all. Every singer that I ever heard, you shall hear. Dear Giulia Grisi shall sing the 'Willow Song' again and again, and you shall hear the applause. Ah, what applause!

"Come into this little room—my favorite; out of *this* window and down these steps we can walk or drive to any place you or I have ever been to, and other places besides. Nothing is far, and we have only to go hand in hand. I don't know yet where my stables and coach-houses are; you must help me to find out. But so far I have never lacked a carriage at the bottom of those steps when I wanted to drive, nor a steam-launch, nor a gondola, nor a lovely place to go to.

"Out of *this* window, from this divan, we can sit and gaze on whatever we like. What shall it be? Just now, you perceive, there is a wild and turbulent sea, with not a ship in sight. Do you hear the waves tumbling and splashing, and see the albatross? I had been reading Keats's 'Ode to the Nightingale,' and was so fascinated by the idea of a lattice opening on the foam

" '*Of perilous seas by faery lands forlorn*'

that I thought it would be nice to have a lattice like that myself. I tried to evolve that sea from my inner consciousness, you know, or rather from seas that I have sailed over. Do you like it? It was done a fortnight ago, and the

waves have been tumbling about ever since. How they roar! and hark at the wind! I couldn't manage the 'faery lands.' It wants one lattice for the sea, and one for the land, I'm afraid. You must help me. Meanwhile, what would you like there to-night—the Yosemite Valley? the Nevski Prospect in the winter, with the sledges? the Rialto? the Bay of Naples after sunset, with Vesuvius in eruption?" . . .

—"Oh Mary—Mimsey—what *do* I care for Vesuvius, and sunsets, and the Bay of Naples . . . *just now?* . . . Vesuvius is in my heart!"

* * * * *

Thus began for us both a period of twenty-five years, during which we passed eight or nine hours out of the twenty-four in each other's company—except on a few rare occasions, when illness or some other cause prevented one of us from sleeping at the proper time.

Mary! Mary!

I idolized her while she lived; I idolize her memory.

For her sake all women are sacred to me, even the lowest and most depraved and God-forsaken. They always found a helping friend in *her*.

How can I pay a fitting tribute to one so near to me—nearer than any woman can ever have been to any man?

I know her mind as I know my own! No two human souls can ever have interpenetrated each other as ours have done, or we should have heard of it. Every thought she ever had from her childhood to her death has been revealed—every thought of mine! Living as we did, it was inevitable. The touch of a finger was enough to establish the strange circuit, and wake a common consciousness of past and present, either hers or mine.

And oh, how thankful am I that some lucky chance has preserved me, murderer and convict as I am, from anything she would have found it impossible to condone!

I try not to think that shyness and poverty, ungainliness and social imbecility combined, have had as much to do as self-restraint and self-respect in keeping me out of so many pitfalls that have been fatal to so many men better and more gifted than myself.

I try to think that her extraordinary affection, the chance result of a persistent impression received in childhood, has followed me through life without my knowing it, and in some occult, mysterious way has kept me from thoughts and deeds that would have rendered me unworthy, even in her too indulgent eyes.

Who knows but that her sweet mother's farewell kiss and blessing, and the tender tears she shed over me when I bade her good-bye at the avenue gate so many years ago, may have had an antiseptic charm? Mary! I have followed her from her sickly, suffering childhood to her girlhood—from her half-ripe, gracefully lanky girlhood to the day of her retirement from the world of which she was so great an ornament. From girl to woman it seems like a triumphal procession through all the courts of Europe—scenes the like of which I have never even dreamed—flattery and strife to have turned the head of any princess! And she was the simple daughter of a working scientist and physician—the granddaughter of a fiddler.

Yet even Austrian court etiquette was waived in favor of the child of plain Dr. Seraskier.

What men have I seen at her feet—how splendid, handsome, gallant, brilliant, chivalrous, lordly, and gay! And to all, from her, the same happy geniality—the same kindly, laughing, frolicsome, innocent gayety, with never a thought of self.

M. le Major was right—"elle avait toutes les intelligences de la tête et du cœur." And old and young, the best and the worst, seemed to love and respect her alike—and women as well as men—for her perfect sincerity, her sweet reasonableness.

And all this time I was plodding at my dull drawing-board in Pentonville, carrying out another's designs for a stable or a pauper's cottage, and not even achieving that poor task particularly well!

It would have driven me mad with humiliation and jealousy to see this past life of hers, but we saw it all hand in hand together—the magical circuit was established! And I knew, as I saw, how it all affected her, and marvelled at her simplicity in thinking all this pomp and splendor of so little consequence.

And I trembled to find that what space in her heart was not filled by the remembrance of her ever-beloved mother and the image of her father (one of the noblest and best of men) enshrined the ridiculous figure of a small boy in a white silk hat and an Eton jacket. And that small boy was I!

Then came a dreadful twelvemonth that I was fain to leave a blank—the twelvemonth during which her girlish fancy for her husband lasted—and then her life was mine again forever!

And *my* life!

The life of a convict is not, as a rule, a happy one; his bed is not generally thought a bed of roses.

Mine was!

If I had been the most miserable leper that ever crawled to his wattled hut in Molokai, I should also have been the happiest of men, could sleep but have found me there, and could I but sleeping have been the friend of sleeping Mary Seraskier. She would have loved me all the more!

She has filled my long life of bondage with such felicity as no monarch has ever dreamed, and has found her own felicity in doing so. That poor, plodding existence I led before my great misadventure, and have tried to describe—she has witnessed almost every hour of it with passionate interest and sympathy, as we went hand in hand together through each other's past. She would at any time have been only too glad to share it, leaving her own.

I dreaded the effect of such a sordid revelation upon one who had lived so brilliantly and at such an altitude. I need have had no fear! Just as she thought me an "angelic hero" at eight years old, she remained persuaded all through her life that I was an Apollo — a misunderstood genius — a martyr!

I am sick with shame when I think of it. But I am not the first unworthy mortal on whom blind, undiscriminating love has chosen to lavish its most priceless treasures. Tarapatapoum is not the only fairy who has idealized a hulking clown with an ass's head into a Prince Charming; the spectacle, alas! is not infrequent. But at least I have been humbly thankful for the undeserved blessing, and known its value. And, moreover, I think I may lay claim to one talent: that of also knowing by intuition when and where and how to love — in a moment — in a flash — and forever!

Twenty-five years!

It seems like a thousand, so much have we seen and felt and done in that busy enchanted quarter of a century. And yet how quickly the time has sped!

And now I must endeavor to give some account of our wonderful inner life — *à deux* — a delicate and difficult task.

There is both an impertinence and a lack of taste in any man's laying bare to the public eye — to any eye — the bliss that has come to him through the love of a devoted woman, with whose life his own has been bound up.

The most sympathetic reader is apt to be repelled by such a revelation — to be sceptical of the beauties and virtues and mental gifts of one he has never seen; at all events, to feel that they are no concern of his, and ought to be the subject of a sacred reticence on the part of her too fortunate lover or husband.

The lack of such reticence has marred the interest of many an autobiography — of many a novel, even; and in private life, who does not know by painful experience how embarrassing to the listener such tender confidences can sometimes be? I will try my best not to transgress in this particular. If I fail (I may have failed already), I can only plead that the circumstances are quite exceptional and not to be matched; and that allowances must be made for the deep gratitude I owe and feel over and above even my passionate admiration and love.

For the next three years of my life has nothing to show but the alternation of such honeymooning as never was before with a dull but contented prison life, not one hour of which is worth recording, or even remembering, except as a foil to its alternative.

It had but one hour for me, the bed hour, and fortunately that was an early one.

Healthily tired in body, blissfully expectant in mind, I would lie on my back, with my hands duly crossed under my head, and sleep would soon steal over me like balm; and before I had forgotten who and what and where I really was, I would reach the goal on which my will was intent, and waking up, find my body in another place, in another garb, on a couch by an enchanted window, still with my arms crossed behind my head—in the sacramental attitude.

Then would I stretch my limbs and slip myself free of my outer life, as a new-born butterfly from the durance of its self-spun cocoon, with an unutterable sense of youth and strength and freshness and felicity; and opening my eyes I would see on the adjacent couch the form of Mary, also supine, but motionless and inanimate as a statue. Nothing could wake her to life till the time came: her hours were somewhat later, and she was still in the toils of the outer life I had just left behind me.

And these toils, in her case, were more complicated than in mine. Although she had given up the world, she had many friends and an immense correspondence. And then, being a woman endowed with boundless health

and energy, splendid buoyancy of animal spirits, and a great capacity for business, she had made for herself many cares and occupations.

She was the virtual mistress of a home for fallen women, a reformatory for juvenile thieves, and a children's convalescent hospital—to all of which she gave her immediate personal superintendence, and almost every penny she had. She had let her house in Hampshire, and lived with a couple of female servants in a small furnished house on Campden Hill. She did without a carriage, and went about in cabs and omnibuses, dressed like a daily governess, though nobody could appear more regally magnificent than she did when we were together.

She still kept her name and title, as a potent weapon of influence on behalf of her charities, and wielded it mercilessly in her constant raid on the purse of the benevolent Philistine, who is fond of great people.

All of which gave rise to much comment that did not affect her equanimity in the least.

She also attended lectures, committees, boards, and councils; opened bazaars and soup kitchens and coffee taverns, etc. The list of her self-imposed tasks was endless. Thus her outer life was filled to overflowing, and, unlike mine, every hour of it was worth record—as I well know, who have witnessed it all. But this is not the place in which to write the outer life of the Duchess of Towers; another hand has done that, as everybody knows.

Every page henceforward must be sacred to Mary Seraskier, the "fée Tarapatapoum" of "Magna sed Apta" (for so we had called the new home and palace of art she had added on to "Parva sed Apta," the home of her childhood).

To return thither, where we left her lying unconscious. Soon the color would come back to her cheeks, the breath to her nostrils, the pulse to her heart, and she would wake to her Eden, as she called it—our common inner

life—that we might spend it in each other's company for the next eight hours.

Pending this happy moment, I would make coffee (such coffee!), and smoke a cigarette or two; and to fully appreciate the bliss of *that* one must be an habitual smoker who lives his real life in an English jail.

When she awoke from her sixteen hours' busy trance in the outer world, such a choice of pleasures lay before us as no other mortal has ever known. She had been all her life a great traveller, and had dwelt in many lands and cities, and seen more of life and the world and nature than most people. I had but to take her hand, and one of us had but to wish, and, lo! wherever either of us had been, whatever either of us had seen or heard or felt, or even eaten or drunk, there it was all over again to choose from, with the other to share in it—such a hypnotism of ourselves and each other as was never dreamed of before.

Everything was as life-like, as real to us both, as it had been to either at the actual time of its occurrence, with an added freshness and charm that never belonged to mortal existence. It was no dream; it was a second life, a better land.

We had, however, to stay within certain bounds, and beware of transgressing certain laws that we discovered for ourselves, but could not quite account for. For instance, it was fatal to attempt exploits that were outside of our real experience: to fly, or to jump from a height, or do any of those non-natural things that make the charm and wonder of ordinary dreams. If we did so our true dream was blurred, and became as an ordinary dream—vague, futile, unreal, and untrue—the baseless fabric of a vision. Nor must we alter ourselves in any way; even to the shape of a finger-nail, we must remain ourselves; although we kept ourselves at our very best, and could choose what age we should be. We chose from twenty-six to twenty-eight, and stuck to it.

TO ST. JAMES'S HALL, PICCADILLY

Yet there were many things, quite as impossible in real life, that we could do with impunity – most delightful things!

For instance, after the waking cup of coffee, it was certainly delightful to spend a couple of hours in the Yosemite Valley, leisurely strolling about and gazing at the giant pines – a never-palling source of delight to both of us – breathing the fragrant fresh air, looking at our fellow-tourists and listening to their talk, with the agreeable consciousness that, solid and substantial as we were to each other, we were quite inaudible, invisible, and intangible to them. Often we would dispense with the tourists, and have the Yosemite Valley all to ourselves. (Always there, and in whatever place she had visited with her husband, we would dispense with the figure of her former self and him, a sight I could not have borne.)

When we had strolled and gazed our fill, it was delightful again, just by a slight effort of her will and a few moments' closing of our eyes, to find ourselves driving along the Via Cornice to an exquisite garden concert in Dresden, or being rowed in a gondola to a Saturday Pop at St. James's Hall. And thence, jumping into a hansom, we would be whisked through Piccadilly and the park to the Arc de Triomphe home to "Magna sed Apta," Rue de la Pompe, Passy (a charming drive, and not a bit too long), just in time for dinner.

A very delicious little dinner, judiciously ordered out of *her* remembrance, not *mine* (and served in the most exquisite little dining-room in all Paris – the Princesse de Chevagné's): "huîtres d'Ostende," let us say, and "soupe à la bonne femme," with a "perdrix aux choux" to follow, and pancakes, and "fromage de Brie"; and to drink, a bottle of "Romané Conti"; without even the bother of waiters to change the dishes; a wish, a moment's shutting of the eyes – *augenblick!* and it was done – and then we could wait on each other.

After my prison fare, and with nothing but tenpenny London dinners to recollect in the immediate past, I trust I shall not be thought a gross materialist for appreciating these small banquets, and in such company. (The only dinner I could recall which was not a tenpenny one, except the old dinners of my childhood, was that famous dinner at Cray, where I had discovered that the Duchess of Towers was Mimsey Seraskier, and I did not eat much of *that.*)

Then a cigarette and a cup of coffee, and a glass of curaçoa; and after, to reach our private box we had but to cross the room and lift a curtain.

And there before us was the theatre or opera-house brilliantly lighted, and the instruments tuning up, and the splendid company pouring in: crowned heads, famous beauties, world-renowned warriors and statesmen, Garibaldi, Gortschakoff, Cavour, Bismarck, and Moltke, now so famous, and who not? Mary would point them out to me. And in the next box Dr. Seraskier and his tall daughter, who seemed friends with all that brilliant crowd.

Now it was St. Petersburg, now Berlin, now Vienna, Paris, Naples, Milan, London – every great city in turn. But our box was always the same, and always the best in the house, and I the one person privileged to smoke my cigar in the face of all that royalty, fashion, and splendor.

Then, after the overture, up went the curtain. If it was a play, and the play was in German or Russian or Italian, I had but to touch Mary's little finger to understand it all – a true but incomprehensible thing. For well as I might understand, I could not have spoken a word of either, and the moment that slight contact was discontinued, they might as well have been acting in Greek or Hebrew, for *me.*

But it was for music we cared the most, and I think I may say that of music during those three years (and ever after) we have had our glut. For all through her busy waking life Mary found time to hear whatever good music was going on in London, that she might bring it back to me at night; and we would rehear it together, again and again, and *da capo.*

TO THE OPERA BOX

It is a rare privilege for two private individuals, and one of them a convict, to assist at a performance honored by the patronage and presence of crowned heads, and yet be able to encore any particular thing that pleases them. How often have we done that!

Oh, Joachim! oh, Clara Schumann! oh, Piatti!—all of whom I know so well, but have never heard with the fleshly ear! Oh, others, whom it would be invidious to mention without mentioning all—a glorious list! How we have made you, all unconscious, repeat the same movements over and over again, without ever from you a sign of impatience or fatigue! How often have we summoned Liszt to play to us on his own favorite piano, which adorned our own favorite sitting-room! How little he knew (or will ever know now, alas!) what exquisite delight he gave us!

Oh, Patti, Angelina! Oh, Santley and Sims Reeves! Oh, De Soria, nightingale of the drawing-room, I wonder you have a note left!

And you, Ristori, and you, Salvini, et vous, divine Sarah, qui débutiez alors! On me dit que votre adorable voix a perdu un peu de sa première fraîcheur. Cela ne m'étonne pas! Bien sûr, nous y sommes pour quelque chose!

* * * * *

And then the picture-galleries, the museums, the botanical and zoological gardens of all countries—"Magna sed Apta" had space for them all, even to the Elgin Marbles room of the British Museum, which I added myself.

What enchanted hours have we spent among the pictures and statues of the world, weeding them here and there, perhaps, or hanging them differently, or placing them in what we thought a better light! The "Venus of Milo" showed to far greater advantage in "Magna sed Apta" than at the Louvre.

And when busied thus delightfully at home, and to enhance the delight, we made it shocking bad weather outside; it rained cats and dogs, or else the north wind piped, and snow fell on the desolate gardens of "Magna sed Apta," and whitened the landscape as far as eye could see.

Nearest to our hearts, however, were many pictures of our own time, for we were moderns of the moderns, after all, in spite of our efforts of self-culture.

There was scarcely a living or recently living master in Europe whose best works were not in our possession, so lighted and hung that even the masters themselves would have been content; for we had plenty of space at our command, and each picture had a wall to itself, so toned as to do full justice to its beauty, and a comfortable sofa for two just opposite.

But in the little room we most lived in, the room with the magic window, we had crowded a few special favorites of the English school, for we had so much foreign blood in us that we were more British than John Bull himself —*plus royalistes que le Roi.*

There was Millais's "Autumn Leaves," his "Youth of Sir Walter Raleigh," his "Chill October"; Watts's "Endymion," and "Orpheus and Eurydice"; Burne-Jones's "Chant d'Amour," and his "Laus Veneris"; Alma-Tadema's "Audience of Agrippa," and the "Women of Amphissa"; J. Whistler's portrait of his mother; the "Venus and Æsculapius," by E. J. Poynter; F. Leighton's "Daphnephoria"; George Mason's "Harvest Moon"; and Frederick Walker's "Harbor of Refuge," and, of course, Merridew's "Sun-God."

While on a screen, designed by H. S. Marks, and exquisitely decorated round the margin with golden plovers and their eggs (which I adore), were smaller gems in oil and water-color that Mary had fallen in love with at one time or another. The immortal "Moonlight Sonata," by Whistler; E. J. Poynter's exquisite "Our Lady of the Fields" (dated Paris, 1857); a pair of adorable "Bimbi" by V. Prinsep, who seems very fond of children; T. R. Lamont's touching "L'Après-Dîner de l'Abbé Constantin," with the sweet girl playing the old spinet; and that admirable work of T. Armstrong, in his earlier and more realistic manner, "Le Zouave et la Nounou," not to mention splendid rough sketches by John Leech, Charles Keene, Tenniel, Sambourne, Furniss, Caldecott, etc.; not to mention, also, endless little sketches in silver point of a most impossibly colossal, black-a-vised, shaggy-coated St. Bernard — signed with the familiar French name of some gay troubadour of the pencil, some stray half-breed like myself, and who seems to have loved his dog as much as I loved mine.

Then suddenly, in the midst of all this unparalleled artistic splendor, we felt that a something was wanting. There was a certain hollowness about it; and we discovered that in our case the principal motives for collecting all these beautiful things were absent.

1. We were not the sole possessors.
2. We had nobody to show them to.
3. Therefore we could take no pride in them.

And found that when we wanted bad weather for a change, and the joys of home, we could be quite as happy in my old school-room, where the squirrels and the monkey and the hedgehog were, with each of us on a cane-bottomed arm-chair by the wood-fire, each roasting chestnuts for the other, and one book between us, for one of us to read out loud; or better still, the morning and evening papers she had read a few hours earlier; and marvellous to relate, she had not even *read* them when awake! she had merely glanced through them carefully, taking in the aspect of each column one after another, from top to bottom — and yet she was able to read out every word from the dream-paper she held in her hands — thus truly chewing the very cud of journalism!

This always seemed to us, in a small but practical way, the most complete and signal triumph of mind over matter we had yet achieved.

Not, indeed, that we could read much, we had so much to talk about.

Unfortunately, the weak part of "Magna sed Apta" was its library.

Naturally it could only consist of books that one or the other of us had read when awake. She had led such an active life that but little leisure had been left her for books, and I had read only as an every-day young man reads who is fond of reading.

However, such books as we *had* read were made the most of, and so magnificently bound that even their authors would have blushed with pride and pleasure had they been there to see. And though we had little time for reading them over again, we could enjoy the true bibliophilous delight of gazing at their backs, and taking them down and fingering them and putting them carefully back again.

In most of these treats, excursions, festivities, and pleasures of the fireside, Mary was naturally leader and hostess; it could scarcely have been otherwise.

There was once a famous Mary, of whom it was said that to know her was a liberal education. I think I may say that to have known Mary Seraskier has been all that to me!

But now and then I would make some small attempt at returning her hospitality.

We have slummed together in Clerkenwell, Smithfield, Cow Cross, Petticoat Lane, Ratcliffe Highway, and the East India and West India docks.

She has been with me to penny gaffs and music-halls; to Greenwich Fair, and Cremorne and Rosherville gardens—and liked them all. She knew Pentonville as well as I do; and my old lodgings there, where we have both leaned over my former shoulder as I read or drew. It was she who rescued from oblivion my little prophetic song about "The Chime," which I had quite forgotten. She has been to Mr. Lintot's parties, and found them most amusing—especially Mr. Lintot.

And going further back into the past, she has roamed with me all over Paris, and climbed with me the towers of Notre Dame, and looked in vain for the mystic word 'Ανάγκη!

But I had also better things to show, untravelled as I was.

She had never seen Hampstead Heath, which I knew by heart; and Hampstead Heath at any time, but especially on a sunny morning in late October, is not to be disdained by any one.

Half the leaves have fallen, so that one can see the fading glory of those that remain; yellow and brown and pale and hectic red, shining like golden guineas and bright copper coins against the rich, dark, business-like green of the trees that mean to flourish all the winter through, like the tall slanting pines near the Spaniards, and the old cedar-trees, and hedges of yew and holly, for which the Hampstead gardens are famous.

Before us lies a sea of fern, gone a russet-brown from decay, in which are isles of dark green gorse, and little trees with little scarlet and orange and lemon-colored leaflets fluttering down, and running after each other on the bright grass, under the brisk west wind which makes the willows rustle, and turn up the whites of their leaves in pious resignation to the coming change.

Harrow-on-the-Hill, with its pointed spire, rises blue in the distance; and distant ridges, like receding waves, rise into blueness, one after the other, out of the low-lying mist; the last ridge bluely melting into space. In the midst of it all gleams the Welsh Harp Lake, like a piece of sky that has become unstuck and tumbled into the landscape with its shiny side up.

On the other side, all London, with nothing but the gilded cross of St. Paul's on a level with the eye; it lies at our feet, as Paris used to do from the heights of Passy, a sight to make true dreamers gaze and think and dream the more; and there we sit thinking and dreaming and gazing our fill, hand in hand, our spirits rushing together.

Once as we sat we heard the clatter of hoofs behind us, and there was a troop of my old regiment out exercising. Invisible to all but ourselves, and each other, we watched the wanton troopers riding by on their meek black chargers.

First came the cornet—a sunny-haired Apollo, a gilded youth, graceful and magnificent to the eye—careless, fearless, but stupid, harsh, and proud—an English Phébus de Châteaupers—the son of a great contractor; I remembered him well, and that he loved me not. Then the rank and file in stable jackets, most of them (but for a stalwart corporal here and there) raw, lanky youths, giving promise of much future strength, and each leading a second horse; and among them, longest and lankiest of them all, but ruddy as a ploughboy, and stolidly whistling "*On revient toujours à ses premiers amours*," rode my former self—a sight (or sound) that seemed to touch some tender chord in Mary's nature, where there were so many, since it filled her eyes with tears.

To describe in full a honeymoon filled with such adventures, and that lasted for three years, is unnecessary. It would be but another superficial record of travel, by another unskilled pen. And what a pen is wanted for such a theme! It was not mere life, it was the very cream and essence of life, that we shared with each other—all the toil and trouble, the friction and fatigue, left out. The necessary earthly journey through time and space from one joy to another was omitted, unless such a journey were a joy in itself.

For instance, a pleasant hour can be spent on the deck of a splendid steamer, as it cleaves its way through a sapphire tropical sea, bound for some lovely West Indian islet; with a good cigar and the dearest companion in the world, watching the dolphins and the flying-fish, and mildly interesting one's self in one's fellow-passengers, the captain, the crew. And then, the hour spent and the cigar smoked out, it is well to shut one's eyes and have one's self quietly lowered down the side of the vessel into a beautiful sledge, and then, half smothered in costly furs, to be whirled along the frozen Neva to a ball at the Winter Palace, there to valse with one's Mary among all the beauty and chivalry of St. Petersburg, and never a soul to find fault with one's valsing, which at first was far from perfect, or one's attire, which was not that of the fashionable world of the day, nor was Mary's either. We were æsthetic people, and very Greek, who made for ourselves fashions of our own, which I will not describe.

Where have we not waltzed together, from Buckingham Palace downward? I confess I grew to take a delight in valsing, or waltzing, or whatever it is properly called; and although it is not much to boast of, I may say that after a year or two no better dancer than I was to be found in all Vienna.

And here, by the way, I may mention what pleasure it gave me (hand in hand with Mary, of course, as usual) to renew and improve my acquaintance with our British aristocracy, begun so agreeably many years ago at Lady Cray's concert.

Our British aristocracy does not waltz well by any means, and lacks lightness generally; but it may gratify and encourage some of its members to hear that Peter Ibbetson (ex-private soldier, architect and surveyor, convict and criminal lunatic), who has had unrivalled opportunities for

mixing with the cream of European society, considers our British aristocracy quite the best-looking, best-dressed, and best-behaved aristocracy of them all, and the most sensible and the least exclusive—perhaps the most sensible *because* the least exclusive.

It often snubs, but does not altogether repulse, those gifted and privileged outsiders who (just for the honor and glory of the thing) are ever so ready to flatter and instruct and amuse it, and run its errands, and fetch and carry, and tumble for its pleasure, and even to marry such of its "ugly ducklings" (or shall we say such of its "unprepossessing cygnets?") as cannot hope to mate with birds of their own feather.

For it has the true English eye for physical beauty.

Indeed, it is much given to throw the handkerchief—successfully, of course—and, most fortunately for itself, beyond the pale of its own narrow precincts—nay, beyond the broad Atlantic, even, to the land where beauty and dollars are to be found in such happy combination.

Nor does it disdain the comeliness of the daughters of Israel, nor their shekels, nor their brains, nor their ancient and most valuable blood. It knows the secret virtue of that mechanical transfusion of fluids familiar to science under the name of "endosmoses" and "exosmoses" (I hope I have spelled them rightly), and practises the same. Whereby it shows itself wise in its generation, and will endure the longer, which cannot be very long.

Peter Ibbetson (etc., etc.), for one, wishes it no manner of harm.

* * * * *

But to return. With all these temptations of travel and amusement and society and the great world, such was our insatiable fondness for "the pretty place of our childhood" and all its associations, that our greatest pleasure of all was to live our old life over again and again, and make Gogo and Mimsey and our parents and cousins and M. le Major go through their old paces once more; and to recall *new* old paces for them, which we were sometimes able to do, out of stray forgotten bits of the past; to hunt for which was the most exciting sport in the world.

Our tenderness for these beloved shades increased with familiarity. We could see all the charm and goodness and kindness of these dear fathers and mothers of ours with the eyes of matured experience, for we were pretty much of an age with them now; no other children could ever say as much since the world began, and how few young parents could bear such a scrutiny as ours!

Ah! what would we not have given to extort just a spark of recognition, but that was impossible; or to have been able to whisper just a word of warning, which would have averted the impending strokes of inexorable fate! They might have been alive now, perhaps—old indeed, but honored and loved as no parents ever were before. How different everything would have been! Alas! alas!

And of all things in the world, we never tired of that walk through the avenue and park and Bois de Boulogne to the Mare d'Auteuil; strolling there leisurely on an early spring afternoon, just in time to spend a mid-summer hour or two on its bank, and watch the old water-rat and the dytiscus and the tadpoles and newts, and see the frogs jump; and then walking home at dusk in the late autumn for tea and roast chestnuts in the school-room of my old home; and then back to warm, well-lighted "Magna sed Apta" by moonlight, through the avenue on New Year's Eve, ankle-deep in snow; all in a few short hours.

Dream winds and dream weathers—what an enchantment! And all real!

Soft caressing rains that do not wet us if we do not wish them to; sharp frosts that brace but never chill; blazing suns that neither scorch nor dazzle.

Blustering winds of early spring, that seem to sweep right through these solid frames of ours, and thrill us to the very marrow with the old heroic excitement and ecstasy we knew so well in happy childhood, but can no longer feel now when awake!

Bland summer breezes, heavy with the scent of long-lost French woods and fields and gardens in full flower; swift, soft, moist equinoctial gales, blowing from the far-off orchards of Meudon, or the old market gardens of Suresnes in their autumnal decay, and laden, we do not know why, with strange, mysterious, troubling reminiscence too subtle and elusive to be expressed in any tongue—too sweet for any words! And then the dark December wind that comes down from the north, and brings the short, early twilights and the snow, and drives us home, pleasantly shivering, to the chimney-corner and the hissing logs—*chez nous!*

It is the last night of an old year—*la veille du jour de l'an.*

Ankle-deep in snow, we walk to warm, well-lighted "Magna sed Apta," up the moonlit avenue. It is dream snow, and yet we feel it crunch beneath our feet; but if we turn to look, the tracks of our footsteps have disappeared—and we cast no shadows, though the moon is full!

M. le Major goes by, and Yverdon the postman, and Père François, with his big sabots, and others, and their footprints remain—and their shadows are strong and sharp!

They wish each other the compliments of the season as they meet and pass; they wish us nothing! We give them *la bonne année* at the tops of our voices; they do not heed us in the least, though our voices are as resonant as theirs. We are wishing them a "Happy New Year," that dawned for good or evil nearly twenty years ago.

Out comes Gogo from the Seraskiers', with Mimsey. He makes a snowball and throws it. It flies straight through me, and splashes itself on Père François's broad back. "Ah, ce polisson de Monsieur Gogo . . . attendez un peu!" and Père François returns the compliment—straight through me again, as it seems; and I do not even feel it! Mary and I are as solid to each other as flesh and blood can make us. We cannot even touch these dream people without their melting away into thin air; we can only hear and see them, but that in perfection!

There goes that little André Corbin, the poulterer's son, running along the slippery top of Madame Pelé's garden wall, which is nearly ten feet high.

"Good heavens," cries Mary, "stop him! Don't you remember? When he gets to the corner he'll fall down and break both his legs!"

I rush and bellow out to him—

"Descends donc, malheureux; tu vas te casser les deux jambes! Saute!

"MAMAN M'A DONNÉ QUAT' SOUS POUR M'EN ALLER À LA FOIRE . . ."

saute!" . . . I cry, holding out my arms. He does not pay the slightest attention: he reaches the corner, followed low down by Gogo and Mimsey, who are beside themselves with generous envy and admiration. Stimulated by their applause, he becomes more foolhardy than ever, and even tries to be droll, and standing on one leg, sings a little song that begins—

> *"Maman m'a donné quat' sous*
> *Pour m'en aller à la foire,*
> *Non pas pour manger ni boire,*
> *Mais pour m'régaler d'joujoux!"*

Then suddenly down he slips, poor boy, and breaks both his legs below the knee on an iron rail, whereby he becomes a cripple for life.

All this sad little tragedy of a New-year's Eve plays itself anew. The sympathetic crowd collects; Mimsey and Gogo weep; the heart-broken parents arrive, and the good little doctor Larcher; and Mary and I look on like criminals, so impossible it seems not to feel that we might have prevented it all!

We two alone are alive and substantial in all this strange world of shadows, who seem, as far as we can hear and see, no less substantial and alive than ourselves. They exist for us; we do not exist for them. We exist for each other only, waking or sleeping; for even the people among whom our waking life is spent know hardly more of us, and what our real existence is, than poor little André Corbin, who has just broken his legs for us over again!

And so, back to "Magna sed Apta," both saddened by this deplorable misadventure, to muse and talk and marvel over these wonders; penetrated to the very heart's core by a dim sense of some vast, mysterious power, latent in the sub-consciousness of man—unheard of, undreamed of as yet, but linking him with the Infinite and the Eternal.

And how many things we always had to talk about besides!

Heaven knows, I am not a brilliant conversationalist, but she was the most easily amusable person in the world—interested in everything that interested me, and I disdamaged myself (to use one of her Anglo-Gallicisms) of the sulky silence of years.

Of her as a companion it is not for me to speak. It would be impertinent, and even ludicrous, for a person in my position to dilate on the social gifts of the famous Duchess of Towers.

MARY, DUCHESS OF TOWERS
From a photograph by Strlkzchuski, Warsaw

Incredible as it may appear, however, most of our conversation was about very common and earthly topics—her homes and refuges, the difficulties of their management, her eternal want of money, her many schemes and plans and experiments and failures and disenchantments—in all of which I naturally took a very warm interest. And then my jail, and all that occurred there—in all of which I became interested myself because it interested her so passionately; she knew every corner of it that I knew, every detail of the life there — the name, appearance, and history of almost every inmate, and criticised its internal economy with a practical knowledge of affairs, a business-like sagacity at which I never ceased to marvel.

One of my drollest recollections is of a visit she paid there *in the flesh*, accompanied by some famous philanthropists of both sexes. I was interviewed by them all as the model prisoner, who, but for his unorthodoxy, was a credit to the institution. She listened demurely to my intelligent answers when I was questioned as to my bodily health, etc., and asked whether I had any complaints to make. Complaints! Never was jail-bird so thoroughly satisfied with his nest — so healthy, so happy, so well-behaved. She took notes all the time.

Eight hours before we had been strolling hand in hand through the Uffizi Gallery in Florence; eight hours later we should be in each other's arms.

* * * * *

Strange to relate, this happiness of ours — so deep, so acute, so transcendent, so unmatched in all the history of human affection — was not always free of unreasonable longings and regrets. Man is never so blessed but what he would have his blessedness still greater.

The reality of our close companionship, of our true possession of each other (during our allotted time), was absolute, complete, and thorough. No Darby that ever lived can ever have had sweeter, warmer, more tender memories of any Joan than I have now of Mary Seraskier! Although each was, in a way, but a seeming illusion of the other's brain, the illusion was no illusion for us. It was an illusion that showed the truth, as does the illusion of sight. Like twin kernels in one shell ("Philipschen," as Mary called it), we touched at more points and were closer than the rest of mankind (with each of them a separate shell of his own). We tried and tested this in every way we could devise, and never found ourselves at fault, and never ceased to marvel at so great a wonder. For instance, I received letters from her in jail (and answered them) in an intricate cipher we had invented and perfected together entirely during sleep, and referring to things that had happened to us both when together.*

Our privileges were such as probably no human beings could have ever enjoyed before. Time and space were annihilated for us at the mere wish of either—we lived in a palace of delight; all conceivable luxuries were ours—and, better than all, and perennially, such freshness and elation as belong only to the morning of life—and such a love for each other (the result of circumstances not to be paralleled) as time could never slake or quench till death should come and part us. All this, and more, was our portion for eight hours out of every twenty-four.

So what must we do sometimes, but fret that the sixteen hours which remained did not belong to us as well; that we must live two-thirds of our lives apart; that we could not share the toils and troubles of our work-a-day, waking existence, as we shared the blissful guerdon of our seeming sleep—the glories of our common dream.

And then we would lament the lost years we had spent in mutual ignorance and separation—a deplorable waste of life; when life, sleeping or waking, was so short.

How different things might have been with us had we but known!

We need never have lost sight and touch of each other; we might have grown up, and learned and worked and struggled together from the first—boy and girl, brother and sister, lovers, man and wife—and yet have found our blessed dream-land and dwelt in it just the same.

Children might have been born to us! Sweet children, *beaux comme le jour*, as in Madame Perrault's fairy tales; even beautiful and good as their mother.

*Note. — *Several of these letters are in my possession.*

Madge Plunket

And as we talked of these imaginary little beings and tried to picture them, we felt in ourselves such a stupendous capacity for loving the same that we would fall to weeping on each other's shoulders. Full well I knew, even as if they had formed part of my own personal experience, all the passion and tenderness, all the wasted anguish of her brief, ill-starred motherhood: the very ache of my jealousy that she should have borne a child to another man was forgotten in that keen and thorough comprehension! Ah, yes . . . that hungry love, that woful pity, which not to know is hardly quite to have lived! Childless as I am (though old enough to be a grandfather) I have it all by heart!

Never could we hope for son or daughter of our own. For us the blessed flower of love in rich, profuse, unfading bloom; but its blessed fruit of life, never, never, never!

Our only children were Mimsey and Gogo, between whom and ourselves was an impassable gulf, and who were unconscious of our very existence, except for Mimsey's strange consciousness that a Fairy Tarapatapoum and a Prince Charming were watching over them.

All this would always end, as it could not but end, in our realizing the more fully our utter dependence on each other for all that made life not only worth living, ingrates that we were, but a heaven on earth for us both; and, indeed, we could not but recognize that merely thus to love and be loved was in itself a thing so immense (without all the other blessings we had) that we were fain to tremble at our audacity in daring to wish for more.

* * * * *

Thus sped three years, and would have sped all the rest, perhaps, but for an incident that made an epoch in our joint lives, and turned all our thoughts and energies in a new direction.

PART SIX

PART SIX

Some petty annoyance to which I had been subjected by one of the prison authorities had kept me awake for a little while after I had gone to bed, so that when at last I awoke in "Magna sed Apta," and lay on my couch there (with that ever-fresh feeling of coming to life in heaven after my daily round of work in an earthly jail), I was conscious that Mary was there already, making coffee, the fragrance of which filled the room, and softly humming a tune as she did so—a quaint, original, but most beautiful tune, that thrilled me with indescribable emotion, for I had never heard it with the bodily ear before, and yet it was as familiar to me as "God save the Queen."

As I listened with rapt ears and closed eyes, wonderful scenes passed before my mental vision: the beautiful white-haired lady of my childish dreams, leading a small *female* child by the hand, and that child was myself; the pigeons and their tower, the stream and the water-mill; the white-haired young man with red heels to his shoes; a very fine lady, very tall, stout, and middle-aged, magnificently dressed in brocaded silk; a park with lawns and alleys and trees cut into trim formal shapes; a turreted castle—all kinds of charming scenes and people of another age and country.

"What on earth is that wonderful tune, Mary?" I exclaimed, when she had finished it.

"It's my favorite tune," she answered; "I seldom hum it for fear of wearing away its charm. I suppose that is why you have never heard it before. Isn't it lovely? I've been trying to lull you awake with it.

"My grandfather, the violinist, used to play it with variations of his own, and made it famous in his time; but it was never published, and it's now forgotten.

"It is called 'Le Chant du Triste Commensal,' and was composed by his grandmother, a beautiful French woman, who played the fiddle too; but not as a profession. He remembered her playing it when he was a child and she was quite an old lady, just as I remember *his* playing it when I was a girl in Vienna, and he was a white-haired old man. She used to play holding her fiddle downward, on her knee, it seems; and always played in perfect tune, quite in the middle of the note, and with excellent taste and expression; it was her playing that decided his career. But she was like 'Single-speech Hamilton,' for this was the only thing she ever composed. She composed it under great grief and excitement, just after her husband had died from the bite of a wolf, and just before the birth of her twin-daughters — her only children — one of whom was my great-grandmother."

"And what was this wonderful old lady's name?"

"Gatienne Aubéry; she married a Breton squire called Budes, who was a *gentilhomme verrier* near St. Prest, in Anjou — that is, he made glass — decanters, water-bottles, tumblers, and all that, I suppose — in spite of his nobility. It was not considered derogatory to do so; indeed, it was the only trade permitted to the *noblesse*, and one had to be at least a squire to engage in it.

"She was a very notable woman, *la belle Verrière*, as she was called; and she managed the glass factory for many years after her husband's death, and made lots of money for her two daughters."

"How strange!" I exclaimed; "Gatienne Aubéry! Dame du Brail — Budes — the names are quite familiar to me. Mathurin Budes, Seigneur de Monhoudéard et de Verny le Moustier."

"Yes, that's it. How wonderful that you should know! One daughter, Jeanne, married my great-grandfather, an officer in the Hungarian army; and Seraskier, the fiddler, was their only child. The other (so like her sister that only her mother could distinguish them) was called Anne, and married a Comte de Bois something."

"Boismorinel. Why, all those names are in my family too. My father used to make me paint their arms and quarterings when I was a child, on Sunday mornings, to keep me quiet. Perhaps we are related by blood, you and I."

"Oh, that would be too delightful!" said Mary. "I wonder how we could find out? Have you no family papers?"

I. "There were lots of them, in a horse-hair trunk, but I don't know where they are now. What good would family papers have been to me? Ibbetson took charge of them when I changed my name. I suppose his lawyers have got them."

She. "Happy thought; we will do without lawyers. Let us go round to your old house, and make Gogo paint the quarterings over again for us, and look over his shoulder."

Happy thought, indeed! We drank our coffee and went straight to my old house, with the wish (immediate father to the deed) that Gogo should be there, once more engaged in his long-forgotten accomplishment of painting coats of arms.

It was a beautiful Sunday morning, and we found Gogo hard at work at a small table by an open window. The floor was covered with old deeds and parchments and family papers; and le beau Pasquier, at another table, was deep in his own pedigree, making notes on the margin—an occupation in which he delighted—and unconsciously humming as he did so. The sunny room was filled with the penetrating soft sound of his voice, as a conservatory is filled with the scent of its flowers.

By the strangest inconsistency my dear father, a genuine republican at heart (for all his fancied loyalty to the white lily of the Bourbons), a would-be scientist, who in reality was far more impressed by a clever and industrious French mechanic than by a prince (and would, I think, have preferred the former's friendship and society), yet took both a pleasure and a pride in his quaint old parchments and obscure quarterings. So would I, perhaps, if things had gone differently with me—for what true democrat, however intolerant of such weakness in others, ever thinks lightly of his own personal claims to aristocratic descent, shadowy as these may be!

He was fond of such proverbs and aphorisms as "noblesse oblige," "bon sang ne sait mentir," "bon chien chasse de race," etc., and had even in-

vented a little aphorism of his own, to comfort him when he was extra hard up, "bon gentilhomme n'a jamais honte de la misère." All of which sayings, to do him justice, he reserved for home consumption exclusively, and he would have been the first to laugh on hearing them in the mouth of any one else.

Of his one great gift, the treasure in his throat, he thought absolutely nothing at all.

"Ce que c'est que de nous!"

Gogo was coloring the quarterings of the Pasquier family—*la maison de Pasquier*, as it was called—in a printed book (*Armorial Général du Maine et de l'Anjou*), according to the instructions that were given underneath. He used one of Madame Liard's three-sou boxes, and the tints left much to be desired.

We looked over his shoulder and read the picturesque old jargon, which sounds even prettier and more comforting and more idiotic in French than in English. It ran thus—

"Pasquier (branche des Seigneurs de la Marière et du Hirel), party de 4 pièces et coupé de 2.

"Au premier, de Hérault, qui est écartelé de gueules et d'argent.

"Au deux, de Budes, qui est d'or au pin de sinople.

"Au trois, d'Aubéry—qui est d'azur à trois croissants d'argent.

"Au quatre, de Busson, qui est d'argent au lyon de sable armé couronné et lampassé d'or." And so on, through the other quarterings: Bigot, Épinay, Malestroit, Mathefelon. And finally, "Sur le tout, de Pasquier qui est d'or à trois lyons d'azur, au franc quartier écartelé des royaumes de Castille et de Léon."

Presently my mother came home from the English chapel in the Rue Marbœuf, where she had been with Sarah, the English maid. Lunch was announced, and we were left alone with the family papers. With infinite precautions, for fear of blurring the dream, we were able to find what we wanted to find—namely, that we were the great-great-grandchildren and only possible living descendants of Gatienne, the fair glassmaker and composer of "Le Chant du Triste Commensal."

Thus runs the descent—

Jean Aubéry, Seigneur du Brail, married Anne Busson. His daughter, Gatienne Aubéry, Dame du Brail, married Mathurin Budes, Seigneur de Verny le Moustier et de Monhoudéard.

Anne Budes, Dame de Verny le Moustier, married Guy Hérault, Comte de Boismorinel.	Jeanne Budes, Dame du Brail et de Monhoudéard, married Ulric Seraskier.
Jeanne Françoise Hérault de Boismorinel married François Pasquier de la Marière.	Otto Seraskier, violinist, married Teresa Pulci.
Jean Pasquier de la Marière married Catherine Ibbetson-Biddulph.	Johann Seraskier, M.D., married Laura Desmond.
Pierre Pasquier de la Marière (*alias* Peter Ibbetson, convict).	Mary Seraskier, Duchess of Towers.

We walked back to "Magna sed Apta" in great joy, and there we celebrated our newly-discovered kinship by a simple repast, out of *my* répertoire this time. It consisted of oysters from Rules's in Maiden Lane, when they were sixpence a dozen, and bottled stout (*l'eau m'en vient à la bouche*); and we spent the rest of the hours allotted to us that night in evolving such visions as we could from the old tune "Le Chant du Triste Commensal," with varying success; she humming it, accompanying herself on the piano in her masterly, musician-like way, with one hand, and seeing all that I saw by holding my hand with the other.

By slow degrees the scenes and people evoked grew less dim, and whenever the splendid and important lady, whom we soon identified for certain as Gatienne, our common great-great-grandmother, appeared—"la belle Verrière de Verny le Moustier"—she was more distinct than the others; no doubt, because we both had part and parcel in her individuality, and also because her individuality was so strongly marked.

And before I was called away at the inexorable hour, we had the supreme satisfaction of seeing her play the fiddle to a shadowy company of patched and powdered and bewigged ladies and gentlemen, who seemed to take much sympathetic delight in her performance, and actually, even, of just hearing the thin, unearthly tones of that most original and exquisite melody, "Le Chant du Triste Commensal," to a quite inaudible accompaniment on the spinet by her daughter, evidently Anne Hérault, Comtesse de Boismorinel (*née* Budes), while the small child Jeanne de Boismorinel (afterwards Dame Pasquier de la Marière) listened with dreamy rapture.

And, just as Mary had said, she played her fiddle with its body downward, and resting on her knees, as though it had been an undersized 'cello. I then vaguely remembered having dreamed of such a figure when a small child.

Within twenty-four hours of this strange adventure the practical and business-like Mary had started, in the flesh and with her maid, for that part of France where these, my ancestors, had lived, and within a fortnight she had made herself mistress of all my French family history, and had visited such of the different houses of my kin as were still in existence.

The turreted castle of my childish dreams, which, with the adjacent glass-factory, was still called Verny le Moustier, was one of these. She found it in the possession of a certain Count Hector du Chamorin, whose grandfather had purchased it at the beginning of the century.

He had built an entirely new plant, and made it one of the first glass-factories in Western France. But the old turreted *corps de logis* still remained, and his foreman lived there with his wife and family. The *pigeonnier* had been pulled down to make room for a shed with a steam-engine, and the whole aspect of the place was revolutionized; but the stream and water-mill (the latter a mere picturesque ruin) were still there; the stream was, however, little more than a ditch, some ten feet deep and twenty broad, with a fringe of gnarled and twisted willows and alders, many of them dead.

It was called "Le Brail," and had given its name to my great-great-grandmother's property, whence it had issued thirty miles away (and many hundred years ago); but the old Château du Brail, the manor of the Aubérys, had become a farm-house.

The Château de la Marière, in its walled park, and with its beautiful, tall, hexagonal tower, dated 1550, and visible for miles around, was now a prosperous cider brewery; it is still, and lies on the high-road from Angers to Le Mans.

The old forest of Boismorinel, that had once belonged to the family of

Hérault, was still in existence; charcoal-burners were to be found in its depths, and a stray roebuck or two; but no more wolves and wild-boars, as in the olden time. And where the old castle had been now stood the new railway station of Boismorinel et Saint Maixent.

Most of such Budes, Bussons, Héraults, Aubérys, and Pasquiers as were still to be found in the country, probably distant kinsmen of Mary's and mine, were lawyers, doctors, or priests, or had gone into trade and become respectably uninteresting; such as they were, they would scarcely have cared to claim kinship with such as I.

But a hundred years ago and more these were names of importance in Maine and Anjou; their bearers were descended for the most part from younger branches of houses which in the Middle Ages had intermarried with all there was of the best in France; and although they were looked down upon by the *noblesse* of the court and Versailles, as were all the provincial nobility, they held their own well in their own country; feasting, hunting, and shooting with each other; dancing and fiddling and making love and intermarrying; and blowing glass, and growing richer and richer, till the Revolution came and blew them and their glass into space, and with them many greater than themselves, but few better. And all record of them and of their doings, pleasant and genial people as they were, is lost, and can only be recalled by a dream.

Verny le Moustier was not the least interesting of these old manors.

It had been built three hundred years ago, on the site of a still older monastery (whence its name); the ruined walls of the old abbey were (and are) still extant in the house-garden, covered with apricot and pear and peach trees, which had been sown or planted by our common ancestress when she was a bride.

Count Hector, who took a great pleasure in explaining all the past history of the place to Mary, had built himself a fine new house in what remained of the old park, and a quarter of a mile away from the old manor-house. Every room of the latter was shown to her; old wood panels still remained, prettily painted in a by-gone fashion; old documents, and parchment deeds, and leases concerning fish-ponds, farms, and the like, were brought out for her inspection, signed by my grandfather Pasquier, my great-grandfather Boismorinel, and our great-great-grandmother and her husband, Mathurin Budes, the lord of Verny le Moustier; and the tradition of Gatienne, *la belle Verrière* (also nicknamed *la reine de Hongrie,* it seems) still lingered in the county; and many old people still remembered, more or less correctly, "Le Chant du Triste Commensal," which a hundred years ago had been in everybody's mouth.

She was said to have been the tallest and handsomest woman in Anjou, of an imperious will and very masculine character, but immensely popular among rich and poor alike; of indomitable energy, and with a finger in every pie; but always more for the good of others than her own—a typical, managing, business-like French woman, and an exquisite musician to boot.

Such was our common ancestress, from whom, no doubt, we drew our love of music and our strange, almost hysterical susceptibility to the power of sound; from whom had issued those two born nightingales of our race—Seraskier, the violinist, and my father, the singer. And, strange to say, her eyebrows met at the bridge of her nose just like mine, and from under them beamed the luminous, black-fringed, gray-blue eyes of Mary, that suffered eclipse whenever their owners laughed or smiled!

During this interesting journey of Mary's in the flesh, we met every night at "Magna sed Apta" in the spirit, as usual; and I was made to participate in every incident of it.

We sat by the magic window, and had for our entertainment, now the Verrerie de Verny le Moustier in its present state, all full of modern life, color, and sound, steam and gas, as she had seen it a few hours before; now the old château as it was a hundred years ago; dim and indistinct, as though seen by near-sighted eyes at the close of a gray, misty afternoon in late autumn through a blurred window-pane, with busy but silent shadows moving about—silent, because at first we could not hear their speech; it was too thin for our mortal ears, even in this dream within our dream! Only Gatienne, the authoritative and commanding Gatienne, was faintly audible.

Then we would go down and mix with them. Thus, at one moment, we would be in the midst of a charming old-fashioned French family group of shadows: Gatienne, with her lovely twin-daughters Jeanne and Anne, and her gardeners round her, all trailing young peach and apricot trees against what still remained of the ancient buttresses and walls of the Abbaye de Verny le Moustier—all this more than a hundred years ago—the pale sun of a long-past noon casting the fainter shadows of these faint shadows on the shadowy garden-path.

Then, presto! Changing the scene as one changes a slide in a magic-lantern, we would skip a century, and behold!

Another French family group, equally charming, on the self-same spot, but in the garb of to-day, and no longer shadowy or mute by any means. Little trees have grown big; big trees have disappeared to make place for industrious workshops and machinery; but the old abbey walls have been respected, and gay, genial father, and handsome mother, and lovely daughters, all pressing on "la belle Duchesse anglaise" peaches and apricots of her great-great-grandmother's growing.

For this amiable family of the Chamorin became devoted to Mary in a very short time—that is, the very moment they first saw her; and she never forgot their kindness, courtesy, and hospitality; they made her feel in five minutes as though she had known them for many years.

I may as well state here that a few months later she received from

Mademoiselle du Chamorin (with a charming letter) the identical violin that had once belonged to *la belle Verrière*, and which Count Hector had found in the possession of an old farmer—the great-grandson of Gatienne's coachman—and had purchased, that he might present it as a New-year's gift to her descendant, the Duchess of Towers.

It is now mine, alas! I cannot play it; but it amuses and comforts me to hold in my hand, when broad and wide awake, an instrument that Mary and I have so often heard and seen in our dream, and which has so often rung in by-gone days with the strange melody that has had so great an influence on our lives. Its aspect, shape, and color, every mark and stain of it, were familiar to us before we had ever seen it with the bodily eye or handled it with the hand of flesh. It thus came straight to us out of the dim and distant past, heralded by the ghost of itself!

*   *   *   *   *

To return. Gradually, by practice and the concentration of our united will, the old-time figures grew to gain substance and color, and their voices became perceptible; till at length there arrived a day when we could move among them, and hear them and see them as distinctly as we could our own immediate progenitors close by—as Gogo and Mimsey, as Monsieur le Major, and the rest.

The child who went about hand in hand with the white-haired lady (whose hair was only powdered) and fed the pigeons was my grandmother, Jeanne de Boismorinel (who married François Pasquier de la Marière). It was her father who wore red heels to his shoes, and made her believe she could manufacture little cocked-hats in colored glass; she had lived again in me whenever, as a child, I had dreamed that exquisite dream.

I could now evoke her at will; and, with her, many buried memories were called out of nothingness into life.

Among other wonderful things, I heard the red-heeled gentleman, M. de Boismorinel (my great-grandfather), sing beautiful old songs by Lulli and others to the spinet, which he played charmingly—a rare accomplishment in those days. And lo! these tunes were tunes that had risen oft and unbidden in my consciousness, and I had fondly imagined that I had composed them myself—little impromptus of my own. And lo, again! His voice, thin, high, nasal, but very sympathetic and musical, was that never still small voice that has been singing unremittingly for more than half a century in the unswept, ungarnished corner of my brain where all the cobwebs are.

And these cobwebs?

Well, I soon became aware, by deeply diving into my inner consciousness when awake and at my daily prison toil (which left the mind singularly clear and free), that I was full, quite full, of slight elusive reminiscences which were neither of my waking life nor of my dream-life with Mary: reminiscences of sub-dreams during sleep, and belonging to the period of my childhood and early youth; sub-dreams which no doubt had been forgotten when I woke, at which time I could only remember the surface dreams that had just preceded my waking.

Ponds, rivers, bridges, roads, and streams, avenues of trees, arbors, windmills and water-mills, corridors and rooms, church functions, village fairs, festivities, men and women and animals, all of another time and of a country where I had never set my foot, were familiar to my remembrance. I had but to dive deep enough into myself, and there they were; and when night came, and sleep, and "Magna sed Apta," I could re-evoke them all, and make them real and complete for Mary and myself.

That these subtle reminiscences were true antenatal memories was soon proved by my excursions with Mary into the past; and her experience of such reminiscences, and their corroboration, were just as my own. We have heard and seen her grandfather play the "Chant du Triste Commensal" to crowded concert-rooms, applauded to the echo by men and women long dead and buried and forgotten!

Now, I believe such reminiscences to form part of the sub-consciousness of others, as well as Mary's and mine, and that by perseverance in self-research many will succeed in reaching them—perhaps even more easily and completely than we have done.

It is something like listening for the overtones of a musical note; we do not hear them at first, though they are there, clamoring for recognition; and when at last we hear them, we wonder at our former obtuseness, so distinct are they.

Let a man with an average ear, however uncultivated, strike the C low down on a good piano-forte, keeping his foot on the loud pedal. At first he will hear nothing but the rich fundamental note C.

But let him become *expectant* of certain other notes; for instance, of the C in the octave immediately above, then the G immediately above that, then the E higher still; he will hear them all in time as clearly as the note originally struck; and, finally, a shrill little ghostly and quite importunate B flat in the treble will pulsate so loudly in his ear that he will never cease to hear it whenever that low C is sounded.

By just such a process, only with infinitely more pains (and in the end with what pleasure and surprise), will he grow aware in time of a dim, latent, antenatal experience that underlies his own personal experience of this life.

We also found that we were able not only to assist as mere spectators at such past scenes as I have described (and they were endless), but also to identify ourselves occasionally with the actors, and cease for the moment to be Mary Seraskier and Peter Ibbetson. Notably was this the case with Gatienne. We could each be Gatienne for a space (though never both of us together), and when we resumed our own personality again we carried back with it a portion of hers, never to be lost again – a strange phenomenon, if the reader will but think of it, and constituting the germ of a comparative personal immortality on earth.

At my work in prison, even, I could distinctly remember having been Gatienne; so that for the time being, Gatienne, a provincial French woman who lived a hundred years ago, was contentedly undergoing penal servitude in an English jail during the latter half of the nineteenth century.

A questionable privilege, perhaps.

But to make up for it, when she was not alive in me she could be brought to life in Mary (only in one at a time, it seemed), and travel by rail and steamer, and know the uses of gas and electricity, and read the telegrams of "our special correspondents" in the *Times*, and taste her nineteenth century under more favorable conditions.

Thus we took *la belle Verrière* by turns, and she saw and heard things she little dreamed of a hundred years ago. Besides, she was made to share in the glories of "Magna sed Apta."

And the better we knew her the more we loved her; she was a very nice person to descend from, and Mary and I were well agreed that we could not have chosen a better great-great-grandmother, and wondered what each of our seven others was like, for we had fifteen of these between us, and as many great-great-grandfathers.

Thirty great-great-grandfathers and great-great-grandmothers had made us what we were; it was no good fighting against them and the millions at their backs.

Which of them all, strong, but gentle and shy, and hating the very sight of blood, yet saw scarlet when he was roused, and thirsted for the blood of his foe?

Which of them all, passionate and tender, but proud, high-minded, and chaste, and with the world at her feet, was yet ready to "throw her cap over the windmills," and give up all for love, deeming the world well lost?

*   *   *   *   *

That we could have thus identified ourselves, only more easily and thoroughly, with our own more immediate progenitors, we felt certain enough. But after mature thought we resolved to desist from any further attempt at such transfusion of identity, for sacred reasons of discretion which the reader will appreciate.

But that this will be done some day (now the way has been made clear), and also that the inconveniences and possible abuses of such a faculty will be obviated or minimized by the ever-active ingenuity of mankind, is to my mind a foregone conclusion.

It is too valuable a faculty to be left in abeyance, and I leave the probable and possible consequences of its culture to the reader's imagination—merely pointing out to him (as an inducement to cultivate that faculty in himself) that if anything can keep us well within the thorny path that leads to happiness and virtue, it is the certainty that those who come after us will remember having been ourselves, if only in a dream—even as the newly-hatched chicken has remembered in its egg the use of eyes and ears and the rest, out of the fulness of its long antenatal experience; and more fortunate than the helpless human infant in this respect, can enter on the business and pleasures of its brief, irresponsible existence at once!

* * * * *

Wherefore, oh reader, if you be but sound in mind and body, it most seriously behooves you (not only for the sake of those who come after you, but your own) to go forth and multiply exceedingly, to marry early and much and often, and to select the very best of your kind in the opposite sex for this most precious, excellent, and blessèd purpose; that all your future reincarnations (and hers), however brief, may be many; and bring you not only joy and peace and pleasurable wonderment and recreation, but the priceless guerdon of well-earned self-approval!

For whoever remembers having once been you, wakes you for the nonce out of—nirvana, shall we say? His strength, his beauty, and his wit are yours; and the felicity he derives from them in this earthly life is for you to share, whenever this subtle remembrance of you stirs in his consciousness; and you can never quite sink back again into—nirvana, till all your future wakers shall cease to be!

It is like a little old-fashioned French game we used to play at Passy, and which is not bad for a dark, rainy afternoon: people sit all round in a circle, and each hands on to his neighbor a spill or a lucifer-match just blown out, but in which a little live spark still lingers; saying, as he does so—

"Petit bonhomme vit encore!"

And he, in whose hand the spark becomes extinct, has to pay forfeit and retire—"Hélas! petit bonhomme n'est plus! . . . Pauv' petit bonhomme!"

Ever thus may a little live spark of your own individual consciousness, when the full, quick flame of your actual life here below is extinguished, be handed down mildly incandescent to your remotest posterity. May it never quite go out—it need not! May you ever be able to say of yourself, from generation to generation, "Petit bonhomme vit encore!" and still keep one finger at least in the pleasant earthly pie!

And, reader, remember so to order your life on earth that the memory of you (like that of Gatienne, la belle Verrière de Verny le Moustier) may smell sweet and blossom in the dust—a memory pleasant to recall—to this end that its recallings and its recallers may be as numerous as filial love and ancestral pride can make them. . . .

And oh! looking *backward* (as *we* did), be tender to the failings of your forbears, who little guessed when alive that the secrets of their long-buried hearts should one day be revealed to *you!* Their faults are really your own, like the faults of your innocent, ignorant childhood, so to say, when you did not know better, as you do now; or will soon, thanks to

"Le Chant du Triste Commensal!"

*　　*　　*　　*　　*

Wherefore, also, beware and be warned in time, ye tenth transmitters of a foolish face, ye reckless begetters of diseased or puny bodies, with hearts and brains to match! Far down the corridors of time shall club-footed retri-

bution follow in your footsteps, and overtake you at every turn! Most remorselessly, most vindictively, will you be aroused, in sleepless hours of unbearable misery (future-waking nightmares), from your false, uneasy dream of death; to participate in an inheritance of woe still worse than yours — worse with all the accumulated interest of long years and centuries of iniquitous self-indulgence, and poisoned by the sting of a self-reproach that shall never cease till the last of your tainted progeny dies out, and finds his true nirvana, and yours, in the dim, forgetful depths of interstellar space!

* * * * *

And here let me most conscientiously affirm that, partly from my keen sense of the solemnity of such an appeal, and the grave responsibility I take upon myself in making it; but more especially in order to impress you, oh reader, with the full significance of this apocalyptic and somewhat minatory utterance (that it may haunt your finer sense during your midnight hours of introspective self-communion), I have done my best, my very best, to couch it in the obscurest and most unintelligible phraseology I could invent. If I have failed to do this, if I have unintentionally made any part of my meaning clear, if I have once deviated by mistake into what might almost appear like sense — mere common-sense — it is the fault of my half-French and wholly imperfect education. I am but a poor scribe!

* * * * *

Thus roughly have I tried to give an account of this, the most important of our joint discoveries in the strange new world revealed to us by chance. More than twenty years of our united lives have been devoted to the following out of this slender clew — with what surprising results will, I trust, be seen in subsequent volumes.

We have not had time to attempt the unravelling of our English ancestry as well — the Crays, and the Desmonds, the Ibbetsons, and Biddulphs, etc. — which connects us with the past history of England. The farther we got back into France, the more fascinating it became, and the easier — and the more difficult to leave.

What an unexampled experience has been ours! To think that we have seen — actually seen — *de nos propres yeux vu* — Napoleon Bonaparte himself, the arch-arbiter of the world, on the very pinnacle of his pride and power; in his little cocked hat and gray double-breasted overcoat, astride his white charger, with all his staff around him, just as he has been so often painted! Surely the most impressive, unforgettable, ineffaceable little figure in all modern history, and clothed in the most cunningly imagined make-up that ever theatrical costumier devised to catch the public eye and haunt the public memory for ages and ages yet to come!

It is a singularly new, piquant, and exciting sensation to stare in person, and as in the present, at by-gone actualities, and be able to foretell the past and remember the future all in one!

To think that we have even beheld him before he was first consul — slim and pale, his lank hair dangling down his neck and cheeks, if possible more impressive still! as innocent as a child of all that lay before him! Europe at his feet — the throne — Waterloo — St. Helena — the Iron English Duke — the pinnacle turned into a pillory so soon!

> *"O corse à cheveux plats, que la France était belle*
> *Au soleil de Messidor!"*

* * * * *

And Mirabeau and Robespierre, and Danton and Marat and Charlotte Corday! we have seen them too; and Marie Antoinette and the fish-wives, and "the beautiful head of Lamballe" (on its pike!) . . . and watched the tumbrils go by to the Place du Carrousel, and gazed at the guillotine by moonlight—silent and terror-stricken, our very hearts in our mouths. . . .

And in the midst of it all, ridiculous stray memories of Madame Tussaud would come stealing into our ghastly dream of blood and retribution, mixing up past and present and future in a manner not to be described, and making us smile through our tears!

Then we were present (several times!) at the taking of the Bastille, and indeed witnessed most of the stormy scenes of that stormy time, with our Carlyle in our hands; and often have we thought, and with many a hearty laugh, what fun it must be to write immortal histories, with never an eye-witness to contradict you!

And going further back we have haunted Versailles in the days of its splendor, and drunk our fill of all the glories of the court of Louis XIV!

What imposing ceremonials, what stupendous royal functions have we not attended—where all the beauty, wit, and chivalry of France, prostrate with reverence and awe (as in the very presence of a god), did loyal homage to the greatest monarch this world has ever seen—while we sat by, on the very steps of his throne, as he solemnly gave out his royal command! and laughed aloud under his very nose—the shallow, silly, pompous little snob—and longed to pull it! and tried to disinfect his greasy, civet-scented, full-bottomed wig with wholesome whiffs from a nineteenth-century regalia!

Nothing of that foolish but fascinating period escaped us. Town, hamlet, river, forest, and field; royal palace, princely castle, and starving peasants' hut; pulpit, stage, and salon; port, camp, and marketplace; tribunal and university; factory, shop, studio, smithy; tavern and gambling-hall and den of thieves; convent and jail, torture-chamber and gibbet-close, and what not all!

And at every successive step our once desponding, over-anxious, over-burdened latter-day souls have swelled with joy and pride and hope at the

triumphs of our own day all along the line! Yea, even though we have heard the illustrious Bossuet preach, and applauded Molière in one of his own plays, and gazed at and listened to (and almost forgiven) Racine and Corneille, and Boileau and Fénélon, and the good La Fontaine—those five ruthless persecutors of our own innocent French childhood!

And still ascending the stream of time, we have hobnobbed with Montaigne and Rabelais, and been personally bored by Malherbe, and sat at Ronsard's feet, and ridden by Froissart's side, and slummed with François Villon—in what enchanted slums! . . .

François Villon! Think of that, ye fond British bards and bardlets of today—ye would-be translators and imitators of that never-to-be-translated, never-to-be-imitated lament, the immortal *Ballade des Dames du Temps jadis!*

And while I speak of it, I may as well mention that we have seen them too, or some of them—those fair ladies *he* had never seen, and who had already melted away before his coming, like the snows of yester year, *les neiges d'antan!* Bertha, with the big feet; Joan of Arc, the good Lorrainer (what would she think of her native province now!); the very learned Héloïse, for love of whom one Peter Esbaillart, or Abélard (a more luckless Peter than even I!), suffered such cruel indignities at monkish hands; and that haughty, naughty queen, in her Tower of Nesle,

> "*Qui commanda que Buridan*
> *Fut jecté en ung sac en Seine. . . .*"

Yes, we have seen them with the eye, and heard them speak and sing, and scold and jest, and laugh and weep, and even pray! And I have sketched them, as you shall see some day, good reader! And let me tell you that their beauty was by no means maddening: the standard of female loveliness has gone up, even in France! Even *la très sage Héloïse* was scarcely

worth such a sacrifice as—but there! Possess your soul in patience; all that, and it is all but endless, will appear in due time, with such descriptions and illustrations as I flatter myself the world has never bargained for, and will value as it has never valued any historical records yet!

Day after day, for more than twenty years, Mary has kept a voluminous diary (in a cipher known to us both); it is now my property, and in it every detail of our long journey into the past has been set down.

Contemporaneously, day by day (during the leisure accorded to me by the kindness of Governor ——) I have drawn over again from memory the sketches of people and places I was able to make straight from nature during those wonderful nights at "Magna sed Apta." I can guarantee the correctness of them, and the fidelity of their likenesses; no doubt their execution leaves much to be desired.

Both her task and mine (to the future publication of which this autobiography is but an introduction) have been performed with the minutest care and conscientiousness; no time or trouble have been spared. For instance, the Massacre of St. Bartholomew alone, which we were able to study from seventeen different points of view, cost us no less than two months' unremitting labor.

As we reached further and further back through the stream of time, the task became easier in a way; but we have had to generalize more, and often, for want of time and space, to use types in lieu of individuals. For with every successive generation the number of our progenitors increased in geometrical progression (as in the problem of the nails in the horseshoe) until a limit of numbers was reached—namely, the sum of the inhabitants of the terrestrial globe. In the seventh century there was not a person living in France (not to mention Europe) who was not in the line of our direct ancestry, excepting, of course, those who had died without issue and were mere collaterals.

We have even just been able to see, as in a glass darkly, the faint shadows of the Mammoth and the cave bear, and of the man who hunted and killed and ate them, that he might live and prevail.

The Mammoth!

We have walked round him and under him as he browsed, and even *through* him where he lay and rested, as one walks through the dun mist in a little hollow on a still, damp morning; and turning round to look (at the proper distance) there was the unmistakable shape again, just thick enough to blot out the lines of the dim primeval landscape beyond, and make a hole in the blank sky. A dread silhouette, thrilling our hearts with awe—blurred and indistinct like a composite photograph—merely the *type*, as it had been seen generally by all who had ever seen it at all, every one of whom (*exceptis excipiendis*) was necessarily an ancestor of ours, and of every man now living.

There it stood or reclined, the monster, like the phantom of an overgrown hairy elephant; we could almost see, or fancy we saw, the expression of his dull, cold, antediluvian eye—almost perceive a suggestion of russet-brown in his fell.

Mary firmly believed that we should have got in time to our hairy ancestor with pointed ears and a tail, and have been able to ascertain whether he was arboreal in his habits or not. With what passionate interest she would have followed and studied and described him! And I! With what eager joy, and yet with what filial reverence, I would have sketched his likeness—with what conscientious fidelity as far as my poor powers would allow! (For all we know to the contrary he may have been the most attractive and engaging little beast that ever was, and far less humiliating to descend from than many a titled yahoo of the present day.)

Fate, alas, has willed that it should be otherwise, and on others, duly trained, must devolve the delightful task of following up the clew we have been so fortunate as to discover.

* * * * *

And now the time has come for me to tell as quickly as I may the story of my bereavement—a bereavement so immense that no man, living or dead, can ever have experienced the like; and to explain how it is that I have not only survived it and kept my wits (which some people seem to doubt), but am here calmly and cheerfully writing my reminiscences, just as if I were a famous Academician, actor, novelist, statesman, or general diner-out—blandly garrulous and well-satisfied with myself and the world.

During the latter years of our joint existence Mary and I, engrossed by

our fascinating journey through the centuries, had seen little or nothing of each other's outer lives, or rather I had seen nothing of hers (for she still came back sometimes with me to my jail); I only saw her as she chose to appear in our dream.

Perhaps at the bottom of this there may have been a feminine dislike on her part to be seen growing older, for at "Magna sed Apta" we were always twenty-eight or thereabouts—at our very best. We had truly discovered the fountain of perennial youth, and had drunk thereof! And in our dream we always felt even younger than we looked; we had the buoyancy of children and their freshness.

Often had we talked of death and separation and the mystery beyond, but only as people do for whom such contingencies are remote; yet in reality time flew as rapidly for us as for others, although we were less sensible of its flight.

There came a day when Mary's exuberant vitality, so constantly overtaxed, broke down, and she was ill for a while; although that did not prevent our meeting as usual, and there was no perceptible difference in her when we met. But I am certain that in reality she was never quite the same again as she had been, and the dread possibility of parting any day would come up oftener in our talk; in our minds, only too often, and our minds were as one.

She knew that if I died first, everything I had brought into "Magna sed Apta" (and little it was) would be there no more; even to my body, ever lying supine on the couch by the enchanted window, if she had woke by chance to our common life before I had, or remained after I had been summoned away to my jail.

And I knew that, if she died, not only her body on the adjacent couch, but all "Magna sed Apta" itself would melt away, and be as if it had never been, with its endless galleries and gardens and magic windows, and all the wonders it contained.

Sometimes I felt a hideous nervous dread, on sinking into sleep, lest I should find it was so, and the ever-heavenly delight of waking there, and finding all as usual, was but the keener. I would kneel by her inanimate body, and gaze at her with a passion of love that seemed made up of all the different kinds of love a human being can feel; even the love of a dog for his mistress was in it, and that of a wild beast for its young.

With eager, tremulous anxiety and aching suspense I would watch for the first light breath from her lips, the first faint tinge of carmine in her cheek, that always heralded her coming back to life. And when she opened her eyes and smiled, and stretched her long young limbs in the joy of waking, what transports of gratitude and relief!

Ah me! the recollection!

*   *   *   *   *

At last a terrible unforgettable night arrived when my presentiment was fulfilled.

I awoke in the little lumber-room of "Parva sed Apta," where the door had always been that led to and from our palace of delight; but there was no door any longer—nothing but a blank wall. . . .

I woke back at once in my cell, in such a state as it is impossible to describe. I felt there must be some mistake, and after much time and effort was able to sink into sleep again, but with the same result: the blank wall, the certainty that "Magna sed Apta" was closed forever, that Mary was dead; and then the terrible jump back into my prison life again.

This happened several times during the night, and when the morning dawned I was a raving madman. I took the warder who first came (attracted by my cries of "Mary!") for Colonel Ibbetson, and tried to kill him, and should have done so, but that he was a very big man, almost as powerful as myself and only half my age.

Other warders came to the rescue, and I took them all for Ibbetsons, and fought like the maniac I was.

When I came to myself, after long horrors and brain-fever and what not, I was removed from the jail infirmary to another place, where I am now.

I had suddenly recovered my reason, and woke to mental agony such as I, who had stood in the dock and been condemned to a shameful death, had never even dreamed of.

I soon had the knowledge of my loss confirmed, and heard (it had been common talk for more than nine days) that the famous Mary, Duchess of Towers, had met her death at the —— station of the Metropolitan Railway.

A woman, carrying a child, had been jostled by a tipsy man just as a train was entering the station, and dropped her child onto the metals. She tried to jump after it but was held back, and Mary, who had just come up, jumped in her stead, and by a miracle of strength and agility was just

able to clutch the child and get onto the six-foot way as the engine came by.

She was able to carry the child to the end of the train, and was helped onto the platform. It was her train, and she got into a carriage, but she was dead before it reached the next station. Her heart (which, it seems, had been diseased for some time) had stopped, and all was over.

So died Mary Seraskier, at fifty-three.

* * * * *

I lay for many weeks convalescent in body, but in a state of dumb, dry, tearless despair, to which there never came a moment's relief, except in the dreamless sleep I got from chloral, which was given to me in large quantities—and then, the *waking!*

I never spoke nor answered a question, and hardly ever stirred. I had one fixed idea—that of self-destruction; and after two unsuccessful attempts, I was so closely bound and watched night and day that any further attempt was impossible. They would not trust me with a toothpick or a button or a piece of common packthread.

I tried to starve myself to death and refused all solid food; but an intolerable thirst (perhaps artificially brought on) made it impossible for me to refuse any liquid that was offered, and I was tempted with milk, beef-tea, port, and sherry, and these kept me alive. . . .

* * * * *

I had lost all wish to dream.

At length, one afternoon, a strange, inexplicable, overwhelming nostalgic desire came over me to see once more the Mare d'Auteuil—only once; to walk thither for the last time through the Chaussée de la Muette, and by the fortifications.

It grew upon me till it became a torture to wait for bedtime, so frantic was my impatience.

When the long-wished-for hour arrived at last, I laid myself down once more (as nearly as I could for my bonds) in the old position I had not tried for so long; my will intent upon the Porte de la Muette, an old stone gateway that separated the Grande Rue de Passy from the entrance to the Bois de Boulogne—a kind of Temple Bar.

It was pulled down forty-five years ago.

I soon found myself there, just where the Grande Rue meets the Rue de la Pompe, and went through the arch and looked towards the Bois.

It was a dull, leaden day in autumn; few people were about, but a gay *repas de noces* was being held at a little restaurant on my right-hand side. It was to celebrate the wedding of Achille Grigoux, the green-grocer, with Félicité Lenormand, who had been the Seraskiers' house-maid. I suddenly remembered all this, and that Mimsey and Gogo were of the party—the latter, indeed, being *premier garçon d'honneur*, on whom would soon devolve the duty of stealing the bride's garter, and cutting it up into little bits to adorn the button-holes of the male guests before the ball began.

In an archway on my left some forlorn, worn-out old rips, broken-kneed and broken-winded, were patiently waiting, ready saddled and bridled, to be hired—Chloris, Murat, Rigolette, and others: I knew and had ridden them all nearly half a century ago. Poor old shadows of the long-dead past, so life-like and real and pathetic—it "split me the heart" to see them!

A handsome young blue-coated, silver-buttoned courier of the name of Lami came trotting along from St. Cloud on a roan horse, with a great jingling of his horse's bells and clacking of his short-handled whip. He stopped at the restaurant and called for a glass of white wine, and rising in his stirrups, shouted gayly for Monsieur et Madame Grigoux. They appeared at the first-floor window, looking very happy, and he drank their

NERS
A
LA
RTE
NOC
E
FEST
DEZVOUS DES AMI
LLARD
CAF
LIQUEU
BIER
du Maurier

"À VOT' SANTÉ!"

health, and they his. I could see Gogo and Mimsey in the crowd behind them, and mildly wondered again, as I had so often wondered before, how I came to see it all from the outside—from another point of view than Gogo's.

Then the courier bowed gallantly, and said, "*Bonne chance!*" and went trotting down the Grande Rue on his way to the Tuileries, and the wedding guests began to sing: they sang a song beginning—

> "*Il était un petit navire,*
> *Qui n'avait jamais navigué. . . .*"

I had quite forgotten it, and listened till the end, and thought it very pretty; and was interested in a dull, mechanical way at discovering that it must be the original of Thackeray's famous ballad of "Little Billee," which I did not hear till many years after.

When they came to the last verse—

> "*Si cette histoire vous embête,*
> *Nous allons la recommencer,*"

I went on my way. This was my last walk in dreamland, perhaps, and dream-hours are uncertain, and I would make the most of them, and look about me.

I walked towards Ranelagh, a kind of casino, where they used to give balls and theatrical performances on Sunday and Thursday nights (and where afterwards Rossini spent the latter years of his life; then it was pulled down, I am told, to make room for many smart little villas).

In the meadow opposite M. Érard's park, Saindou's school-boys were playing rounders—*la balle au camp*—from which I concluded it was a Thursday afternoon, a half-holiday; if they had had clean shirts on (which they had not) it would have been Sunday, and the holiday a whole one.

I knew them all, and the two *pions*, or ushers, M. Lartigue and *le petit Cazal;* but no longer cared for them or found them amusing or interesting in the least.

Opposite the Ranelagh a few old hackney-coachmen were pacifically killing time by a game of *bouchon*—knocking sous off a cork with other sous—great fat sous and double sous long gone out of fashion. It is a very good game, and I watched it for a while and envied the long-dead players.

Close by was a small wooden shed, or *baraque*, prettily painted and glazed, and ornamented at the top with little tricolor flags; it belonged to a couple of old ladies, Mère Manette and Grand'mère Manette—the two oldest women ever seen. They were very keen about business, and would not give credit for a centime—not even to English boys. They were said to be immensely rich and quite alone in the world. How very dead they must be now! I thought. And I gazed at them and wondered at their liveliness and the pleasure they took in living. They sold many things: nougat, *pain d'épices*, mirlitons, hoops, drums, noisy battledoors and shuttlecocks; and little ten-sou hand-mirrors, neatly bound in zinc, that could open and shut.

I looked at myself in one of these that was hanging outside; I was old and worn and gray—my face badly shaven—my hair almost white. I had never been old in a dream before.

I walked through the gate in the fortifications on to the outer Talus (which was quite bare in those days), in the direction of the Mare d'Auteuil. The place seemed very deserted and dull for a Thursday. It was a sad and sober walk; my melancholy was not to be borne—my heart was utterly broken, and my body so tired I could scarcely drag myself along. Never before had I known in a dream what it was to be tired.

I gazed at the famous fortifications in all their brand-new pinkness, the scaffoldings barely removed—some of them still lying in the dry ditch between—and smiled to think how little these brick and granite walls

would avail to keep the Germans out of Paris thirty years later (twenty years ago). I tried to throw a stone across the narrow part, and found I could no longer throw stones; so I sat down and rested. How thin my legs were! and how miserably clad—in old prison trousers, greasy, stained, and frayed, and ignobly kneed—and what boots!

Never had I been shabby in a dream before.

Why could not I, once for all, walk round to the other side, and take a header *à la hussarde* off those lofty bulwarks, and kill myself for good and all? Alas! I should only blur the dream, and perhaps even wake in my miserable strait-waistcoat. And I wanted to see the *mare* once more, very badly.

This set me thinking. I would fill my pockets with stones, and throw myself into the Mare d'Auteuil after I had taken a last good look at it, and around. Perhaps the shock of emotion, in my present state of weakness,

might really kill me in my sleep. Who knows? it was worth trying, anyhow.

I got up and dragged myself to the *mare*. It was deserted but for one solitary female figure, soberly clad in black and gray, that sat motionless on the bench by the old willow.

I walked slowly round in her direction, picking up stones and putting them into my pockets, and saw that she was gray-haired and middle-aged, with very dark eyebrows, and extremely tall, and that her magnificent eyes were following me.

Then, as I drew nearer, she smiled and showed gleaming white teeth, and her eyes crinkled and nearly closed up as she did so.

"Oh, my God!" I shrieked; "it is Mary Seraskier!"

* * * * *

I ran to her—I threw myself at her feet, and buried my face in her lap, and there I sobbed like a hysterical child, while she tried to soothe me as one soothes a child.

After a while I looked up into her face. It was old and worn and gray, and her hair nearly white, like mine. I had never seen her like that before; she had always been eight-and-twenty. But age became her well—she looked so benignly beautiful and calm and grand that I was awed—and quick, chill waves went down my backbone.

Her dress and bonnet were old and shabby; her gloves had been mended—old kid gloves with fur about the wrists. She drew them off, and took my hands and made me sit beside her, and looked at me for a while with all her might in silence.

At length she said: "Gogo mio, I know all you have been through by the touch of your hands. Does the touch of mine tell you nothing?"

It told me nothing but her huge love for me, which was all I cared for, and I said so.

She sighed, and said: "I was afraid it would be like this. The old circuit is broken, and can't be restored—not yet!"

We tried again hard; but it was useless.

She looked round and about and up at the treetops, everywhere; and then at me again, with great wistfulness, and shivered, and finally began to speak; with hesitation at first, and in a manner foreign to her. But soon she became apparently herself, and found her old swift smile and laugh, her happy slight shrugs and gestures, and quaint polyglot colloquialisms (which I omit, as I cannot always spell them); her homely, simple ways of speech, her fluent, magnetic energy, the winning and sympathetic modulations of her voice, its quick humorous changes from grave to gay—all that made everything she said so suggestive of all she wanted to say besides.

"Gogo, I knew you would come. I *wished* it! How dreadfully you have suffered! How thin you are! It shocks me to see you! But that will not be any more; we are going to change all that.

"Gogo, you have no idea how difficult it has been for me to come back, even for a few short hours, for I can't hold on very long. It is like hanging on to the window-sill by one's wrists. This time it is Hero swimming to Leander, or Juliet climbing up to Romeo.

"Nobody has ever come back before.

"I am but a poor husk of my former self, put together at great pains for you to know me by. I could not make myself again what I have always been to you. I had to be content with this, and so must you. These are the clothes I died in. But you knew me directly, dear Gogo.

"I have come a long way—such a long way—to have an *abboccamento* with you. I had so many things to say. And now we are both here, hand in hand as we used to be, I can't even understand what they were; and if I could, I couldn't make *you* understand. But you will know some day, and there is no hurry whatever.

"Every thought you have had since I died, I know already; *your* share of the circuit is unbroken at least. I know now why you picked up those stones and put them in your pockets. You must never think of *that* again—you never will. Besides, it would be of no use, poor Gogo!"

Then she looked up at the sky and all round her again, and smiled in her old happy manner, and rubbed her eyes with the backs of her hands, and seemed to settle herself for a good long talk—an *abboccamento!*

* * * * *

Of all she said I can only give a few fragments—whatever I can recall and understand when awake. Wherever I have forgotten I will put a line of little dots. Only when I sleep and dream can I recall and understand the rest. It seems all very simple then. I often say to myself, "I will fix it well in my mind, and put it into well-chosen words—*her* words—and learn them by heart; and then wake cautiously and remember them, and write them all down in a book, so that they shall do for others all they have done for me, and turn doubt into happy certainty, and despair into patience and hope and high elation."

But the bell rings and I wake, and my memory plays me false. Nothing remains but the knowledge *that all will be well for us all, and of such a kind that those who do not sigh for the moon will be well content.*

Alas, this knowledge: I cannot impart it to others. Like many who have lived before me, I cannot prove—I can only affirm. . . .

* * *

"How odd and old-fashioned it feels," she began, "to have eyes and ears again, and all that—little open windows on to what is near us. They are very clumsy contrivances! I had already forgotten them.

* * *

"Look, there goes our old friend, the water-rat, under the bank—the old fat father—*le bon gros père*—as we used to call him. He is only a little flat picture moving upside-down in the opposite direction across the backs of our eyes, and the farther he goes the smaller he seems. A couple of hundred yards off we shouldn't see him at all. As it is, we can only see the outside of him, and that only on one side at a time; and yet he is full of important and wonderful things that have taken millions of years to make—like us! And to see him at all we have to look straight at him—and then we can't

see what's behind us or around—and if it was dark we couldn't see anything whatever.

"Poor eyes! Little bags full of water, with a little magnifying-glass inside, and a nasturtium leaf behind—to catch the light and feel it!

"A celebrated German oculist once told papa that if his instrument-maker were to send him such an ill-made machine as a human eye, he would send it back and refuse to pay the bill. I can understand that now; and yet on earth where should we be without eyes? And afterwards where should we be if some of us hadn't once had them on earth?

* * *

"I can hear your dear voice, Gogo, with both ears. Why two ears? Why only two? What you want, or think, or feel, you try to tell me in sounds that you have been taught—English, French. If I didn't know English and French, it would be no good whatever. Language is a poor thing. You fill your lungs with wind and shake a little slit in your throat, and make mouths, and that shakes the air; and the air shakes a pair of little drums in my head—a very complicated arrangement, with lots of bones behind—and my brain seizes your meaning in the rough. What a roundabout way, and what a waste of time!

* * *

"And so with all the rest. We can't even smell straight! A dog would laugh at us—not that even a dog knows much!

"And feeling! We can feel too hot or too cold, and it sometimes makes us ill, or even kills us. But we can't feel the coming storm, or which is north and south, or where the new moon is, or the sun at midnight, or the stars at noon, or even what o'clock it is by our own measurement. We cannot even find our way home blindfolded—not even a pigeon can do that, nor a swallow, nor an owl! Only a mole, or a blind man, perhaps, feebly groping with a stick, if he has already been that way before.

"And taste! It is well said there is no accounting for it.

"And then, to keep all this going, we have to eat, and drink, and sleep, and all the rest. What a burden!

* * *

"And you and I are the only mortals that I know of who ever found a way to each other's inner being by the touch of the hands. And then we had to go to sleep first. Our bodies were miles apart; not that *that* would have made any difference, for we could never have done it waking—never; not if we hugged each other to extinction!

* * *

"Gogo, I cannot find any words to tell you *how*, for there are none in any language that *I* ever knew to tell it; but where I am it is all ear and eye and the rest in *one*, and there is, oh, how much more besides! Things a homing-pigeon has known, and an ant, and a mole, and a water-beetle, and an earthworm, and a leaf, and a root, and a magnet—even a lump of chalk, and more. One can see and smell and touch and taste a sound, as well as hear it, and *vice versa*. It is very simple, though it may not seem so to you now.

"And the sounds! Ah, what sounds! The thick atmosphere of earth is no conductor for such as *they*, and earthly ear-drums no receiver. Sound is everything. Sound and light are one.

* * *

"And what does it all mean?

"I knew what it meant when I was there—part of it, at least—and should know again in a few hours. But this poor old earth-brain of mine, which I have had to put on once more as an old woman puts on a nightcap, is like my eyes and ears. It can now only understand what is of the earth—what *you* can understand, Gogo, who are still of the earth. I forget, as one forgets an ordinary dream, as one sometimes forgets the answer to a riddle, or the last verse of a song. It is on the tip of the tongue; but there it sticks, and won't come any farther.

"Remember, it is only in your brain I am living now—your earthly brain, that has been my only home for so many happy years, as mine has been yours.

"How we have nestled!

* * *

"But this I know: one must have had them all once—brains, ears, eyes, and the rest—on earth. 'Il faut avoir passé par là!' or no after-existence for man or beast would be possible or even conceivable.

"One cannot teach a born deaf-mute how to understand a musical score, nor a born blind man how to feel color. To Beethoven, who had once heard with the ear, his deafness made no difference, nor their blindness to Homer and Milton.

"Can you make out my little parable?

* * *

"Sound and light and heat, and electricity and motion, and will and thought and remembrance, and love and hate and pity, and the desire to be born and to live, and the longing of all things alive and dead to get near each other, or to fly apart—and lots of other things besides! All that comes to the same—'C'est comme qui dirait bonnet blanc et blanc bonnet,' as Monsieur le Major used to say. 'C'est simple comme bonjour!'

"Where I am, Gogo, I can hear the sun shining on the earth and making the flowers blow, and the birds sing, and the bells peal for birth and marriage and death — happy, happy death, if you only knew — 'C'est la clef des champs!'

"It shines on moons and planets, and I can hear it, and hear the echo they give back again. The very stars are singing; rather a long way off! but it is well worth their while with such an audience as lies between us and them; and they can't help it. . . .

"I can't hear it here — not a bit — now that I've got my ears on; besides, the winds of the earth are too loud. . . .

"Ah, that *is* music, if you like; but men and women are stone-deaf to it — their ears are in the way! . . .

"Those poor unseen flat fish that live in the darkness and mud at the bottom of deep seas can't catch the music men and women make upon the earth — such poor music as it is! But if ever so faint a murmur, borne on the wings and fins of a sunbeam, reaches them for a few minutes at mid-day, and they have a speck of marrow in their spines to feel it, and no ears or eyes to come between, they are better off than any man, Gogo. Their dull existence is more blessed than his.

"But alas for them, as yet! They haven't got the memory of the eye and ear, and without that no speck of spinal marrow will avail; they must be content to wait, like you. . . .

"The blind and deaf?

"Oh yes; *là-bas*, it is all right for the poor deaf-mutes and born blind of the earth; they can remember with the past eyes and ears of all the rest. Besides, it is no longer *they*. There is no *they!* That is only a detail.

* * *

"You must try and realize that it is just as though all space between us and the sun and stars were full of little specks of spinal marrow, much too small to be seen in any microscope—smaller than anything in the world. All space is full of them, shoulder to shoulder—almost as close as sardines in a box—and there is still room for more! Yet a single drop of water would hold them all, and not be the less transparent. They all remember having been alive on earth or elsewhere, in some form or other, and each knows all the others remember. I can only compare it to that.

"Once all that space was only full of stones, rushing, whirling, meeting, and crushing together, and melting and steaming in the white-heat of their own hurry. But now there's a crop of something better than stones, I can promise you! It goes on gathering, and being garnered and mingled and sifted and winnowed—the precious, indestructible harvest of how many millions of years of life.

* * *

"And this I know: the longer and more strenuously and completely one lives one's life on earth the better for all. It is the foundation of everything. Though if men could guess what is in store for them when they die, without also knowing *that*, they would not have the patience to live—they wouldn't wait! For who would fardels bear? They would just put stones in their pockets, as you did, and make for the nearest pond.

"They mustn't!

* * *

"Nothing is lost—nothing! From the ineffable, high, fleeting thought a Shakespeare can't find words to express, to the slightest sensation of an earthworm—nothing! Not a leaf's feeling of the light, not a loadstone's sense of the pole, not a single volcanic or electric thrill of the mother earth.

"All knowledge must begin on earth for *us*. It is the most favored planet in this poor system of ours just now, and for a few short millions of years to come. There are just a couple of others, perhaps three; but they are not of great consequence. 'Il y fait trop chaud—ou pas assez!' They are failures.

"The sun, the father sun, *le bon gros père,* rains life on to the mother earth. A poor little life it was at first, as you know—grasses and moss, and little wriggling, transparent things—all stomach; it is quite true! That is what we come from—Shakespeare, and you, and I!

* * *

"After each individual death the earth retains each individual clay to be used again and again; and, as far as I can see, it rains back each individual essence to the sun—or somewhere near it—like a precious water-drop returned to the sea, where it mingles, after having been about and seen something of the world, and learned the use of five small wits—and remembering all! Yes, like that poor little exiled wandering water-drop in the pretty song your father used to sing, and which always manages to find its home at last—

> " '*Va passaggier' in fiume,*
> *Va prigionier' in fonte,*
> *Ma sempre ritorn' al mar.*'

* * *

"Or else it is as if little grains of salt were being showered into the Mare d'Auteuil, to melt and mingle with the water and each other till the Mare d'Auteuil itself was as salt as salt can be.

"Not till that Mare d'Auteuil of the sun is saturated with the salt of the earth, of earthly life and knowledge, will the purpose be complete, and then old mother earth may well dry up into a cinder like the moon; its occupation will be gone, like hers—'adieu, panier, les vendanges sont faites!'

"And as for the sun and its surrounding ocean of life—ah, that is beyond

me! but the sun will dry up, too, and its ocean of life no doubt be drawn to other greater suns. For everything seems to go on more or less in the same way, only crescendo, everywhere and forever.

*　　　*　　　*

"You must understand that it is not a bit like an ocean, nor a bit like water-drops, or grains of salt, or specks of spinal marrow; but it is only by such poor metaphors that I can give you a glimpse of what I mean, since you can no longer understand me, as you used to do on earthly things, by the mere touch of our hands.

*　　　*　　　*

"Gogo, I am the only little water-drop, the one grain of salt that has not yet been able to dissolve and melt away in that universal sea; I am the exception.

"It is as though a long, invisible chain bound me still to the earth, and I were hung at the other end of it in a little transparent locket, a kind of cage, which lets me see and hear things all round, but keeps me from melting away.

"And soon I found that this locket was made of that half of you that is still in me, so that I couldn't dissolve, because half of me wasn't dead at all; for the chain linked me to that half of myself I had left in you, so that half of me actually wasn't there to be dissolved. . . . I am getting rather mixed!

"But oh, my heart's true love, how I hugged my chain, with you at the other end of it!

"With such pain and effort as you cannot conceive, I have crept along it back to you, like a spider on an endless thread of its own spinning. Such love as mine is stronger than death indeed!

*　　　*　　　*

"I have come to tell you that we are inseparable forever, you and I, one double speck of spinal marrow — 'Philipschen!' — one little grain of salt, one drop. There is to be no parting for *us* — I can see that; but such extraordinary luck seems reserved for you and me alone up to now; and it is all our own doing.

"But not till you join me shall you and I be complete, and free to melt away in that universal ocean, and take our part, as One, in all that is to be.

"That moment — you must not hasten it by a moment. Time is nothing. I'm even beginning to believe there's no such thing; there is so little difference, *là-bas*, between a year and a day. And as for space — dear me, an inch is as good as an ell!

"Things cannot be measured like that.

"A midge's life is as long as a man's, for it has time to learn its business, and do all the harm it can, and fight, and make love, and marry, and reproduce its kind, and grow disenchanted and bored and sick and content to die — all in a summer afternoon. An average man can live to seventy years without doing much more.

"And then there are tall midges, and clever and good-looking ones, and midges of great personal strength and cunning, who can fly a little faster and a little farther than the rest, and live an hour longer to drink a whole drop more of some other creature's blood; but it does not make a very great difference!

* * *

"No, time and space mean just the same as 'nothing.'

"But for you they mean much, as you have much to do. Our joint life must be revealed — that long, sweet life of make-believe, that has been so much more real than reality. Ah! where and what were time or space to us then?

* * *

"And you must tell all we have found out, and how; the way must be shown to others with better brains and better training than *we* had. The value to mankind—to mankind here and hereafter—may be incalculable.

* * *

"For some day, when all is found out that can be found out on earth, and made the common property of all (or even before that), the great man will perhaps arise and make the great guess that is to set us all free, here and hereafter. Who knows?

"I feel this splendid guesser will be some inspired musician of the future, as simple as a little child in all things but his knowledge of the power of sound; but even little children will have learned much in those days. He will want new notes and find them—new notes between the black and white keys. He will go blind like Milton and Homer, and deaf like Beethoven; and then, all in the stillness and the dark, all in the depths of his forlorn and lonely soul, he will make his best music, and out of the endless mazes of its counterpoint he will evolve a secret, as we did from the 'Chant du Triste Commensal,' but it will be a greater secret than ours. Others will have been very near this hidden treasure; but he will happen right *on* it, and unearth it, and bring it to light.

"I think I see him sitting at the key-board, so familiar of old to the feel of his consummate fingers; painfully dictating his score to some most patient and devoted friend—mother, sister, daughter, wife—that score that he will never see or hear.

"What a stammerer! Not only blind and deaf, but *mad*—mad in the world's eyes, for fifty, a hundred, a thousand years. Time is nothing; but that score will survive. . . .

"He will die of it, of course; and when he dies and comes to us, there will be joy from here to Sirius, and beyond.

"And one day they will find out on earth that he was only deaf and blind—not mad at all. They will hear and *understand*—they will know that he saw and heard as none had ever heard or seen before!

*   *   *

"For 'as we sow we reap'; that is a true saying, and all the sowing is done here on earth, and the reaping beyond. Man is a grub; his dead clay, as he lies coffined in his grave, is the left-off cocoon he has spun for himself during his earthly life, to burst open and soar from with all his memories about him, even his lost ones. Like the dragon-fly, the butterfly, the moth . . . and when *they* die it is the same, and the same with a blade of grass. We are all, *tous tant que nous sommes*, little bags of remembrance that never dies; that's what we're *for*. But we can only bring with us to the common stock what we've got. As Père François used to say, 'La plus belle fille au monde ne peut donner que ce qu'elle a.'

*   *   *

"Besides all this I am your earthly wife, Gogo—your loving, faithful, devoted wife, and I wish it to be known.

*   *   *

"And then at last, in the fulness of time—a very few years—ah, then—

"Once more shall Neuha lead her Torquil by the hand."

*   *   *

"Oh, Mary!" I cried, "shall we be transcendently happy again? As happy as we were—*happier* even?"

"Ah, Gogo, is a man happier than a mouse, or a mouse than a turnip, or a turnip than a lump of chalk? But what man would be a mouse or a turnip, or *vice versa?* What turnip would be a lump—of anything but itself? Are two people happier than one? You and I, yes; because we *are* one; but who else? It is one and all. Happiness is like time and space—we make and measure it ourselves; it is a fancy—as big, as little, as you please; just a thing of contrasts and comparisons, like health or strength or beauty or any other good—that wouldn't even be noticed but for sad personal experience of its opposite!—or its greater!

"I have forgotten all I know but this, which is for you and me: we are inseparable forever. Be sure we shall not want to go back again for a moment."

"And is there no punishment or reward?"

"Oh, there again! What a detail! Poor little naughty perverse midges—who were *born* so—and *can't* keep straight! poor little exemplary midges who couldn't go wrong if they tried! Is it worth while? Isn't it enough for either punishment or reward that the secrets of all midges' hearts shall be revealed, and for all other midges to see? Think of it!

* * *

"There are battles to be fought and races to be won, but no longer against '*each other*.' And strength and swiftness to win them; but no longer any strong and swift. There is weakness and cowardice, but no longer any cowards or weaklings. The good and the bad and the worst and the best—it is all mixed up. But the good comes to the top; the bad goes to the bottom—it is precipitated, as papa used to say. It is not an agreeable sediment, with its once useful cruelty at the lowest bottom of all—out of sight, out of mind—all but forgotten. *C'est déjà le ciel.*

* * *

"And the goal? The cause, the whither, and the why of it all? Ah! Gogo —as inscrutable, as unthinkable as ever, till the great guesser comes! At least so it seems to me, speaking as a fool, out of the depths of my poor ignorance; for I am a new arrival, and a complete outsider, with my chain and locket, waiting for you.

"I have only picked up a few grains of sand on the shore of that sea—a few little shells, and I can't even show you what they are like. I see that it is no good even talking of it, alas! And I had promised myself *so* much.

"Oh! how my earthly education was neglected, and yours! and how I feel it now, with so much to say in words, mere words! Why, to tell you in words the little I can see, the very little—so that you could understand—would require that each of us should be the greatest poet and the greatest mathematician that ever were, rolled into one! How I pity you, Gogo—with your untrained, unskilled, innocent pen, poor scribe! having to write all this down—for you *must*—and do your poor little best, as I have done mine in telling you! You must let the heart speak, and not mind style or manner! Write *any*how! write for the greatest need and the greatest number.

"But do just try and see this, dearest, and make the best of it you can: as far as *I* can make it out, everything everywhere seems to be an ever-deepening, ever-broadening stream that makes with inconceivable velocity for its own proper level, WHERE PERFECTION IS! . . . and ever gets nearer and nearer, and never finds it, and fortunately never will!

"Only that, unlike an earthly stream, and more like a fresh flowing tide up an endless, boundless, shoreless creek (if you can imagine that), the level it seeks is immeasurably higher than its source. And everywhere in it is Life, Life, Life! ever renewing and doubling itself and ever swelling that mighty river which has no banks!

"And everywhere in it like begets like, *plus* a little better or a little worse; and the little worse finds its way into some backwater and sticks there, and finally goes to the bottom, and nobody cares. And the little better goes on bettering and bettering—not all man's folly or perverseness can hinder *that*, nor make that headlong torrent stay, or ebb, or roll backward for a moment—*c'est plus fort que nous!* . . . The record goes on beating itself, the high-water-mark gets higher and higher till the highest on earth is reached that can be—and then, I suppose, the earth grows cold and the sun goes out—to be broken up into bits, and used all over again, perhaps! And betterness flies to warmer climes and huger systems, to better itself still! And so on, from better to better, from higher to higher, from warmer to warmer, and bigger to bigger—for ever and ever and ever!

"But the final superlative of all, absolute all-goodness and all-highness, absolute all-wisdom, absolute omnipotence, beyond which there neither is nor can be anything more, will never be reached at all—since there are no such things; they are abstractions; besides which, attainment means rest, and rest stagnation, and stagnation an end of all! And there is no end, and never can be—no end to Time and all the things that are done in it—no end to Space and all the things that fill it, or all would come together in a heap and smash up in the middle—and there *is* no middle!—no end, no beginning, no middle! *no middle*, Gogo! think of *that!* it is the most inconceivable thing of all!!!

"So who shall say where Shakespeare and you and I come in—tiny links in an endless chain, so tiny that even Shakespeare is no bigger than we! And just a little way behind us, those little wriggling transparent things, all stomach, that we descend from; and far ahead of ourselves, but in the direct line of a long descent from *us*, an ever-growing conscious Power, so strong, so glad, so simple, so wise, so mild, and so beneficent, that what can we do, even now, but fall on our knees with our foreheads in the dust, and our hearts brimful of wonder, hope, and love, and tender shivering awe; and worship as a yet unborn, barely conceived, and scarce begotten *Child*

—that which we have always been taught to worship as a *Father*—That which is not now, but *is* to be—That which we shall all share in and be part and parcel of in the dim future—That which is slowly, surely, painfully weaving Itself out of us and the likes of us all through the limitless Universe, and Whose coming we can but faintly foretell by the casting of its shadow on our own slowly, surely, painfully awakening souls!"

* * *

Then she went on to speak of earthly things, and ask questions in her old practical way. First of my bodily health, with the tenderest solicitude and the wisest advice—as a mother to a son. She even insisted on listening to my heart, like a doctor.

Then she spoke at great length of the charities in which she had been interested, and gave me many directions which I was to write, as coming from myself, to certain people whose names and addresses she impressed upon me with great care.

I have done as she wished, and most of these directions have been followed to the letter, with no little wonder on the world's part (as the world well knows) that such sagacious and useful reforms should have originated with the inmate of a criminal lunatic asylum.

* * *

At last the time came for us to part. She foresaw that I should have to wake in a few minutes, and said, rising—

"And now, Gogo, the best beloved that ever was on earth, take me once more in your dear arms, and kiss me good-bye for a little while—*auf Wiedersehen*. Come here to rest and think and remember when your body sleeps. My spirit will always be here with you. I may even be able to come back again myself—just this poor husk of me—hardly more to look at than a bundle of old clothes; but yet a world made up of love for *you*. Good-bye, good-bye, dearest and best. Time is nothing, but I shall count the hours. Good-bye. . . ."

Even as she strained me to her breast I awoke.

* * * * *

I awoke, and knew that the dread black shadow of melancholia had passed away from me like a hideous nightmare — like a long and horrible winter. My heart was full of the sunshine of spring — the gladness of awaking to a new life.

I smiled at my night attendant, who stared back at me in astonishment, and exclaimed —

"Why, sir, blest if you ain't a new man altogether. There, now!"

I wrung his hand, and thanked him for all his past patience, kindness, and forbearance with such effusion that his eyes had tears in them. I had not spoken for weeks, and he heard my voice for the first time.

That day, also, without any preamble or explanation, I gave the doctor and the chaplain and the governor my word of honor